The Little Lame Prince

by

Miss Mulock--Pseudonym of Maria Dinah Craik

The Echo Library 2007

Published by

The Echo Library

Echo Library
131 High St.
Teddington
Middlesex TW11 8HH

www.echo-library.com

Please report serious faults in the text to complaints@echo-library.com

ISBN 978-1-40684-908-0

CONTENTS

THE LITTLE LAME PRINCE

CHAPTER I

Yes, he was the most beautiful Prince that ever was born.

Of course, being a prince, people said this; but it was true besides. When he looked at the candle, his eyes had an expression of earnest inquiry quite startling in a new born baby. His nose—there was not much of it certainly, but what there was seemed an aquiline shape; his complexion was a charming, healthy purple; he was round and fat, straight-limbed and long—in fact, a splendid baby, and everybody was exceedingly proud of him, especially his father and mother, the King and Queen of Nomansland, who had waited for him during their happy reign of ten years—now made happier than ever, to themselves and their subjects, by the appearance of a son and heir.

The only person who was not quite happy was the King's brother, the heir presumptive, who would have been king one day had the baby not been born. But as his majesty was very kind to him, and even rather sorry for him—insomuch that at the Queen's request he gave him a dukedom almost as big as a county—the Crown-Prince, as he was called, tried to seem pleased also; and let us hope he succeeded.

The Prince's christening was to be a grand affair. According to the custom of the country, there were chosen for him four-and-twenty god-fathers and godmothers, who each had to give him a name, and promise to do their utmost for him. When he came of age, he himself had to choose the name—and the godfather or god-mother—that he liked the best, for the rest of his days.

Meantime all was rejoicing. Subscriptions were made among the rich to give pleasure to the poor; dinners in town-halls for the workingmen; tea-parties in the streets for their wives; and milk-and-bun feasts for the children in the schoolrooms. For Nomansland, though I cannot point it out in any map, or read of it in any history, was, I believe, much like our own or many another country.

As for the palace—which was no different from other palaces—it was clean "turned out of the windows," as people say, with the preparations going on. The only quiet place in it was the room which, though the Prince was six weeks old, his mother the Queen had never quitted. Nobody said she was ill, however—it would have been so inconvenient; and as she said nothing about it herself, but lay pale and placid, giving no trouble to anybody, nobody thought much about her. All the world was absorbed in admiring the baby.

The christening-day came at last, and it was as lovely as the Prince himself. All the people in the palace were lovely too—or thought themselves so—in the elegant new clothes which the Queen, who thought of everybody, had taken care to give them, from the ladies-in-waiting down to the poor little kitchen-maid, who looked at herself in her pink cotton gown, and thought, doubtless, that there never was such a pretty girl as she.

By six in the morning all the royal household had dressed itself in its very best; and then the little Prince was dressed in his best—his magnificent christening robe; which proceeding his Royal Highness did not like at all, but kicked and screamed like any common baby. When he had a little calmed down, they carried him to be looked at by the Queen his mother, who, though her royal robes had been brought and laid upon the bed, was, as everybody well knew, quite unable to rise and put them on.

She admired her baby very much; kissed and blessed him, and lay looking at him, as she did for hours sometimes, when he was placed beside her fast asleep; then she gave him up with a gentle smile, and, saying she hoped he would be very good, that it would be a very nice christening, and all the guests would enjoy themselves, turned peacefully over on her bed, saying nothing more to anybody. She was a very uncomplaining person, the Queen—and her name was Dolorez.

Everything went on exactly as if she had been present. All, even the king himself, had grown used to her absence; for she was not strong, and for years had not joined in any gayeties. She always did her royal duties, but as to pleasures, they could go on quite well without her, or it seemed so. The company arrived: great and notable persons in this and neighboring countries; also the four-and-twenty godfathers and godmothers, who had been chosen with care, as the people who would be most useful to his royal highness should he ever want friends, which did not seem likely. What such want could possibly happen to the heir of the powerful monarch of Nomansland?

They came, walking two and two, with their coronets on their heads—being dukes and duchesses, princes and princesses, or the like; they all kissed the child and pronounced the name each had given him. Then the four-and-twenty names were shouted out with great energy by six heralds, one after the other, and afterward written down, to be preserved in the state records, in readiness for the next time they were wanted, which would be either on his Royal Highness' coronation or his funeral.

Soon the ceremony was over, and everybody satisfied; except, perhaps, the little Prince himself, who moaned faintly under his christening robes, which nearly smothered him.

In truth, though very few knew, the Prince in coming to the chapel had met with a slight disaster. His nurse,—not his ordinary one, but the state nurse-maid,—an elegant and fashionable young lady of rank, whose duty it was to carry him to and from the chapel, had been so occupied in arranging her train with one hand, while she held the baby with the other, that she stumbled and let him fall, just at the foot of the marble staircase.

To be sure, she contrived to pick him up again the next minute; and the accident was so slight it seemed hardly worth speaking of. Consequently nobody did speak of it. The baby had turned deadly pale, but did not cry, so no person a step or two behind could discover anything wrong; afterward, even if he had moaned, the silver trumpets were loud enough to drown his voice. It would have been a pity to let anything trouble such a day of felicity.

So, after a minute's pause, the procession had moved on. Such a procession t Heralds in blue and silver; pages in crimson and gold; and a troop of little girls in dazzling white, carrying baskets of flowers, which they strewed all the way before the nurse and child—finally the four-and-twenty godfathers and godmothers, as proud as possible, and so splendid to look at that they would have quite extinguished their small godson—merely a heap of lace and muslin with a baby face inside—had it not been for a canopy of white satin and ostrich feathers which was held over him wherever he was carried.

Thus, with the sun shining on them through the painted windows, they stood; the king and his train on one side, the Prince and his attendants on the other, as pretty a sight as ever was seen out of fairyland.

"It's just like fairyland," whispered the eldest little girl to the next eldest, as she shook the last rose out of her basket; "and I think the only thing the Prince wants now is a fairy god-mother."

"Does he?" said a shrill but soft and not unpleasant voice behind; and there was seen among the group of children somebody,—not a child, yet no bigger than a child,—somebody whom nobody had seen before, and who certainly had not been invited, for she had no christening clothes on.

She was a little old woman dressed all in gray: gray gown; gray hooded cloak, of a material excessively fine, and a tint that seemed perpetually changing, like the gray of an evening sky. Her hair was gray, and her eyes also—even her complexion had a soft gray shadow over it. But there was nothing unpleasantly old about her, and her smile was as sweet and childlike as the Prince's own, which stole over his pale little face the instant she came near enough to touch him.

"Take care! Don't let the baby fall again."

The grand young lady nurse started, flushing angrily.

"Who spoke to me? How did anybody know?—I mean, what business has anybody——" Then frightened, but still speaking in a much sharper tone than I hope young ladies of rank are in the habit of speaking—"Old woman, you will be kind enough not to say 'the baby,' but 'the Prince.' Keep away; his Royal Highness is just going to sleep."

"Nevertheless I must kiss him. I am his god-mother."

"You!" cried the elegant lady nurse.

"You!" repeated all the gentlemen and ladies-in-waiting.

"You!" echoed the heralds and pages—and they began to blow the silver trumpets in order to stop all further conversation.

The Prince's procession formed itself for returning,—the King and his train having already moved off toward the palace,—but on the top-most step of the marble stairs stood, right in front of all, the little old woman clothed in gray.

She stretched herself on tiptoe by the help of her stick, and gave the little Prince three kisses.

"This is intolerable!" cried the young lady nurse, wiping the kisses off rapidly with her lace handkerchief. "Such an insult to his Royal Highness! Take yourself out of the way, old woman, or the King shall be informed immediately."

"The King knows nothing of me, more's the pity," replied the old woman, with an indifferent air, as if she thought the loss was more on his Majesty's side than hers. "My friend in the palace is the King's wife."

"King's have not wives, but queens," said the lady nurse, with a contemptuous air.

"You are right," replied the old woman. "Nevertheless I know her Majesty well, and I love her and her child. And—since you dropped him on the marble stairs (this she said in a mysterious whisper, which made the young lady tremble in spite of her anger)—I choose to take him for my own, and be his godmother, ready to help him whenever he wants me."

"You help him!" cried all the group breaking into shouts of laughter, to which the little old woman paid not the slightest attention. Her soft gray eyes were fixed on the Prince, who seemed to answer to the look, smiling again and again in the causeless, aimless fashion that babies do smile.

"His Majesty must hear of this," said a gentleman-in-waiting.

"His Majesty will hear quite enough news in a minute or two," said the old woman sadly. And again stretching up to the little Prince, she kissed him on the forehead solemnly.

"Be called by a new name which nobody has ever thought of. Be Prince Dolor, in memory of your mother Dolorez."

"In memory of!" Everybody started at the ominous phrase, and also at a most terrible breach of etiquette which the old woman had committed. In Nomansland, neither the king nor the queen was supposed to have any Christian name at all. They dropped it on their coronation day, and it never was mentioned again till it was engraved on their coffins when they died.

"Old woman, you are exceedingly ill-bred," cried the eldest lady-in-waiting, much horrified. "How you could know the fact passes my comprehension. But even if you did know it, how dared you presume to hint that her most gracious Majesty is called Dolorez?"

"WAS called Dolorez," said the old woman, with a tender solemnity.

The first gentleman, called the Gold-stick-in-waiting, raised it to strike her, and all the rest stretched out their hands to seize her; but the gray mantle melted from between their fingers like air; and, before anybody had time to do anything more, there came a heavy, muffled, startling sound.

The great bell of the palace the bell which was only heard on the death of some one of the royal family, and for as many times as he or she was years old—began to toll. They listened, mute and horror-stricken. Some one counted: one—two—three—four—up to nine-and-twenty—just the Queen's age.

It was, indeed, the Queen. Her Majesty was dead! In the midst of the festivities she had slipped away out of her new happiness and her old sufferings, not few nor small. Sending away all her women to see the grand sight,—at least they said afterward, in excuse, that she had done so, and it was very like her to do it,—she had turned with her face to the window, whence one could just see the tops of the distant mountains—the Beautiful Mountains, as they were called—where she was born. So gazing, she had quietly died.

When the little Prince was carried back to his mother's room, there was no mother to kiss him. And, though he did not know it, there would be for him no mother's kiss any more. As for his godmother,—the little old woman in gray who called herself so,—whether she melted into air, like her gown when they touched it, or whether she flew out of the chapel window, or slipped through the doorway among the bewildered crowd, nobody knew—nobody ever thought about her.

Only the nurse, the ordinary homely one, coming out of the Prince's nursery in the middle of the night in search of a cordial to quiet his continual moans, saw, sitting in the doorway, something which she would have thought a mere shadow, had she not seen shining out of it two eyes, gray and soft and sweet. She put her hand before her own, screaming loudly. When she took them away the old woman was gone.

CHAPTER II

Everybody was very kind to the poor little prince. I think people generally are kind to motherless children, whether princes or peasants. He had a magnificent nursery and a regular suite of attendants, and was treated with the greatest respect and state. Nobody was allowed to talk to him in silly baby language, or dandle him, or, above all to kiss him, though perhaps some people did it surreptitiously, for he was such a sweet baby that it was difficult to help it.

It could not be said that the Prince missed his mother—children of his age cannot do that; but somehow after she died everything seemed to go wrong with him. From a beautiful baby he became sickly and pale, seeming to have almost ceased growing, especially in his legs, which had been so fat and strong.

But after the day of his christening they withered and shrank; he no longer kicked them out either in passion or play, and when, as he got to be nearly a year old, his nurse tried to make him stand upon them, he only tumbled down.

This happened so many times that at last people began to talk about it. A prince, and not able to stand on his own legs! What a dreadful thing! What a misfortune for the country!

Rather a misfortune to him also, poor little boy! but nobody seemed to think of that. And when, after a while, his health revived, and the old bright look came back to his sweet little face, and his body grew larger and stronger, though still his legs remained the same, people continued to speak of him in whispers, and with grave shakes of the head. Everybody knew, though nobody said it, that something, it was impossible to guess what, was not quite right with the poor little Prince.

Of course, nobody hinted this to the King his father: it does not do to tell great people anything unpleasant. And besides, his Majesty took very little notice of his son, or of his other affairs, beyond the necessary duties of his kingdom.

People had said he would not miss the Queen at all, she having been so long an invalid, but he did. After her death he never was quite the same. He established himself in her empty rooms, the only rooms in the palace whence one could see the Beautiful Mountains, and was often observed looking at them as if he thought she had flown away thither, and that his longing could bring her back again. And by a curious coincidence, which nobody dared inquire into, he desired that the Prince might be called, not by any of the four-and-twenty grand names given him by his godfathers and godmothers, but by the identical name mentioned by the little old woman in gray—Dolor, after his mother Dolorez.

Once a week, according to established state custom, the Prince, dressed in his very best, was brought to the King his father for half an hour, but his Majesty was generally too ill and too melancholy to pay much heed to the child.

Only once, when he and the Crown-Prince, who was exceedingly attentive to his royal brother, were sitting together, with Prince Dolor playing in a corner of the room, dragging himself about with his arms rather than his legs, and sometimes trying feebly to crawl from one chair to another, it seemed to strike the father that all was not right with his son.

"How old is his Royal Highness?" said he suddenly to the nurse.

"Two years, three months, and five days, please your Majesty."

"It does not please me," said the King, with a sigh. "He ought to be far more forward than he is now ought he not, brother? You, who have so many children, must know. Is there not something wrong about him?"

"Oh, no," said the Crown-Prince, exchanging meaning looks with the nurse, who did not understand at all, but stood frightened and trembling with the tears in her eyes. "Nothing to make your Majesty at all uneasy. No doubt his Royal Highness will outgrow it in time."

"Outgrow—what?"

"A slight delicacy—ahem!—in the spine; something inherited, perhaps, from his dear mother."

"Ah, she was always delicate; but she was the sweetest woman that ever lived. Come here, my little son."

And as the Prince turned round upon his father a small, sweet, grave face,— so like his mother's,—his Majesty the King smiled and held out his arms. But when the boy came to him, not running like a boy, but wriggling awkwardly along the floor, the royal countenance clouded over.

"I ought to have been told of this. It is terrible—terrible! And for a prince too. Send for all the doctors in my kingdom immediately."

They came, and each gave a different opinion and ordered a different mode of treatment. The only thing they agreed in was what had been pretty well known before, that the Prince must have been hurt when he was an infant—let fall, perhaps, so as to injure his spine and lower limbs. Did nobody remember?

No, nobody. Indignantly, all the nurses denied that any such accident had happened, was possible to have happened, until the faithful country nurse recollected that it really had happened on the day of the christening. For which unluckily good memory all the others scolded her so severely that she had no peace of her life, and soon after, by the influence of the young lady nurse who had carried the baby that fatal day, and who was a sort of connection of the Crown-Prince—being his wife's second cousin once removed—the poor woman was pensioned off and sent to the Beautiful Mountains from whence she came, with orders to remain there for the rest of her days.

But of all this the King knew nothing, for, indeed, after the first shock of finding out that his son could not walk, and seemed never likely to he interfered very little concerning him. The whole thing was too painful, and his Majesty never liked painful things. Sometimes he inquired after Prince Dolor, and they told him his Royal Highness was going on as well as could be expected, which really was the case. For, after worrying the poor child and perplexing themselves with one remedy after another, the Crown-Prince, not wishing to offend any of the differing doctors, had proposed leaving him to Nature; and Nature, the safest doctor of all, had come to his help and done her best.

He could not walk, it is true; his limbs were mere useless appendages to his body; but the body itself was strong and sound. And his face was the same as ever—just his mother's face, one of the sweetest in the world.

Even the King, indifferent as he was, sometimes looked at the little fellow with sad tenderness, noticing how cleverly he learned to crawl and swing himself about by his arms, so that in his own awkward way he was as active in motion as most children of his age.

"Poor little man! he does his best, and he is not unhappy—not half so unhappy as I, brother," addressing the Crown-Prince, who was more constant than ever in his attendance upon the sick monarch. "If anything should befall me, I have appointed you Regent. In case of my death, you will take care of my poor little boy?"

"Certainly, certainly; but do not let us imagine any such misfortune. I assure your Majesty—everybody will assure you—that it is not in the least likely."

He knew, however, and everybody knew, that it was likely, and soon after it actually did happen. The King died as suddenly and quietly as the Queen had done—indeed, in her very room and bed; and Prince Dolor was left without either father or mother—as sad a thing as could happen, even to a prince.

He was more than that now, though. He was a king. In Nomansland, as in other countries, the people were struck with grief one day and revived the next. "The king is dead—long live the king!" was the cry that rang through the nation, and almost before his late Majesty had been laid beside the Queen in their splendid mausoleum, crowds came thronging from all parts to the royal palace, eager to see the new monarch.

They did see him,—the Prince Regent took care they should,—sitting on the floor of the council chamber, sucking his thumb! And when one of the gentlemen-in-waiting lifted him up and carried him—fancy carrying a king!—to the chair of state, and put the crown on his head, he shook it off again, it was so heavy and uncomfortable. Sliding down to the foot of the throne he began playing with the golden lions that supported it, stroking their paws and putting his tiny fingers into their eyes, and laughing—laughing as if he had at last found something to amuse him.

"There's a fine king for you!" said the first lord-in-waiting, a friend of the Prince Regent's (the Crown-Prince that used to be, who, in the deepest mourning, stood silently beside the throne of his young nephew. He was a handsome man, very grand and clever-looking). "What a king! who can never stand to receive his subjects, never walk in processions, who to the last day of his life will have to be carried about like a baby. Very unfortunate!"

"Exceedingly unfortunate," repeated the second lord. "It is always bad for a nation when its king is a child; but such a child—a permanent cripple, if not worse."

"Let us hope not worse," said the first lord in a very hopeless tone, and looking toward the Regent, who stood erect and pretended to hear nothing. "I have heard that these sort of children with very large heads, and great broad fore-heads and staring eyes, are—well, well, let us hope for the best and be prepared for the worst. In the meantime——"

"I swear," said the Crown-Prince, coming forward and kissing the hilt of his sword—"I swear to perform my duties as Regent, to take all care of his Royal

Highness—his Majesty, I mean," with a grand bow to the little child, who laughed innocently back again. "And I will do my humble best to govern the country. Still, if the country has the slightest objection——"

But the Crown-Prince being generalissimo, having the whole army at his beck and call, so that he could have begun a civil war in no time, the country had, of course, not the slightest objection.

So the King and Queen slept together in peace, and Prince Dolor reigned over the land—that is, his uncle did; and everybody said what a fortunate thing it was for the poor little Prince to have such a clever uncle to take care of him.

All things went on as usual; indeed, after the Regent had brought his wife and her seven sons, and established them in the palace, rather better than usual. For they gave such splendid entertainments and made the capital so lively that trade revived, and the country was said to be more flourishing than it had been for a century. Whenever the Regent and his sons appeared, they were received with shouts: "Long live the Crown-Prince!" "Long live the royal family!" And, in truth, they were very fine children, the whole seven of them, and made a great show when they rode out together on seven beautiful horses, one height above another, down to the youngest, on his tiny black pony, no bigger than a large dog.

As for the other child, his Royal Highness Prince Dolor,—for somehow people soon ceased to call him his Majesty, which seemed such a ridiculous title for a poor little fellow, a helpless cripple,—with only head and trunk, and no legs to speak of,—he was seen very seldom by anybody.

Sometimes people daring enough to peer over the high wall of the palace garden noticed there, carried in a footman's arms, or drawn in a chair, or left to play on the grass, often with nobody to mind him, a pretty little boy, with a bright, intelligent face and large, melancholy eyes—no, not exactly melancholy, for they were his mother's, and she was by no means sad-minded, but thoughtful and dreamy. They rather perplexed people, those childish eyes; they were so exceedingly innocent and yet so penetrating. If anybody did a wrong thing—told a lie, for instance they would turn round with such a grave, silent surprise the child never talked much—that every naughty person in the palace was rather afraid of Prince Dolor.

He could not help it, and perhaps he did not even know it, being no better a child than many other children, but there was something about him which made bad people sorry, and grumbling people ashamed of themselves, and ill-natured people gentle and kind.

I suppose because they were touched to see a poor little fellow who did not in the least know what had befallen him or what lay before him, living his baby life as happy as the day is long. Thus, whether or not he was good himself, the sight of him and his affliction made other people good, and, above all, made everybody love him—so much so, that his uncle the Regent began to feel a little uncomfortable.

Now, I have nothing to say against uncles in general. They are usually very excellent people, and very convenient to little boys and girls. Even the "cruel uncle" of the "Babes in the Wood" I believe to be quite an exceptional character. And this "cruel uncle" of whom I am telling was, I hope, an exception, too.

He did not mean to be cruel. If anybody had called him so, he would have resented it extremely: he would have said that what he did was done entirely for the good of the country. But he was a man who had always been accustomed to consider himself first and foremost, believing that whatever he wanted was sure to be right, and therefore he ought to have it. So he tried to get it, and got it too, as people like him very often do. Whether they enjoy it when they have it is another question.

Therefore he went one day to the council chamber, determined on making a speech, and informing the ministers and the country at large that the young King was in failing health, and that it would be advisable to send him for a time to the Beautiful Mountains. Whether he really meant to do this, or whether it occurred to him afterward that there would be an easier way of attaining his great desire, the crown of Nomansland, is a point which I cannot decide.

But soon after, when he had obtained an order in council to send the King away, which was done in great state, with a guard of honor composed of two whole regiments of soldiers,—the nation learned, without much surprise, that the poor little Prince—nobody ever called him king now—had gone a much longer journey than to the Beautiful Mountains.

He had fallen ill on the road and died within a few hours; at least so declared the physician in attendance and the nurse who had been sent to take care of him. They brought his coffin back in great state, and buried it in the mausoleum with his parents.

So Prince Dolor was seen no more. The country went into deep mourning for him, and then forgot him, and his uncle reigned in his stead. That illustrious personage accepted his crown with great decorum, and wore it with great dignity to the last. But whether he enjoyed it or not there is no evidence to show.

CHAPTER III

And what of the little lame Prince, whom everybody seemed so easily to have forgotten?

Not everybody. There were a few kind souls, mothers of families, who had heard his sad story, and some servants about the palace, who had been familiar with his sweet ways—these many a time sighed and said, "Poor Prince Dolor!" Or, looking at the Beautiful Mountains, which were visible all over Nomansland, though few people ever visited them, "Well, perhaps his Royal Highness is better where he is than even there."

They did not know—indeed, hardly anybody did know—that beyond the mountains, between them and the sea, lay a tract of country, barren, level, bare, except for short, stunted grass, and here and there a patch of tiny flowers. Not a bush—not a tree not a resting place for bird or beast was in that dreary plain. In summer the sunshine fell upon it hour after hour with a blinding glare; in winter the winds and rains swept over it unhindered, and the snow came down steadily, noiselessly, covering it from end to end in one great white sheet, which lay for days and weeks unmarked by a single footprint.

Not a pleasant place to live in—and nobody did live there, apparently. The only sign that human creatures had ever been near the spot was one large round tower which rose up in the center of the plain, and might be seen all over it—if there had been anybody to see, which there never was. Rose right up out of the ground, as if it had grown of itself, like a mushroom. But it was not at all mushroom-like; on the contrary, it was very solidly built. In form it resembled the Irish round towers, which have puzzled people for so long, nobody being able to find out when, or by whom, or for what purpose they were made; seemingly for no use at all, like this tower. It was circular, of very firm brickwork, with neither doors nor windows, until near the top, when you could perceive some slits in the wall through which one might possibly creep in or look out. Its height was nearly a hundred feet, and it had a battlemented parapet showing sharp against the sky.

As the plain was quite desolate—almost like a desert, only without sand, and led to nowhere except the still more desolate seacoast—nobody ever crossed it. Whatever mystery there was about the tower, it and the sky and the plain kept their secret to themselves.

It was a very great secret indeed,—a state secret,—which none but so clever a man as the present King of Nomansland would ever have thought of. How he carried it out, undiscovered, I cannot tell. People said, long afterward, that it was by means of a gang of condemned criminals, who were set to work, and executed immediately after they had done, so that nobody knew anything, or in the least suspected the real fact.

And what was the fact? Why, that this tower, which seemed a mere mass of masonry, utterly forsaken and uninhabited, was not so at all. Within twenty feet of the top some ingenious architect had planned a perfect little house, divided into four rooms—as by drawing a cross within a circle you will see might easily be done. By making skylights, and a few slits in the walls for windows, and raising a peaked roof which was hidden by the parapet, here was a dwelling complete, eighty feet from the ground, and as inaccessible as a rook's nest on the top of a tree.

A charming place to live in! if you once got up there,—and never wanted to come down again.

Inside—though nobody could have looked inside except a bird, and hardly even a bird flew past that lonely tower—inside it was furnished with all the comfort and elegance imaginable; with lots of books and toys, and everything that the heart of a child could desire. For its only inhabitant, except a nurse of course, was a poor solitary child.

One winter night, when all the plain was white with moonlight, there was seen crossing it a great tall black horse, ridden by a man also big and equally black, carrying before him on the saddle a woman and a child. The woman—she had a sad, fierce look, and no wonder, for she was a criminal under sentence of death, but her sentence had been changed to almost as severe a punishment. She was to inhabit the lonely tower with the child, and was allowed to live as long as the child lived—no longer. This in order that she might take the utmost care of him; for those who put him there were equally afraid of his dying and of his living.

Yet he was only a little gentle boy, with a sweet, sleepy smile—he had been very tired with his long journey—and clinging arms, which held tight to the man's neck, for he was rather frightened, and the face, black as it was, looked kindly at him. And he was very helpless, with his poor, small shriveled legs, which could neither stand nor run away—for the little forlorn boy was Prince Dolor.

He had not been dead at all—or buried either. His grand funeral had been a mere pretense: a wax figure having been put in his place, while he himself was spirited away under charge of these two, the condemned woman and the black man. The latter was deaf and dumb, so could neither tell nor repeat anything.

When they reached the foot of the tower, there was light enough to see a huge chain dangling from the parapet, but dangling only halfway. The deaf-mute took from his saddle-wallet a sort of ladder, arranged in pieces like a puzzle, fitted it together, and lifted it up to meet the chain. Then he mounted to the top of the tower, and slung from it a sort of chair, in which the woman and the child placed themselves and were drawn up, never to come down again as long as they lived. Leaving them there, the man descended the ladder, took it to pieces again and packed it in his pack, mounted the horse and disappeared across the plain.

Every month they used to watch for him, appearing like a speck in the distance. He fastened his horse to the foot of the tower, and climbed it, as before, laden with provisions and many other things. He always saw the Prince, so as to make sure that the child was alive and well, and then went away until the following month.

While his first childhood lasted Prince Dolor was happy enough. He had every luxury that even a prince could need, and the one thing wanting,—love,—

never having known, he did not miss. His nurse was very kind to him though she was a wicked woman. But either she had not been quite so wicked as people said, or she grew better through being shut up continually with a little innocent child who was dependent upon her for every comfort and pleasure of his life.

It was not an unhappy life. There was nobody to tease or ill-use him, and he was never ill. He played about from room to room—there were four rooms, parlor, kitchen, his nurse's bedroom, and his own; learned to crawl like a fly, and to jump like a frog, and to run about on all-fours almost as fast as a puppy. In fact, he was very much like a puppy or a kitten, as thoughtless and as merry—scarcely ever cross, though sometimes a little weary.

As he grew older, he occasionally liked to be quiet for a while, and then he would sit at the slits of windows—which were, however, much bigger than they looked from the bottom of the tower—and watch the sky above and the ground below, with the storms sweeping over and the sunshine coming and going, and the shadows of the clouds running races across the blank plain.

By and by he began to learn lessons—not that his nurse had been ordered to teach him, but she did it partly to amuse herself. She was not a stupid woman, and Prince Dolor was by no means a stupid boy; so they got on very well, and his continual entreaty, "What can I do? what can you find me to do?" was stopped, at least for an hour or two in the day.

It was a dull life, but he had never known any other; anyhow, he remembered no other, and he did not pity himself at all. Not for a long time, till he grew quite a big little boy, and could read quite easily. Then he suddenly took to books, which the deaf-mute brought him from time to time—books which, not being acquainted with the literature of Nomansland, I cannot describe, but no doubt they were very interesting; and they informed him of everything in the outside world, and filled him with an intense longing to see it.

From this time a change came over the boy. He began to look sad and thin, and to shut himself up for hours without speaking. For his nurse hardly spoke, and whatever questions he asked beyond their ordinary daily life she never answered. She had, indeed, been forbidden, on pain of death, to tell him anything about himself, who he was, or what he might have been.

He knew he was Prince Dolor, because she always addressed him as "My Prince" and "Your Royal Highness," but what a prince was he had not the least idea. He had no idea of anything in the world, except what he found in his books.

He sat one day surrounded by them, having built them up round him like a little castle wall. He had been reading them half the day, but feeling all the while that to read about things which you never can see is like hearing about a beautiful dinner while you are starving. For almost the first time in his life he grew melancholy; his hands fell on his lap; he sat gazing out of the window-slit upon the view outside—the view he had looked at every day of his life, and might look at for endless days more.

Not a very cheerful view,—just the plain and the sky,—but he liked it. He used to think, if he could only fly out of that window, up to the sky or down to the plain, how nice it would be! Perhaps when he died—his nurse had told him once in anger that he would never leave the tower till he died—he might be able to do this. Not that he understood much what dying meant, but it must be a change, and any change seemed to him a blessing.

"And I wish I had somebody to tell me all about it—about that and many other things; somebody that would be fond of me, like my poor white kitten."

Here the tears came into his eyes, for the boy's one friend, the one interest of his life, had been a little white kitten, which the deaf-mute, kindly smiling, once took out of his pocket and gave him—the only living creature Prince Dolor had ever seen.

For four weeks it was his constant plaything and companion, till one moonlight night it took a fancy for wandering, climbed on to the parapet of the tower, dropped over and disappeared. It was not killed, he hoped, for cats have nine lives; indeed, he almost fancied he saw it pick itself up and scamper away; but he never caught sight of it more.

"Yes, I wish I had something better than a kitten—a person, a real live person, who would be fond of me and kind to me. Oh, I want somebody— dreadfully, dreadfully!"

As he spoke, there sounded behind him a slight tap-tap-tap, as of a stick or a cane, and twisting himself round, he saw—what do you think he saw?

Nothing either frightening or ugly, but still exceedingly curious. A little woman, no bigger than he might himself have been had his legs grown like those of other children; but she was not a child—she was an old woman. Her hair was gray, and her dress was gray, and there was a gray shadow over her wherever she moved. But she had the sweetest smile, the prettiest hands, and when she spoke it was in the softest voice imaginable.

"My dear little boy,"—and dropping her cane, the only bright and rich thing about her, she laid those two tiny hands on his shoulders,—"my own little boy, I could not come to you until you had said you wanted me; but now you do want me, here I am."

"And you are very welcome, madam," replied the Prince, trying to speak politely, as princes always did in books; "and I am exceedingly obliged to you. May I ask who you are? Perhaps my mother?" For he knew that little boys usually had a mother, and had occasionally wondered what had become of his own.

"No," said the visitor, with a tender, half-sad smile, putting back the hair from his forehead, and looking right into his eyes—"no, I am not your mother, though she was a dear friend of mine; and you are as like her as ever you can be."

"Will you tell her to come and see me, then?"

"She cannot; but I dare say she knows all about you. And she loves you very much—and so do I; and I want to help you all I can, my poor little boy."

"Why do you call me poor?" asked Prince Dolor, in surprise.

The little old woman glanced down on his legs and feet, which he did not know were different from those of other children, and then at his sweet, bright face, which, though he knew not that either, was exceedingly different from many children's faces, which are often so fretful, cross, sullen. Looking at him, instead of sighing, she smiled. "I beg your pardon, my Prince," said she.

"Yes, I am a prince, and my name is Dolor; will you tell me yours, madam?"

The little old woman laughed like a chime of silver bells.

"I have not got a name—or, rather, I have so many names that I don't know which to choose. However, it was I who gave you yours, and you will belong to me all your days. I am your godmother."

"Hurrah!" cried the little Prince; "I am glad I belong to you, for I like you very much. Will you come and play with me?"

So they sat down together and played. By and by they began to talk.

"Are you very dull here?" asked the little old woman.

"Not particularly, thank you, godmother. I have plenty to eat and drink, and my lessons to do, and my books to read—lots of books."

"And you want nothing?"

"Nothing. Yes—perhaps——If you please, godmother, could you bring me just one more thing?"

"What sort of thing!"

"A little boy to play with."

The old woman looked very sad. "Just the thing, alas I which I cannot give you. My child, I cannot alter your lot in any way, but I can help you to bear it."

"Thank you. But why do you talk of bearing it? I have nothing to bear."

"My poor little man!" said the old woman in the very tenderest tone of her tender voice. "Kiss me!"

"What is kissing?" asked the wondering child.

His godmother took him in her arms and embraced him many times. By and by he kissed her back again—at first awkwardly and shyly, then with all the strength of his warm little heart.

"You are better to cuddle than even my white kitten, I think. Promise me that you will never go away."

"I must; but I will leave a present behind me,—something as good as myself to amuse you,—something that will take you wherever you want to go, and show you all that you wish to see."

"What is it?"

"A traveling-cloak."

The Prince's countenance fell. "I don't want a cloak, for I never go out. Sometimes nurse hoists me on to the roof, and carries me round by the parapet; but that is all. I can't walk, you know, as she does."

"The more reason why you should ride; and besides, this traveling-cloak——"

"Hush!—she's coming."

There sounded outside the room door a heavy step and a grumpy voice, and a rattle of plates and dishes.

"It's my nurse, and she is bringing my dinner; but I don't want dinner at all—I only want you. Will her coming drive you away, godmother?"

"Perhaps; but only for a little while. Never mind; all the bolts and bars in the world couldn't keep me out. I'd fly in at the window, or down through the chimney. Only wish for me, and I come."

"Thank you," said Prince Dolor, but almost in a whisper, for he was very uneasy at what might happen next. His nurse and his godmother—what would they say to one another? how would they look at one another?—two such different faces: one harsh-lined, sullen, cross, and sad; the other sweet and bright and calm as a summer evening before the dark begins.

When the door was flung open, Prince Dolor shut his eyes, trembling all over; opening them again, he saw he need fear nothing—his lovely old godmother had melted away just like the rainbow out of the sky, as he had watched it many a time. Nobody but his nurse was in the room.

"What a muddle your Royal Highness is sitting in," said she sharply. "Such a heap of untidy books; and what's this rubbish?" knocking a little bundle that lay beside them.

"Oh, nothing, nothing—give it me!" cried the Prince, and, darting after it, he hid it under his pinafore, and then pushed it quickly into his pocket. Rubbish as it was, it was left in the place where she sat, and might be something belonging to her—his dear, kind godmother, whom already he loved with all his lonely, tender, passionate heart.

It was, though he did not know this, his wonderful traveling-cloak.

CHAPTER IV

And what of the traveling-cloak? What sort of cloak was it, and what A good did it do the Prince?

Stay, and I'll tell you all about it. Outside it was the commonest-looking bundle imaginable—shabby and small; and the instant Prince Dolor touched it, it grew smaller still, dwindling down till he could put it in his trousers pocket, like a handkerchief rolled up into a ball. He did this at once, for fear his nurse should see it, and kept it there all day—all night, too. Till after his next morning's lessons he had no opportunity of examining his treasure.

When he did, it seemed no treasure at all; but a mere piece of cloth—circular in form, dark green in color—that is, if it had any color at all, being so worn and shabby, though not dirty. It had a split cut to the center, forming a round hole for the neck—and that was all its shape; the shape, in fact, of those cloaks which in South America are called ponchos—very simple, but most graceful and convenient.

Prince Dolor had never seen anything like it. In spite of his disappointment, he examined it curiously; spread it out on the door, then arranged it on his shoulders. It felt very warm and comfortable; but it was so exceedingly shabby—the only shabby thing that the Prince had ever seen in his life.

"And what use will it be to me?" said he sadly. "I have no need of outdoor clothes, as I never go out. Why was this given me, I wonder? and what in the world am I to do with it? She must be a rather funny person, this dear godmother of mine."

Nevertheless, because she was his godmother, and had given him the cloak, he folded it carefully and put it away, poor and shabby as it was, hiding it in a safe corner of his top cupboard, which his nurse never meddled with. He did not want her to find it, or to laugh at it or at his godmother—as he felt sure she would, if she knew all.

There it lay, and by and by he forgot all about it; nay, I am sorry to say that, being but a child, and not seeing her again, he almost forgot his sweet old godmother, or thought of her only as he did of the angels or fairies that he read of in his books, and of her visit as if it had been a mere dream of the night.

There were times, certainly, when he recalled her: of early mornings, like that morning when she appeared beside him, and late evenings, when the gray twilight reminded him of the color of her hair and her pretty soft garments; above all, when, waking in the middle of the night, with the stars peering in at his window, or the moonlight shining across his little bed, he would not have been surprised to see her standing beside it, looking at him with those beautiful tender eyes, which seemed to have a pleasantness and comfort in them different from anything he had ever known.

But she never came, and gradually she slipped out of his memory—only a boy's memory, after all; until something happened which made him remember her, and want her as he had never wanted anything before.

Prince Dolor fell ill. He caught—his nurse could not tell how—a complaint common to the people of Nomansland, called the doldrums, as unpleasant as measles or any other of our complaints; and it made him restless, cross, and disagreeable. Even when a little better, he was too weak to enjoy anything, but lay all day long on his sofa, fidgeting his nurse extremely—while, in her intense terror lest he might die, she fidgeted him still more. At last, seeing he really was getting well, she left him to himself—which he was most glad of, in spite of his dullness and dreariness. There he lay, alone, quite alone.

Now and then an irritable fit came over him, in which he longed to get up and do something, or to go somewhere—would have liked to imitate his white kitten—jump down from the tower and run away, taking the chance of whatever might happen.

Only one thing, alas! was likely to happen; for the kitten, he remembered, had four active legs, while he——

"I wonder what my godmother meant when she looked at my legs and sighed so bitterly? I wonder why I can't walk straight and steady like my nurse only I wouldn't like to have her great, noisy, clumping shoes. Still it would be very nice to move about quickly—perhaps to fly, like a bird, like that string of birds I saw the other day skimming across the sky, one after the other."

These were the passage-birds—the only living creatures that ever crossed the lonely plain; and he had been much interested in them, wondering whence they came and whither they were going.

"How nice it must be to be a bird! If legs are no good, why cannot one have wings? People have wings when they die—perhaps; I wish I were dead, that I do. I am so tired, so tired; and nobody cares for me. Nobody ever did care for me, except perhaps my godmother. Godmother, dear, have you quite forsaken me?"

He stretched himself wearily, gathered himself up, and dropped his head upon his hands; as he did so, he felt somebody kiss him at the back of his neck, and, turning, found that he was resting, not on the sofa pillows, but on a warm shoulder—that of the little old woman clothed in gray.

How glad he was to see her! How he looked into her kind eyes and felt her hands, to see if she were all real and alive! then put both his arms round her neck, and kissed her as if he would never have done kissing.

"Stop, stop!" cried she, pretending to be smothered. "I see you have not forgotten my teachings. Kissing is a good thing—in moderation. Only just let me have breath to speak one word."

"A dozen!" he said.

"Well, then, tell me all that has happened to you since I saw you—or, rather, since you saw me, which is quite a different thing."

"Nothing has happened—nothing ever does happen to me," answered the Prince dolefully.

"And are you very dull, my boy?"

"So dull that I was just thinking whether I could not jump down to the bottom of the tower, like my white kitten."

"Don't do that, not being a white kitten."

"I wish I were—I wish I were anything but what I am."

"And you can't make yourself any different, nor can I do it either. You must be content to stay just what you are."

The little old woman said this—very firmly, but gently, too—with her arms round his neck and her lips on his forehead. It was the first time the boy had ever heard any one talk like this, and he looked up in surprise—but not in pain, for her sweet manner softened the hardness of her words.

"Now, my Prince,—for you are a prince, and must behave as such,—let us see what we can do; how much I can do for you, or show you how to do for yourself. Where is your traveling-cloak?"

Prince Dolor blushed extremely. "I—I put it away in the cupboard; I suppose it is there still."

"You have never used it; you dislike it?"

He hesitated, no; wishing to be impolite. "Don't you think it's—just a little old and shabby for a prince?"

The old woman laughed—long and loud, though very sweetly.

"Prince, indeed! Why, if all the princes in the world craved for it, they couldn't get it, unless I gave it them. Old and shabby! It's the most valuable thing imaginable! Very few ever have it; but I thought I would give it to you, because—because you are different from other people."

"Am I?" said the Prince, and looked first with curiosity, then with a sort of anxiety, into his godmother's face, which was sad and grave, with slow tears beginning to steal down.

She touched his poor little legs. "These are not like those of other little boys."

"Indeed!—my nurse never told me that."

"Very likely not. But it is time you were told; and I tell you, because I love you."

"Tell me what, dear godmother?"

"That you will never be able to walk or run or jump or play—that your life will be quite different from most people's lives; but it may be a very happy life for all that. Do not be afraid."

"I am not afraid," said the boy; but he turned very pale, and his lips began to quiver, though he did not actually cry—he was too old for that, and, perhaps, too proud.

Though not wholly comprehending, he began dimly to guess what his godmother meant. He had never seen any real live boys, but he had seen pictures of them running and jumping; which he had admired and tried hard to imitate but always failed. Now he began to understand why he failed, and that he always should fail—that, in fact, he was not like other little boys; and it was of no use his wishing to do as they did, and play as they played, even if he had had them to play with. His was a separate life, in which he must find out new work and new pleasures for himself.

The sense of THE INEVITABLE, as grown-up people call it—that we cannot have things as we want them to be, but as they are, and that we must learn to bear them and make the best of them—this lesson, which everybody has to learn soon or late—came, alas! sadly soon, to the poor boy. He fought against it for a while, and then, quite overcome, turned and sobbed bitterly in his godmother's arms.

She comforted him—I do not know how, except that love always comforts; and then she whispered to him, in her sweet, strong, cheerful voice: "Never mind!"

"No, I don't think I do mind—that is, I WON'T mind," replied he, catching the courage of her tone and speaking like a man, though he was still such a mere boy.

"That is right, my Prince!—that is being like a prince. Now we know exactly where we are; let us put our shoulders to the wheel and——"

"We are in Hopeless Tower" (this was its name, if it had a name), "and there is no wheel to put our shoulders to," said the child sadly.

"You little matter-of-fact goose! Well for you that you have a godmother called——"

"What?" he eagerly asked.

"Stuff-and-nonsense."

"Stuff-and-nonsense! What a funny name!"

"Some people give it me, but they are not my most intimate friends. These call me—never mind what," added the old woman, with a soft twinkle in her eyes. "So as you know me, and know me well, you may give me any name you please; it doesn't matter. But I am your godmother, child. I have few godchildren; those I have love me dearly, and find me the greatest blessing in all the world."

"I can well believe it," cried the little lame Prince, and forgot his troubles in looking at her—as her figure dilated, her eyes grew lustrous as stars, her very raiment brightened, and the whole room seemed filled with her beautiful and beneficent presence like light.

He could have looked at her forever—half in love, half in awe; but she suddenly dwindled down into the little old woman all in gray, and, with a malicious twinkle in her eyes, asked for the traveling-cloak.

"Bring it out of the rubbish cupboard, and shake the dust off it, quick!" said she to Prince Dolor, who hung his head, rather ashamed. "Spread it out on the floor, and wait till the split closes and the edges turn up like a rim all round. Then go and open the skylight,—mind, I say OPEN THE SKYLIGHT,—set yourself down in the middle of it, like a frog on a water-lily leaf; say 'Abracadabra, dum dum dum,' and—see what will happen!"

The Prince burst into a fit of laughing. It all seemed so exceedingly silly; he wondered that a wise old woman like his godmother should talk such nonsense.

"Stuff-and-nonsense, you mean," said she, answering, to his great alarm, his unspoken thoughts. "Did I not tell you some people called me by that name? Never mind; it doesn't harm me."

And she laughed—her merry laugh—as child-like as if she were the Prince's age instead of her own, whatever that might be. She certainly was a most extraordinary old woman.

"Believe me or not, it doesn't matter," said she. "Here is the cloak: when you want to go traveling on it, say 'Abracadabra, dum, dum, dum'; when you want to come back again, say 'Abracadabra, tum tum ti.' That's all; good-by."

A puff of most pleasant air passing by him, and making him feel for the moment quite strong and well, was all the Prince was conscious of. His most extraordinary godmother was gone.

"Really now, how rosy your Royal Highness' cheeks have grown! You seem to have got well already," said the nurse, entering the room.

"I think I have," replied the Prince very gently—he felt gently and kindly even to his grim nurse. "And now let me have my dinner, and go you to your sewing as usual."

The instant she was gone, however, taking with her the plates and dishes, which for the first time since his illness he had satisfactorily cleared, Prince Dolor sprang down from his sofa, and with one or two of his frog-like jumps reached the cupboard where he kept his toys, and looked everywhere for his traveling-cloak.

Alas! it was not there.

While he was ill of the doldrums, his nurse, thinking it a good opportunity for putting things to rights, had made a grand clearance of all his "rubbish"—as she considered it: his beloved headless horses, broken carts, sheep without feet, and birds without wings—all the treasures of his baby days, which he could not bear to part with. Though he seldom played with them now, he liked just to feel they were there.

They were all gone and with them the traveling-cloak. He sat down on the floor, looking at the empty shelves, so beautifully clean and tidy, then burst out sobbing as if his heart would break.

But quietly—always quietly. He never let his nurse hear him cry. She only laughed at him, as he felt she would laugh now.

"And it is all my own fault!" he cried. "I ought to have taken better care of my godmother's gift. Oh, godmother, forgive me! I'll never be so careless again. I don't know what the cloak is exactly, but I am sure it is something precious. Help me to find it again. Oh, don't let it be stolen from me—don't, please!"

"Ha, ha, ha!" laughed a silvery voice. "Why, that traveling-cloak is the one thing in the world which nobody can steal. It is of no use to anybody except the owner. Open your eyes, my Prince, and see what you shall see."

His dear old godmother, he thought, and turned eagerly round. But no; he only beheld, lying in a corner of the room, all dust and cobwebs, his precious traveling-cloak.

Prince Dolor darted toward it, tumbling several times on the way, as he often did tumble, poor boy! and pick himself up again, never complaining. Snatching it to his breast, he hugged and kissed it, cobwebs and all, as if it had been something alive. Then he began unrolling it, wondering each minute what would happen. What did happen was so curious that I must leave it for another chapter.

CHAPTER V

If any reader, big or little, should wonder whether there is a meaning in this story deeper than that of an ordinary fairy tale, I will own that there is. But I have hidden it so carefully that the smaller people, and many larger folk, will never find it out, and meantime the book may be read straight on, like "Cinderella," or "Blue-Beard," or "Hop-o'my-Thumb," for what interest it has, or what amusement it may bring.

Having said this, I return to Prince Dolor, that little lame boy whom many may think so exceedingly to be pitied. But if you had seen him as he sat patiently untying his wonderful cloak, which was done up in a very tight and perplexing parcel, using skillfully his deft little hands, and knitting his brows with firm determination, while his eyes glistened with pleasure and energy and eager anticipation—if you had beheld him thus, you might have changed your opinion.

When we see people suffering or unfortunate, we feel very sorry for them; but when we see them bravely bearing their sufferings and making the best of their misfortunes, it is quite a different feeling. We respect, we admire them. One can respect and admire even a little child.

When Prince Dolor had patiently untied all the knots, a remarkable thing happened. The cloak began to undo itself. Slowly unfolding, it laid itself down on the carpet, as flat as if it had been ironed; the split joined with a little sharp crick-crack, and the rim turned up all round till it was breast-high; for meantime the cloak had grown and grown, and become quite large enough for one person to sit in it as comfortable as if in a boat.

The Prince watched it rather anxiously; it was such an extraordinary, not to say a frightening, thing. However, he was no coward, but a thorough boy, who, if he had been like other boys, would doubtless have grown up daring and adventurous—a soldier, a sailor, or the like. As it was, he could only show his courage morally, not physically, by being afraid of nothing, and by doing boldly all that it was in his narrow powers to do. And I am not sure but that in this way he showed more real valor than if he had had six pairs of proper legs.

He said to himself: "What a goose I am! As if my dear godmother would ever have given me anything to hurt me. Here goes!"

So, with one of his active leaps, he sprang right into the middle of the cloak, where he squatted down, wrapping his arms tight round his knees, for they shook a little and his heart beat fast. But there he sat, steady and silent, waiting for what might happen next.

Nothing did happen, and he began to think nothing would, and to feel rather disappointed, when he recollected the words he had been told to repeat—"Abracadabra, dum dum dum!"

He repeated them, laughing all the while, they seemed such nonsense. And then—and then——

Now I don't expect anybody to believe what I am going to relate, though a good many wise people have believed a good many sillier things. And as seeing's believing, and I never saw it, I cannot be expected implicitly to believe it myself, except in a sort of a way; and yet there is truth in it—for some people.

The cloak rose, slowly and steadily, at first only a few inches, then gradually higher and higher, till it nearly touched the skylight. Prince Dolor's head actually bumped against the glass, or would have done so had he not crouched down, crying "Oh, please don't hurt me!" in a most melancholy voice.

Then he suddenly remembered his godmother's express command—"Open the skylight!"

Regaining his courage at once, without a moment's delay he lifted up his head and began searching for the bolt—the cloak meanwhile remaining perfectly still, balanced in the air. But the minute the window was opened, out it sailed— right out into the clear, fresh air, with nothing between it and the cloudless blue.

Prince Dolor had never felt any such delicious sensation before. I can understand it. Cannot you? Did you never think, in watching the rooks going home singly or in pairs, soaring their way across the calm evening sky till they vanish like black dots in the misty gray, how pleasant it must feel to be up there, quite out of the noise and din of the world, able to hear and see everything down below, yet troubled by nothing and teased by no one—all alone, but perfectly content?

Something like this was the happiness of the little lame Prince when he got out of Hopeless Tower, and found himself for the first time in the pure open air, with the sky above him and the earth below.

True, there was nothing but earth and sky; no houses, no trees, no rivers, mountains, seas—not a beast on the ground, or a bird in the air. But to him even the level plain looked beautiful; and then there was the glorious arch of the sky, with a little young moon sitting in the west like a baby queen. And the evening breeze was so sweet and fresh—it kissed him like his godmother's kisses; and by and by a few stars came out—first two or three, and then quantities—quantities! so that when he began to count them he was utterly bewildered.

By this time, however, the cool breeze had become cold; the mist gathered; and as he had, as he said, no outdoor clothes, poor Prince Dolor was not very comfortable. The dews fell damp on his curls—he began to shiver.

"Perhaps I had better go home," thought he.

But how? For in his excitement the other words which his godmother had told him to use had slipped his memory. They were only a little different from the first, but in that slight difference all the importance lay. As he repeated his "Abracadabra," trying ever so many other syllables after it, the cloak only went faster and faster, skimming on through the dusky, empty air.

The poor little Prince began to feel frightened. What if his wonderful traveling-cloak should keep on thus traveling, perhaps to the world's end, carrying with it a poor, tired, hungry boy, who, after all, was beginning to think there was something very pleasant in supper and bed!

"Dear godmother," he cried pitifully, "do help me! Tell me just this once and I'll never forget again."

Instantly the words came rushing into his head—"Abracadabra, tum tum ti!" Was that it? Ah! yes—for the cloak began to turn slowly. He repeated the charm again, more distinctly and firmly, when it gave a gentle dip, like a nod of satisfaction, and immediately started back, as fast as ever, in the direction of the tower.

He reached the skylight, which he found exactly as he had left it, and slipped in, cloak and all, as easily as he had got out. He had scarcely reached the floor, and was still sitting in the middle of his traveling-cloak,—like a frog on a water-lily leaf, as his godmother had expressed it,—when he heard his nurse's voice outside.

"Bless us! what has become of your Royal Highness all this time? To sit stupidly here at the window till it is quite dark, and leave the skylight open, too. Prince! what can you be thinking of? You are the silliest boy I ever knew."

"Am I?" said he absently, and never heeding her crossness; for his only anxiety was lest she might find out anything.

She would have been a very clever person to have done so. The instant Prince Dolor got off it, the cloak folded itself up into the tiniest possible parcel, tied all its own knots, and rolled itself of its own accord into the farthest and darkest corner of the room. If the nurse had seen it, which she didn't, she would have taken it for a mere bundle of rubbish not worth noticing.

Shutting the skylight with an angry bang, she brought in the supper and lit the candles with her usual unhappy expression of countenance. But Prince Dolor hardly saw it; he only saw, hid in the corner where nobody else would see it, his wonderful traveling-cloak. And though his supper was not particularly nice, he ate it heartily, scarcely hearing a word of his nurse's grumbling, which to-night seemed to have taken the place of her sullen silence.

"Poor woman!" he thought, when he paused a minute to listen and look at her with those quiet, happy eyes, so like his mother's. "Poor woman! she hasn't got a traveling-cloak!"

And when he was left alone at last, and crept into his little bed, where he lay awake a good while, watching what he called his "sky-garden," all planted with stars, like flowers, his chief thought was—"I must be up very early to-morrow morning, and get my lessons done, and then I'll go traveling all over the world on my beautiful cloak."

So next day he opened his eyes with the sun, and went with a good heart to his lessons. They had hitherto been the chief amusement of his dull life; now, I am afraid, he found them also a little dull. But he tried to be good,—I don't say Prince Dolor always was good, but he generally tried to be,—and when his mind went wandering after the dark, dusty corner where lay his precious treasure, he resolutely called it back again.

"For," he said, "how ashamed my godmother would be of me if I grew up a stupid boy!"

But the instant lessons were done, and he was alone in the empty room, he crept across the floor, undid the shabby little bundle, his fingers trembling with eagerness, climbed on the chair, and thence to the table, so as to unbar the skylight,—he forgot nothing now,—said his magic charm, and was away out of the window, as children say, "in a few minutes less than no time."

Nobody missed him. He was accustomed to sit so quietly always that his nurse, though only in the next room, perceived no difference. And besides, she might have gone in and out a dozen times, and it would have been just the same; she never could have found out his absence.

For what do you think the clever godmother did? She took a quantity of moonshine, or some equally convenient material, and made an image, which she set on the window-sill reading, or by the table drawing, where it looked so like Prince Dolor that any common observer would never have guessed the deception; and even the boy would have been puzzled to know which was the image and which was himself.

And all this while the happy little fellow was away, floating in the air on his magic cloak, and seeing all sorts of wonderful things—or they seemed wonderful to him, who had hitherto seen nothing at all.

First, there were the flowers that grew on the plain, which, whenever the cloak came near enough, he strained his eyes to look at; they were very tiny, but very beautiful—white saxifrage, and yellow lotus, and ground-thistles, purple and bright, with many others the names of which I do not know. No more did Prince Dolor, though he tried to find them out by recalling any pictures he had seen of them. But he was too far off; and though it was pleasant enough to admire them as brilliant patches of color, still he would have liked to examine them all. He was, as a little girl I know once said of a playfellow, "a very examining boy."

"I wonder," he thought, "whether I could see better through a pair of glasses like those my nurse reads with, and takes such care of. How I would take care of them, too, if I only had a pair!"

Immediately he felt something queer and hard fixing itself to the bridge of his nose. It was a pair of the prettiest gold spectacles ever seen; and looking downward, he found that, though ever so high above the ground, he could see every minute blade of grass, every tiny bud and flower—nay, even the insects that walked over them.

"Thank you, thank you!" he cried, in a gush of gratitude—to anybody or everybody, but especially to his dear godmother, who he felt sure had given him this new present. He amused himself with it for ever so long, with his chin pressed on the rim of the cloak, gazing down upon the grass, every square foot of which was a mine of wonders.

Then, just to rest his eyes, he turned them up to the sky—the blue, bright, empty sky, which he had looked at so often and seen nothing.

Now surely there was something. A long, black, wavy line, moving on in the distance, not by chance, as the clouds move apparently, but deliberately, as if it were alive. He might have seen it before—he almost thought he had; but then he could not tell what it was. Looking at it through his spectacles, he discovered that it really was alive; being a long string of birds, flying one after the other, their wings moving steadily and their heads pointed in one direction, as steadily as if each were a little ship, guided invisibly by an unerring helm.

"They must be the passage-birds flying seaward!" cried the boy, who had read a little about them, and had a great talent for putting two and two together and finding out all he could. "Oh, how I should like to see them quite close, and to know where they come from and whither they are going! How I wish I knew everything in all the world!"

A silly speech for even an "examining" little boy to make; because, as we grow older, the more we know the more we find out there is to know. And Prince Dolor blushed when he had said it, and hoped nobody had heard him.

Apparently somebody had, however; for the cloak gave a sudden bound forward, and presently he found himself high in the air, in the very middle of that band of aerial travelers, who had mo magic cloak to travel on—nothing except their wings. Yet there they were, making their fearless way through the sky.

Prince Dolor looked at them as one after the other they glided past him; and they looked at him—those pretty swallows, with their changing necks and bright eyes—as if wondering to meet in mid-air such an extraordinary sort of bird.

"Oh, I wish I were going with you, you lovely creatures! I'm getting so tired of this dull plain, and the dreary and lonely tower. I do so want to see the world! Pretty swallows, dear swallows! tell me what it looks like—the beautiful, wonderful world!"

But the swallows flew past him—steadily, slowly pursuing their course as if inside each little head had been a mariner's compass, to guide them safe over land and sea, direct to the place where they wished to go.

The boy looked after them with envy. For a long time he followed with his eyes the faint, wavy black line as it floated away, sometimes changing its curves a little, but never deviating from its settled course, till it vanished entirely out of sight.

Then he settled himself down in the center of the cloak, feeling quite sad and lonely.

"I think I'll go home," said he, and repeated his "Abracadabra, tum tum ti!" with a rather heavy heart. The more he had, the more he wanted; and it is not always one can have everything one wants—at least, at the exact minute one craves for it; not even though one is a prince, and has a powerful and beneficent godmother.

He did not like to vex her by calling for her and telling her how unhappy he was, in spite of all her goodness; so he just kept his trouble to himself, went back to his lonely tower, and spent three days in silent melancholy, without even attempting another journey on his traveling-cloak.

CHAPTER VI

The fourth day it happened that the deaf-mute paid his accustomed visit, after which Prince Dolor's spirits rose. They always did when he got the new books which, just to relieve his conscience, the King of Nomansland regularly sent to his nephew; with many new toys also, though the latter were disregarded now.

"Toys, indeed! when I'm a big boy," said the Prince, with disdain, and would scarcely condescend to mount a rocking-horse which had come, somehow or other,—I can't be expected to explain things very exactly,—packed on the back of the other, the great black horse, which stood and fed contentedly at the bottom of the tower.

Prince Dolor leaned over and looked at it, and thought how grand it must be to get upon its back—this grand live steed—and ride away, like the pictures of knights.

"Suppose I was a knight," he said to himself; "then I should be obliged to ride out and see the world."

But he kept all these thoughts to himself, and just sat still, devouring his new books till he had come to the end of them all. It was a repast not unlike the Barmecide's feast which you read of in the "Arabian Nights," which consisted of very elegant but empty dishes, or that supper of Sancho Panza in "Don Quixote," where, the minute the smoking dishes came on the table, the physician waved his hand and they were all taken away.

Thus almost all the ordinary delights of boy-life had been taken away from, or rather never given to this poor little prince.

"I wonder," he would sometimes think—"I wonder what it feels like to be on the back of a horse, galloping away, or holding the reins in a carriage, and tearing across the country, or jumping a ditch, or running a race, such as I read of or see in pictures. What a lot of things there are that I should like to do! But first I should like to go and see the world. I'll try."

Apparently it was his godmother's plan always to let him try, and try hard, before he gained anything. This day the knots that tied up his traveling-cloak were more than usually troublesome, and he was a full half-hour before he got out into the open air, and found himself floating merrily over the top of the tower.

Hitherto, in all his journeys, he had never let himself go out of sight of home, for the dreary building, after all, was home—he remembered no other; but now he felt sick of the very look of his tower, with its round smooth walls and level battlements.

"Off we go!" cried he, when the cloak stirred itself with a slight, slow motion, as if waiting his orders. "Anywhere anywhere, so that I am away from here, and out into the world."

As he spoke, the cloak, as if seized suddenly with a new idea, bounded forward and went skimming through the air, faster than the very fastest railway train.

"Gee-up! gee-up!" cried Prince Dolor in great excitement. "This is as good as riding a race."

And he patted the cloak as if it had been a horse—that is, in the way he supposed horses ought to be patted—and tossed his head back to meet the fresh breeze, and pulled his coat collar up and his hat down as he felt the wind grow keener and colder—colder than anything he had ever known.

"What does it matter, though?" said he. "I'm a boy, and boys ought not to mind anything."

Still, for all his good-will, by and by, he began to shiver exceedingly; also, he had come away without his dinner, and he grew frightfully hungry. And to add to everything, the sunshiny day changed into rain, and being high up, in the very midst of the clouds, he got soaked through and through in a very few minutes.

"Shall I turn back?" meditated he. "Suppose I say 'Abracadabra?'"

Here he stopped, for already the cloak gave an obedient lurch, as if it were expecting to be sent home immediately.

"No—I can't—I can't go back! I must go forward and see the world. But oh! if I had but the shabbiest old rug to shelter me from the rain, or the driest morsel of bread and cheese, just to keep me from starving! Still, I don't much mind; I'm a prince, and ought to be able to stand anything. Hold on, cloak, we'll make the best of it."

It was a most curious circumstance, but no sooner had he said this than he felt stealing over his knees something warm and soft; in fact, a most beautiful bearskin, which folded itself round him quite naturally, and cuddled him up as closely as if he had been the cub of the kind old mother-bear that once owned it. Then feeling in his pocket, which suddenly stuck out in a marvelous way, he found, not exactly bread and cheese, nor even sandwiches, but a packet of the most delicious food he had ever tasted. It was not meat, nor pudding, but a combination of both, and it served him excellently for both. He ate his dinner with the greatest gusto imaginable, till he grew so thirsty he did not know what to do.

"Couldn't I have just one drop of water, if it didn't trouble you too much, kindest of godmothers?"

For he really thought this want was beyond her power to supply. All the water which supplied Hopeless Tower was pumped up with difficulty from a deep artesian well—there were such things known in Nomansland—which had been made at the foot of it. But around, for miles upon miles, the desolate plain was perfectly dry. And above it, high in the air, how could he expect to find a well, or to get even a drop of water?

He forgot one thing—the rain. While he spoke, it came on in another wild burst, as if the clouds had poured themselves out in a passion of crying, wetting him certainly, but leaving behind, in a large glass vessel which he had never noticed before, enough water to quench the thirst of two or three boys at least. And it was so fresh, so pure—as water from the clouds always is when it does not catch the soot from city chimneys and other defilements—that he drank it, every drop, with the greatest delight and content.

Also, as soon as it was empty the rain filled it again, so that he was able to wash his face and hands and refresh himself exceedingly. Then the sun came out and dried him in no time. After that he curled himself up under the bear-skin rug, and though he determined to be the most wide-awake boy imaginable, being so exceedingly snug and warm and comfortable, Prince Dolor condescended to shut his eyes just for one minute. The next minute he was sound asleep.

When he awoke, he found himself floating over a country quite unlike anything he had ever seen before.

Yet it was nothing but what most of you children see every day and never notice it—a pretty country landscape, like England, Scotland, France, or any other land you choose to name. It had no particular features—nothing in it grand or lovely—was simply pretty, nothing more; yet to Prince Dolor, who had never gone beyond his lonely tower and level plain, it appeared the most charming sight imaginable.

First, there was a river. It came tumbling down the hillside, frothing and foaming, playing at hide-and-seek among the rocks, then bursting out in noisy fun like a child, to bury itself in deep, still pools. Afterward it went steadily on for a while, like a good grown-up person, till it came to another big rock, where it misbehaved itself extremely. It turned into a cataract, and went tumbling over and over, after a fashion that made the prince—who had never seen water before, except in his bath or his drinking-cup—clap his hands with delight.

"It is so active, so alive! I like things active and alive!" cried he, and watched it shimmering and dancing, whirling and leaping, till, after a few windings and vagaries, it settled into a respectable stream. After that it went along, deep and quiet, but flowing steadily on, till it reached a large lake, into which it slipped and so ended its course.

All this the boy saw, either with his own naked eye or through his gold spectacles. He saw also as in a picture, beautiful but silent, many other things which struck him with wonder, especially a grove of trees.

Only think, to have lived to his age (which he himself did not know, as he did not know his own birthday) and never to have seen trees! As he floated over these oaks, they seemed to him—trunk, branches, and leaves—the most curious sight imaginable.

"If I could only get nearer, so as to touch them," said he, and immediately the obedient cloak ducked down; Prince Dolor made a snatch at the topmost twig of the tallest tree, and caught a bunch of leaves in his hand.

Just a bunch of green leaves—such as we see in myriads; watching them bud, grow, fall, and then kicking them along on the ground as if they were worth nothing. Yet how wonderful they are—every one of them a little different. I don't suppose you could ever find two leaves exactly alike in form, color, and size—no more than you could find two faces alike, or two characters exactly the same. The plan of this world is infinite similarity and yet infinite variety.

Prince Dolor examined his leaves with the greatest curiosity—and also a little caterpillar that he found walking over one of them. He coaxed it to take an additional walk over his finger, which it did with the greatest dignity and decorum, as if it, Mr. Caterpillar, were the most important individual in existence. It amused him for a long time; and when a sudden gust of wind blew it overboard, leaves and all, he felt quite disconsolate.

"Still there must be many live creatures in the world besides caterpillars. I should like to see a few of them."

The cloak gave a little dip down, as if to say "All right, my Prince," and bore him across the oak forest to a long fertile valley—called in Scotland a strath and in England a weald, but what they call it in the tongue of Nomansland I do not know. It was made up of cornfields, pasturefields, lanes, hedges, brooks, and ponds. Also, in it were what the prince desired to see—a quantity of living creatures, wild and tame. Cows and horses, lambs and sheep, fed in the meadows; pigs and fowls walked about the farm-yards; and in lonelier places hares scudded, rabbits burrowed, and pheasants and partridges, with many other smaller birds, inhabited the fields and woods.

Through his wonderful spectacles the Prince could see everything; but, as I said, it was a silent picture; he was too high up to catch anything except a faint murmur, which only aroused his anxiety to hear more.

"I have as good as two pairs of eyes," he thought. "I wonder if my godmother would give me a second pair of ears."

Scarcely had he spoken than he found lying on his lap the most curious little parcel, all done up in silvery paper. And it contained—what do you think? Actually a pair of silver ears, which, when he tried them on, fitted so exactly over his own that he hardly felt them, except for the difference they made in his hearing.

There is something which we listen to daily and never notice. I mean the sounds of the visible world, animate and inanimate. Winds blowing, waters flowing, trees stirring, insects whirring (dear me! I am quite unconsciously writing rhyme), with the various cries of birds and beasts,—lowing cattle, bleating sheep, grunting pigs, and cackling hens,—all the infinite discords that somehow or other make a beautiful harmony.

We hear this, and are so accustomed to it that we think nothing of it; but Prince Dolor, who had lived all his days in the dead silence of Hopeless Tower, heard it for the first time. And oh! if you had seen his face.

He listened, listened, as if he could never have done listening. And he looked and looked, as if he could not gaze enough. Above all, the motion of the animals delighted him: cows walking, horses galloping, little lambs and calves running races across the meadows, were such a treat for him to watch—he that was always so quiet. But, these creatures having four legs, and he only two, the difference did not strike him painfully.

Still, by and by, after the fashion of children,—and I fear, of many big people too,—he began to want something more than he had, something fresh and new.

"Godmother," he said, having now begun to believe that, whether he saw her or not, he could always speak to her with full confidence that she would hear him—"Godmother, all these creatures I like exceedingly; but I should like better to see a creature like myself. Couldn't you show me just one little boy?"

There was a sigh behind him,—it might have been only the wind,—and the cloak remained so long balanced motionless in air that he was half afraid his godmother had forgotten him, or was offended with him for asking too much. Suddenly a shrill whistle startled him, even through his silver ears, and looking downward, he saw start up from behind a bush on a common, something——

Neither a sheep nor a horse nor a cow—nothing upon four legs. This creature had only two; but they were long, straight, and strong. And it had a lithe, active body, and a curly head of black hair set upon its shoulders. It was a boy, a shepherd-boy, about the Prince's own age—but, oh! so different.

Not that he was an ugly boy—though his face was almost as red as his hands, and his shaggy hair matted like the backs of his own sheep. He was rather a nice-looking lad; and seemed so bright and healthy and good-tempered— "jolly" would be the word, only I am not sure if they have such a one in the elegant language of Nomansland—that the little Prince watched him with great admiration.

"Might he come and play with me? I would drop down to the ground to him, or fetch him up to me here. Oh, how nice it would be if I only had a little boy to play with me."

But the cloak, usually so obedient to his wishes, disobeyed him now. There were evidently some things which his godmother either could not or would not give. The cloak hung stationary, high in air, never attempting to descend. The shepherd-lad evidently took it for a large bird, and, shading his eyes, looked up at it, making the Prince's heart beat fast.

However, nothing ensued. The boy turned round, with a long, loud whistle—seemingly his usual and only way of expressing his feelings. He could not make the thing out exactly—it was a rather mysterious affair, but it did not trouble him much—he was not an "examining" boy.

Then, stretching himself, for he had been evidently half asleep, he began flopping his shoulders with his arms to wake and warm himself; while his dog, a rough collie, who had been guarding the sheep meanwhile, began to jump upon him, barking with delight.

"Down, Snap, down: Stop that, or I'll thrash you," the Prince heard him say; though with such a rough, hard voice and queer pronunciation that it was difficult to make the words out. "Hollo! Let's warm ourselves by a race."

They started off together, boy and dog—barking and shouting, till it was doubtful which made the more noise or ran the faster. A regular steeplechase it was: first across the level common, greatly disturbing the quiet sheep; and then tearing away across country, scrambling through hedges and leaping ditches, and tumbling up and down over plowed fields. They did not seem to have anything to run for—but as if they did it, both of them, for the mere pleasure of motion.

And what a pleasure that seemed! To the dog of course, but scarcely less so to the boy. How he skimmed along over the ground—his cheeks glowing, and his hair flying, and his legs—oh, what a pair of legs he had!

Prince Dolor watched him with great intentness, and in a state of excitement almost equal to that of the runner himself—for a while. Then the sweet, pale face grew a trifle paler, the lips began to quiver, and the eyes to fill.

"How nice it must be to run like that!" he said softly, thinking that never—no, never in this world—would he be able to do the same.

Now he understood what his godmother had meant when she gave him his traveling-cloak, and why he had heard that sigh—he was sure it was hers—when he had asked to see "just one little boy."

"I think I had rather not look at him again," said the poor little Prince, drawing himself back into the center of his cloak, and resuming his favorite posture, sitting like a Turk, with his arms wrapped round his feeble, useless legs.

"You're no good to me," he said, patting them mournfully. "You never will be any good to me. I wonder why I had you at all. I wonder why I was born at all, since I was not to grow up like other boys. Why not?"

A question so strange, so sad, yet so often occurring in some form or other in this world—as you will find, my children, when you are older—that even if he had put it to his mother she could only have answered it, as we have to answer many as difficult things, by simply saying, "I don't know." There is much that we do not know and cannot understand—we big folks no more than you little ones. We have to accept it all just as you have to accept anything which your parents may tell you, even though you don't as yet see the reason of it. You may sometime, if you do exactly as they tell you, and are content to wait.

Prince Dolor sat a good while thus, or it appeared to him a good while, so many thoughts came and went through his poor young mind—thoughts of great bitterness, which, little though he was, seemed to make him grow years older in a few minutes.

Then he fancied the cloak began to rock gently to and fro, with a soothing kind of motion, as if he were in somebody's arms: somebody who did not speak, but loved him and comforted him without need of words; not by deceiving him with false encouragement or hope, but by making him see the plain, hard truth in all its hardness, and thus letting him quietly face it, till it grew softened down, and did not seem nearly so dreadful after all.

Through the dreary silence and blankness, for he had placed himself so that he could see nothing but the sky, and had taken off his silver ears as well as his gold spectacles—what was the use of either when he had no legs with which to walk or run?—up from below there rose a delicious sound.

You have heard it hundreds of times, my children, and so have I. When I was a child I thought there was nothing so sweet; and I think so still. It was just the song of a skylark, mounting higher and higher from the ground, till it came so close that Prince Dolor could distinguish his quivering wings and tiny body, almost too tiny to contain such a gush of music.

"Oh, you beautiful, beautiful bird!" cried he; "I should dearly like to take you in and cuddle you. That is, if I could—if I dared."

But he hesitated. The little brown creature with its loud heavenly voice almost made him afraid. Nevertheless, it also made him happy; and he watched and listened—so absorbed that he forgot all regret and pain, forgot everything in the world except the little lark.

It soared and soared, and he was just wondering if it would soar out of sight, and what in the world he should do when it was gone, when it suddenly closed its wings, as larks do when they mean to drop to the ground. But, instead of dropping to the ground, it dropped right into the little boy's breast.

What felicity! If it would only stay! A tiny, soft thing to fondle and kiss, to sing to him all day long, and be his playfellow and companion, tame and tender, while to the rest of the world it was a wild bird of the air. What a pride, what a delight! To have something that nobody else had—something all his own. As the traveling-cloak traveled on, he little heeded where, and the lark still stayed, nestled down in his bosom, hopped from his hand to his shoulder, and kissed him with its dainty beak, as if it loved him, Prince Dolor forgot all his grief, and was entirely happy.

But when he got in sight of Hopeless Tower a painful thought struck him.

"My pretty bird, what am I to do with you? If I take you into my room and shut you up there, you, a wild skylark of the air, what will become of you? I am used to this, but you are not. You will be so miserable; and suppose my nurse should find you—she who can't bear the sound of singing? Besides, I remember her once telling me that the nicest thing she ever ate in her life was lark pie!"

The little boy shivered all over at the thought. And, though the merry lark immediately broke into the loudest carol, as if saying derisively that he defied anybody to eat him, still, Prince Dolor was very uneasy. In another minute he had made up his mind.

"No, my bird, nothing so dreadful shall happen to you if I can help it; I would rather do without you altogether. Yes, I'll try. Fly away, my darling, my beautiful! Good-by, my merry, merry bird."

Opening his two caressing hands, in which, as if for protection, he had folded it, he let the lark go. It lingered a minute, perching on the rim of the cloak, and looking at him with eyes of almost human tenderness; then away it flew, far up into the blue sky. It was only a bird.

But some time after, when Prince Dolor had eaten his supper—somewhat drearily, except for the thought that he could not possibly sup off lark pie now—and gone quietly to bed, the old familiar little bed, where he was accustomed to sleep, or lie awake contentedly thinking—suddenly he heard outside the window a little faint carol—faint but cheerful—cheerful even though it was the middle of the night.

The dear little lark! it had not flown away, after all. And it was truly the most extraordinary bird, for, unlike ordinary larks, it kept hovering about the tower in the silence and darkness of the night, outside the window or over the roof. Whenever he listened for a moment, he heard it singing still.

He went to sleep as happy as a king.

CHAPTER VII

"Happy as a king." How far kings are happy I cannot say, no more than could Prince Dolor, though he had once been a king himself. But he remembered nothing about it, and there was nobody to tell him, except his nurse, who had been forbidden upon pain of death to let him know anything about his dead parents, or the king his uncle, or indeed any part of his own history.

Sometimes he speculated about himself, whether he had had a father and mother as other little boys had what they had been like, and why he had never seen them. But, knowing nothing about them, he did not miss them—only once or twice, reading pretty stories about little children and their mothers, who helped them when they were in difficulty and comforted them when they were sick, he feeling ill and dull and lonely, wondered what had become of his mother and why she never came to see him.

Then, in his history lessons, of course he read about kings and princes, and the governments of different countries, and the events that happened there. And though he but faintly took in all this, still he did take it in a little, and worried his young brain about it, and perplexed his nurse with questions, to which she returned sharp and mysterious answers, which only set him thinking the more.

He had plenty of time for thinking. After his last journey in the traveling-cloak, the journey which had given him so much pain, his desire to see the world somehow faded away. He contented himself with reading his books, and looking out of the tower windows, and listening to his beloved little lark, which had come home with him that day, and never left him again.

True, it kept out of the way; and though his nurse sometimes dimly heard it, and said "What is that horrid noise outside?" she never got the faintest chance of making it into a lark pie. Prince Dolor had his pet all to himself, and though he seldom saw it, he knew it was near him, and he caught continually, at odd hours of the day, and even in the night, fragments of its delicious song.

All during the winter—so far as there ever was any difference between summer and winter in Hopeless Tower—the little bird cheered and amused him. He scarcely needed anything more—not even his traveling-cloak, which lay bundled up unnoticed in a corner, tied up in its innumerable knots.

Nor did his godmother come near him. It seemed as if she had given these treasures and left him alone—to use them or lose them, apply them or misapply them, according to his own choice. That is all we can do with children when they grow into big children old enough to distinguish between right and wrong, and too old to be forced to do either.

Prince Dolor was now quite a big boy. Not tall—alas! he never could be that, with his poor little shrunken legs, which were of no use, only an encumbrance. But he was stout and strong, with great sturdy shoulders, and muscular arms, upon which he could swing himself about almost like a monkey. As if in compensation for his useless lower limbs, Nature had given to these extra strength and activity. His face, too, was very handsome; thinner, firmer, more manly; but still the sweet face of his childhood—his mother's own face.

How his mother would have liked to look at him! Perhaps she did—who knows?

The boy was not a stupid boy either. He could learn almost anything he chose—and he did choose, which was more than half the battle. He never gave up his lessons till he had learned them all—never thought it a punishment that he had to work at them, and that they cost him a deal of trouble sometimes.

"But," thought he, "men work, and it must be so grand to be a man—a prince too; and I fancy princes work harder than anybody—except kings. The princes I read about generally turn into kings. I wonder"—the boy was always wondering—"Nurse,"—and one day he startled her with a sudden question,—"tell me—shall I ever be a king?"

The woman stood, perplexed beyond expression. So long a time had passed by since her crime—if it were a crime—and her sentence, that she now seldom thought of either. Even her punishment—to be shut up for life in Hopeless Tower—she had gradually got used to. Used also to the little lame Prince, her charge—whom at first she had hated, though she carefully did everything to keep him alive, since upon him her own life hung.

But latterly she had ceased to hate him, and, in a sort of way, almost loved him—at least, enough to be sorry for him—an innocent child, imprisoned here till he grew into an old man, and became a dull, worn-out creature like herself. Sometimes, watching him, she felt more sorry for him than even for herself; and then, seeing she looked a less miserable and ugly woman, he did not shrink from her as usual.

He did not now. "Nurse—dear nurse," said he, "I don't mean to vex you, but tell me what is a king? shall I ever be one?"

When she began to think less of herself and more of the child, the woman's courage increased. The idea came to her—what harm would it be, even if he did know his own history? Perhaps he ought to know it—for there had been various ups and downs, usurpations, revolutions, and restorations in Nomansland, as in most other countries. Something might happen—who could tell? Changes might occur. Possibly a crown would even yet be set upon those pretty, fair curls—which she began to think prettier than ever when she saw the imaginary coronet upon them.

She sat down, considering whether her oath, never to "say a word" to Prince Dolor about himself, would be broken if she were to take a pencil and write what was to be told. A mere quibble—a mean, miserable quibble. But then she was a miserable woman, more to be pitied than scorned.

After long doubt, and with great trepidation, she put her fingers to her lips, and taking the Prince's slate—with the sponge tied to it, ready to rub out the writing in a minute—she wrote:

"You are a king."

Prince Dolor started. His face grew pale, and then flushed all over; he held himself erect. Lame as he was, anybody could see he was born to be a king.

"Hush!" said the nurse, as he was beginning to speak. And then, terribly frightened all the while,—people who have done wrong always are frightened,— she wrote down in a few hurried sentences his history. How his parents had died—his uncle had usurped his throne, and sent him to end his days in this lonely tower.

"I, too," added she, bursting into tears. "Unless, indeed, you could get out into the world, and fight for your rights like a man. And fight for me also, my Prince, that I may not die in this desolate place."

"Poor old nurse!" said the boy compassionately. For somehow, boy as he was, when he heard he was born to be a king, he felt like a man—like a king— who could afford to be tender because he was strong.

He scarcely slept that night, and even though he heard his little lark singing in the sunrise, he barely listened to it. Things more serious and important had taken possession of his mind.

"Suppose," thought he, "I were to do as she says, and go out in the world, no matter how it hurts me—the world of people, active people, as that boy I saw. They might only laugh at me—poor helpless creature that I am; but still I might show them I could do something. At any rate, I might go and see if there were anything for me to do. Godmother, help me!"

It was so long since he had asked her help that he was hardly surprised when he got no answer—only the little lark outside the window sang louder and louder, and the sun rose, flooding the room with light.

Prince Dolor sprang out of bed, and began dressing himself, which was hard work, for he was not used to it—he had always been accustomed to depend upon his nurse for everything.

"But I must now learn to be independent," thought he. "Fancy a king being dressed like a baby!"

So he did the best he could,—awkwardly but cheerily,—and then he leaped to the corner where lay his traveling-cloak, untied it as before, and watched it unrolling itself—which it did rapidly, with a hearty good-will, as if quite tired of idleness. So was Prince Dolor—or felt as if he were. He jumped into the middle of it, said his charm, and was out through the skylight immediately.

"Good-by, pretty lark!" he shouted, as he passed it on the wing, still warbling its carol to the newly risen sun. "You have been my pleasure, my delight; now I must go and work. Sing to old nurse till I come back again. Perhaps she'll hear you—perhaps she won't—but it will do her good all the same. Good-by!"

But, as the cloak hung irresolute in air, he suddenly remembered that he had not determined where to go—indeed, he did not know, and there was nobody to tell him.

"Godmother," he cried, in much perplexity, "you know what I want,—at least, I hope you do, for I hardly do myself—take me where I ought to go; show me whatever I ought to see—never mind what I like to see," as a sudden idea came into his mind that he might see many painful and disagreeable things. But this journey was not for pleasure as before. He was not a baby now, to do nothing but play—big boys do not always play. Nor men neither—they work. Thus much Prince Dolor knew—though very little more.

As the cloak started off, traveling faster than he had ever known it to do,—through sky-land and cloud land, over freezing mountain-tops, and desolate stretches of forest, and smiling cultivated plains, and great lakes that seemed to him almost as shoreless as the sea,—he was often rather frightened. But he crouched down, silent and quiet; what was the use of making a fuss? and, wrapping himself up in his bear-skin, waited for what was to happen.

After some time he heard a murmur in the distance, increasing more and more till it grew like the hum of a gigantic hive of bees. And, stretching his chin over the rim of his cloak, Prince Dolor saw—far, far below him, yet, with his gold spectacles and silver ears on, he could distinctly hear and see—what?

Most of us have some time or other visited a great metropolis—have wandered through its network of streets—lost ourselves in its crowds of people—looked up at its tall rows of houses, its grand public buildings, churches, and squares. Also, perhaps, we have peeped into its miserable little back alleys, where dirty children play in gutters all day and half the night—even young boys go about picking pockets, with nobody to tell them it is wrong except the policeman, and he simply takes them off to prison. And all this wretchedness is close behind the grandeur—like the two sides of the leaf of a book.

An awful sight is a large city, seen any how from any where. But, suppose you were to see it from the upper air, where, with your eyes and ears open, you could take in everything at once? What would it look like? How would you feel about it? I hardly know myself. Do you?

Prince Dolor had need to be a king—that is, a boy with a kingly nature—to be able to stand such a sight without being utterly overcome. But he was very much bewildered—as bewildered as a blind person who is suddenly made to see.

He gazed down on the city below him, and then put his hand over his eyes.

"I can't bear to look at it, it is so beautiful—so dreadful. And I don't understand it—not one bit. There is nobody to tell me about it. I wish I had somebody to speak to."

"Do you? Then pray speak to me. I was always considered good at conversation."

The voice that squeaked out this reply was an excellent imitation of the human one, though it came only from a bird. No lark this time, however, but a great black and white creature that flew into the cloak, and began walking round and round on the edge of it with a dignified stride, one foot before the other, like any unfeathered biped you could name.

"I haven't the honor of your acquaintance, sir," said the boy politely.

"Ma'am, if you please. I am a mother bird, and my name is Mag, and I shall be happy to tell you everything you want to know. For I know a great deal; and I enjoy talking. My family is of great antiquity; we have built in this palace for hundreds—that is to say, dozens of years. I am intimately acquainted with the king, the queen, and the little princes and princesses—also the maids of honor, and all the inhabitants of the city. I talk a good deal, but I always talk sense, and I daresay I should be exceedingly useful to a poor little ignorant boy like you."

"I am a prince," said the other gently.

"All right. And I am a magpie. You will find me a most respectable bird."

"I have no doubt of it," was the polite answer—though he thought in his own mind that Mag must have a very good opinion of herself. But she was a lady and a stranger, so of course he was civil to her.

She settled herself at his elbow, and began to chatter away, pointing out with one skinny claw, while she balanced herself on the other, every object of interest, evidently believing, as no doubt all its inhabitants did, that there was no capital in the world like the great metropolis of Nomansland.

I have not seen it, and therefore cannot describe it, so we will just take it upon trust, and suppose it to be, like every other fine city, the finest city that ever was built. Mag said so—and of course she knew.

Nevertheless, there were a few things in it which surprised Prince Dolor—and, as he had said, he could not understand them at all. One half the people seemed so happy and busy—hurrying up and down the full streets, or driving lazily along the parks in their grand carriages, while the other half were so wretched and miserable.

"Can't the world be made a little more level? I would try to do it if I were a king."

"But you're not the king: only a little goose of a boy," returned the magpie loftily. "And I'm here not to explain things, only to show them. Shall I show you the royal palace?"

It was a very magnificent palace. It had terraces and gardens, battlements and towers. It extended over acres of ground, and had in it rooms enough to accommodate half the city. Its windows looked in all directions, but none of them had any particular view—except a small one, high up toward the roof, which looked out on the Beautiful Mountains. But since the queen died there it had been closed, boarded up, indeed, the magpie said. It was so little and inconvenient that nobody cared to live in it. Besides, the lower apartments, which had no view, were magnificent—worthy of being inhabited by the king.

"I should like to see the king," said Prince Dolor.

CHAPTER VIII

What, I wonder, would be people's idea of a king? What was Prince Dolor's?

Perhaps a very splendid personage, with a crown on his head and a scepter in his hand, sitting on a throne and judging the people. Always doing right, and never wrong—"The king can do no wrong" was a law laid down in olden times. Never cross, or tired, or sick, or suffering; perfectly handsome and well dressed, calm and good-tempered, ready to see and hear everybody, and discourteous to nobody; all things always going well with him, and nothing unpleasant ever happening.

This, probably, was what Prince Dolor expected to see. And what did he see? But I must tell you how he saw it.

"Ah," said the magpie, "no levee to-day. The King is ill, though his Majesty does not wish it to be generally known—it would be so very inconvenient. He can't see you, but perhaps you might like to go and take a look at him in a way I often do? It is so very amusing."

Amusing, indeed!

The prince was just now too much excited to talk much. Was he not going to see the king his uncle, who had succeeded his father and dethroned himself; had stepped into all the pleasant things that he, Prince Dolor, ought to have had, and shut him up in a desolate tower? What was he like, this great, bad, clever man? Had he got all the things he wanted, which another ought to have had? And did he enjoy them?

"Nobody knows," answered the magpie, just as if she had been sitting inside the prince's heart, instead of on the top of his shoulder. "He is a king, and that's enough. For the rest nobody knows."

As she spoke, Mag flew down on to the palace roof, where the cloak had rested, settling down between the great stacks of chimneys as comfortably as if on the ground. She pecked at the tiles with her beak—truly she was a wonderful bird—and immediately a little hole opened, a sort of door, through which could be seen distinctly the chamber below.

"Now look in, my Prince. Make haste, for I must soon shut it up again."

But the boy hesitated. "Isn't it rude?—won't they think us intruding?"

"Oh, dear no! there's a hole like this in every palace; dozens of holes, indeed. Everybody knows it, but nobody speaks of it. Intrusion! Why, though the royal family are supposed to live shut up behind stone walls ever so thick, all the world knows that they live in a glass house where everybody can see them and throw a stone at them. Now pop down on your knees, and take a peep at his Majesty."

His Majesty!

The Prince gazed eagerly down into a large room, the largest room he had ever beheld, with furniture and hangings grander than anything he could have ever imagined. A stray sunbeam, coming through a crevice of the darkened windows, struck across the carpet, and it was the loveliest carpet ever woven—

just like a bed of flowers to walk over; only nobody walked over it, the room being perfectly empty and silent.

"Where is the King?" asked the puzzled boy.

"There," said Mag, pointing with one wrinkled claw to a magnificent bed, large enough to contain six people. In the center of it, just visible under the silken counterpane,—quite straight and still,—with its head on the lace pillow, lay a small figure, something like wax-work, fast asleep—very fast asleep! There was a number of sparkling rings on the tiny yellow hands, that were curled a little, helplessly, like a baby's, outside the coverlet; the eyes were shut, the nose looked sharp and thin, and the long gray beard hid the mouth and lay over the breast. A sight not ugly nor frightening, only solemn and quiet. And so very silent—two little flies buzzing about the curtains of the bed being the only audible sound.

"Is that the King?" whispered Prince Dolor.

"Yes," replied the bird.

He had been angry—furiously angry—ever since he knew how his uncle had taken the crown, and sent him, a poor little helpless child, to be shut up for life, just as if he had been dead. Many times the boy had felt as if, king as he was, he should like to strike him, this great, strong, wicked man.

Why, you might as well have struck a baby! How helpless he lay, with his eyes shut, and his idle hands folded: they had no more work to do, bad or good.

"What is the matter with him?" asked the Prince.

"He is dead," said the Magpie, with a croak.

No, there was not the least use in being angry with him now. On the contrary, the Prince felt almost sorry for him, except that he looked so peaceful with all his cares at rest. And this was being dead? So even kings died?

"Well, well, he hadn't an easy life, folk say, for all his grandeur. Perhaps he is glad it is over. Good-by, your Majesty."

With another cheerful tap of her beak, Mistress Mag shut down the little door in the tiles, and Prince Dolor's first and last sight of his uncle was ended.

He sat in the center of his traveling-cloak, silent and thoughtful.

"What shall we do now?" said the magpie. "There's nothing much more to be done with his majesty, except a fine funeral, which I shall certainly go and see. All the world will. He interested the world exceedingly when he was alive, and he ought to do it now he's dead—just once more. And since he can't hear me, I may as well say that, on the whole, his majesty is much better dead than alive—if we can only get somebody in his place. There'll be such a row in the city presently. Suppose we float up again and see it all—at a safe distance, though. It will be such fun!"

"What will be fun?"

"A revolution."

Whether anybody except a magpie would have called it "fun" I don't know, but it certainly was a remarkable scene.

As soon as the cathedral bell began to toll and the minute-guns to fire, announcing to the kingdom that it was without a king, the people gathered in crowds, stopping at street corners to talk together. The murmur now and then rose into a shout, and the shout into a roar. When Prince Dolor, quietly floating in upper air, caught the sound of their different and opposite cries, it seemed to him as if the whole city had gone mad together.

"Long live the king!" "The king is dead—down with the king!" "Down with the crown, and the king too!" "Hurrah for the republic!" "Hurrah for no government at all!"

Such were the shouts which traveled up to the traveling-cloak. And then began—oh, what a scene!

When you children are grown men and women—or before—you will hear and read in books about what are called revolutions—earnestly I trust that neither I nor you may ever see one. But they have happened, and may happen again, in other countries besides Nomansland, when wicked kings have helped to make their people wicked too, or out of an unrighteous nation have sprung rulers equally bad; or, without either of these causes, when a restless country has fancied any change better than no change at all.

For me, I don't like changes, unless pretty sure that they are for good. And how good can come out of absolute evil—the horrible evil that went on this night under Prince Dolor's very eyes—soldiers shooting down people by hundreds in the streets, scaffolds erected, and heads dropping off—houses burned, and women and children murdered—this is more than I can understand.

But all these things you will find in history, my children, and must by and by judge for yourselves the right and wrong of them, as far as anybody ever can judge.

Prince Dolor saw it all. Things happened so fast one after another that they quite confused his faculties.

"Oh, let me go home," he cried at last, stopping his ears and shutting his eyes; "only let me go home!" for even his lonely tower seemed home, and its dreariness and silence absolute paradise after all this.

"Good-by, then," said the magpie, flapping her wings. She had been chatting incessantly all day and all night, for it was actually thus long that Prince Dolor had been hovering over the city, neither eating nor sleeping, with all these terrible things happening under his very eyes. "You've had enough, I suppose, of seeing the world?"

"Oh, I have—I have!" cried the prince, with a shudder.

"That is, till next time. All right, your royal highness. You don't know me, but I know you. We may meet again some time."

She looked at him with her clear, piercing eyes, sharp enough to see through everything, and it seemed as if they changed from bird's eyes to human eyes—the very eyes of his godmother, whom he had not seen for ever so long. But the minute afterward she became only a bird, and with a screech and a chatter, spread her wings and flew away.

Prince Dolor fell into a kind of swoon of utter misery, bewilderment, and exhaustion, and when he awoke he found himself in his own room—alone and quiet—with the dawn just breaking, and the long rim of yellow light in the horizon glimmering through the window-panes.

CHAPTER IX

When Prince Dolor sat up in bed, trying to remember where he was, whither he had been, and what he had seen the day before, he perceived that his room was empty.

Generally his nurse rather worried him by breaking his slumbers, coming in and "setting things to rights," as she called it. Now the dust lay thick upon chairs and tables; there was no harsh voice heard to scold him for not getting up immediately, which, I am sorry to say, this boy did not always do. For he so enjoyed lying still, and thinking lazily about everything or nothing, that, if he had not tried hard against it, he would certainly have become like those celebrated "Two little men

Who lay in their bed till the clock struck ten."

It was striking ten now, and still no nurse was to be seen. He was rather relieved at first, for he felt so tired; and besides, when he stretched out his arm, he found to his dismay that he had gone to bed in his clothes.

Very uncomfortable he felt, of course; and just a little frightened. Especially when he began to call and call again, but nobody answered. Often he used to think how nice it would be to get rid of his nurse and live in this tower all by himself—like a sort of monarch able to do everything he liked, and leave undone all that he did not want to do; but now that this seemed really to have happened, he did not like it at all.

"Nurse,—dear nurse,—please come back!" he called out. "Come back, and I will be the best boy in all the land."

And when she did not come back, and nothing but silence answered his lamentable call, he very nearly began to cry.

"This won't do," he said at last, dashing the tears from his eyes. "It's just like a baby, and I'm a big boy—shall be a man some day. What has happened, I wonder? I'll go and see."

He sprang out of bed,—not to his feet, alas! but to his poor little weak knees, and crawled on them from room to room. All the four chambers were deserted—not forlorn or untidy, for everything seemed to have been done for his comfort—the breakfast and dinner things were laid, the food spread in order. He might live "like a prince," as the proverb is, for several days. But the place was entirely forsaken—there was evidently not a creature but himself in the solitary tower.

A great fear came upon the poor boy. Lonely as his life had been, he had never known what it was to be absolutely alone. A kind of despair seized him— no violent anger or terror, but a sort of patient desolation.

"What in the world am I to do?" thought he, and sat down in the middle of the floor, half inclined to believe that it would be better to give up entirely, lay himself down, and die.

This feeling, however, did not last long, for he was young and strong, and, I said before, by nature a very courageous boy. There came into his head, somehow or other, a proverb that his nurse had taught him—the people of Nomansland were very fond of proverbs:

"For every evil under the sun
There is a remedy, or there's none;
If there is one, try to find it—
If there isn't, never mind it."

"I wonder is there a remedy now, and could I find it?" cried the Prince, jumping up and looking out of the window.

No help there. He only saw the broad, bleak, sunshiny plain—that is, at first. But by and by, in the circle of mud that surrounded the base of the tower, he perceived distinctly the marks of a horse's feet, and just in the spot where the deaf-mute was accustomed to tie up his great black charger, while he himself ascended, there lay the remains of a bundle of hay and a feed of corn.

"Yes, that's it. He has come and gone, taking nurse away with him. Poor nurse! how glad she would be to go!"

That was Prince Dolor's first thought. His second—wasn't it natural?—was a passionate indignation at her cruelty—at the cruelty of all the world toward him, a poor little helpless boy. Then he determined, forsaken as he was, to try and hold on to the last, and not to die as long as he could possibly help it.

Anyhow, it would be easier to die here than out in the world, among the terrible doings which he had just beheld—from the midst of which, it suddenly struck him, the deaf-mute had come, contriving somehow to make the nurse understand that the king was dead, and she need have no fear in going back to the capital, where there was a grand revolution, and everything turned upside down. So, of course, she had gone. "I hope she'll enjoy it, miserable woman—if they don't cut off her head too."

And then a kind of remorse smote him for feeling so bitterly toward her, after all the years she had taken care of him—grudgingly, perhaps, and coldly; still she had taken care of him, and that even to the last: for, as I have said, all his four rooms were as tidy as possible, and his meals laid out, that he might have no more trouble than could be helped.

"Possibly she did not mean to be cruel. I won't judge her," said he. And afterward he was very glad that he had so determined.

For the second time he tried to dress himself, and then to do everything he could for himself—even to sweeping up the hearth and putting on more coals. "It's a funny thing for a prince to have to do," said he, laughing. "But my godmother once said princes need never mind doing anything."

And then he thought a little of his godmother. Not of summoning her, or asking her to help him,—she had evidently left him to help himself, and he was determined to try his best to do it, being a very proud and independent boy,— but he remembered her tenderly and regret-fully, as if even she had been a little hard upon him—poor, forlorn boy that he was. But he seemed to have seen and learned so much within the last few days that he scarcely felt like a boy, but a man—until he went to bed at night.

When I was a child, I used often to think how nice it would be to live in a little house all by my own self—a house built high up in a tree, or far away in a forest, or halfway up a hillside so deliciously alone and independent. Not a lesson to learn—but no! I always liked learning my lessons. Anyhow, to choose the lessons I liked best, to have as many books to read and dolls to play with as ever I wanted: above all, to be free and at rest, with nobody to tease or trouble or scold me, would be charming. For I was a lonely little thing, who liked quietness—as many children do; which other children, and sometimes grown-up people even, cannot understand. And so I can understand Prince Dolor.

After his first despair, he was not merely comfortable, but actually happy in his solitude, doing everything for himself, and enjoying everything by himself— until bedtime. Then he did not like it at all. No more, I suppose, than other children would have liked my imaginary house in a tree when they had had sufficient of their own company.

But the Prince had to bear it—and he did bear it, like a prince—for fully five days. All that time he got up in the morning and went to bed at night without having spoken to a creature, or, indeed, heard a single sound. For even his little lark was silent; and as for his traveling-cloak, either he never thought about it, or else it had been spirited away—for he made no use of it, nor attempted to do so.

A very strange existence it was, those five lonely days. He never entirely forgot it. It threw him back upon himself, and into himself—in a way that all of us have to learn when we grow up, and are the better for it; but it is somewhat hard learning.

On the sixth day Prince Dolor had a strange composure in his look, but he was very grave and thin and white. He had nearly come to the end of his provisions—and what was to happen next? Get out of the tower he could not: the ladder the deaf-mute used was always carried away again; and if it had not been, how could the poor boy have used it? And even if he slung or flung himself down, and by miraculous chance came alive to the foot of the tower, how could he run away?

Fate had been very hard to him, or so it seemed.

He made up his mind to die. Not that he wished to die; on the contrary, there was a great deal that he wished to live to do; but if he must die, he must. Dying did not seem so very dreadful; not even to lie quiet like his uncle, whom he had entirely forgiven now, and neither be miserable nor naughty any more, and escape all those horrible things that he had seen going on outside the palace, in that awful place which was called "the world."

"It's a great deal nicer here," said the poor little Prince, and collected all his pretty things round him: his favorite pictures, which he thought he should like to have near him when he died; his books and toys—no, he had ceased to care for toys now; he only liked them because he had done so as a child. And there he sat very calm and patient, like a king in his castle, waiting for the end.

"Still, I wish I had done something first—something worth doing, that somebody might remember me by," thought he. "Suppose I had grown a man, and had had work to do, and people to care for, and was so useful and busy that they liked me, and perhaps even forgot I was lame? Then it would have been nice to live, I think."

A tear came into the little fellow's eyes, and he listened intently through the dead silence for some hopeful sound.

Was there one?—was it his little lark, whom he had almost forgotten? No, nothing half so sweet. But it really was something—something which came nearer and nearer, so that there was no mistaking it. It was the sound of a trumpet, one of the great silver trumpets so admired in Nomansland. Not pleasant music, but very bold, grand, and inspiring.

As he listened to it the boy seemed to recall many things which had slipped his memory for years, and to nerve himself for whatever might be going to happen.

What had happened was this.

The poor condemned woman had not been such a wicked woman after all. Perhaps her courage was not wholly disinterested, but she had done a very heroic thing. As soon as she heard of the death and burial of the King and of the changes that were taking place in the country, a daring idea came into her head—to set upon the throne of Nomansland its rightful heir. Thereupon she persuaded the deaf-mute to take her away with him, and they galloped like the wind from city to city, spreading everywhere the news that Prince Dolor's death and burial had been an invention concocted by his wicked uncle that he was alive and well, and the noblest young prince that ever was born.

It was a bold stroke, but it succeeded. The country, weary perhaps of the late King's harsh rule, and yet glad to save itself from the horrors of the last few days, and the still further horrors of no rule at all, and having no particular interest in the other young princes, jumped at the idea of this Prince, who was the son of their late good King and the beloved Queen Dolorez.

"Hurrah for Prince Dolor! Let Prince Dolor be our sovereign!" rang from end to end of the kingdom. Everybody tried to remember what a dear baby he once was—how like his mother, who had been so sweet and kind, and his father, the finest-looking king that ever reigned. Nobody remembered his lameness—or, if they did, they passed it over as a matter of no consequence. They were determined to have him reign over them, boy as he was—perhaps just because he was a boy, since in that case the great nobles thought they should be able to do as they liked with the country.

Accordingly, with a fickleness not confined to the people of Nomansland, no sooner was the late King laid in his grave than they pronounced him to have been a usurper; turned all his family out of the palace, and left it empty for the reception of the new sovereign, whom they went to fetch with great rejoicing, a select body of lords, gentlemen, and soldiers traveling night and day in solemn procession through the country until they reached Hopeless Tower.

There they found the Prince, sitting calmly on the floor—deadly pale, indeed, for he expected a quite different end from this, and was resolved, if he had to die, to die courageously, like a Prince and a King.

But when they hailed him as Prince and King, and explained to him how matters stood, and went down on their knees before him, offering the crown (on a velvet cushion, with four golden tassels, each nearly as big as his head),—small though he was and lame, which lameness the courtiers pretended not to notice,—there came such a glow into his face, such a dignity into his demeanor, that he became beautiful, king-like.

"Yes," he said, "if you desire it, I will be your king. And I will do my best to make my people happy."

Then there arose, from inside and outside the tower, such a shout as never yet was heard across the lonely plain.

Prince Dolor shrank a little from the deafening sound. "How shall I be able to rule all this great people? You forget, my lords, that I am only a little boy still."

"Not so very little," was the respectful answer. "We have searched in the records, and found that your Royal Highness—your Majesty, I mean—is fifteen years old."

"Am I?" said Prince Dolor; and his first thought was a thoroughly childish pleasure that he should now have a birthday, with a whole nation to keep it. Then he remembered that his childish days were done. He was a monarch now. Even his nurse, to whom, the moment he saw her, he had held out his hand, kissed it reverently, and called him ceremoniously "his Majesty the King."

"A king must be always a king, I suppose," said he half-sadly, when, the ceremonies over, he had been left to himself for just ten minutes, to put off his boy's clothes and be reattired in magnificent robes, before he was conveyed away from his tower to the royal palace.

He could take nothing with him; indeed, he soon saw that, however politely they spoke, they would not allow him to take anything. If he was to be their king, he must give up his old life forever. So he looked with tender farewell on his old books, old toys, the furniture he knew so well, and the familiar plain in all its levelness—ugly yet pleasant, simply because it was familiar.

"It will be a new life in a new world," said he to himself; "but I'll remember the old things still. And, oh! if before I go I could but once see my dear old godmother."

While he spoke he had laid himself down on the bed for a minute or two, rather tired with his grandeur, and confused by the noise of the trumpets which kept playing incessantly down below. He gazed, half sadly, up to the skylight, whence there came pouring a stream of sunrays, with innumerable motes floating there, like a bridge thrown between heaven and earth. Sliding down it, as if she had been made of air, came the little old woman in gray.

So beautiful looked she—old as she was—that Prince Dolor was at first quite startled by the apparition. Then he held out his arms in eager delight.

"Oh, godmother, you have not forsaken me!"

"Not at all, my son. You may not have seen me, but I have seen you many a time."

"How?"

"Oh, never mind. I can turn into anything I please, you know. And I have been a bearskin rug, and a crystal goblet—and sometimes I have changed from inanimate to animate nature, put on feathers, and made myself very comfortable as a bird."

"Ha!" laughed the prince, a new light breaking in upon him as he caught the infection of her tone, lively and mischievous. "Ha! ha! a lark, for instance?"

"Or a magpie," answered she, with a capital imitation of Mistress Mag's croaky voice. "Do you suppose I am always sentimental, and never funny? If anything makes you happy, gay, or grave, don't you think it is more than likely to come through your old godmother?"

"I believe that," said the boy tenderly, holding out his arms. They clasped one another in a close embrace.

Suddenly Prince Dolor looked very anxious. "You will not leave me now that I am a king? Otherwise I had rather not be a king at all. Promise never to forsake me!"

The little old woman laughed gayly. "Forsake you? that is impossible. But it is just possible you may forsake me. Not probable though. Your mother never did, and she was a queen. The sweetest queen in all the world was the Lady Dolorez."

"Tell me about her," said the boy eagerly. "As I get older I think I can understand more. Do tell me."

"Not now. You couldn't hear me for the trumpets and the shouting. But when you are come to the palace, ask for a long-closed upper room, which looks out upon the Beautiful Mountains; open it and take it for your own. Whenever you go there you will always find me, and we will talk together about all sorts of things."

"And about my mother?"

The little old woman nodded—and kept nodding and smiling to herself many times, as the boy repeated over and over again the sweet words he had never known or understood—"my mother—my mother."

"Now I must go," said she, as the trumpets blared louder and louder, and the shouts of the people showed that they would not endure any delay. "Good-by, good-by! Open the window and out I fly."

Prince Dolor repeated gayly the musical rhyme—but all the while tried to hold his godmother fast.

Vain, vain! for the moment that a knocking was heard at his door the sun went behind a cloud, the bright stream of dancing motes vanished, and the little old woman with them—he knew not where.

So Prince Dolor quitted his tower—which he had entered so mournfully and ignominiously as a little helpless baby carried in the deaf-mute's arms—quitted it as the great King of Nomansland.

The only thing he took away with him was something so insignificant that none of the lords, gentlemen, and soldiers who escorted him with such triumphant splendor could possibly notice it—a tiny bundle, which he had found lying on the floor just where the bridge of sunbeams had rested. At once he had pounced upon it, and thrust it secretly into his bosom, where it dwindled into such small proportions that it might have been taken for a mere chest-comforter, a bit of flannel, or an old pocket-handkerchief. It was his traveling-cloak!

CHAPTER X

Did Prince Dolar become a great king? Was he, though little more than a boy, "the father of his people," as all kings ought to be? Did his reign last long— long and happy? and what were the principal events of it, as chronicled in the history of Nomansland?

Why, if I were to answer all these questions I should have to write another book. And I'm tired, children, tired—as grown-up people sometimes are, though not always with play. (Besides, I have a small person belonging to me, who, though she likes extremely to listen to the word-of-mouth story of this book, grumbles much at the writing of it, and has run about the house clapping her hands with joy when mamma told her that it was nearly finished. But that is neither here nor there.)

I have related as well as I could the history of Prince Dolor, but with the history of Nomansland I am as yet unacquainted. If anybody knows it, perhaps he or she will kindly write it all down in another book. But mine is done.

However, of this I am sure, that Prince Dolor made an excellent king. Nobody ever does anything less well, not even the commonest duty of common daily life, for having such a godmother as the little old woman clothed in gray, whose name is—well, I leave you to guess. Nor, I think, is anybody less good, less capable of both work and enjoyment in after-life, for having been a little unhappy in his youth, as the prince had been.

I cannot take upon myself to say that he was always happy now—who is?— or that he had no cares; just show me the person who is quite free from them! But whenever people worried and bothered him—as they did sometimes, with state etiquette, state squabbles, and the like, setting up themselves and pulling down their neighbors—he would take refuge in that upper room which looked out on the Beautiful Mountains, and, laying his head on his godmother's shoulder, become calmed and at rest.

Also, she helped him out of any difficulty which now and then occurred— for there never was such a wise old woman. When the people of Nomansland raised the alarm—as sometimes they did—for what people can exist without a little fault-finding?—and began to cry out, "Un-happy is the nation whose king is a child," she would say to him gently, "You are a child. Accept the fact. Be humble—be teachable. Lean upon the wisdom of others till you have gained your own."

He did so. He learned how to take advice before attempting to give it, to obey before he could righteously command. He assembled round him all the good and wise of his kingdom—laid all its affairs before them, and was guided by their opinions until he had maturely formed his own.

This he did sooner than anybody would have imagined who did not know of his godmother and his traveling-cloak—two secret blessings, which, though many guessed at, nobody quite understood. Nor did they understand why he loved so the little upper room, except that it had been his mother's room, from the window of which, as people remembered now, she had used to sit for hours watching the Beautiful Mountains.

Out of that window he used to fly—not very often; as he grew older, the labors of state prevented the frequent use of his traveling-cloak; still he did use it sometimes. Only now it was less for his own pleasure and amusement than to see something or investigate something for the good of the country. But he prized his godmother's gift as dearly as ever. It was a comfort to him in all his vexations, an enhancement of all his joys. It made him almost forget his lameness—which was never cured.

However, the cruel things which had been once foreboded of him did not happen. His misfortune was not such a heavy one, after all. It proved to be of much less inconvenience, even to himself, than had been feared. A council of eminent surgeons and mechanicians invented for him a wonderful pair of crutches, with the help of which, though he never walked easily or gracefully, he did manage to walk so as to be quite independent. And such was the love his people bore him that they never heard the sound of his crutches on the marble palace floors without a leap of the heart, for they knew that good was coming to them whenever he approached.

Thus, though he never walked in processions, never reviewed his troops mounted on a magnificent charger, nor did any of the things which make a show monarch so much appreciated, he was able for all the duties and a great many of the pleasures of his rank. When he held his levees, not standing, but seated on a throne ingeniously contrived to hide his infirmity, the people thronged to greet him; when he drove out through the city streets, shouts followed him wherever he went—every countenance brightened as he passed, and his own, perhaps, was the brightest of all.

First, because, accepting his affliction as inevitable, he took it patiently; second, because, being a brave man, he bore it bravely, trying to forget himself, and live out of himself, and in and for other people. Therefore other people grew to love him so well that I think hundreds of his subjects might have been found who were almost ready to die for their poor lame king.

He never gave them a queen. When they implored him to choose one, he replied that his country was his bride, and he desired no other. But perhaps the real reason was that he shrank from any change; and that no wife in all the world would have been found so perfect, so lovable, so tender to him in all his weaknesses as his beautiful old godmother.

His twenty-four other godfathers and godmothers, or as many of them as were still alive, crowded round him as soon as he ascended the throne. He was very civil to them all, but adopted none of the names they had given him, keeping to the one by which he had been always known, though it had now almost lost its meaning; for King Dolor was one of the happiest and cheerfulest men alive.

He did a good many things, however, unlike most men and most kings, which a little astonished his subjects. First, he pardoned the condemned woman who had been his nurse, and ordained that from henceforth there should be no such thing as the punishment of death in Nomansland. All capital criminals were to be sent to perpetual imprisonment in Hopeless Tower and the plain round about it, where they could do no harm to anybody, and might in time do a little good, as the woman had done.

Another surprise he shortly afterward gave the nation. He recalled his uncle's family, who had fled away in terror to another country, and restored them to all their honors in their own. By and by he chose the eldest son of his eldest cousin (who had been dead a year), and had him educated in the royal palace, as the heir to the throne. This little prince was a quiet, unobtrusive boy, so that everybody wondered at the King's choosing him when there were so many more; but as he grew into a fine young fellow, good and brave, they agreed that the King judged more wisely than they.

"Not a lame prince, either," his Majesty observed one day, watching him affectionately; for he was the best runner, the highest leaper, the keenest and most active sportsman in the country. "One cannot make one's self, but one can sometimes help a little in the making of somebody else. It is well."

This was said, not to any of his great lords and ladies, but to a good old woman—his first homely nurse whom he had sought for far and wide, and at last found in her cottage among the Beautiful Mountains. He sent for her to visit him once a year, and treated her with great honor until she died. He was equally kind, though somewhat less tender, to his other nurse, who, after receiving her pardon, returned to her native town and grew into a great lady, and I hope a good one. But as she was so grand a personage now, any little faults she had did not show.

Thus King Dolor's reign passed year after year, long and prosperous. Whether he were happy—"as happy as a king"—is a question no human being can decide. But I think he was, because he had the power of making everybody about him happy, and did it too; also because he was his godmother's godson, and could shut himself up with her whenever he liked, in that quiet little room in view of the Beautiful Mountains, which nobody else ever saw or cared to see. They were too far off, and the city lay so low. But there they were, all the time. No change ever came to them; and I think, at any day throughout his long reign, the King would sooner have lost his crown than have lost sight of the Beautiful Mountains.

In course of time, when the little Prince, his cousin, was grown into a tall young man, capable of all the duties of a man, his Majesty did one of the most extraordinary acts ever known in a sovereign beloved by his people and prosperous in his reign. He announced that he wished to invest his heir with the royal purple—at any rate, for a time—while he himself went away on a distant journey, whither he had long desired to go.

Everybody marveled, but nobody opposed him. Who could oppose the good King, who was not a young king now? And besides, the nation had a great admiration for the young regent—and possibly a lurking pleasure in change.

So there was a fixed day when all the people whom it would hold assembled in the great square of the capital, to see the young prince installed solemnly in his new duties, and undertaking his new vows. He was a very fine young fellow; tall and straight as a poplar tree, with a frank, handsome face—a great deal handsomer than the king, some people said, but others thought differently. However, as his Majesty sat on his throne, with his gray hair falling from underneath his crown, and a few wrinkles showing in spite of his smile, there was something about his countenance which made his people, even while they shouted, regard him with a tenderness mixed with awe.

He lifted up his thin, slender hand, and there came a silence over the vast crowd immediately. Then he spoke, in his own accustomed way, using no grand words, but saying what he had to say in the simplest fashion, though with a clearness that struck their ears like the first song of a bird in the dusk of the morning.

"My people, I am tired: I want to rest. I have had a long reign, and done much work—at least, as much as I was able to do. Many might have done it better than I—but none with a better will. Now I leave it to others; I am tired, very tired. Let me go home."

There arose a murmur—of content or discontent none could well tell; then it died down again, and the assembly listened silently once more.

"I am not anxious about you, my people—my children," continued the King. "You are prosperous and at peace. I leave you in good hands. The Prince Regent will be a fitter king for you than I."

"No, no, no!" rose the universal shout—and those who had sometimes found fault with him shouted louder than anybody. But he seemed as if he heard them not.

"Yes, yes," said he, as soon as the tumult had a little subsided: and his voice sounded firm and clear; and some very old people, who boasted of having seen him as a child, declared that his face took a sudden change, and grew as young and sweet as that of the little Prince Dolor. "Yes, I must go. It is time for me to go. Remember me sometimes, my people, for I have loved you well. And I am going a long way, and I do not think I shall come back any more."

He drew a little bundle out of his breast pocket—a bundle that nobody had ever seen before. It was small and shabby-looking, and tied up with many knots, which untied themselves in an instant. With a joyful countenance, he muttered over it a few half-intelligible words. Then, so suddenly that even those nearest to his Majesty could not tell how it came about, the King was away—away—floating right up in the air—upon something, they knew not what, except that it appeared to be as safe and pleasant as the wings of a bird.

And after him sprang a bird—a dear little lark, rising from whence no one could say, since larks do not usually build their nests in the pavement of city squares. But there it was, a real lark, singing far over their heads, louder and clearer and more joyful as it vanished further into the blue sky.

Shading their eyes, and straining their ears, the astonished people stood until the whole vision disappeared like a speck in the clouds—the rosy clouds that overhung the Beautiful Mountains.

King Dolor was never again beheld or heard of in his own country. But the good he had done there lasted for years and years; he was long missed and deeply mourned—at least, so far as anybody could mourn one who was gone on such a happy journey.

Whither he went, or who went with him, it is impossible to say. But I myself believe that his godmother took him on his traveling-cloak to the Beautiful Mountains. What he did there, or where he is now, who can tell? I cannot. But one thing I am quite sure of, that, wherever he is, he is perfectly happy.

And so, when I think of him, am I.

THE INVISIBLE PRINCE

THERE were a king and queen who were dotingly fond of their only son, notwithstanding that he was equally deformed in mind and person. The king was quite sensible of the evil disposition of his son, but the queen in her excessive fondness saw no fault whatever in her dear Furibon, as he was named. The surest way to win her favor was to praise Furibon for charms he did not possess. When he came of age to have a governor, the king made choice of a prince who had an ancient right to the crown, but was not able to support it. This prince had a son, named Leander, handsome, accomplished, amiable—in every respect the opposite of Prince Furibon. The two were frequently together, which only made the deformed prince more repulsive.

One day, certain ambassadors having arrived from a far country, the prince stood in a gallery to see them; when, taking Leander for the king's son, they made their obeisance to him, treating Furibon as a mere dwarf, at which the latter was so offended that he drew his sword, and would have done them a mischief had not the king just then appeared. As it was, the affair produced a quarrel, which ended in Leander's being sent to a far-away castle belonging to his father.

There, however, he was quite happy, for he was a great lover of hunting, fishing, and walking: he understood painting, read much, and played upon several instruments, so that he was glad to be freed from the fantastic humors of Furibon. One day as he was walking in the garden, finding the heat increase, he retired into a shady grove and began to play upon the flute to amuse himself. As he played, he felt something wind about his leg, and looking down saw a great adder: he took his handkerchief, and catching it by the head was going to kill it. But the adder, looking steadfastly in his face, seemed to beg his pardon. At this instant one of the gardeners happened to come to the place where Leander was, and spying the snake, cried out to his master: "Hold him fast, sir; it is but an hour since we ran after him to kill him: it is the most mischievous creature in the world."

Leander, casting his eyes a second time upon the snake, which was speckled with a thousand extraordinary colors, perceived the poor creature still looked upon him with an aspect that seemed to implore compassion, and never tried in the least to defend itself.

"Though thou hast such a mind to kill it," said he to the gardener, "yet, as it came to me for refuge, I forbid thee to do it any harm; for I will keep it, and when it has cast its beautiful skin I will let it go." He then returned home, and carrying the snake with him, put it into a large chamber, the key of which he kept himself, and ordered bran, milk, and flowers to be given to it, for its delight and sustenance; so that never was snake so happy. Leander went sometimes to see it, and when it perceived him it made haste to meet him, showing him all the little marks of love and gratitude of which a poor snake was capable, which did not a little surprise him, though he took no further notice of it.

In the meantime all the court ladies were extremely troubled at his absence, and he was the subject of all their discourse. "Alas!" cried they, "there is no pleasure at court since Leander is gone, of whose absence the wicked Furibon is the cause!" Furibon also had his parasites, for his power over the queen made him feared; they told him what the ladies said, which enraged him to such a degree that in his passion he flew to the queen's chamber, and vowed he would kill himself before her face if she did not find means to destroy Leander. The queen, who also hated Leander, because he was handsomer than her son, replied that she had long looked upon him as a traitor, and therefore would willingly consent to his death. To which purpose she advised Furibon to go a-hunting with some of his confidants, and contrive it so that Leander should make one of the party.

"Then," said she, "you may find some way to punish him for pleasing everybody."

Furibon understood her, and accordingly went a-hunting; and Leander, when he heard the horns and the hounds, mounted his horse and rode to see who it was. But he was surprised to meet the prince so unexpectedly; he alighted immediately and saluted him with respect; and Furibon received him more graciously than usual and bade follow him. All of a sudden he turned his horse and rode another way, making a sign to the ruffians to take the first opportunity to kill him; but before he had got quite out of sight, a lion of prodigious size, coming out of his den, leaped upon Furibon; all his followers fled, and only Leander remained; who, attacking the animal sword in hand, by his valor and agility saved the life of his most cruel enemy, who had fallen in a swoon from fear. When he recovered, Leander presented him his horse to remount. Now, any other than such a wretch would have been grateful, but Furibon did not even look upon him; nay, mounting the horse, he rode in quest of the ruffians, to whom he repeated his orders to kill him. They accordingly surrounded Leander, who, setting his back to a tree, behaved with so much bravery that he laid them all dead at his feet. Furibon, believing him by this time slain, rode eagerly up to the spot. When Leander saw him he advanced to meet him. "Sir," said he, "if it was by your order that these assassins came to kill me, I am sorry I made any defense."

"You are an insolent villain!" replied Furibon, "and if ever you come into my presence again, you shall surely die."

Leander made no answer, but retired sad and pensive to his own home, where he spent the night in pondering what was best for him to do; for there was no likelihood he should be able to defend himself against the power of the king's son; therefore he at length concluded he would travel abroad and see the world. Being ready to depart, he recollected his snake, and, calling for some milk and fruits, carried them to the poor creature for the last time; but on opening the door he perceived an extraordinary luster in one corner of the room, and casting his eye on the place he was surprised to see a lady, whose noble and majestic air made him immediately conclude she was a princess of royal birth.

Her habit was of purple satin, embroidered with pearls and diamonds; she advanced toward him with a gracious smile.

"Young prince," said she, "you find no longer your pet snake, but me, the fairy Gentilla, ready to requite your generosity. For know that we fairies live a hundred years in flourishing youth, without diseases, without trouble or pain; and this term being expired, we become snakes for eight days. During that time it is not in our power to prevent any misfortune that may befall us; and if we happen to be killed, we never revive again. But these eight days being expired, we resume our usual form and recover our beauty, our power, and our riches. Now you know how much I am obliged to your goodness, and it is but just that I should repay my debt of gratitude; think how I can serve you and depend on me."

The young prince, who had never conversed with a fairy till now, was so surprised that it was a long time before he could speak. But at length, making a profound reverence, "Madam," said he, "since I have had the honor to serve you, I know not any other happiness that I can wish for."

"I should be sorry," replied she, "not to be of service to you in something; consider, it is in my power to bestow on you long life, kingdoms, riches; to give you mines of diamonds and houses full of gold; I can make you an excellent orator, poet, musician, and painter; or, if you desire it, a spirit of the air, the water, or the earth."

Here Leander interrupted her. "Permit me, madam," said he, "to ask you what benefit it would be to me to be a spirit?"

"Much," replied the fairy, "you would be invisible when you pleased, and might in an instant traverse the whole earth; you would be able to fly without wings, to descend into the abyss of the earth without dying, and walk at the bottom of the sea without being drowned; nor doors, nor windows, though fast shut and locked, could hinder you from entering anywhere; and whenever you had a mind, you might resume your natural form."

"Oh, madam!" cried Leander, "then let me be a spirit; I am going to travel, and should prefer it above all those other advantages you have so generously offered me."

Gentilla thereupon stroking his face three times, "Be a spirit," said she; and then, embracing him, she gave him a little red cap with a plume of feathers. "When you put on this cap you shall be invisible; but when you take it off you shall again become visible."

Leander, overjoyed, put his little red cap upon his head and wished himself in the forest, that he might gather some wild roses which he had observed there: his body immediately became as light as thought; he flew through the window like a bird; though, in flying over the river, he was not without fear lest he should fall into it, and the power of the fairy not be able to save him. But he arrived in safety at the rose-bushes, plucked the three roses, and returned immediately to his chamber; presented his roses to the fairy, overjoyed that his first experiments had succeeded so well. She bade him keep the roses, for that one of them would supply him with money whenever he wanted it; that if he put the other into his mistress' bosom, he would know whether she was faithful or not; and that the third would keep him always in good health. Then, without staying to receive his thanks, she wished him success in his travels and disappeared.

Leander, infinitely pleased, settled his affairs, mounted the finest horse in the stable, called Gris-de-line, and attended by some of his servants in livery, made his return to court. Now you must know Furibon had given out that had it not been for his courage Leander would have murdered him when they were a-hunting; so the king, being importuned by the queen, gave orders that Leander should be apprehended. But when he came, he showed so much courage and resolution that Furibon ran to the queen's chamber and prayed her to order him to be seized. The queen, who was extremely diligent in everything that her son desired, went immediately to the king. Furibon, being impatient to know what would be resolved, followed her; but stopped at the door and laid his ear to the keyhole, putting his hair aside that he might the better hear what was said. At the same time, Leander entered the court-hall of the palace with his red cap upon his head, and perceiving Furibon listening at the door of the king's chamber, he took a nail and a hammer and nailed his ear to the door. Furibon began to roar, so that the queen, hearing her son's voice, ran and opened the door, and, pulling it hastily, tore her son's ear from his head. Half out of her wits, she set him in her lap, took up his ear, kissed it, and clapped it again upon its place; but the invisible Leander, seizing upon a handful of twigs, with which they corrected the king's little dogs, gave the queen several lashes upon her hands, and her son as many on the nose: upon which the queen cried out, "Murder! murder!" and the king looked about, and the people came running in; but nothing was to be seen. Some cried that the queen was mad, and that her madness proceeded from her grief to see that her son had lost one ear; and the king was as ready as any to believe it, so that when she came near him he avoided her, which made a very ridiculous scene. Leander, then leaving the chamber, went into the garden, and there, assuming his own shape, he boldly began to pluck the queen's cherries, apricots, strawberries, and flowers, though he knew she set such a high value on them that it was as much as a man's life was worth to touch one. The gardeners, all amazed, came and told their majesties that Prince Leander was making havoc of all the fruits and flowers in the queen's gardens.

"What insolence!" said the queen: then turning to Furibon, "my pretty child, forget the pain of thy ear but for a moment, and fetch that vile wretch hither; take our guards, both horse and foot, seize him, and punish him as he deserves."

Furibon, encouraged by his mother, and attended by a great number of armed soldiers, entered the garden and saw Leander; who, taking refuge under a tree, pelted them all with oranges. But when they came running toward him, thinking to have seized him, he was not to be seen; he had slipped behind Furibon, who was in a bad condition already. But Leander played him one trick more; for he pushed him down upon the gravel walk, and frightened him so that the soldiers had to take him up, carry him away, and put him to bed.

Satisfied with this revenge, he returned to his servants, who waited for him, and giving them money, sent them back to his castle, that none might know the secret of his red cap and roses. As yet he had not determined whither to go; however, he mounted his fine horse Gris-de-line, and, laying the reins upon his neck, let him take his own road: at length he arrived in a forest, where he stopped to shelter himself from the heat. He had not been above a minute there before he heard a lamentable noise of sighing and sobbing; and looking about him, beheld a man, who ran, stopped, then ran again, sometimes crying, sometimes silent, then tearing his hair, then thumping his breast like some unfortunate madman. Yet he seemed to be both handsome and young: his garments had been magnificent, but he had torn them all to tatters. The prince, moved with compassion, made toward him, and mildly accosted him. "Sir," said he, "your condition appears so deplorable that I must ask the cause of your sorrow, assuring you of every assistance in my power."

"Oh, sir," answered the young man, "nothing can cure my grief; this day my dear mistress is to be sacrificed to a rich old ruffian of a husband who will make her miserable."

"Does she love you, then?" asked Leander.

"I flatter myself so," answered the young man.

"Where is she?" continued Leander.

"In the castle at the end of this forest," replied the lover.

"Very well," said Leander; "stay you here till I come again, and in a little while I will bring you good news."

He then put on his little red cap and wished himself in the castle. He had hardly got thither before he heard all sorts of music; he entered into a great room, where the friends and kindred of the old man and the young lady were assembled. No one could look more amiable than she; but the paleness of her complexion, the melancholy that appeared in her countenance, and the tears that now and then dropped, as it were by stealth from her eyes, betrayed the trouble of her mind.

Leander now became invisible, and placed himself in a corner of the room. He soon perceived the father and mother of the bride; and coming behind the mother's chair, whispered in her ear, "If you marry your daughter to that old dotard, before eight days are over you shall certainly die." The woman, frightened to hear such a terrible sentence pronounced upon her, and yet not know from whence it came, gave a loud shriek and dropped upon the floor. Her husband asked what ailed her: she cried that she was a dead woman if the marriage of her daughter went forward, and therefore she would not consent to it for all the world. Her husband laughed at her and called her a fool. But the invisible Leander accosting the man, threatened him in the same way, which frightened him so terribly that he also insisted on the marriage being broken off. When the lover complained, Leander trod hard upon his gouty toes and rang such an alarm in his ears that, not being able any longer to hear himself speak, away he limped, glad enough to go. The real lover soon appeared, and he and his fair mistress fell joyfully into one another's arms, the parents consenting to their union. Leander, assuming his own shape, appeared at the hall door, as if he were a stranger drawn thither by the report of this extraordinary wedding.

From hence he traveled on, and came to a great city, where, upon his arrival, he understood there was a great and solemn procession, in order to shut up a young woman against her will among the vestal-nuns. The prince was touched with compassion; and thinking the best use he could make of his cap was to redress public wrongs and relieve the oppressed, he flew to the temple, where he saw the young woman, crowned with flowers, clad in white, and with her disheveled hair flowing about her shoulders. Two of her brothers led her by each hand, and her mother followed her with a great crowd of men and women. Leander, being invisible, cried out, "Stop, stop, wicked brethren: stop, rash and inconsiderate mother; if you proceed any further, you shall be squeezed to death like so many frogs." They looked about, but could not conceive from whence these terrible menaces came. The brothers said it was only their sister's lover, who had hid himself in some hole; at which Leander, in wrath, took a long cudgel, and they had no reason to say the blows were not well laid on. The multitude fled, the vestals ran away, and Leander was left alone with the victim; immediately he pulled off his red cap and asked her wherein he might serve her. She answered him that there was a certain gentleman whom she would be glad to marry, but that he wanted an estate. Leander then shook his rose so long that he supplied them with ten millions; after which they were married and lived happily together.

But his last adventure was the most agreeable. Entering into a wide forest, he heard lamentable cries. Looking about him every way, at length he spied four men well armed, who were carrying away by force a young lady, thirteen or fourteen years of age; upon which, making up to them as fast as he could, "What harm has that girl done?" said he.

"Ha! ha! my little master," cried he who seemed to be the ringleader of the rest, "who bade you inquire?"

"Let her alone," said Leander, "and go about your business."

"Oh, yes, to be sure," cried they, laughing; whereupon the prince, alighting, put on his red cap, not thinking it otherwise prudent to attack four who seemed strong enough to fight a dozen. One of them stayed to take care of the young lady, while the three others went after Gris-de-line, who gave them a great deal of unwelcome exercise.

Meantime the young lady continued her cries and complaints. "Oh, my dear princess," said she, "how happy was I in your palace! Did you but know my sad misfortune, you would send your Amazons to rescue poor Abricotina."

Leander, having listened to what she said, without delay seized the ruffian that held her, and bound him fast to a tree before he had time or strength to defend himself. He then went to the second, and taking him by both arms, bound him in the same manner to another tree. In the meantime Abricotina made the best of her good fortune and betook herself to her heels, not knowing which way she went. But Leander, missing her, called out to his horse Gris-de-line; who, by two kicks with his hoof, rid himself of the two ruffians who had pursued him: one of them had his head broken and the other three of his ribs. And now Leander only wanted to overtake Abricotina; for he thought her so handsome that he wished to see her again. He found her leaning against a tree. When she saw Gris-de-line coming toward her, "How lucky am I!" cried she; "this pretty little horse will carry me to the palace of pleasure." Leander heard her, though she saw him not: he rode up to her; Gris-de-line stopped, and when Abricotina mounted him, Leander clasped her in his arms and placed her gently before him. Oh, how great was Abricotina's fear to feel herself fast embraced, and yet see nobody! She durst not stir, and shut her eyes for fear of seeing a spirit. But Leander took off his little cap. "How comes it, fair Abricotina," said he, "that you are afraid of me, who delivered you out of the hands of the ruffians?"

With that she opened her eyes, and knowing him again, "Oh, sir," said she, "I am infinitely obliged to you; but I was afraid, for I felt myself held fast and could see no one."

"Surely," replied Leander, "the danger you have been in has disturbed you and cast a mist before your eyes."

Abricotina would not seem to doubt him, though she was otherwise extremely sensible. And after they had talked for some time of indifferent things, Leander requested her to tell him her age, her country, and by what accident she fell into the hands of the ruffians.

"Know then, sir," said she, "there was a certain very great fairy married to a prince who wearied of her: she therefore banished him from her presence, and established herself and daughter in the Island of Calm Delights. The princess, who is my mistress, being very fair, has many lovers—among others, one named Furibon, whom she detests; he it was whose ruffians seized me to-day when I was wandering in search of a stray parrot. Accept, noble prince, my best thanks for your valor, which I shall never forget."

Leander said how happy he was to have served her, and asked if he could not obtain admission into the island. Abricotina assured him this was impossible, and therefore he had better forget all about it. While they were thus conversing, they came to the bank of a large river. Abricotina alighted with a nimble jump from the horse.

"Farewell, sir," said she to the prince, making a profound reverence; "I wish you every happiness."

"And I," said Leander, "wish that I may now and then have a small share in your remembrance."

So saying, he galloped away and soon entered into the thickest part of the wood, near a river, where he unbridled and unsaddled Gris-de-line; then, putting on his little cap, wished himself in the Island of Calm Delights, and his wish was immediately accomplished.

The palace was of pure gold, and stood upon pillars of crystal and precious stones, which represented the zodiac and all the wonders of nature; all the arts and sciences; the sea, with all the variety of fish therein contained; the earth, with all the various creatures which it produces; the chases of Diana and her nymphs; the noble exercises of the Amazons; the amusements of a country life; flocks of sheep with their shepherds and dogs; the toils of agriculture, harvesting, gardening. And among all this variety of representations there was neither man nor boy to be seen—not so much as a little winged Cupid; so highly had the princess been incensed against her inconstant husband as not to show the least favor to his fickle sex.

"Abricotina did not deceive me," said Leander to himself; "they have banished from hence the very idea of men; now let us see what they have lost by it." With that he entered into the palaces and at every step he took he met with objects so wonderful that when he had once fixed his eyes upon them he had much ado to take them off again. He viewed a vast number of these apartments, some full of china, no less fine than curious; others lined with porcelain, so delicate that the walls were quite transparent. Coral, jasper, agates, and cornelians adorned the rooms of state, and the presence-chamber was one entire mirror. The throne was one great pearl, hollowed like a shell; the princess sat, surrounded by her maidens, none of whom could compare with herself. In her was all the innocent sweetness of youth, joined to the dignity of maturity; in truth, she was perfection; and so thought the invisible Leander.

Not seeing Abricotina, she asked where she was. Upon that, Leander, being very desirous to speak, assumed the tone of a parrot, for there were many in the room, and addressed himself invisibly to the princess.

"Most charming princess," said he, "Abricotina will return immediately. She was in great danger of being carried away from this place but for a young prince who rescued her."

The princess was surprised at the parrot, his answer was so extremely pertinent.

"You are very rude, little parrot," said the princess; "and Abricotina, when she comes, shall chastise you for it."

"I shall not be chastised," answered Leander, still counterfeiting the parrot's voice; "moreover, she will let you know the great desire that stranger had to be admitted into this palace, that he might convince you of the falsehood of those ideas which you have conceived against his sex."

"In truth, pretty parrot," cried the princess, "it is a pity you are not every day so diverting; I should love you dearly."

"Ah! if prattling will please you, princess," replied Leander, "I will prate from morning till night."

"But," continued the princess, "how shall I be sure my parrot is not a sorcerer?"

"He is more in love than any sorcerer can be," replied the prince.

At this moment Abricotina entered the room, and falling at her lovely mistress' feet, gave her a full account of what had befallen her, and described the prince in the most glowing colors.

"I should have hated all men," added she, "had I not seen him! Oh, madam, how charming he is! His air and all his behavior have something in them so noble; and though whatever he spoke was infinitely pleasing, yet I think I did well in not bringing him hither."

To this the princess said nothing, but she asked Abricotina a hundred other questions concerning the prince; whether she knew his name, his country, his birth, from whence he came, and whither he was going; and after this she fell into a profound thoughtfulness.

Leander observed everything, and continued to chatter as he had begun.

"Abricotina is ungrateful, madam," said he; "that poor stranger will die for grief if he sees you not."

"Well, parrot, let him die," answered the princess with a sigh; "and since thou undertakest to reason like a person of wit, and not a little bird, I forbid thee to talk to me any more of this unknown person."

Leander was overjoyed to find that Abricotina's and the parrot's discourse had made such an impression on the princess. He looked upon her with pleasure and delight. "Can it be," said he to himself, "that the masterpiece of nature, that the wonder of our age, should be confined eternally in an island, and no mortal dare to approach her? But," continued he, "wherefore am I concerned that others are banished hence, since I have the happiness to be with her, to hear and to admire her; nay, more, to love her above all the women in the universe?"

It was late, and the princess retired into a large room of marble and porphyry, where several bubbling fountains, refreshed the air with an agreeable coolness. As soon as she entered the music began, a sumptuous supper was served up, and the birds from several aviaries on each side of the room, of which Abricotina had the chief care, opened their little throats in the most agreeable manner.

Leander had traveled a journey long enough to give him a good appetite, which made him draw near the table, where the very smell of such viands was agreeable and refreshing. The princess had a curious tabby-cat, for which she had a great kindness. This cat one of the maids of honor held in her arms, saying, "Madam, Bluet is hungry!" With that a chair was presently brought for the cat; for he was a cat of quality, and had a necklace of pearl about his neck. He was served on a golden plate with a laced napkin before him; and the plate being supplied with meat, Bluet sat with the solemn importance of an alderman.

"Ho! ho!" cried Leander to himself; "an idle tabby malkin, that perhaps never caught a mouse in his life, and I dare say is not descended from a better family than myself, has the honor to sit at table with my mistress: I would fain know whether he loves her so well as I do."

Saying this, he placed himself in the chair with the cat upon his knee, for nobody saw him, because he had his little red cap on; finding Bluet's plate well supplied with partridge, quails, and pheasants, he made so free with them that whatever was set before Master Puss disappeared in a trice. The whole court said no cat ever ate with a better appetite. There were excellent ragouts, and the prince made use of the cat's paw to taste them; but he sometimes pulled his paw too roughly, and Bluet, not understanding raillery, began to mew and be quite out of patience. The princess observing it, "Bring that fricassee and that tart to poor Bluet," said she; "see how he cries to have them."

Leander laughed to himself at the pleasantness of this adventure; but he was very thirsty, not being accustomed to make such large meals without drinking. By the help of the cat's paw he got a melon, with which he somewhat quenched his thirst; and when supper was quite over, he went to the buffet and took two bottles of delicious wine.

The princess now retired into her boudoir, ordering Abricotina to follow her and make fast the door; but they could not keep out Leander, who was there as soon as they. However, the princess, believing herself alone with her confidante:

"Abricotina," said she, "tell me truly, did you exaggerate in your description of the unknown prince, for methinks it is impossible he should be as amiable as you say?"

"Madam," replied the damsel, "if I have failed in anything, it was in coming short of what was due to him."

The princess sighed and was silent for a time; then resuming her speech: "I am glad," said she, "thou didst not bring him with thee."

"But, madam," answered Abricotina, who was a cunning girl, and already penetrated her mistress' thoughts, "suppose he had come to admire the wonders of these beautiful mansions, what harm could he have done us? Will you live eternally unknown in a corner of the world, concealed from the rest of human kind? Of what use is all your grandeur, pomp, magnificence, if nobody sees it?"

"Hold thy peace, prattler," replied the princess, "and do not disturb that happy repose which I have enjoyed so long."

Abricotina durst make no reply; and the princess, having waited her answer for some time, asked her whether she had anything to say. Abricotina then said she thought it was to very little purpose her mistress having sent her picture to the courts of several princes, where it only served to make those who saw it miserable; that every one would be desirous to marry her, and as she could not marry them all, indeed none of them, it would make them desperate.

"Yet, for all that," said the princess, "I could wish my picture were in the hands of this same stranger."

"Oh, madam," answered Abricotina, "is not his desire to see you violent enough already? Would you augment it?"

"Yes," cried the princess; "a certain impulse of vanity, which I was never sensible of till now, has bred this foolish fancy in me."

Leander heard all this discourse, and lost not a tittle of what she said; some of her expressions gave him hope, others absolutely destroyed it. The princess presently asked Abricotina whether she had seen anything extraordinary during her short travels.

"Madam," said she, "I passed through one forest where I saw certain creatures that resembled little children: they skip and dance upon the trees like squirrels; they are very ugly, but have wonderful agility and address."

"I wish I had one of them," said the princess; "but if they are so nimble as you say they are, it is impossible to catch one."

Leander, who passed through the same forest, knew what Abricotina meant, and presently wished himself in the place. He caught a dozen of little monkeys, some bigger, some less, and all of different colors, and with much ado put them into a large sack; then, wishing himself at Paris, where, he had heard, a man might have everything for money, he went and bought a little gold chariot. He taught six green monkeys to draw it; they were harnessed with fine traces of flame-colored morocco leather. He went to another place, where he met with two monkeys of merit, the most pleasant of which was called Briscambril, the other Pierceforest—both very spruce and well educated. He dressed Briscambril like a king and placed him in the coach; Pierceforest he made the coachman; the others were dressed like pages; all which he put into his sack, coach and all.

The princess not being gone to bed, heard a rumbling of a little coach in the long gallery; at the same time, her ladies came to tell her that the king of the dwarfs was arrived, and the chariot immediately entered her chamber with all the monkey train. The country monkeys began to show a thousand tricks, which far surpassed those of Briscambril and Pierceforest. To say the truth, Leander conducted the whole machine. He drew the chariot where Briscambril sat arrayed as a king, and making him hold a box of diamonds in his hand, he presented it with a becoming grace to the princess. The princess' surprise may be easily imagined. Moreover, Briscambril made a sign for Pierceforest to come and dance with him. The most celebrated dancers were not to be compared with them in activity. But the princess, troubled that she could not guess from whence this curious present came, dismissed the dancers sooner than she would otherwise have done, though she was extremely pleased with them.

Leander, satisfied with having seen the delight the princess had taken in beholding the monkeys, thought of nothing now but to get a little repose, which he greatly wanted. He stayed sometime in the great gallery; afterward, going down a pair of stairs, and finding a door open, he entered into an apartment the most delightful that ever was seen. There was in it a bed of cloth-of-gold, enriched with pearls, intermixed with rubies and emeralds: for by this time there appeared daylight sufficient for him to view and admire the magnificence of this sumptuous furniture. Having made fast the door, he composed himself to sleep. Next day he rose very early, and looking about on every side, he spied a painter's pallet, with colors ready prepared and pencils. Remembering what the princess had said to Abricotina touching her own portrait, he immediately (for he could paint as well as the most excellent masters) seated himself before a mirror and drew his own picture first; then, in an oval, that of the princess. He had all her features so strong in his imagination that he had no occasion for her sitting; and as his desire to please her had set him to work, never did portrait bear a stronger resemblance. He had painted himself upon one knee, holding the princess' picture in one hand, and in the other a label with this inscription, "She is better in my heart." When the princess went into her cabinet, she was amazed to see the portrait of a man; and she fixed her eyes upon it with so much the more surprise, because she also saw her own with it, and because the words which were written upon the label afforded her ample room for curiosity. She persuaded herself that it was Abricotina's doing; and all she desired to know was whether the portrait was real or imaginary. Rising in haste, she called Abricotina, while the invisible Leander, with his little red cap, slipped into the cabinet, impatient to know what passed. The princess bade Abricotina look upon the picture and tell her what she thought of it.

After she had viewed it, "I protest!" said she, "'tis the picture of that generous stranger to whom I am indebted for my life. Yes, yes, I am sure it is he; his very features, shape, and hair."

"Thou pretendest surprise," said the princess, "but I know it was thou thyself who put it there."

"Who! I, madam?" replied Abricotina. "I protest I never saw the picture before in my life. Should I be so bold as to conceal from your knowledge a thing that so nearly concerns you? And by what miracle could I come by it? I never could paint, nor did any man ever enter this place; yet here he is painted with you?"

"Some spirit, then, must have brought it hither," cried the princess.

"How I tremble for fear, madam!" said Abricotina. "Was it not rather some lover? And therefore, if you will take my advice, let us burn it immediately."

"'Twere a pity to burn it," cried the princess, sighing; "a finer piece, methinks, cannot adorn my cabinet." And saying these words, she cast her eyes upon it. But Abricotina continued obstinate in her opinion that it ought to be burned, as a thing that could not come there but by the power of magic.

"And these words—'She is better in my heart,'" said the princess; "must we burn them too?"

"No favor must be shown to anything," said Abricotina, "not even to your own portrait."

Abricotina ran away immediately for some fire, while the princess went to look out at the window. Leander, unwilling to let his performance be burned, took this opportunity to convey it away without being perceived. He had hardly quitted the cabinet, when the princess turned about to look once more upon that enchanting picture, which had so delighted her. But how was she surprised to find it gone! She sought for it all the room over; and Abricotina, returning, was no less surprised than her mistress; so that this last adventure put them both in the most terrible fright.

Leander took great delight in hearing and seeing his incomparable mistress; even though he had to eat every day at her table with the tabby-cat, who fared never the worse for that; but his satisfaction was far from being complete, seeing he durst neither speak nor show himself; and he knew it was not a common thing for ladies to fall in love with persons invisible.

The princess had a universal taste for amusement. One day, she was saying to her attend-ants that it would give her great pleasure to know how the ladies were dressed in all the courts of the universe. There needed no more words to send Leander all over the world. He wished himself in China, where he bought the richest stuffs he could lay his hands on, and got patterns of all the court fashions. From thence he flew to Siam, where he did the same; in three days he traveled over all the four parts of the world, and from time to time brought what he bought to the Palace of Calm Delights, and hid it all in a chamber, which he kept always locked. When he had thus collected together all the rarities he could meet with—for he never wanted money, his rose always supplying him—he went and bought five or six dozen of dolls, which he caused to be dressed at Paris, the place in the world where most regard is paid to fashions. They were all dressed differently, and as magnificent as could be, and Leander placed them all in the princess' closet. When she entered it, she was agreeably surprised to see such company of little mutes, every one decked with watches bracelets, diamond buckles, or necklaces; and the most remarkable of them held a picture box in its hand, which the princess opening, found it contained Leander's portrait. She gave a loud shriek, and looking upon Abricotina, "There have appeared of late," said she, "so many wonders in this place, that I know not what to think of them: my birds are all grown witty; I cannot so much as wish, but presently I have my desires; twice have I now seen the portrait of him who rescued thee from the ruffians; and here are silks of all sorts, diamonds, embroideries, laces, and an infinite number of other rarities. What fairy is it that takes such care to pay me these agreeable civilities?"

Leander was overjoyed to hear and see her so much interested about his picture, and calling to mind that there was in a grotto which she often frequented a certain pedestal, on which a Diana, not yet finished, was to be erected, on this pedestal he resolved to place himself, crowned with laurel, and holding a lyre in his hand, on which he played like another Apollo. He most anxiously waited the princess' retiring to the grotto, which she did every day since her thoughts had taken up with this unknown person; for what Abricotina had said, joined to the sight of the picture, had almost destroyed her repose: her lively humor changed into a pensive melancholy, and she grew a great lover of solitude. When she entered the grotto, she made a sign that nobody should follow her, so that her young damsels dispersed themselves into the neighboring walks. The princess threw herself upon a bank of green turf, sighed, wept, and even talked, but so softly that Leander could not hear what she said. He had put his red cap on, that she might not see him at first; but having taken it off, she beheld him standing on the pedestal. At first she took him for a real statue, for he observed exactly the attitude in which he had placed himself, without moving so much as a finger. She beheld with a kind of pleasure intermixed with fear, but pleasure soon dispelled her fear, and she continued to view the pleasing figure, which so exactly resembled life. The prince having tuned his lyre, began to play; at which the princess, greatly surprised, could not resist the fear that seized her; she grew pale and fell into a swoon. Leander leaped from the pedestal, and putting on his little red cap, that he might not be perceived, took the princess in his arms and gave her all the assistance that his zeal and tenderness could inspire. At length she opened her charming eyes and looked about in search of him, but she could perceive nobody; yet she felt somebody who held her hands, kissed them, and bedewed them with his tears. It was a long time before she durst speak, and her spirits were in a confused agitation between fear and hope.

She was afraid of the spirit, but loved the figure of the unknown. At length she said: "Courtly invisible, why are you not the person I desire you should be?" At these words Leander was going to declare himself, but durst not do it yet. "For," thought he, "if I again affright the object I adore and make her fear me, she will not love me." This consideration caused him to keep silence.

The princess, then, believing herself alone, called Abricotina and told her all the wonders of the animated statue; that it had played divinely, and that the invisible person had given her great assistance when she lay in a swoon.

"What pity 'tis," said she, "that this person should be so frightful, for nothing can be more amiable or acceptable than his behavior!"

"Who told you, madam," answered Abricotina, "that he is frightful? If he is the youth who saved me, he is beautiful as Cupid himself."

"If Cupid and the unknown are the same," replied the princess, blushing, "I could be content to love Cupid; but alas! how far am I from such a happiness! I love a mere shadow; and this fatal picture, joined to what thou hast told me, have inspired me with inclinations so contrary to the precepts which I received from my mother that I am daily afraid of being punished for them."

"Oh! madam," said Abricotina, interrupting her, "have you not troubles enough already? Why should you anticipate afflictions which may never come to pass?"

It is easy to imagine what pleasure Leander took in this conversation.

In the meantime the little Furibon, still enamored of the princess whom he had never seen, expected with impatience the return of the four servants whom he had sent to the Island of Calm Delights. One of them at last came back, and after he had given the prince a particular account of what had passed, told him that the island was defended by Amazons, and that unless he sent a very powerful army, it would be impossible to get into it. The king his father was dead, and Furibon was now lord of all: disdaining, therefore, any repulse, he raised an army of four hundred thousand men, and put himself at the head of them, appearing like another Tom Thumb upon a war-horse. Now, when the Amazons perceived his mighty host, they gave the princess notice of its who immediately dispatched away her trusty Abricotina to the kingdom of the fairies, to beg her mother's instructions as to what she should do to drive the little Furibon from her territories. But Abricotina found the fairy in an angry humor.

"Nothing that my daughter does," said she, "escapes my knowledge. The Prince Leander is now in her palace; he loves her, and she has a tenderness for him. All my cares and precepts have not been able to guard her from the tyranny of love, and she is now under its fatal dominion. But it is the decree of destiny, and I must submit; therefore, Abricotina, begone! nor let me hear a word more of a daughter whose behavior has so much displeased me."

Abricotina returned with these ill tidings, whereat the princess was almost distracted; and this was soon perceived by Leander, who was near her, though she did not see him. He beheld her grief with the greatest pain. However, he durst not then open his lips; but recollecting that Furibon was exceedingly covetous, he thought that, by giving him a sum of money, he might perhaps prevail with him to retire. Thereupon, he dressed himself like an Amazon, and wished himself in the forest, to catch his horse. He had no sooner called him than Gris-de-line came leaping, prancing, and neighing for joy, for he was grown quite weary of being so long absent from his dear master; but when he beheld him dressed as a woman he hardly knew him. However, at the sound of his voice, he suffered the prince to mount, and they soon arrived in the camp at Furibon, where they gave notice that a lady was come to speak with him from the Princess of Calm Delights. Immediately the little fellow put on his royal robes, and having placed himself upon his throne, he looked like a great toad counterfeiting a king.

Leander harangued him, and told him that the princess, preferring a quiet and peaceable life to the fatigues of war, had sent to offer his majesty as much money as he pleased to demand, provided he would suffer her to continue in peace; but if he refused her proposal, she would omit no means that might serve for her defense. Furibon replied that he took pity on her, and would grant her the honor of his protection; but that he demanded a hundred thousand millions of pounds, and without which he would not return to his kingdom. Leander answered that such a vast sum would be too long a-counting, and therefore, if he would say how many rooms full he desired to have, the princess was generous and rich enough to satisfy him. Furibon was astonished to hear that, instead of entreating, she would rather offer more; and it came into his wicked mind to take all the money he could get, and then seize the Amazon and kill her, that she might never return to her mistress. He told Leander, therefore, that he would have thirty chambers of gold, all full to the ceiling. Leander, being conducted into the chambers, took his rose and shook it, till every room was filled with all sorts of coin. Furibon was in an ecstasy, and the more gold he saw the greater was his desire to get hold of the Amazon; so that when all the rooms were full, he commanded his guards to seize her, alleging she had brought him counterfeit money. Immediately Leander put on his little red cap and disappeared. The guards, believing that the lady had escaped, ran out and left Furibon alone; when Leander, availing himself of the opportunity, took the tyrant by the hair, and twisted his head off with the same ease he would a pullet's; nor did the little wretch of a king see that hand that killed him.

Leander having got his enemy's head, wished himself in the Palace of Calm Delights, where he found the princess walking, and with grief considering the message which her mother had sent her, and on the means to repel Furibon.

Suddenly she beheld a head hanging in the air, with nobody to hold it. This prodigy astonished her so that she could not tell what to think of it; but her amazement was increased when she saw the head laid at her feet, and heard a voice utter these words:
"Charming Princess, cease your fear
Of Furibon; whose head see here."

Abricotina, knowing Leander's voice, cried:
"I protest, madam, the invisible person who speaks is the very stranger that rescued me."

The princess seemed astonished, but yet pleased.

"Oh," said she, "if it be true that the invisible and the stranger are the same person, I confess I shall be glad to make him my acknowledgments."

Leander, still invisible, replied, "I will yet do more to deserve them;" and so saying he returned to Furibon's army, where the report of the king's death was already spread throughout the camp. As soon as Leander appeared there in his usual habit, everybody knew him; all the officers and soldiers surrounded him, uttering the loudest acclamations of joy. In short, they acknowledged him for their king, and that the crown of right belonged to him, for which he thanked them, and, as the first mark of his royal bounty, divided the thirty rooms of gold among the soldiers. This done he returned to his princess, ordering his army to march back into his kingdom.

The princess was gone to bed. Leander, therefore, retired into his own apartment, for he was very sleepy—so sleepy that he forgot to bolt his door; and so it happened that the princess, rising early to taste the morning air, chanced to enter into this very chamber, and was astonished to find a young prince asleep upon the bed. She took a full view of him, and was convinced that he was the person whose picture she had in her diamond box. "It is impossible," said she, "that this should be a spirit; for can spirits sleep? Is this a body composed of air and fire, without substance, as Abricotina told me?" She softly touched his hair, and heard him breathe, and looked at him as if she could have looked forever. While she was thus occupied, her mother, the fairy entered with such a noise that Leander started out of his sleep. But how deeply was he afflicted to behold his beloved princess in the most deplorable condition! Her mother dragged her by the hair and loaded her with a thousand bitter reproaches. In what grief and consternation were the two young lovers, who saw themselves now upon the point of being separated forever! The princess durst not open her lips, but cast her eyes upon Leander, as if to beg his assistance. He judged rightly that he ought not to deal rudely with a power superior to his own, and therefore he sought, by his eloquence and submission, to move the incensed fairy. He ran to her, threw himself at her feet, and besought her to have pity upon a young prince who would never change in his affection for her daughter. The princess, encouraged, also embraced her mother's knees, and declared that without Leander she should never be happy.

"Happy!" cried the fairy; "you know not the miseries of love nor the treacheries of which lovers are capable. They bewitch us only to poison our lives; I have known it by experience; and will you suffer the same?"

"Is there no exception, madam?" replied Leander, and his countenance showed him to be one.

But neither tears nor entreaties could move the implacable fairy; and it is very probable that she would have never pardoned them, had not the lovely Gentilla appeared at that instant in the chamber, more brilliant than the sun. Embracing the old fairy:

"Dear sister," said she, "I am persuaded you cannot have forgotten the good office I did you when, after your unhappy marriage, you besought a readmittance into Fairyland; since then I never desired any favor at your hands, but now the time is come. Pardon, then, this lovely princess; consent to her nuptials with this young prince. I will engage he shall be ever constant to her; the thread of their days shall be spun of gold and silk; they shall live to complete your happiness; and I will never forget the obligation you lay upon me."

"Charming Gentilla," cried the fairy, "I consent to whatever you desire. Come, my dear children, and receive my love." So saying, she embraced them both.

Abricotina, just then entering, cast her eyes upon Leander; she knew him again, and saw he was perfectly happy, at which she, too, was quite satisfied.

"Prince," condescendingly said the fairy-mother, "I will remove the Island of Calm Delights into your own kingdom, live with you myself, and do you great services."

Whether or not Prince Leander appreciated this offer, he bowed low, and assured his mother-in-law that no favor could be equal to the one he had that day received from her hands. This short compliment pleased the fairy exceedingly, for she belonged to those ancient days when people used to stand a whole day upon one leg complimenting one another. The nuptials were performed in a most splendid manner, and the young prince and princess lived together happily many years, beloved by all around them.

PRINCE CHERRY

LONG ago there lived a monarch, who was such a very, honest man that his subjects entitled him the Good King. One day, when he was out hunting, a little white rabbit, which had been half-killed by his hounds, leaped right into his majesty's arms. Said he, caressing it: "This poor creature has put itself under my protection, and I will allow no one to injure it." So he carried it to his palace, had prepared for it a neat little rabbit-hutch, with abundance of the daintiest food, such as rabbits love, and there he left it.

The same night, when he was alone in his chamber, there appeared to him a beautiful lady. She was dressed neither in gold, nor silver, nor brocade; but her flowing robes were white as snow, and she wore a garland of white roses on her head. The Good King was greatly astonished at the sight; for his door was locked, and he wondered how so dazzling a lady could possibly enter; but she soon removed his doubts.

"I am the fairy Candide," said she, with a smiling and gracious air. "Passing through the wood where you were hunting, I took a desire to know if you were as good as men say you are I therefore changed myself into a white rabbit and took refuge in your arms. You saved me and now I know that those who are merciful to dum beasts will be ten times more so to human beings. You merit the name your subjects give you: you are the Good King. I thank you for your protection, and shall be always one of your best friends. You have but to say what you most desire, and I promise you your wish shall be granted."

"Madam," replied the king, "if you are a fairy, you must know, without my telling you, the wish of my heart. I have one well-beloved son, Prince Cherry: whatever kindly feeling you have toward me, extend it to him."

"Willingly," said Candide. "I will make him the handsomest, richest, or most powerful prince in the world: choose whichever you desire for him."

"None of the three," returned the father. "I only wish him to be good—the best prince in the whole world. Of what use would riches, power, or beauty be to him if he were a bad man?"

"You are right," said the fairy; "but I can not make him good: he must do that himself. I can only change his external fortunes; for his personal character, the utmost I can promise is to give him good counsel, reprove him for his faults, and even punish him, if he will not punish himself. You mortals can do the same with your children."

"Ah, yes!" said the king, sighing. Still, he felt that the kindness of a fairy was something gained for his son, and died not long after, content and at peace.

Prince Cherry mourned deeply, for he dearly loved his father, and would have gladly given all his kingdoms and treasures to keep him in life a little longer. Two days after the Good King was no more, Prince Cherry was sleeping in his chamber, when he saw the same dazzling vision of the fairy Candide.

"I promised your father," said she, "to be your best friend, and in pledge of this take what I now give you;" and she placed a small gold ring upon his finger. "Poor as it looks, it is more precious than diamonds; for whenever you do ill it will prick your finger. If, after that warning, you still continue in evil, you will lose my friendship, and I shall become your direst enemy.'"

So saying, she disappeared, leaving Cherry in such amazement that he would have believed it all a dream, save for the ring on his finger.

He was for a long time so good that the ring never pricked him at all; and this made him so cheerful and pleasant in his humor that everybody called him "Happy Prince Cherry." But one unlucky day he was out hunting and found no sport, which vexed him so much that he showed his ill temper by his looks and ways. He fancied his ring felt very tight and uncomfortable, but as it did not prick him he took no heed of this: until, re-entering his palace, his little pet dog, Bibi, jumped up upon him and was sharply told to get away. The creature, accustomed to nothing but caresses, tried to attract his attention by pulling at his garments, when Prince Cherry turned and gave it a severe kick. At this moment he felt in his finger a prick like a pin.

"What nonsense!" said he to himself. "The fairy must be making game of me. Why, what great evil have I done! I, the master of a great empire, cannot I kick my own dog?"

A voice replied, or else Prince Cherry imagined it, "No, sire; the master of a great empire has a right to do good, but not evil. I—a fairy—am as much above you as you are above your dog. I might punish you, kill you, if I chose; but I prefer leaving you to amend your ways. You have been guilty of three faults today—bad temper, passion, cruelty: do better to-morrow."

The prince promised, and kept his word a while; but he had been brought up by a foolish nurse, who indulged him in every way and was always telling him that he would be a king one day, when he might do as he liked in all things. He found out now that even a king cannot always do that; it vexed him and made him angry. His ring began to prick him so often that his little finger was continually bleeding. He disliked this, as was natural, and soon began to consider whether it would not be easier to throw the ring away altogether than to be constantly annoyed by it. It was such a queer thing for a king to have a spot of blood on his finger! At last, unable to put up with it any more, he took his ring off and hid it where he would never see it; and believed himself the happiest of men, for he could now do exactly what he liked. He did it, and became every day more and more miserable.

One day he saw a young girl, so beautiful that, being always accustomed to have his own way, he immediately determined to espouse her. He never doubted that she would be only too glad to be made a queen, for she was very poor. But Zelia—that was her name—answered, to his great astonishment, that she would rather not marry him.

"Do I displease you?" asked the prince, into whose mind it had never entered that he could displease anybody.

"Not at all, my prince," said the honest peasant maiden. "You are very handsome, very charming; but you are not like your father the Good King. I will not be your queen, for you would make me miserable."

At these words the prince's love seemed all to turn to hatred: he gave orders to his guards to convey Zelia to a prison near the palace, and then took counsel with his foster brother, the one of all his ill companions who most incited him to do wrong.

"Sir," said this man, "if I were in your majesty's place, I would never vex myself about a poor silly girl. Feed her on bread and water till she comes to her senses; and if she still refuses you, let her die in torment, as a warning to your other subjects should they venture to dispute your will. You will be disgraced should you suffer yourself to be conquered by a simple girl."

"But," said Prince Cherry, "shall I not be disgraced if I harm a creature so perfectly innocent?"

"No one is innocent who disputes your majesty's authority," said the courtier, bowing; "and it is better to commit an injustice than allow it to be supposed you can ever be contradicted with impunity."

This touched Cherry on his weak point—his good impulses faded; he resolved once more to ask Zelia if she would marry him, and if she again refused, to sell her as a slave. Arrived at the cell in which she was confined, what was his astonishment to find her gone! He knew not whom to accuse, for he had kept the key in his pocket the whole time. At last, the foster-brother suggested that the escape of Zelia might have been contrived by an old man, Suliman by name, the prince's former tutor, who was the only one who now ventured to blame him for anything that he did. Cherry sent immediately, and ordered his old friend to be brought to him, loaded heavily with irons. Then, full of fury, he went and shut himself up in his own chamber, where he went raging to and fro, till startled by a noise like a clap of thunder. The fairy Candide stood before him.

"Prince," said she, in a severe voice, "I promised your father to give you good counsels and to punish you if you refused to follow them. My counsels were forgotten, my punishment despised. Under the figure of a man, you have been no better than the beasts you chase: like a lion in fury, a wolf in gluttony, a serpent in revenge, and a bull in brutality. Take, therefore, in your new form the likeness of all these animals."

Scarcely had Prince Cherry heard these words than to his horror he found himself transformed into what the Fairy had named. He was a creature with the head of a lion, the horns of a bull, the feet of a wolf, and the tail of a serpent. At the same time he felt himself transported to a distant forest, where, standing on the bank of a stream, he saw reflected in the water his own frightful shape, and heard a voice saying:

"Look at thyself, and know thy soul has become a thousand times uglier even than thy body."

Cherry recognized the voice of Candide, and in his rage would have sprung upon her and devoured her; but he saw nothing and the same voice said behind him:

"Cease thy feeble fury, and learn to conquer thy pride by being in submission to thine own subjects."

Hearing no more, he soon quitted the stream, hoping at least to get rid of the sight of himself; but he had scarcely gone twenty paces when he tumbled into a pitfall that was laid to catch bears; the bear-hunters, descending from some trees hard by, caught him, chained him, and only too delighted to get hold of such a curious-looking animal, led him along with them to the capital of his own kingdom.

There great rejoicings were taking place, and the bear-hunters, asking what it was all about, were told that it was because Prince Cherry, the torment of his subjects, had just been struck dead by a thunderbolt—just punishment of all his crimes. Four courtiers, his wicked companions, had wished to divide his throne between them; but the people had risen up against them and offered the crown to Suliman, the old tutor whom Cherry had ordered to be arrested.

All this the poor monster heard. He even saw Suliman sitting upon his own throne and trying to calm the populace by representing to them that it was not certain Prince Cherry was dead; that he might return one day to reassume with honor the crown which Suliman only consented to wear as a sort of viceroy.

"I know his heart," said the honest and faithful old man; "it is tainted, but not corrupt. If alive, he may reform yet, and be all his father over again to you, his people, whom he has caused to suffer so much."

These words touched the poor beast so deeply that he ceased to beat himself against the iron bars of the cage in which the hunters carried him about, became gentle as a lamb, and suffered himself to be taken quietly to a menagerie, where were kept all sorts of strange and ferocious animals a place which he had himself often visited as a boy, but never thought he should be shut up there himself.

However, he owned he had deserved it all, and began to make amends by showing himself very obedient to his keeper. This man was almost as great a brute as the animals he had charge of, and when he was in ill humor he used to beat them without rhyme or reason. One day, while he was sleeping, a tiger broke loose and leaped upon him, eager to devour him. Cherry at first felt a thrill of pleasure at the thought of being revenged; then, seeing how helpless the man was, he wished himself free, that he might defend him. Immediately the doors of his cage opened. The keeper, waking up, saw the strange beast leap out, and imagined, of course, that he was going to be slain at once. Instead, he saw the tiger lying dead, and the strange beast creeping up and laying itself at his feet to be caressed. But as he lifted up his hand to stroke it, a voice was heard saying, "Good actions never go unrewarded;" and instead of the frightful monster, there crouched on the ground nothing but a pretty little dog.

Cherry, delighted to find himself thus metamorphosed, caressed the keeper in every possible way, till at last the man took him up into his arms and carried him to the king, to whom he related this wonderful story, from beginning to end. The queen wished to have the charming little dog; and Cherry would have been exceedingly happy could he have forgotten that he was originally a man and a king. He was lodged most elegantly, had the richest of collars to adorn his neck, and heard himself praised continually. But his beauty rather brought him into trouble, for the queen, afraid lest he might grow too large for a pet, took advice of dog-doctors, who ordered that he should be fed entirely upon bread, and that very sparingly; so poor Cherry was sometimes nearly starved.

One day, when they gave him his crust for breakfast, a fancy seized him to go and eat it in the palace garden; so he took the bread in his mouth and trotted away toward a stream which he knew, and where he sometimes stopped to drink. But instead of the stream he saw a splendid palace, glittering with gold and precious stones. Entering the doors was a crowd of men and women, magnificently dressed; and within there was singing and dancing and good cheer of all sorts. Yet, however grandly and gayly the people went in, Cherry noticed that those who came out were pale, thin, ragged, half-naked, covered with wounds and sores. Some of them dropped dead at once; others dragged themselves on a little way and then lay down, dying of hunger, and vainly begged a morsel of bread from others who were entering in—who never took the least notice of them.

Cherry perceived one woman, who was trying feebly to gather and eat some green herbs. "Poor thing!" said he to himself; "I know what it is to be hungry, and I want my breakfast badly enough; but still it will kill me to wait till dinner time, and my crust may save the life of this poor woman."

So the little dog ran up to her and dropped his bread at her feet; she picked it up and ate it with avidity. Soon she looked quite recovered, and Cherry, delighted, was trotting back again to his kennel, when he heard loud cries, and saw a young girl dragged by four men to the door of the palace, which they were trying to compel her to enter. Oh, how he wished himself a monster again, as when he slew the tiger!—for the young girl was no other than his beloved Zelia. Alas! what could a poor little dog do to defend her? But he ran forward and barked at the men, and bit their heels, until at last they chased him away with heavy blows. And then he lay down outside the palace door, determined to watch and see what had become of Zelia.

Conscience pricked him now. "What!" thought he, "I am furious against these wicked men, who are carrying her away; and did I not do the same myself? Did I not cast her into prison, and intend to sell her as a slave? Who knows how much more wickedness I might not have done to her and others, if Heaven's justice had not stopped me in time?"

While he lay thinking and repenting, he heard a window open and saw Zelia throw out of it a bit of dainty meat. Cherry, who felt hungry enough by this time, was just about to eat it, when the woman to whom he had given his crust snatched him up in her arms.

"Poor little beast!" cried she, patting him, "every bit of food in that palace is poisoned: you shall not touch a morsel."

And at the same time the voice in the air repeated again, "Good actions never go unrewarded;" and Cherry found himself changed into a beautiful little white pigeon. He remembered with joy that white was the color of the fairy Candide, and began to hope that she was taking him into favor again.

So he stretched his wings, delighted that he might now have a chance of approaching his fair Zelia. He flew up to the palace windows, and, finding one of them open, entered and sought everywhere, but he could not find Zelia. Then, in despair, he flew out again, resolved to go over the world until he beheld her once more.

He took flight at once and traversed many countries, swiftly as a bird can, but found no trace of his beloved. At length in a desert, sitting beside an old hermit in his cave and par-taking with him his frugal repast, Cherry saw a poor peasant girl and recognized Zelia. Transported with joy, he flew in, perched on her shoulder, and expressed his delight and affection by a thousand caresses.

She, charmed with the pretty little pigeon, caressed it in her turn, and promised it that if it would stay with her she would love it always.

"What have you done, Zelia?" said the hermit, smiling; and while he spoke the white pigeon vanished, and there stood Prince Cherry in his own natural form. "Your enchantment ended, prince, when Zelia promised to love you. Indeed, she has loved you always, but your many faults constrained her to hide her love. These are now amended, and you may both live happy if you will, because your union is founded upon mutual esteem."

Cherry and Zelia threw themselves at the feet of the hermit, whose form also began to change. His soiled garments became of dazzling whiteness, and his long beard and withered face grew into the flowing hair and lovely countenance of the fairy Candide.

"Rise up, my children," said she; "I must now transport you to your palace and restore to Prince Cherry his father's crown, of which he is now worthy."

She had scarcely ceased speaking when they found themselves in the chamber of Suliman, who, delighted to find again his beloved pupil and master, willingly resigned the throne, and became the most faithful of his subjects.

King Cherry and Queen Zelia reigned together for many years, and it is said that the former was so blameless and strict in all his duties that though he constantly wore the ring which Candide had restored to him, it never once pricked his finger enough to make it bleed.

THE PRINCE WITH THE NOSE

THERE was once a king who was passionately in love with a beautiful princess, but she could not be married because a magician had enchanted her. The king went to a good fairy to inquire what he should do. Said the fairy, after receiving him graciously: "Sir, I will tell you a great secret. The princess has a great cat whom she loves so well that she cares for nothing and nobody else; but she will be obliged to marry any person who is adroit enough to walk upon the cat's tail."

"That will not be very difficult," thought the king to himself, and departed, resolving to trample the cat's tail to pieces rather than not succeed in walking upon it. He went immediately to the palace of his fair mistress and the cat; the animal came in front of him, arching its back in anger as it was wont to do. The king lifted up his foot, thinking nothing would be so easy as to tread on the tail, but he found himself mistaken. Minon—that was the creature's name—twisted itself round so sharply that the king only hurt his own foot by stamping on the floor. For eight days did he pursue the cat everywhere: up and down the palace he was after it from morning till night, but with no better success; the tail seemed made of quicksilver, so very lively was it. At last the king had the good fortune to catch Minon sleeping, when tramp! tramp! he trod on the tail with all his force.

Minon woke up, mewed horribly, and immediately changed from a cat into a large, fierce-looking man, who regarded the king with flashing eyes.

"You must marry the princess," cried he, "because you have broken the enchantment in which I held her; but I will be revenged on you. You shall have a son with a nose as long as—that;" he made in the air a curve of half a foot; "yet he shall believe it is just like all other noses, and shall be always unfortunate till he has found out it is not. And if you ever tell anybody of this threat of mine, you shall die on the spot." So saying the magician disappeared.

The king, who was at first much terrified, soon began to laugh at this adventure. "My son might have a worse misfortune than too long a nose," thought he. "At least it will hinder him neither in seeing nor hearing. I will go and find the princess and marry her at once."

He did so, but he only lived a few months after, and died before his little son was born, so that nobody knew anything about the secret of the nose.

The little prince was so much wished for that when he came into the world they agreed to call him Prince Wish. He had beautiful blue eyes and a sweet little mouth, but his nose was so big that it covered half his face. The queen, his mother, was inconsolable; but her ladies tried to satisfy her by telling her that the nose was not nearly so large as it seemed, that it would grow smaller as the prince grew bigger, and that if it did not a large nose was indispensable to a hero. All great soldiers, they said, had great noses, as everybody knew. The queen was so very fond of her son that she listened eagerly to all this comfort. Shortly she grew so used to the princes's nose that it did not seem to her any larger than ordinary noses of the court; where, in process of time, everybody with a long nose was very much admired, and the unfortunate people who had only snubs were taken very little notice of.

Great care was observed in the education of the prince; and as soon as he could speak they told him all sorts of amusing tales, in which all the bad people had short noses, and all the good people had long ones. No person was suffered to come near him who had not a nose of more than ordinary length; nay, to such an extent did the countries carry their fancy, that the noses of all the little babies were ordered to be pulled out as far as possible several times a day, in order to make them grow. But grow as they would, they never could grow as long as that of Prince Wish. When he was old enough his tutor taught him history; and whenever any great king or lovely princess was referred to, the tutor always took care to mention that he or she had a long nose. All the royal apartments were filled with pictures and portraits having this peculiarity, so that at last Prince Wish began to regard the length of his nose as his greatest perfection, and would not have had it an inch less even to save his crown.

When he was twenty years old his mother and his people wished him to marry. They procured for him the likenesses of many princesses, but the one he preferred was Princess Darling, daughter of a powerful monarch and heiress to several kingdoms. Alas! with all her beauty, this princess had one great misfortune, a little turned-up nose, which, every one else said made her only the more bewitching. But here, in the kingdom of Prince Wish, the courtiers were thrown by it into the utmost perplexity. They were in the habit of laughing at all small noses; but how dared they make fun of the nose of Princess Darling? Two unfortunate gentlemen, whom Prince Wish had overheard doing so, were ignominiously banished from the court and capital.

After this, the courtiers became alarmed, and tried to correct their habit of speech; but they would have found themselves in constant difficulties, had not one clever person struck out a bright idea. He said that though it was indispensably necessary for a man to have a great nose, women were very different; and that a learned man had discovered in a very old manuscript that the celebrated Cleopatra, Queen of Egypt, the beauty of the ancient world, had a turned-up nose. At this information Prince Wish was so delighted that he made the courtier a very handsome present, and immediately sent off ambassadors to demand Princess Darling in marriage.

She accepted his offer at once, and returned with the ambassadors. He made all haste to meet and welcome her, but when she was only three leagues distant from his capital, before he had time even to kiss her hand, the magician who had once assumed the shape of his mother's cat, Minon, appeared in the air and carried her off before the lover's very eyes.

Prince Wish, almost beside himself with grief, declared that nothing should induce him to return to his throne and kingdom till he had found Darling. He would suffer none of his courtiers or attendants to follow him; but bidding them all adieu, mounted a good horse, laid the reins on the animal's neck, and let him take him wherever he would.

The horse entered a wide-extended plain, and trotted on steadily the whole day without finding a single house. Master and beast began almost to faint with hunger; and Prince Wish might have wished himself at home again, had he not discovered, just at dusk, a cavern, where there sat, beside a bright lantern, a little woman who might have been more than a hundred years old.

She put on her spectacles the better to look at the stranger, and he noticed that her nose was so small that the spectacles would hardly stay on; then the prince and the fairy—for she was a fairy—burst into laughter.

"What a funny nose!" cried the one.

"Not so funny as yours, madam," returned the other. "But pray let us leave our noses alone, and be good enough to give me something to eat, for I am dying with hunger, and so is my poor horse."

"With all my heart," answered the fairy. "Although your nose is ridiculously long, you are no less the son of one of my best friends. I loved your father like a brother; he had a very handsome nose."

"What is wanting to my nose?" asked Wish rather savagely.

"Oh! nothing at all. On the contrary, there is a great deal too much of it; but never mind, one may be a very honest man, and yet have too big a nose. As I said, I was a great friend of your father's; he came often to see me. I was very pretty then, and oftentimes he used to say to me, 'My sister——'"

"I will hear the rest, madam, with pleasure, when I have supped; but will you condescend to remember that I have tasted nothing all day?"

"Poor boy," said the fairy, "I will give you some supper directly; and while you eat it I will tell you my history in six words, for I hate much talking. A long tongue is as insupportable as a long nose; and I remember when I was young how much I used to be admired because I was not a talker; indeed, some one said to the queen my mother—for poor as you see me now, I am the daughter of a great king, who always——"

"Ate when he was hungry, I hope," interrupted the prince, whose patience was fast departing.

"You are right," said the imperturbable old fairy; "and I will bring you your supper directly, only I wish first just to say that the king my father——"

"Hang the king your father!" Prince Wish was about to exclaim, but he stopped himself, and only observed that however the pleasure of her conversation might make him forget his hunger, it could not have the same effect upon his horse, who was really starving.

The fairy, pleased at his civility, called her servants and bade them supply him at once with all he needed. "And," added she, "I must say you are very polite and very good-tempered, in spite of your nose."

"What has the old woman to do with my nose?" thought the prince. "If I were not so very hungry, I would soon show her what she is—a regular old gossip and chatterbox. She to fancy she talks little, indeed! One must be very foolish not to know one's own defects. This comes of being born a princess. Flatterers have spoiled her and persuaded her that she talks little. Little, indeed! I never knew anybody chatter so much."

While the prince thus meditated, the servants were laying the table, the fairy asking them a hundred unnecessary questions, simply for the pleasure of hearing herself talk. "Well," thought Wish, "I am delighted that I came hither, if only to learn how wise I have been in never listening to flatterers, who hide from us our faults, or make us believe they are perfections. But they could never deceive me. I know all my own weak points, I trust." As truly he believed he did.

So he went on eating contentedly, nor stopped till the old fairy began to address him.

"Prince," said she, "will you be kind enough to turn a little? Your nose casts such a shadow that I cannot see what is on my plate. And, as I was saying, your father admired me and always made me welcome at court. What is the court etiquette there now? Do the ladies still go to assemblies, promenades, balls?—I beg your pardon for laughing, but how very long your nose is."

"I wish you would cease to speak of my nose," said the prince, becoming annoyed. "It is what it is, and I do not desire it any shorter."

"Oh! I see that I have vexed you," returned the fairy. "Nevertheless, I am one of your best friends, and so I shall take the liberty of always——" She would doubtless have gone on talking till midnight; but the prince, unable to bear it any longer, here interrupted her, thanked her for her hospitality, bade her a hasty adieu, and rode away.

He traveled for a long time, half over the world, but he heard no news of Princess Darling. However, in each place he went to, he heard one remarkable fact—the great length of his own nose. The little boys in the streets jeered at him, the peasants stared at him, and the more polite ladies and gentlemen whom he met in society used to try in vain to keep from laughing, and to get out of his way as soon as they could. So the poor prince became gradually quite forlorn and solitary; he thought all the world was mad, but still he never thought of there being anything queer about his own nose. At last the old fairy, who, though she was a chatterbox, was very good-natured; saw that he was almost breaking his heart. She felt sorry for him and wished to help him in spite of himself, for she knew the enchantment which hid from him the Princess Darling could never be broken till he had discovered his own defect. So she went in search of the princess, and being more powerful than the magician, since she was a good fairy and he was an evil magician, she got her away from him and shut her up in a palace of crystal, which she placed on the road which Prince Wish had to pass.

He was riding along, very melancholy, when he saw the palace; and at its entrance was a room, made of the purest glass, in which sat his beloved princess, smiling and beautiful as ever. He leaped from his horse and ran toward her. She held out her hand for him to kiss, but he could not get at it for the glass. Transported with eagerness and delight, he dashed his sword through the crystal and succeeded in breaking a small opening, to which she put up her beautiful rosy mouth. But it was in vain; Prince Wish could not approach it. He twisted his neck about, and turned his head on all sides, till at length, putting up his hand to his face, he discovered the impediment.

"It must be confessed," exclaimed he, "that my nose is too long."

That moment the glass walls all split asunder, and the old fairy appeared, leading Princess Darling.

"Avow, prince," said she, "that you are very much obliged to me, for now the enchantment is ended. You may marry the object of your choice. But," added she, smiling, "I fear I might have talked to you forever on the subject of your nose, and you would not have believed me in its length, till it became an obstacle to your own inclinations. Now behold it!" and she held up a crystal mirror. "Are you satisfied to be no different from other people?"

"Perfectly," said Prince Wish, who found his nose had shrunk to an ordinary length. And taking the Princess Darling by the hand, he kissed her courteously, affectionately, and satisfactorily. Then they departed to their own country, and lived very happily all their days.

THE FROG-PRINCE

IN times of yore, when wishes were both heard and granted, lived a king whose daughters were all beautiful but the youngest was so lovely that the sun himself, who has seen so much, wondered at her beauty every time he looked in her face. Now, near the king's castle was a large dark forest; and in the forest, under an old linden tree, was a deep well. When the day was very hot, the king's daughter used to go to the wood and seat herself at the edge of the cool well; and when she became wearied, she would take a golden ball, throw it up in the air, and catch it again. This was her favorite amusement. Once it happened that her golden ball, instead of falling back into the little hand that she stretched out for it, dropped on the ground, and immediately rolled away into the water. The king's daughter followed it with her eyes, but the ball had vanished, and the well was so deep that no one could see down to the bottom. Then she began to weep, wept louder and louder every minute, and could not console herself at all.

While she was thus lamenting some one called to her: "What is the matter with you, king's daughter? You weep so that you would touch the heart of a stone."

She looked around to see whence the voice came, and saw a frog stretching his thick ugly head out of the water.

"Ah! it is you, old water-paddler!" said she. "I am crying for my golden ball, which has fallen into the well."

"Be content," answered the frog; "I dare say I can give you some good advice; but what will you give me if I bring back your plaything to you?"

"Whatever you like, dear frog," said she, "my clothes, my pearls and jewels, even the golden crown I wear."

The frog answered, "Your clothes, your pearls and jewels, even your golden crown, I do not care for; but if you will love me, and let me be your companion and play-fellow, sit near you at your little table, eat from your little golden plate, drink from your little cup, and sleep in your little bed—if you will promise me this, then I will bring you back your golden ball from the bottom of the well."

"Oh, yes!" said she; "I promise you every-thing, if you will only bring me back my golden ball."

She thought to herself, meanwhile: "What nonsense the silly frog talks! He sits in the water with the other frogs, and croaks, and cannot be anybody's playfellow!"

But the frog, as soon as he had received the promise dipped his head under the water and sank down. In a little while up he came again with the ball in his mouth, and threw it on the grass. The king's daughter was overjoyed when she beheld her pretty plaything again, picked it up, and ran away with it.

"Wait! wait!" cried the frog; "take me with you. I cannot run as fast as you."

Alas! of what use was it that he croaked after her as loud as he could. She would not listen to him, but hastened home, and soon forgot the poor frog, who was obliged to plunge again to the bottom of his well.

The next day, when she was sitting at dinner with the king and all the courtiers, eating from her little gold plate, there came a sound of something creeping up the marble staircase—splish, splash; and when it had reached the top, it knocked at the door and cried, "Youngest king's daughter, open to me."

She ran, wishing to see who was outside; but when she opened the door and there sat the frog, she flung it hastily to again and sat down at table, feeling very, very uncomfortable. The king saw that her heart was beating violently, and said, "How, my child, why are you afraid? Is a giant standing outside the door to carry you off?"

"Oh, no!" answered she, "it is no giant, but a nasty frog, who yesterday, when I was playing in the wood near the well, fetched my golden ball out of the water. For this I promised him he should be my companion, but I never thought he could come out of his well. Now he is at the door, and wants to come in."

Again, the second time there was a knock, and a voice cried:

"Youngest king's daughter,
Open to me;
Know you what yesterday
You promised me,
By the cool water?
Youngest king's daughter,
Open to me."

Then said the king, "What you promised you must perform. Go and open the door."

She went and opened the door; the frog hopped in, always following and following her till he came up to her chair. There he sat and cried out, "Lift me up to you on the table."

She refused, till the king, her father, commanded her to do it. When the frog was on the table, he said, "Now push your little golden plate nearer to me, that we may eat together." She did as he desired, but one could easily see that she did it unwillingly. The frog seemed to enjoy his dinner very much, but every morsel she ate stuck in the throat of the poor little princess.

Then said the frog, "I have eaten enough, and am tired; carry me to your little room, and make your little silken bed smooth, and we will lay ourselves down to sleep together."

At this the daughter of the king began to weep; for she was afraid of the cold frog, who wanted to sleep in her pretty clean bed.

But the king looked angrily at her, and said again: "What you have promised you must perform. The frog is your companion."

It was no use to complain; whether she liked it or not, she was obliged to take the frog with her up to her little bed. So she picked him up with two fingers, hating him bitterly the while, and carried him upstairs: but when she got into bed, instead of lifting him up to her, she threw him with all her strength against the wall, saying, "Now you nasty frog, there will be an end of you."

But what fell down from the wall was not a dead frog, but a living young prince, with beautiful and loving eyes, who at once became, by her own promise and her father's will, her dear companion and husband. He told her how he had been cursed by a wicked sorceress, and that no one but the king's youngest daughter could release him from his enchantment and take him out of the well.

The next day a carriage drove up to the palace gates with eight white horses, having white feathers on their heads and golden reins. Behind it stood the servant of the young prince, called the faithful Henry. This faithful Henry had been so grieved when his master was changed into a frog that he had been compelled to have three iron bands fastened round his heart, lest it should break. Now the carriage came to convey the prince to his kingdom, so the faithful Henry lifted in the bride and bridegroom and mounted behind, full of joy at his lord's release. But when they had gone a short distance, the prince heard behind him a noise as if something was breaking. He cried out, "Henry, the carriage is breaking!"

But Henry replied: "No, sir, it is not the carriage but one of the bands from my heart, with which I was forced to bind it up, or it would have broken with grief while you sat as a frog at the bottom of the well."

Twice again this happened, and the prince always thought the carriage was breaking; but it was only the bands breaking off from the heart of the faithful Henry, out of joy that his lord, the frog-prince, was a frog no more.

CLEVER ALICE

ONCE upon a time there was a man who had a daughter who was called "Clever Alice," and when she was grown up, her father said, "We must see about her marrying."

"Yes," replied her mother, "whenever a young man shall appear who is worthy of her."

At last a certain youth, by name Hans, came from a distance to make a proposal of marriage; but he required one condition, that the clever Alice should be very prudent.

"Oh," said her father, "no fear of that! she has got a head full of brains;" and the mother added, "ah, she can see the wind blow up the street, and hear the flies cough!"

"Very well," replied Hans; "but remember, if she is not very prudent, I will not take her." Soon afterward they sat down to dinner, and her mother said, "Alice, go down into the cellar and draw some beer."

So Clever Alice took the jug down from the wall, and went into the cellar, jerking the lid up and down on her way, to pass away the time. As soon as she got downstairs she drew a stool and placed it before the cask, in order that she might not have to stoop, for she thought stooping might in some way injure her back and give it an undesirable bend. Then she placed the can before her and turned the tap, and while the beer was running, as she did not wish her eyes to be idle, she looked about upon the wall above and below. Presently she perceived, after much peeping into this corner and that corner, a hatchet, which the bricklayers had left behind? sticking out of the ceiling right above her head. At the sight of this Clever Alice began to cry, saying, "Oh! if I marry Hans, and we have a child, and he grows up, and we send him into the cellar to draw beer, the hatchet will fall upon his head and kill him," and so she sat there weeping with all her might over the impending misfortune.

Meanwhile the good folks upstairs were waiting for the beer, but as Clever Alice did not come, her mother told the maid to go and see what she was stopping for. The maid went down into the cellar and found Alice sitting before the cask crying heartily, and she asked, "Alice, what are you weeping about?"

"Ah," she replied, "have I not cause? If I marry Hans, and we have a child, and he grows up, and we send him here to draw beer, that hatchet will fall upon his head and kill him."

"Oh," said the maid, "what a clever Alice we have!" And sitting down, she began to weep, too, for the misfortune that was to happen.

After a while, when the servant did not return, the good folks above began to feel very thirsty; so the husband told the boy to go down into the cellar and see what had become of Alice and the maid. The boy went down, and there sat Clever Alice and the maid both crying, so he asked the reason; and Alice told him the same tale, of the hatchet that was to fall on her child, if she married Hans, and if they had a child. When she had finished, the boy exclaimed, "What a clever Alice we have!" and fell weeping and howling with the others.

Upstairs they were still waiting, and the husband said, when the boy did not return, "Do you go down, wife, into the cellar and see why Alice stays so long." So she went down, and finding all three sitting there crying, asked the reason, and Alice told her about the hatchet which must inevitably fall upon the head of her son. Then the mother likewise exclaimed, "Oh, what a clever Alice we have!" and, sitting down, began to weep as much as any of the rest.

Meanwhile the husband waited for his wife's return; but at last he felt so very thirsty that he said, "I must go myself down into the cellar and see what is keeping our Alice." As soon as he entered the cellar, there he found the four sitting and crying together, and when he heard the reason, he also exclaimed, "Oh, what a clever Alice we have!" and sat down to cry with the whole strength of his lungs.

All this time the bridegroom above sat waiting, but when nobody returned, he thought they must be waiting for him, and so he went down to see what was the matter. When he entered, there sat the five crying and groaning, each one in a louder key than his neighbor.

"What misfortune has happened?" he asked.

"Ah, dear Hans!" cried Alice, "if you and I should marry one another, and have a child, and he grew up, and we, perhaps, send him down to this cellar to tap the beer, the hatchet which has been left sticking up there may fall on his head, and so kill him; and do you not think this is enough to weep about?"

"Now," said Hans, "more prudence than this is not necessary for my housekeeping; because you are such a clever Alice, I will have you for my wife." And, taking her hand, he led her home, and celebrated the wedding directly.

After they had been married a little while, Hans, said one morning, "Wife, I will go out to work and earn some money; do you go into the field and gather some corn wherewith to make bread."

"Yes," she answered, "I will do so, dear Hans." And when he was gone, she cooked herself a nice mess of pottage to take with her. As she came to the field, she said to herself, "What shall I do? Shall I cut first, or eat first? Aye, I will eat first!" Then she ate up the contents of her pot, and when it was finished, she thought to herself, "Now, shall I reap first or sleep first? Well, I think I will have a nap!" and so she laid herself down among the corn, and went to sleep.

Meanwhile Hans returned home, but Alice did not come, and so he said, "Oh, what a prudent Alice I have! She is so industrious that she does not even come home to eat anything." By and by, however, evening came on, and still she did not return; so Hans went out to see how much she had reaped; but, behold, nothing at all, and there lay Alice fast asleep among the corn! So home he ran very fast, and brought a net with little bells hanging on it, which he threw over her head while she still slept on. When he had done this, he went back again and shut to the house door, and, seating himself on his stool, began working very industriously.

At last, when it was nearly dark, the clever Alice awoke, and as soon as she stood up, the net fell all over her hair, and the bells jingled at every step she took. This quite frightened her, and she began to doubt whether she were really

Clever Alice, and said to herself, "Am I she, or am I not?" This was a question she could not answer, and she stood still a long while considering about it. At last she thought she would go home and ask whether she was really herself—supposing somebody would be able to tell her.

When she came up to the house door it was shut; so she tapped at the window, and asked, "Hans, is Alice within?" "Yes," he replied, "she is." At which answer she became really terrified, and exclaiming, "Ah, heaven, then I am not Alice!" she ran up to another house, intending to ask the same question. But as soon as the folks within heard the jingling of the bells in her net, they refused to open their doors, and nobody would receive her. So she ran straight away from the village, and no one has ever seen her since.

Echo Library
www.echo-library.com

Echo Library uses advanced digital print-on-demand technology to build and preserve an exciting world class collection of rare and out-of-print books, making them readily available for everyone to enjoy.

Situated just yards from Teddington Lock on the River Thames, Echo Library was founded in 2005 by Tom Cherrington, a specialist dealer in rare and antiquarian books with a passion for literature.

Please visit our website for a complete catalogue of our books, which includes foreign language titles.

The Right to Read

Echo Library actively supports the Royal National Institute of the Blind's Right to Read initiative by publishing a comprehensive range of large print and clear print titles.

Large Print titles are in 16 point Tiresias font as recommended by the RNIB.

Clear Print titles are in 13 point Tiresias font and designed for those who find standard print difficult to read.

Customer Service

If there is a serious error in the text or layout please send details to feedback@echo-library.com and we will supply a corrected copy. If there is a printing fault or the book is damaged please refer to your supplier.

CPSIA information can be obtained
at www.ICGtesting.com
Printed in the USA
LVOW11s1619100717

540843LV00002B/575/P

THE
BIG THREE

PAUL PIERCE, KEVIN GARNETT, RAY ALLEN, AND THE REBIRTH OF THE BOSTON CELTICS

MICHAEL HOLLEY

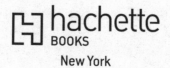

hachette
BOOKS
New York

ALSO BY MICHAEL HOLLEY

Belichick and Brady
War Room
Red Sox Rule
Patriot Reign

Hachette Books
Hachette Book Group
1290 Avenue of the Americas
New York, NY 10104
HachetteBooks.com
Twitter.com/HachetteBooks
Instagram.com/HachetteBooks

First Trade Paperback Edition: December 2021

Published by Hachette Books, an imprint of Perseus Books, LLC, a subsidiary of Hachette Book Group, Inc. The Hachette Books name and logo is a trademark of the Hachette Book Group.

The Hachette Speakers Bureau provides a wide range of authors for speaking events. To find out more, go to www.hachettespeakersbureau.com or call (866) 376-6591.

The publisher is not responsible for websites (or their content) that are not owned by the publisher.

Library of Congress Control Number: 2020945284

ISBNs: 9780316489928 (trade paperback), 9780316489942 (hardcover),
       9780316489935 (ebook)

Printed in the United States of America

LSC-C

Printing 1, 2021

For Nana and Grandpa—Kathryn Sales Darnell and Goldman Booker—whose proverbs continually guide me Proverbs 4:20–22, NRSV

CONTENTS

Contents

PROLOGUE

That day's business meeting in Phoenix was supposed to be a simple one. The plan in the spring of 2003 was for Danny Ainge to go to Sky Harbor International Airport in the morning, personally pick up a friend arriving from Boston at eleven o'clock, and eventually recommend some candidates for an executive position.

They'd get in a round of golf, with tee time scheduled for one thirty. Go over some dynamic names. Have dinner. Easy.

Ainge was perfect for assignments like these. Not only did he have an abundance of contacts and opinions, but he was also an expert on the topic: pro basketball—specifically, the Boston Celtics.

His friend was Steve Pagliuca, one of the Celtics' new co-owners. Months earlier, Pagliuca, Wyc Grousbeck, Bob Epstein, and several partners had paid more for the Celtics, $360 million, than anyone had paid for a team in NBA history. That was 2002. Pagliuca and Grousbeck, longtime and excitable Boston fans, spoke publicly of bringing championship basketball to the city; in private, to confidants like Ainge, they confessed that they wanted to hire a championship team-builder, too.

Pagliuca respected Ainge and liked the way he thought. The two of them attended the 2000 U.S. Open at Pebble Beach, which Tiger Woods dominated with a 15-stroke victory. When they weren't talking about golf as they walked the famed course, they discussed pro basketball. Pagliuca remembered those conversations when his group bought the Celtics, and he asked Ainge then to take the job. But Ainge was enjoying his life as a TV analyst. He turned Pagliuca down, but that didn't stop them from joyfully debating basketball in the lounge of Boston's Four Seasons Hotel, sometimes until one a.m., whenever Ainge was in New England.

The last great Celtics team, from 1986, included four Hall of Famers in the starting five: Larry Bird, Kevin McHale, Robert Parish, Dennis Johnson. The fifth starter was a six-foot-four guard named Ainge, born to be a gamesman. He could backflip off a diving board before he was five. Growing up in Oregon, he was the teenager who was All-State in three sports. He was twenty when he got three hits in his Major League Baseball debut, weeks after completing his sophomore year of college. When he returned to Brigham Young University as a junior, he earned all-conference and All-American. In basketball. He became a Celtic at twenty-two. He won his first Boston title at twenty-five.

It was hard to pin down Ainge precisely as just one thing all the time. He'd touched all sides of the basketball business. By the time he retired in 1995, he'd played in six NBA Finals. Been an All-Star. Been traded. Traveled with and teased by Bird. Tangled with and taunted by Michael Jordan. He was the prankster who became a coach, briefly, and won 70 percent of his games in his first full season. He'd done national TV, too: an analyst who wasn't partial to his era of ball. He was no *in my day* type. He often praised modern players and took mythology away from ones he'd traded elbows with. In fact, he once scolded his boss, basketball deity Red Auerbach, at a Christmas party in 1988. He looked around the room and saw his best friend, McHale, limping. He pointed to Bird's surgically repaired feet. He shook his head and told Auerbach, the sport's original front-office genius, "I'd trade these guys."

Pagliuca knew Ainge wouldn't give him convenient clichés. The ownership group wanted names of elite team-builders. What's the point of spending all that money if you don't have a creative visionary making basketball decisions? Ainge promised to help.

When Pagliuca arrived in Phoenix, he saw Ainge waiting for him outside. The owner got into Ainge's gray Ford Taurus, and as they began to drive, it was clear that their original plan was being tweaked. Pagliuca and Ainge were supposed to meet with a candidate, and the three of them would play golf and talk about the Celtics job. But Ainge wasn't hurried.

"Let's drive for a while," he told Pagliuca. "We've got some time. You know, I've given a lot of thought to this . . ."

Ainge was trying to get to a point, and it was that he knew the perfect man for the job that Pagliuca had flown hours to discuss.

Him.

That was his recommendation. He could be the one to go back to Boston, twenty-two years after he first stepped on the court there, to make a series of bold basketball decisions. When he stopped coaching, he and his wife, Michelle, had six kids at home, and he needed to spend more time there. But now three of the six were out of the house, and Michelle was open to the idea of a Boston return.

As for Ainge's decisions, frankly, many of them might confuse people, in and out of the office. Some people would be confused due to their own assumptions. For example, in Boston, the story naturally could be positioned as a sentimental homecoming. But that wasn't quite it. He wasn't invested in the 1980s or in the way the Celtics typically did business, and not even in what Auerbach imagined as the best way to win again. If anything, he was attached to social experiments. He'd do it to his friends all the time with the intention of getting to some pure, objective truth.

He'd take an indefensible position on something he didn't believe just to see if you'd buy the indefensibility. Because if you did, well, maybe it meant that you could be swayed too easily. Or that you don't want to argue with him just because he played in the NBA and you didn't. He certainly wasn't *that* guy. Either way, he was always trying to sniff out that personality type because that in itself was an obstacle to improvement.

If he took that job in Boston, there'd have to be some firm principles.

There could be no player or topic protected from analytical scrutiny.

There could be no quick acceptance of so-called basketball truisms without a challenge.

There could be no exasperation or hopelessness about how hard it is to scout unrealized talent, recruit and coach known talent, manage the salary cap, and ultimately win in pro basketball.

That last one is where many NBA executives lose their spirit.

The contemporary player has been scouted since he was a high school freshman, and a general manager must have some sense of who that player projects to be by the time he's nineteen or twenty. Even so, that player's motivations might change when given guaranteed millions and international attention. For those who find talent, develop and expertly coach it, the heartbreak is sometimes crass and sudden: The talent might want to play elsewhere, in a better city, for a better team, or leave simply in the name of change. It wasn't that way in the 1980s for several reasons, and intelligent team-builders understand that they don't have time to rant about it. Too much looking back will get you fired.

From the outside looking in, Boston was just fine. The Celtics won forty-nine games in the 2001–2002 season and advanced to the Eastern Conference Finals. When Pagliuca made his trip to Phoenix to visit with Ainge, the 2002–2003 Celtics were back in the playoffs again, headed toward the Eastern Conference Semifinals. The fans weren't asking for a change. The players were content. Things were comfortable.

But Ainge, then forty-four years old, had matured from games-man to strategist. His TV listeners could hear his discomfort when he analyzed Celtics games. You could see it on screen, underneath the half smile for the benefit of the cameras. Real basketball observers were not fooled; he wasn't impressed with the Celtics. He didn't believe that they were anywhere close to winning a championship.

They were stuck: too good to be bad and not good enough to be great. There was only so far they could go as they were, so the trick for Ainge was to do what had never been done in his life. He was to inherit a situation, temporarily make it worse, and then rise from that subterranean point to the top of the industry.

This would be tougher than that magic he pulled in the spring of 1981. Then, he and two future NBA players from BYU were up against six future NBA players from Notre Dame. They trailed by 1 point with eight seconds to play. Ainge got the ball and was on the move fast. He dribbled with his right hand past John Paxson, then went behind his back to elude Kelly Tripucka and another defender. He'd blown up a triple-team in four seconds. He was college basketball's player of the year and an academic All-American. It was obvious. He was fast but not frantic, smarts blurring perfectly with style and cool urgency. He was in the lane now, with a slow-footed center named Tim Andree in front of him and an athletic six-foot-nine forward, Orlando Woolridge, close by. It took him a second and a half to get there. He had time for one more left-to-right switch, and the right was a beauty: a soft finger roll over Woolridge. Ainge hadn't been great that game, but it didn't matter. He dribbled BYU to a win.

Ainge was outnumbered, and Ainge prevailed.

This would be tougher than the fall of 1981. He'd picked the wrong pro sport, baseball, and he knew it. He wasn't even hitting .200. The best thing he could say about the year was that as a third baseman, he got to stand next to shortstop Alfredo Griffin, who was on his way to being the American League's Rookie of the Year. At the end of May and the first week and a half of June, his Toronto Blue Jays lost eleven games in a row. Then baseball went on strike. The basketball team that drafted him, the Celtics, had lost ten games combined in all of March, April, and May. Then it won the NBA title. This wasn't working. He told the Jays that he didn't want to play baseball anymore and that he'd return their signing bonus money. He thought their soothing words equaled a verbal release from the contract; the Jays disagreed. They took him to court, and the court agreed with them. But he still got out of the contract and joined the Celtics.

Ainge took on an entire baseball franchise, and Ainge somehow prevailed.

This would be tougher, more humbling, than the winter of 1997. He was back in Boston as head coach of the Phoenix Suns. He had a frustrated player, Robert Horry, who wasn't playing well, and the player took out his frustration on him. Horry threw a towel in the coach's face as he walked back to the bench. Why do that to him in Boston, of all places? In front of his people? Embarrassing. But less than a week later, Horry was traded, and Ainge remained on the bench.

Ainge didn't agree with a player, and the player had to leave. How many times does that happen in the NBA?

This task was going to take something new. In the previous ones, he was left with things in his hands, literally and figuratively, and he had to make a good choice. With the basketball. With baseball. With, remarkably, the towel. In Boston, he had to create a winning plan and then sell it to groups with competing agendas: players, coaches, fans, media, ownership. Some of the people he'd sell it to knew that, long term, they wouldn't be around if a championship parade ever were to happen.

Ainge said he was intrigued by the job, and Pagliuca, a man who had presided over multiple billion-dollar deals at his private investment firm, thought he knew what that meant: Ainge really wanted the job. Pags, as everyone called him, started thinking about how excited his ownership group would be with this development. Pags, Ainge, and the would-be candidate played golf for five hours that day, and then it was time for two of them to think about reshaping the Celtics.

When he was a gamesman in his twenties, Ainge played with teammates who were known as the Big Three. As a strategist in his forties, his mission was to find the updated version of it. Pags and the owners liked Ainge's chances because of the way he blended the old and new eras of basketball. They soon found out, as they negotiated a contract with him, that he had a lot more than basketball instincts. They were composed dealmakers, and so was he. And he was using his skills on them.

The owners wanted his first-year salary to be $2 million. Ainge said it should be $3 million. The owners kept talking with him over the next two weeks and going up incrementally—$2.1 million, $2.3 million, $2.5 million. Ainge had something else in mind, and he was determined to get it. He wasn't trying to be the highest-paid team-builder in the NBA or get to a number that someone could proudly leak to the media. He didn't care about any of that. This really was about him as an evaluator and negotiator. This was their first opportunity to see him work up close, to see how he placed a value on something—in this case, himself—and how he got the result he wanted.

As they negotiated with him over two weeks, they noticed what was happening. Pags and Grousbeck were venture capitalists, a position that Grousbeck summed up as "finding people to believe in and bet on." They'd found one, and he was already at work. Ainge remained firm and patient with them, yet the numbers from their side continued to rise: $2.6 million, $2.7 million, $2.8 million . . .

Auerbach, then eighty-five years old, had already told the new owners that Ainge was lucky, and the wise man winked when he said it. He knew that you could create a mess for Ainge, and somehow he'd find a way to sort it out and make it better.

That was his task in Boston. Pags and Grousbeck had negotiated with him, and he'd finally accepted their final offer to take the job. His first-year salary was $3 million.

CHAPTER ONE

IT'S A NEW GAME

Wyc Grousbeck stood outside the gorgeous townhouse on the Upper East Side of Manhattan and took a breath. He'd been in and closed dozens of million-dollar meetings before, but none like this one in the summer of 2002.

In a few seconds, he planned to enter the building, go to the second floor, shake hands with a man he'd never met, and ask him to sell the Boston Celtics. And the Celtics weren't for sale.

None of that made him nervous.

He was thinking more about his life. He had degrees from Princeton, Michigan, and Stanford. He'd graduated from law and business school. As a venture capitalist, he'd invested in software and biotech in Silicon Valley and made a lot of money, enough of it to be taken seriously in this meeting. All those things were a part of him, but they weren't what made him feel most alive.

He was at his authentic peak when connected to team sports, just like he'd been as a college rower with his championship crew. He'd searched nearly twenty years for an echo of that, and now at forty-one years old, he was convinced that this would be the last of Boston's professional teams to sell in his lifetime.

He was a Celtics fan from Worcester, Massachusetts, so he knew about the team's legends and history. He didn't know much about the owner, Paul Gaston. He had two dealmakers from Boston set up a meeting at Gaston's office in New York. Before that introduction, Grousbeck looked up the publicly traded franchise's income statement and got an idea. The Celtics hadn't been to the NBA Finals in fifteen years, and they'd ended the 1990s with seven consecutive losing seasons, but they still made money. He'd factor that into the big offer he planned to make for the team.

Things moved faster than he expected when he met Gaston. He'd gone over numbers in his head, with a ceiling of what he couldn't exceed. He'd rehearsed how it would go, and in his vision, things were more formal. In reality, he was barely in the office, just after the pleasantries, when Gaston got right to the point.

"Why are we here?" he asked.

"I'd like to buy the Celtics," Grousbeck replied.

"But they're not for sale."

"Well, there must be a number, a crazy number, that you'd sell them for."

Gaston's family had owned the team since 1983. It was theirs for the franchise's fifteenth and sixteenth championship seasons, in 1984 and 1986. It was theirs for the lean years, too. Gaston didn't live in Boston, and he'd been to only a handful of his own team's games in the previous three years. This just might be his time to cash out.

"There is a crazy number," he said. "It's $360 million."

Grousbeck couldn't believe it. It was as if Gaston was in his head. That was exactly his maximum figure.

When he saw that income statement with its numbers, slim but still positive, he'd put together his strategy then. He thought he could offer $360 million if necessary, borrow half of it, and pay it off with the team's profits. It would support some debt, and it would be similar to paying a mortgage.

Yes, that was one half of the plan.

The other?

He'd have to raise it with investors in Boston, and he'd have to do it quickly. He'd also have to ask those investors, who were trained not to make emotional financial decisions, to do just that. Not to mention the crazy number—it really was insane. It was $75 million more than the Dallas Mavericks had sold for two years earlier, and they had their own arena. The Celtics were arena tenants.

There was no credible comp for what Grousbeck was about to say and do.

"If I pay you $360 million, you'll give me the Celtics?"

Gaston hesitated briefly. Then he nodded. Grousbeck had already decided that he wouldn't negotiate for a better deal. He wouldn't suggest a knockdown by $10 or $15 million. The Celtics were right here in his grasp, in New York City. If he screwed this up, if Gaston changed his mind and auctioned off the Celtics, he'd be out of his element. He'd never win an investment-bank auction. He had to do this now. He had a joke in his head: *If I'd gone to Harvard Business School, I'd still be doing the math on this. But I went to Stanford, so I'm just going to fucking do it.*

He smiled and extended his hand.

"You've got a deal."

The meeting had been intense, if short—no more than twenty minutes. After the rush of it was over, and after Grousbeck laughed at himself for violating every principle taught in business school, it started to sink in. He'd agreed to purchase the Celtics for a record price, and he needed a monied team of investors to help him make it official. He had a commitment from his father, Irving, cofounder of Continental Cablevision and also a business professor. He needed his father's contribution and the contributions of, roughly, ten to twenty others. If he asked everyone to contribute $20 million, it would be ten. If the ask was $10 million per, he needed twenty. His first surprise on the fundraising trail: His projection of needing to raise $180 million was off; the actual number was closer to $200 million.

As he searched for people who would, as he put it, "be in because it's about Banner 17 and not a 17 percent return on your money," his wife thought of someone who could partner with him. His name was Steve Pagliuca, also known as Pags.

"He must be some basketball freak," Corrine Grousbeck reasoned. "He's got a basketball court in his house."

She was right. Pags was the father of four, and he'd installed the home gym for his basketball-playing kids and himself. Pags knew Grousbeck, but not well. They lived in the same Boston suburb, Weston, and their daughters, Stephanie Pagliuca and Kelsey Grousbeck, were seventh-grade classmates.

Pags played in college, on the freshman team at Duke. He'd never gotten over ball, even after going through Harvard Business School and working at Bain Capital, a global investment firm. When Grousbeck initially called with a request to invest, Pags was in his office and smiled at his desk. When another call came a week later, with an offer for Pags to be a co-owner, he showed up at Grousbeck's house, beaming and wearing Celtics gear.

Then he looked at those income statements and had a thought that he tried to quiet: *How can somebody pay $360 million for something that has declining attendance and hardly makes any money? It doesn't make any sense to me.*

He was in anyway.

Soon after agreeing to partner with Grousbeck, the scrutiny of NBA life became real to him. In late September, he and Grousbeck walked into a packed press conference at the Celtics' practice facility for the sale announcement. Pags had negotiated bigger deals than this one. At Bain, they'd bought Domino's as a private company, taken it public, and watched it become a giant. They'd founded Staples as a venture capitalist company, and it became huge, too. Yet those deals didn't draw a crowd like this.

Everyone was paying attention to what they did and said, including a man in the balcony who was staring at them intently. He was Jim O'Brien, set to enter his second full season as the Celtics' head coach. Grousbeck and Pags made eye contact with him and gave him a wave, and the stare became a glare.

They had a problem. No one had told O'Brien about this. And since they had just been introduced as the owners—even though they were far from the money target—they'd eventually be the ones to explain to O'Brien what this meant for him and everyone else on the basketball side of the business.

In a lot of ways, O'Brien had saved Paul Gaston's Celtics. He'd taken over as head coach after Rick Pitino, who had been installed as a franchise savior in 1997, walked away from the job in January 2001. Pitino was a complicated mix of brilliance, generosity, intensity, and, most notoriously, impatience.

Everywhere he went in his coaching career, his teams delivered more than anyone expected. He led a Providence College team with no first-round NBA prospects to the 1987 Final Four. His 1996 University of Kentucky team, stacked with six first-rounders, won the national title. But even that came with something extra: a twenty-seven-game winning streak. One of those high draft picks from Kentucky, Antoine Walker, was selected by the Celtics one year ahead of Pitino's arrival.

When Pitino got to Boston, he planned to surround second-year star Walker with talent and then win games fast. He got the city's attention in his first game, a win over Michael Jordan's Bulls, and then toasted with the city afterward. He went to a sports bar, the Fours, across the street from the arena and savored every sip of victory. He coached the Celtics to a twenty-one-win improvement in his first year, but they still had more losses than wins, and the slow build toward contention made him miserable.

He wanted quick turnarounds with everything, including physical appearances. He was so obsessed with having well-conditioned players that he raised the stakes off the court. In Boston, he was the weight watcher who required members of his staff to reduce their size. The first general manager he hired, Chris Wallace, got a letter from Pitino, and the message was simple: drop weight. Wallace lost fifty-three pounds. Pitino rode him relentlessly but then bought him a $3,000 suit from a high-end boutique, Louis Boston, at the end of the journey.

Pitino was generous: He once endorsed a $25,000 check he'd received from a speaking engagement and dropped it into an offering basket. Saint Patrick's Church in Natick needed funds to help retired nuns and priests. The request happened to be made on a morning when Pitino had slipped into Mass there, not far from his house, before going to work.

Pitino was insecure and offbeat: When he took the job in Boston, one of his conditions was being named team president, a title that Red Auerbach always had. While Pitino had an eye for talented coaching and support staff, with his hiring of O'Brien, Wallace, and Frank Vogel, he also relied on the other Red. He was a high school home ec teacher known as Jersey Red, who cooked for Pitino when he was a college student. Jersey Red, a Pitino sycophant, was more privy to basketball decisions than Auerbach. He was so much a part of Pitino's inner circle that he traveled on the team plane, shared staff members' hotel rooms, and occupied a seat in the draft room.

The Celtics' atmosphere was wild and unpredictable. It could have derailed if the steady O'Brien hadn't stabilized things in 2001. He earned the trust of the team's two best players, Walker and Paul Pierce, and they immediately responded to his hands-off approach. In fact, "hands off" had become the organizational mantra, with everyone taking ownership of their own plots. Wallace and Leo Papile handled basketball operations, O'Brien coached, and Walker and Pierce called the shots—lots of them—on the court.

That's why Grousbeck and Pags got that glare. No one just dropped in like this. Who in the hell were these guys? There was already an undercurrent of resistance, and they hadn't done anything yet.

Gaston wasn't an owner who hovered, so the franchise often ran itself. When Wallace made a controversial trade two months earlier for former All-Star Vin Baker, Gaston didn't stop by the office or call for an exhaustive review. As it was, Baker had four years and $50 million remaining on his contract, and his game was in decline. It was an open secret around the league that Baker had a drinking problem, although not many knew the extent of it. The trade was a mistake, on multiple levels, and it wouldn't be long before the new Celtics owners would ask questions about why it was made.

In their day jobs, Grousbeck and Pags craved precise information and details. The Celtics' way of doing business in every corner of the organization was about to change.

As November approached, Grousbeck and Pags still didn't have the money they needed to satisfy Gaston's terms. He'd given them until the end of December, so they needed to continue meeting with investors. It was what they spent most of their time doing. There was the pressure of the deadline and the pressure of getting into a business that they didn't know well enough.

Fortunately for them, New England was populated with wealthy businesspeople whose love for the Celtics rivaled their love of business. Bob Epstein, cofounder of the Abbey Group, a high-end real estate company, was one of those people. He grew up in Newton, a quick Green Line trip away from Boston Garden. As a kid, he'd played basketball constantly and once had a brief conversation with Bob Cousy; he considered that chat a highlight of his childhood. But that was years ago. In 2002, he knew better than to put a lot of financial faith in a pro sports team. One of his friends warned him, "Forget everything you know about business when you get involved in pro sports."

It didn't matter. It was the Celtics, and he'd dreamed of owning them for years. Once, in his thirties, he thought of making an offer for them and soon realized he and his group were in over their heads. He comforted himself after that with his own mission statement: *I buy real estate; I don't buy companies.* And then Grousbeck called, looking for a second co-owner. He'd never said no to the Celtics in his life, and he wasn't going to do it now. He was in.

One Friday afternoon, it became obvious that Grousbeck felt the enormity of what was at stake. He was agitated. He had a Monday-morning meeting with even more investors, and he wanted to be sure he could answer any questions they had. But he knew he was deficient in a key area. Surrounded by members of the consulting group the Celtics hired, he said aloud, "You know, I don't understand the salary cap well enough yet. I just need to know. What can we spend, and what can't we spend? What kind of players can we get? I just need to know more."

He was frustrated, so he didn't notice that his complaint spurred a thirty-year-old case team leader of consultants into action. He was an analytics savant, an MIT graduate who secretly wanted to be involved with basketball one day. His name was Daryl Morey.

He started making phone calls to the NBA office immediately after Grousbeck spoke. He was dogged with this assignment, and he'd been persistent enough to get the NBA commissioner, David Stern, on the phone.

After a brief exchange, a plan was in motion, and suddenly Morey was out of the room in Boston and on his way to NBA headquarters in New York. Stern had agreed to open the building to him for the weekend, and a team of half a dozen NBA staffers gave Morey a rushed tutorial on the various pockets, spins, and twists of the salary cap. He spent all day on it Saturday and parts of Sunday.

He left New York on Sunday and called Grousbeck.

"I prepared a memo," he said.

Did he ever. The memo was a beautifully presented booklet with a fountain of data. They spent hours going over the major points of the cap, with Sunday night turning into the early hours of Monday morning, and Grousbeck was prepared for his meeting a few hours later. He also had a new hire.

"Daryl, you're going to look good in green," Grousbeck said. "You're coming with me."

After Grousbeck and Pags reached their financial goals, they were able to focus fully on the organization. It had the Celtic quaintness and charm that they all loved, but the franchise was outdated. That meant upgrades, and most of those would be welcome.

In basketball operations, no one in the office had computers. They were using calculators and notebooks to tally salary-cap information. Their international scouting wasn't competitive at a time when the league was becoming more global. They were spending about $6 million in operations, well below the top teams in the league, and Pags's recommendation was that the number had to at least triple.

On the court, with front-row seats at opposing baselines, Grousbeck and Pags were able to see the best players in the world up close. Grousbeck didn't view himself as a basketball expert, so he knew that he didn't have the vision to remake the basketball-playing Celtics. He could do that in other parts of the organization by expanding its sponsorships, reenergizing its sales approach, and embracing the concept of marketing, which the organization had been historically reluctant to develop. It was as if the love of pure basketball couldn't coexist with an aggressive and fun marketing plan, which was somehow viewed as the ugly other.

One of the first things Grousbeck did when the sale became official was write a letter to each season ticket holder. He introduced himself and the group, said he wanted to win a championship, and left his email and phone number if anyone wanted to share feedback.

Grousbeck knew he could identify creative and quick-thinking individuals, collaborate with them, and make the total Celtics experience more modern and lucrative. He was content to find them through his own experience, as he did with Morey (his vice president of strategy and information), or by leaning on the advice of his friends in business.

One week, he had multiple meetings in which Rich Gotham's name came up. He didn't know Gotham, but he took that as a sign that they needed to meet. Grousbeck got his number, told him that he sounded like someone who would be good for the Celtics, and then told him that, if not, "the worst case is you can tell me what you think of the team and consult a little, and I'll flip you some playoff tickets."

Grousbeck had done his homework, so he knew exactly what he was doing. Gotham was an internet media executive with a company named Lycos, yes, but he was also a Celtics fan from Milford, Massachusetts. He grew up idolizing Larry Bird, Kevin McHale, and Robert Parish. This was a dream offer. Grousbeck was prepared for him to accept it and had a title waiting for him when he did: vice president of sales and marketing.

The new strategy of the Celtics was simple. Find the best people, and waste no time hiring them. That could be done efficiently on the business side. If only that were the case for bringing in players. Pags was all in, spending the bulk of his time in basketball operations. He sometimes slept on the couch in the office there, trying to understand everything he could about running an NBA team in general and the Celtics in particular.

There were some good things to see early in 2003. Pitino may have tried to trade every other player on his roster years ago, but he never thought of moving Paul Pierce. He knew how fortunate he was that the Celtics had been able to draft him in 1998. Pierce, a Los Angeles kid who attended the University of Kansas, was supposed to be a top five pick that year. He didn't visit teams with lower selections. The Celtics had the tenth choice, and when Pierce started to slide toward them, Pitino got nervous.

"What's wrong with him?" he asked Wallace. "What do these other teams know about him that we don't?"

He was too good to be coming their way, and the rest of the league finally figured it out just before Boston picked. The Celtics got multiple offers for their slot, with some packages including as many as three first-round picks. They stayed put and took Pierce. In his fifth season, he was no longer a basketball secret.

He was six foot seven, and he had a knack for looking at a player directly in front of him, fifteen feet from the basket, and then suddenly having that same player on his hip while Pierce was at the rim. It was a trick that defenders couldn't quite figure out.

Pierce was faster than he looked, thanks to his expert footwork and uncanny instincts. He was strong near the basket, too, so he could take a hard push and score at the same time. He looked around the league and saw peers, like him, who could score with ease. There was Kobe Bryant and Allen Iverson and Tracy McGrady. But no one, not those three and not even the big men like Shaquille O'Neal and Tim Duncan, attempted and made more free throws than Pierce.

In fact, after he put 42 points on the Los Angeles Lakers in the spring of 2001, an approving O'Neal excitedly declared, "Paul Pierce is the motherfucking truth." The comment stuck, with edits, and Pierce had a nickname that was as simple and thorough as everything he brought to a game: "the Truth."

He and Walker looked for each other on the court constantly, and it wasn't unusual for the six-foot-nine Walker to venture to the high post and call a play for Pierce to post up. They'd mastered that two-man game, and it was a big reason that for three years in a row, Pierce led the Celtics in scoring while Walker topped them in assists.

In February, both Walker, twenty-six, and Pierce, twenty-five, represented the Celtics in the All-Star Game. They had the profile of two young building blocks for a team on the rise. But Grousbeck and Pags didn't see it that way, and neither did an opinionated former Celtic, Danny Ainge. Pags and Ainge were both board members for Hall of Fame quarterback Steve Young's Forever Young Foundation. They were friends who loved basketball, so conversations about the Celtics were inevitable.

Ainge had it easy. All he had to do was watch the games, share his thoughts on what he liked and didn't for his TNT audience, and then go home. Pags, meanwhile, was one of the people charged with fixing it. He, Epstein, and Grousbeck never told Wallace that they were looking to hire someone who would become his boss, but Wallace knew they weren't happy. They were accustomed to excellence and success in their industry, and they had the same expectation for the Celtics.

The Baker trade had become such a costly and embarrassing disaster that it followed Wallace wherever he went. He was driving on Cambridge Street, near the arena, with his wife and six-year-old son. At a red light, a man in the car next to Wallace looked, recognized him, and motioned for him to roll down his window.

"You ruined our cap, Wallace!" he yelled. "Terrible trade."

Baker never became a starter during the season, and as the playoffs approached, he was suspended for them. He was headed to rehab. He averaged five points and four rebounds, negligible production for such a substantial salary. It was awkward to discuss, but it was obvious that Baker was fighting for his sobriety and the millions remaining on his contract.

Beyond Baker, there wasn't ownership excitement about how the Celtics were built. From afar, Ainge thought they were scrappy and defensive-minded, but he actually saw a team getting worse. He also didn't see the two stars that many people in Boston did. He saw one, Pierce, as critical to any championship plan the Celtics had.

Pags knew the ownership group had to do something about it. They'd all structured complex multimillion-dollar deals on their own, but they wanted a blessing of sorts before they moved forward. Auerbach had arrived in Boston for one of his organizational check-ins, so Grousbeck and Epstein decided to get his advice on what to do next.

"Red, we're going to be searching for a new GM," Epstein said. "Can you think of anyone we should be talking to?"

Auerbach looked at the two men. Whether they followed his suggestions or not was secondary. He liked that they sought his opinion.

"Oh, I can think of a couple," he said. "Call Wayne Embry. Or Danny Ainge."

CHAPTER TWO

PIVOT

In early May 2003, Chris Wallace received a wake-up call that he didn't request.

He was in Madrid for a scouting trip. At five a.m., while fast asleep in his hotel room, he was first surprised by a ringing phone. Then, when he picked it up, there was the slightly recognizable voice of his wife, Debby. He tried to piece together her report, but he was so groggy and she sounded scared, so it was hard to get a grip on what this was all about. He thought, *Is the house burning down or something?*

It was eleven p.m. in Boston, and Debby was watching the local news. The lead story was that an old Celtic, Danny Ainge, was returning to be the organization's top man in basketball operations. He was here to do Wallace's job. And Debby Wallace had been on enough NBA adventures with Chris that she thought she knew what was coming next. They had to be on the way out. Fired. That was how this usually worked.

The Wallaces knew how fun, and fragile, an NBA life could be. There couldn't have been a bigger gap between Ainge and Chris Wallace. One was a gifted athlete in multiple sports, a two-time NBA champion, a smart and respected TV analyst. The other was an NBA outsider: He wasn't an athlete; he grew up in Buckhannon, West Virginia, a four-hour drive from the closest NBA city (Washington, DC); and he got the league's attention by his basketball publishing rather than playing.

When Ainge was celebrating the last Celtics' championship, in 1986, Wallace was breaking into the league as a $9,000-a-year Portland Trail Blazers employee. He thought he'd made it big in 1990 when the man who hired him in Portland, Jon Spoelstra, got a job with the Denver Nuggets. Spoelstra brought Wallace with him and presented him with the biggest salary of his life: $60,000. An ecstatic Wallace called Debby, his fiancée then, and when she picked up the phone, he began singing "Rocky Mountain High."

It's a tough business. When Wallace returned from their honeymoon, he found out that Spoelstra and everyone connected to him had been fired.

With that context, of course, anyone associated with basketball operations would expect to be replaced. Grousbeck and Pags aggressively recruited Ainge for the position, not the other way around, so they'd give him what he wanted right now in *his* version of a honeymoon period.

But what a lot of people were about to learn about Ainge is that he wasn't a conventional thinker. On one hand, he'd been unequivocal with his scouting report of the team on the court. It needed to change. He'd also told Grousbeck and Pags how much he valued franchise stability and alignment. He looked around the league at teams that casually removed coaches and GMs, good basketball people, as if they were changing computer wallpaper. How do you expect to be taken seriously, and have players take you seriously, if all people see is upheaval?

Frankly, it was one of the big concerns he expressed to Grousbeck, Pags, and Epstein, given the size of their ownership group.

There were a lot of hands in there, men and women who'd contributed millions of dollars to be a part of this team. Ainge wanted to be assured that there wouldn't be a problem if, for example, he stood by a coach who'd piled up a bunch of losses. Or a coach who was doing a good job, even if that wasn't the public perception.

It was an important point that needed to be resolved before he could accept the assignment. He was more prescient than he realized.

Things were all right, personally, in the O'Brien-ownership relationship. O'Brien was seen as a devoted family man, and that resonated with the owners, who wanted to celebrate that throughout the organization. But there was friction when O'Brien was asked to consider things that no one had ever asked him to consider. He didn't like it when he was questioned about the team's style of play. He didn't want to hear it when he was asked why the Celtics got so many technical fouls, and that conversation got worse when someone pointed out that analytics suggested berating the officials actually made things worse for your team.

Ah, analytics. Grousbeck and Pags valued them, and it was one of the reasons Daryl Morey was now a team vice president. But the only coach on O'Brien's staff who seemed intrigued by the numbers was Frank Vogel, who also happened to be the staff's youngest coach.

If Ainge had said he wanted to fire O'Brien, ownership wasn't going to stand in the way of it. But he wasn't interested in firing him. He met with the coach over five days, felt a strong bond with him, and instead wanted to give him a contract extension. A week and a half after taking the job, Ainge announced that O'Brien had been extended two years. Wallace was staying, too. The new boss believed he had a lot to figure out and not much time to do it and that he needed help from all angles.

It was already mid-May, and the NBA draft was approaching quickly.

It was going to take a couple of sizable mistakes from teams in front of the Celtics for Boston to acquire a future superstar in the draft. Pags was stunned when he saw the results from one of Morey's studies. The point was to find out, over twenty years of research, the value of each draft position. The standard was simple: What percent chance does a team have of finding a starting NBA player from each slot?

The numbers were humbling.

Teams with the number one overall pick: 90 percent chance of finding a starter.

Teams with pick sixteen: 1 percent.

Teams with pick twenty: Scant results.

The Celtics had two picks in the first round, numbers sixteen and twenty. But Ainge made a deal with Memphis, and those picks became thirteen and twenty-seven. That left him a dozen picks and a lifetime away from the prize of the draft, an eighteen-year-old forward named LeBron James. Ainge had a running joke in the office, claiming that he'd trade the entire Celtics' roster for James. But the more he said it, the less it sounded like a joke. James was going to be a number one choice destined to boost those grim analytics.

James was from the same midwestern city, Akron, Ohio, as Nate Thurmond and Gus Johnson, both in the Basketball Hall of Fame. Same city, different tradition. At six foot eight, James was taller than Johnson and bulkier than the lean, nearly seven-foot Thurmond. Still, when scouts looked for comparisons, they brought up Magic Johnson and Michael Jordan.

Antoine Walker had already played against James, and so had Jordan. Some of the top players in the league traveled to Chicago's near West Side to play in a gym called Hoops. James was there, too, following the gym tradition of waiting his turn to play so the veterans could go first and lead off the pickup games.

That waiting was the perfect metaphor for James, who was already projected as the league's next superstar. The team thirty miles away from his hometown, the Cleveland Cavaliers, had the top pick. James was the most anticipated selection in that franchise's history, as the Cavs viewed James as a one-man revival for the team and the city.

For Ainge, this was his first opportunity to show supportive owners, and skeptical players and coaches, how he planned to shape the team. This draft was historically strong in the top five, and then it became a subjective exercise. At the end of the night on June 26, the newest Celtics were point guard Marcus Banks and center Kendrick Perkins, an eighteen-year-old high schooler from Texas. Walker was excited because he felt those were the two positions where the New Jersey Nets silenced the Celtics on their way to sweeping them out of the playoffs.

Paul Pierce remained curious two weeks later when he made the forty-minute drive from his house to the campus of the University of Massachusetts Boston. There was a weeklong NBA Summer League tournament happening there, and the rookies and free agents from the Celtics and Cavs were scheduled to play. Most people in the building were there to see James in person. Pierce said he was there for something else.

"I want to see Banks," he said.

While that may have been the initial reason for the trip, it changed quickly. Banks looked like most rookie point guards with promise: a few good plays mixed with some decision-making that's only acceptable for basketball in July. James, meanwhile, was clearly in the wrong league. He was more advanced, physically and mentally, than everyone around him. He was strong, quick, and charismatic. Pierce, who averaged 26 points per night, was usually in the position of having rookies worry about him. But he'd have to keep his eye on this one.

Cleveland had been so bad in the previous season that even a generational prodigy couldn't make the Cavs an instant contender. Pierce and Walker were thinking about how they matched up with the Nets and Pistons, the other contenders in the East. Vin Baker had gone through rehab and was now projected to be the team's starting center. He looked and sounded good, and he drew compliments from all of his teammates. He knew his consequences were different this season because he'd agreed to daily alcohol testing. A relapse could affect his career and his contract.

The progress and status of Baker was one of the major preseason stories—until Ainge gave the region and league a jolt with something else.

He traded Walker and his college teammate, Tony Delk, to Dallas in exchange for Raef LaFrentz, Jiri Welsch, Chris Mills, and a 2004 first-round pick. The deal wasn't surprising to a handful of people—Grousbeck, Pags, and O'Brien, who were aware of how Ainge viewed Walker. Everyone else was shocked.

Walker was devastated. He'd been hanging out with friends at Mohegan Sun Casino and had a hard time concentrating on what Ainge was saying over the phone.

"We're going in a different direction. But I'm trading you to a really good team and good situation."

Walker was from Chicago, but he'd adopted Boston as his own. He loved the tradition and stories he learned when people like Red Auerbach, Bill Russell, and Tommy Heinsohn would pull him aside to chat. His first coach, former Celtic M. L. Carr, treated him like a son. He was amazed when he went around town and heard the passion and basketball knowledge of the fans. He relished being a Celtics captain, and members of the support staff could feel it in tangible ways; he bought them suits and shoes, split his playoff shares with them, and picked up meals on the road.

After that phone call with Ainge, he immediately called his agent. He just needed help wrapping his head around this thing. He was going to Dallas? He'd convinced himself that he'd have a fifteen-year career, with all of it spent in Boston.

It wasn't just that the trade was hard for Walker to process. The return for Walker, whose contract was set to expire in two seasons, seemed uninspired. LaFrentz, who played at Kansas with Pierce, had been disappointing in his career and had five years remaining on his contract. Mills was injured. Welsch was unproven. As for the pick, it would likely be in the mid- to late twenties—the longshot / no shot zone of Daryl Morey's study—if Dallas played as well as expected.

Ainge didn't think the Celtics were a contender when others did. Now everyone could see that they weren't. They split their first ten games of the season, but this wasn't about winning. This was about acquiring assets in all forms—promising players, players with expiring contracts, first- and second-round picks, good role-players—shuffling them around, and making incremental progress toward some ideal that only Ainge could imagine.

O'Brien was on board with the Walker trade, but he wasn't totally comfortable with how Ainge viewed the season. O'Brien, naturally, thought like a coach—that is, he didn't believe anyone was going to look at his record and make excuses for him. No one was going to remember that he began to lose games that his team used to win because his franchise, overnight, began to play a shell game with his roster.

He'd seen too much of the coaching pattern: When they win, they stay. As soon as they start to lose, even the slightest lull, they're out.

It had just happened in Orlando.

It wasn't that long ago when everyone in the NBA was applauding Magic coach Glenn "Doc" Rivers. He'd been the Coach of the Year in 2000 when he got his team, with an unheard of four undrafted players in the starting five, to win as often as it lost. It was quite an achievement. Then, by dint of his eloquence and elite salesmanship, he was able to recruit free agents Tracy McGrady and Grant Hill to Orlando. They became a playoff team then. Injuries and expectations crushed them at the beginning of the season, and after a 1–10 start, Rivers was fired.

O'Brien didn't know Ainge well enough to understand that Ainge was rebelling against that pattern. That's exactly the thing he'd talked about with Grousbeck and Pags. Ainge was a bit of a riddle for sure: a bold dealmaker who appreciated stability.

In December, O'Brien finally got his imperfect team to win several games in a row. They'd pushed their winning streak to a modest five, and now they were close to even on the season. Not many people in Boston were paying attention to them because the New England Patriots hadn't lost a game since October, and the Red Sox were trying to trade for Alex Rodriguez, the best player in baseball. Boston, as a whole, was becoming what Ainge's Celtics had been in the 1980s: a place with an appetite for champions. Still, O'Brien was proud of what they'd done. If this were his job review, he'd highlight this; this was the employee displaying creativity with limited resources.

Then Ainge called. Those resources were about to be remixed and reshuffled again. Ainge had completed a trade with Cleveland. Boston was getting a second-round pick and Ricky Davis, a skilled player with a questionable attitude and lack of defensive intensity. To get him, the Celtics had to part with two more of O'Brien's trusted veteran players, Tony Battie and Eric Williams.

As the season moved into January, leading the Celtics became more challenging. The new players had to be managed, and one veteran player, Baker, needed professional help. He'd begun the season with a flourish. He had All-Star Games and Olympic Games on his résumé, and it showed. He had more double-digit scoring nights in the first ten games than he'd had all of the previous season. But when his performance abruptly dipped, his coworkers knew what it meant. It was confirmed by the tests that he'd agreed to as well. He'd begun drinking again, and he was suspended indefinitely on January 20. His Celtics career was effectively over.

One week later, O'Brien began to reflect on his own job. He'd signed that extension in May, and here he was in January, unhappy. He had a lot of things on his mind, and he wanted to share them. Ainge liked hearing different opinions from everyone in the organization, and he was about to receive them from his head coach.

They needed to talk.

Ainge and Grousbeck were already at the practice facility with O'Brien, and Pags was at Bain in a meeting. In the middle of that meeting, he learned O'Brien was thinking about leaving the Celtics. He rushed out of the office, got into his car, and found himself in thick Boston traffic. He knew then he'd be a few minutes late, and he was hopeful that nothing got out of hand before he arrived.

As traffic lightened and Pags sped to the facility, O'Brien began speaking to Ainge and Grousbeck. He listed all the things he didn't like, such as the uncertain roster, the trade for Ricky Davis, and what he perceived as heavy-handedness and meddling from ownership. He could have gone on. Ainge listened; Grousbeck got annoyed. O'Brien began raising his voice, and Grousbeck did the same. Pags, still hustling in, was missing a heated disagreement.

Honestly, Grousbeck and O'Brien were really arguing about the current season plus their time together before Ainge was hired. The organization had changed dramatically in just fifteen months. O'Brien worked for Paul Gaston for five and a half years, yet he'd already seen more of Grousbeck and Pags than he ever did of Gaston. The radical culture change wasn't for him.

By the time Pags arrived at the meeting, three minutes late, he saw the flushed faces and understood that the hard-line positions were clear: O'Brien said he didn't like how things were going, and Grousbeck asked for his resignation.

Pags tried to suggest cooling down a bit before any rash decisions were made, but O'Brien was convinced that stepping away from the job was the best decision, and Grousbeck agreed with him. Ainge saw it for what it was. He had a coach who didn't see the big picture and a man who was honest enough to say that he wasn't okay with where they were headed. If he wasn't on board, Ainge thought, now was the time to jump off.

They wished each other well and came to their first unanimous decision of the season: This was over.

Forty-two games into year one, Ainge needed to find a coach who could be firmly planted in this rubble and, like him, still glimpse a championship horizon beyond it.

CHAPTER THREE

SMART AND HUNGRY

When Doc Rivers got fired eleven games into the 2003–2004 season, dozens of his friends reached out just to make sure he was all right. His Orlando team had lost ten games in a row. After number ten, on the road in Salt Lake City, Rivers flew back home to Orlando.

There was one message that he didn't see coming: David Stern, NBA commissioner, was on the phone and wanted to talk.

"David Stern?" Rivers said to his administrative assistant. "I guess when you get fired as a coach, the commissioner calls to commiserate."

Rivers soon discovered that Stern had a different agenda.

"Doc," the commissioner began, "I'm so sorry about you and the Magic . . . but, hey, TNT and ABC are going to call you. Both of them are going to offer you jobs. Listen, as you know, Doc, I'm impartial. But ABC has Al Michaels. I'm impartial, but Al Michaels doesn't have a partner."

The NBA wanted the same big-game distinction for its prime-time games that Michaels brought to *Monday Night Football*. Stern had personally asked Michaels to be involved in marquee games, and now he was working on Rivers.

"Can you believe it, Doc?" he concluded. "We're about a month away from Christmas, and Al Michaels, at ABC, doesn't have a partner."

Rivers got off the phone and called his agent, Lonnie Cooper. He told him what the commissioner said, they laughed about it . . . and Rivers joined Michaels on the ABC telecasts. He was good on TV, and having this job for the rest of his career would be comfortable. He and Michaels played golf at Michaels's club, Bel-Air. They frequently ate at Toscana, one of their favorite Los Angeles restaurants. They watched the best basketball in the world and never worried about correcting mistakes that some player made in the third quarter.

The problem with Rivers was that something in him couldn't resist competition or the desire to redeem what others had written off. Doing TV was fun, and it allowed for a flexible golf schedule, but it couldn't provide the rush and sense of belonging and achieving like the games—and all that went into them—did.

As soon as Jim O'Brien decided the Celtics were no longer for him, Danny Ainge began the search for his next coach. Rivers's intelligence, personality, and leadership made him the top target.

His quick smile for the camera hid the fighter in him. His father, Grady Rivers, was a Chicago policeman who loved watching his son play ball. But when the police scanner beckoned and Grady had to miss the games, he'd ask his son about one stat. It wasn't points. Rivers was reminded of that after a game his sophomore year at Proviso East High School.

He and his brother came home raving about Doc's 48 points. And on varsity, no less. His brother gave details. His mother hugged him. Grady, sitting at the kitchen table, continued to eat. When Doc joined him there, he asked his familiar question.

"How many fouls did you have?"

His son told him that he had one or two.

"You played hard with one foul? You think that's possible?"

"Well, I did have forty-eight—"

"How can you leave fouls out there? How will you ever know how physical you can be if you don't push the envelope?"

Rivers played well and hard for the Atlanta Hawks in the 1980s and was often the assist man for some of Dominique Wilkins's ferocious and artistic dunks. Wilkins was nicknamed "the Human Highlight Film," and what he and the Hawks did during that span really was avant-garde. The problem was that they could never get past the two teams, the Celtics and the Pistons, who represented the East in the finals for seven consecutive seasons.

Rivers and the Hawks never made it to the NBA Finals. By the time he left the East for a year and returned in 1992, Rivers and his New York Knicks were stopped short of the stage by Michael Jordan one year and stopped on it in a heartbreaking game seven loss to Hakeem Olajuwon the next.

The blessing there, though, was playing for New York coach Pat Riley. Before going to the Knicks, Rivers's postcareer plan was to be a broadcaster. He'd been a sports intern at CNN in Atlanta, so he'd studied the pros in that field up close. But then he watched and listened to Riley, who made coaching seem cool. Riley knew the game, but that wasn't what engaged Rivers; a lot of coaches knew the technical aspects of the sport. He saw Riley as a team-builder and riveting speaker. Plus, Riley's philosophy on fouls was the same as his father's. No coach had ever captured his total attention the way Riley did.

Man, he thought, *I want to be able to do that. I want to be able to lead and get guys to buy it.*

If Ainge wanted to win a championship, Rivers wanted one more. Some former players were unaffected by the titles that they'd missed, but he wasn't one of them. He prayed often, and starting in second grade, he didn't leave his knees until he'd asked God to help him reach his three big goals. He wanted to play in the NBA, which became official in 1983. He wanted to make the All-Star team, which happened in 1988 (alongside Ainge). He wanted to win an NBA title.

The absence of a title bothered him, and he was savvy enough to keep it to himself when the New York media talked about getting a ring for Patrick Ewing. He loved Ewing and thought he was a great teammate. But it wasn't just the great players. He wanted a championship, too.

Being fired by Orlando turned out to be a positive, if forced, sabbatical. As an analyst, he got a courtside view of what everyone was doing, and he could see up close how faint the line between winning and elimination often is. As an ex-player, he knew that sometimes the problem was team construction; there were really good—no, great—players around the league who didn't win because there wasn't enough talent or spirit around them.

Sometimes that was perceived as the player's problem. Sometimes the blame was placed on the head coach. That was one of the reasons he got so many mixed reviews in the spring of 2004, when he told his friends that Ainge was trying to recruit him to Boston.

They brought up the general negatives: bad talent on the roster, they hadn't won in years, the fans were tough. They brought up the negatives specific to the treatment of black coaches: not getting a fair chance; being criticized for things that other coaches weren't; and, from one of his smartest friends, the fear that "a two-times-fired black coach is the worst disease you can ever catch. If you go there, you're going to get fired, and then you'll never coach again."

He listened to and weighed all the good advice. He also listened to the tenets of Ainge's vision, with an emphasis on stability and total investment in the head coach, even when that coach was unpopular. Rivers had played basketball against and golf with Ainge. They'd shared the same All-Star Game locker room and TV studio. He liked and trusted him. If the offer hadn't been from the Celtics, with Ainge leading them, he might have passed. But this was something to strongly consider.

Al Michaels knew something was up in early April when, sitting in his room at the Four Seasons in Houston, he got a call from his analyst.

"Can I come up to your room for a second?" Rivers asked.

"Sure."

Rivers was there a few minutes later. He began explaining to Michaels how much he enjoyed working with him and that there were only a few jobs that would make him even consider walking away from what he and Michaels had quickly established. He didn't get a chance to tell Michaels the team he had in mind because the broadcaster guessed it first.

"Boston!" Michaels said. "Doc, you *have* to take it."

The rebuilding of the Celtics continued officially three weeks later, when Rivers was introduced as the team's new coach. The announcement came forty-eight hours after interim coach John Carroll was fired. Rivers planned to start his coaching work in Boston as soon as Rivers, the broadcaster, finished his duties at the end of the 2004 playoffs.

Near the one-year mark of Ainge's hiring, the Celtics had one of the deepest and most talented rosters in the league—in management positions. The fans didn't pay to see the best and brightest of suites and boardrooms. The hope, though, was that smarts, passion, and hunger from the inside of the organization would eventually show up on the court.

Grousbeck, Pags, and Epstein had added Daryl Morey and Rich Gotham to a business and marketing team that already had employees worthy of promotion. In basketball operations, Ainge brought Rivers in as his head coach, retained the staff he inherited, added young scout Ryan McDonough, benefited from a dramatic budget increase, and experienced the thing that Red Auerbach always said he had: good luck.

One of the Celtics' most devout fans and lifelong season ticket holders was also someone who could make them smarter in basketball operations and more secure in their legal department. His name was Mike Zarren, a third-year Harvard Law School student who grew up in Swampscott, on Boston's North Shore. His schedule had been built around Celtics games for as long as he could remember. One of his childhood highlights was meeting Kevin McHale, his favorite player. He held McHale's attention when he shared that he was more interested in a basketball discussion than an autograph. McHale happily talked ball with nine-year-old Zarren for ten minutes.

After graduating from the University of Chicago with quiz bowl bragging rights (he was his team's player-GM, so to speak) and an econometrics degree, Zarren had his choice between law school there and at Harvard. He chose Harvard simply because he missed going to Celtics games with his father. When Grousbeck and Pags became Celtics co-owners, he wrote them a letter and asked if they needed help on the legal side. He didn't hear back, so he proceeded with his summer plan to work for a law firm in New York City.

Shortly after, he got an email from the Harvard statistics department. The Celtics were looking for their own version of *Moneyball*. Michael Lewis's 2003 book had become a bestseller. In it, those who stood up for groupthink were left behind, while the best team-builders recognized "market inefficiencies" and took advantage of those who essentially stopped asking questions: questions about the sport, its players, its scouts, its contracts, its most sensible path to winning.

The book had its detractors, of course, especially those who perceived a jocks-versus-geeks tension, with the geeks finally winning. But that was too simplistic for multidimensional personalities, like Ainge, who played at the highest level of two sports but appreciated the conversations that analytics provoked. The more people got to know him, the more they could see the point-counterpoint positions he tried to create when discussing players, policy, politics, everything. The surface debates were too polite and didn't dig in enough. If it didn't get there organically, he didn't assume it would happen. Not asking questions was not a problem for him. He'd do it and manufacture a fight if he had to.

Morey brought in Zarren for an interview with Ainge, and in typical Ainge fashion, he spent most of the session talking to Morey about how stupid some of the advanced stats were. It was a test, of course. He believed half of what he said and wanted to see the law student's reaction to the other stuff.

It must have worked. Zarren got the job. His time was divided between attending law school, working for a law journal at Harvard, and doing whatever was needed with the Celtics. He blew their minds when he built an Excel spreadsheet they could use to do the math on, potentially, twenty trades in five minutes instead of using their old system with a tedious printing calculator. In an office of increasingly dazzling minds, Zarren was a rising star.

In the spring of 2004, Rivers's other gig, ABC, provided joy and escapism for a few weeks. Eventually, the NBA playoffs would end, and he'd have to devote all his focus to remaking the Celtics.

For now, he was excited to be an informed observer of the league's final four teams: the Lakers of O'Neal and Bryant, the Timberwolves, the Pistons, and the Pacers. The Lakers were favored to win it all because of the Shaq-Kobe combination, which featured superior athleticism and force that few in the NBA could match. The Wolves had the best record in the West and the league's MVP, Kevin Garnett.

Garnett was a player Rivers could admire and with whom he could empathize. The admiration was universal. No one got himself into more of a lather than Garnett, pointing and cussing and sprinting toward both baskets. That was just the pregame routine. When the game began, the energy spiked. He was over seven feet tall and didn't want to be; he told people that he was "six foot thirteen." He was a versatile and passionate player, a perennial all-league defender, rebounding champion, and someone who could consistently make a twenty-foot jumper.

When Ainge coached in Phoenix, he was amazed by a matchup he saw on the court. There was Garnett, defending Kevin Johnson one-on-one, with flawless technique. This was not normal; Johnson was a speedy point guard, a full foot shorter than his opponent.

Garnett arrived in Minnesota as a nineteen-year-old experiment. He was the first player in two decades to go from high school to the pros, and people were unsure how he'd handle it. In many ways, Garnett was the test to determine how the league valued teenagers on a similar track. He was drafted by the Wolves, the rare franchise that was younger than he was. Their general manager was Kevin McHale, Ainge's best friend and former Celtics teammate. The Kevins talked all the time, with the younger one constantly asking questions about improvement. And winning. He had all the gifts that stars have, but he yearned to win more than he yearned for stardom.

Stardom came in bundles. As for the winning . . . it was complicated.

The Wolves had successful regular seasons but couldn't advance past the first round of the playoffs. That happened seven years in a row, and it frustrated him. Everybody knew, or should have known, that he was one of the best players in the history of the game. But why couldn't he win? He looked to rebound and defend and pass before looking to score, and they still lost. He scored more and still rebounded; they still lost. The Kobe to his Shaq, Stephon Marbury, forced a trade out of Minnesota, and Garnett never asked to leave. He was intensely loyal. And they still couldn't win.

Rivers knew that feeling, that helplessness, from his time playing with Wilkins and Patrick Ewing—two great players who did all they could and were blocked by something far beyond their talents. It was something that was never explained well enough when commentators praised the winners or patronized/downgraded/ignored the greats who had it all except, you know, that.

When Rivers still had the Orlando job, one of the teams on the Magic's early schedule was Minnesota. Garnett didn't even have one of his top games of the season and still finished with 22 points and 17 rebounds. It was going to be that kind of year. He gave everything that he'd given in the previous seven seasons, and more, and he produced the type of year that the league had seen just a few times. He led the NBA in total points and rebounds, something that hadn't been done since Hall of Famer Bob McAdoo did it in 1975.

It was difficult to find an individual deficiency with KG. But that wasn't the issue; Shaq and Kobe—especially Shaq—were. The Wolves won their first two playoff rounds for the first time in team history. When they faced the Lakers in the conference finals, they lost in six games. As Garnett slowly packed his bags after yet another unsatisfying elimination game, there was a sense of rage and anxiety. His rage happened during games and sometimes after them, so he knew that part was temporary. The anxiety was starting to stick to him. He wasn't some wide-eyed kid anymore. He had just turned twenty-eight, and he'd never been to the finals. He'd achieved everything in the sport, everything, except that. He feared that 2004 had been his team's best opportunity. Maybe it would never happen for him.

Meanwhile, one of his old teammates was there in the finals, taking on the Lakers. Chauncey Billups entered the league as a Celtic, Rick Pitino's first draft pick. Pitino traded Billups during his rookie year, and the guard bounced around the league. When he played in Minnesota for two years, Billups was on his fourth team. The Wolves let his contract expire, and as a free agent he found a GM in Joe Dumars and a city, Detroit, that got him.

Over the course of two incredible weeks, Billups and the Pistons were able to relieve some pressure from Garnett, Rivers, and dozens of NBA players, coaches, and general managers who didn't have a title. It was nothing that Billups and the Pistons said. It was what they did. They resolved on a court what the analytics people tried to work out in formulas: They found a way to defeat the established NBA machine.

The Pistons did *not* have one of the league's top five players on their roster. They had two All-Stars, both of whom had scars and were on their third NBA team. Ben Wallace, six foot nine, was their heavy rebounding, light scoring, undersized center. Their recently acquired power forward, Rasheed Wallace, had played just twenty-two games for them in the regular season. They also had the NBA Finals MVP, the well-traveled Billups, who was the team's regulator all series and season.

They lost the first game of the finals and then went on a four-game winning streak to capture the championship in Detroit. It was an extraordinary thing to witness on the pro stage, a scene out of college basketball. The underdog didn't just win one game. It was four in a row, with each more emphatic than the last. It gave hope to those who dreamed of building title teams without the benefit of number one overall picks and historical greats like O'Neal, Bryant, and Tim Duncan on their side.

NBA players and fans alike marveled at the unlikeliest league champion in decades. The game's commentators, Michaels and Rivers, were still in awe as they wrapped up their coverage for the season.

"There's a lot of people smiling at this basketball team," Rivers said.

He was one of them. He continued to smile as long as he could, and then Michaels, extending a hand, brought him back to reality.

"My man is going to the Celtics," the broadcaster said with a smile. He said he would be there when Rivers lofted a championship one day in Boston. They smiled, and a nation laughed. The Celtics had no shot. Going to Boston was even tougher than it appeared because Rivers knew a secret that Michaels had shared with him a month earlier. When they were in LA for the conference semifinals, Michaels bumped into Lakers owner Dr. Jerry Buss. He asked Buss about the future of head coach Phil Jackson.

"You know Phil," Buss told him. "You never know what he's going to do. But I'll tell you this: If your guy hadn't been hired by the Celtics, your guy would be our guy."

Michaels debated whether to tell Rivers what Buss said. Finally, he decided to do it during one of the broadcast breaks. Rivers listened, thought about what it would be like to coach a championship-level team in LA, and replied, "Well, I'm not sure the ink on the Celtics contract is totally dry."

As Detroit lined up a parade, the Celtics set their draft board.

The numbers that mattered in June 2004 were the first-round draft slots for the Celtics: fifteen, twenty-four, and twenty-five. The two players considered to be the best in the draft, centers Dwight Howard and Emeka Okafor, were expected to go one and two. What it meant for Ainge, for the second year in a row, was that he was out of franchise-player range. According to the numbers from Morey's study last season, that top pick, fifteen, had the slightest chance of landing an NBA starter. Last year's top Boston selection, number thirteen Marcus Banks, struggled and looked like a good pro player off the bench. This year, with more time to personally scout prospects and train a deeper staff to look for what he wanted, Ainge felt more confident going into the draft. He'd also begun to settle into his contrarian role around the office.

One day, intentionally, Pags approached Ainge and told him that he was a huge fan of Jameer Nelson, a point guard from St. Joseph's. Ainge raised his eyebrows and told the team's co-owner about all the problems with Nelson's game. *Perfect*, Pags thought, *this is classic Danny.*

A couple of days later, the owner went to Ainge with a strong anti-Nelson take. And, just as Pags imagined, Ainge countered with a list of positives. Despite the comedy that Pags got out of it, he appreciated that Ainge was consistently pushing everyone around him to look at players thoroughly and not just tell him what they thought he wanted to hear.

There was some predictability on draft night when Howard and Okafor were selected with the top choices. At fifteen, the hope for the Celtics was to get someone who, unlike Banks, could be a consistent rookie contributor. To do that, a few teams in front of them needed to make mistakes. The Raptors, picking eighth, and the Cavs, at ten, both took players who were of no interest to the

Celtics. Ten picks in, Ainge focused on two high school centers, Robert Swift and Al Jefferson.

Sometimes you get better when other teams make mistakes. Sometimes it happens when the mistakes are yours and you're spared from them anyway. Ainge was intrigued by Swift and might have taken him if Seattle hadn't done it at twelve. So that left Jefferson, who wasn't Howard but still showed up in most scouts' top-five high school prospect rankings.

This was like the old Celtics again: They'd gotten lucky on draft night.

At one point during the night, cigar smoke wafted in the draft room. That's because the godfather himself, Auerbach, was brought in. For five minutes, he and Zarren sat side by side, and not a word was spoken. Zarren was awed into silence. Someone should have taken a picture, because the illustration is all the things the new Celtics were: built on and in reverence of Auerbach, plus informed by modern analytics, practices, and strategies.

The Celtics' good fortune continued with both of their picks in the twenties. Those choices were there to be made due to the aggressiveness of Ainge. They acquired number twenty-four the year before in the Antoine Walker trade with Dallas and used it to select Delonte West, the "other" guard from St. Joseph's (Nelson went to Denver at number twenty). The story of number twenty-five was a story Celtics fans were going to have to get used to with Ainge. The overarching theme of the narrative: Prepare to move.

That's what happened with Mike James, a guard Ainge signed as a free agent in 2003. He was traded to Detroit six months later. James got a championship ring. The Celtics got a first-round pick. Everyone was happy then, and now, because the Celtics used the pick on Tony Allen, the Oklahoma State guard whom they'd graded as the best defender in college basketball.

No one knew if the Celtics were better, but it did feel that way. They were busier, for sure, and more direct. Paul Pierce could feel the difference, and he didn't perceive it as pleasant. While Jim O'Brien talked with him about his game and improvement, he never challenged—or confronted—him about his game. Rivers took that approach after he grew tired of watching Pierce hold the ball too long during practices and preseason games.

He called the franchise player into his office.

"Paul, are you a great shooter?" he asked.

"I'm a great shooter. Yeah."

"I don't know," the coach replied. "You're shooting forty percent, bro."

Pierce paused. Not only had he shot 40 percent from the field last season, he'd also shot 30 percent from 3-point range the last two years, well below the league average.

"Listen, either you're a great shooter, or you're taking bad shots. So which one is it? Because if you're a great shooter, you'd be shooting at least above forty-five. But maybe you're not a great shooter. Or you're taking bad shots. But it can't be both."

Pierce had no answer, but he was angry. He left the office that way, and it got worse during the season. The coach felt that Pierce hadn't shaken his habit of holding the ball too long, so he took him out of a close game that the Celtics eventually lost.

Now Rivers was angry. On his way to the locker room, he knew that Pierce would be in there stewing. So he wanted to enter and verbally strike first. He wanted the whole team to hear the message.

"Tough loss, guys. And Paul? I will get fired first before I give in on this. And that's a guarantee. So we're either going to move the ball and play right, or you're going to get your way and do it and I get fired. And I'm completely fine with that. But I am not fucking changing, and I'm telling you right the fuck now. I'm telling everybody that right now."

Pierce waited a few days and then initiated a visit with Rivers.

"Hey," he said to the coach. "We're good. Me and you, we're good. I'm going to do it. I don't really understand why you're doing this; I think I do. But I'm going to do it."

Rivers explained that a gifted scorer like Pierce was much harder to defend when the ball was moving to him rather than a hold, where everybody knew where he was. Pierce saw that for himself when he moved the ball and was often wide open when it came back to him.

Pierce continued to play as if he'd absorbed the advice. At the All-Star break, the Celtics were 27–26. Pierce and his improved shooting once again represented the franchise in the All-Star Game. By now, everyone who had been around Ainge knew what was coming next.

Trades.

Lots of them.

He was going to keep doing that until he had the players he wanted or the assets to get them.

While his fearlessness with trades was known, the depths he'd go to to make moves were shocking. In the fall of 2003, he'd been outspoken about his Welsch excitement. In February 2005, he admitted his mistake. He traded Welsch to Cleveland and managed to pocket a first-round pick from the Cavs in return for someone who clearly wasn't an impressive NBA player.

That was nothing compared to what Ainge did later in the same day. It was astonishing, actually. In another trade, with Atlanta, the Celtics reacquired one of their former players. His name was Antoine Walker.

Walker was in the final year of his contract now after just one season in Dallas. He didn't fit in with the Mavericks as he or they expected, and he'd been traded to a bad Hawks team. The Celtics needed another scorer for their playoff run, and Walker was the best person to fill that need.

The return of Walker led to a few standing ovations from Boston crowds and nice words from some of his former teammates. But this felt temporary. If Ainge didn't think Walker was someone to build around in 2003, he probably wasn't going to change his mind in 2005.

One big difference between now and two years ago was that the Celtics now had more in their organizational reserves. They had several young players and draft picks, and at times it seemed as if they acquired players because they were of interest to other teams and not the Celtics themselves.

They got lots of phone calls from teams asking about young Jefferson and Allen. Asking about future first- and second-round picks. And after another first-round playoff loss to the Pacers, there was speculation of whether there would be an ask about, or offer of, Pierce.

CHAPTER FOUR

ATTACKED

Paul Pierce had many reasons to believe that his day to be traded was on its way. He understood that, technically, the NBA didn't have any franchise players. There were magnetic and impactful players, attractive showmen for marketing, merchandising, and TV ratings, but even they got traded or forcefully pushed aside. This was business: The players moved, and the franchises—most of them, anyway—stayed put.

It happened just last season. Shaquille O'Neal, seven foot one and 370 pounds, literally the league's biggest star and three-time NBA Finals MVP, was traded from the Lakers to the Miami Heat. He and teammate Kobe Bryant clashed, very publicly, and the Lakers kept Bryant and parted with O'Neal. Phil Jackson, whose championship rings grew from six to nine while he led the Lakers, was fired, so he went from coaching the game to writing about it in a memoir. Their departures had come weeks after their fourth finals appearance in the last five years.

Pierce grew up in LA. He knew how people there adored the Lakers, especially the iconic ones. If O'Neal and Jackson could be dismissed after what they'd done in the league, so could he.

This was only a conversation because of the last two games of the 2005 season. A couple of images from that next-to-last one, in Indianapolis, would play and replay all summer and fall.

Pierce had been fouled late in game six against the Pacers, inadvertently slapped in the face by an opponent. It was an obvious hit, but the officials either didn't see it or didn't think enough of it to respond. Pierce reacted with a high swing of his elbow, one that missed his defender but still looked bad. The officials were no longer thinking about the slap that Pierce took. They saw that elbow, looked at the replay to confirm it was what they thought, and then handed him his second technical foul of the game. Automatic ejection. From a playoff game.

Once Pierce realized that he'd been thrown out, he responded to the jeers of Pacers players and fans by removing his jersey and swinging it over his head as he walked through a tunnel toward the locker room. It was his version of a middle finger to them all: players, fans, officials. That was the image that people, loyal Celtics fans among them, couldn't get past. Why did he act like that after being thrown out of a game? Why did he put himself in position to be thrown out? What if the Celtics had lost (they didn't) and that was his final act of the season?

It got worse later that night, following a Celtics overtime win that forced a game seven in Boston. He decided to play a joke, a sight gag, that missed its mark. He attended his postgame press conference with a bandage wrapped around his head. He announced that he had a broken jaw, which he didn't, and he said he did because he was trying to bring attention to the poor officiating.

Between the swinging jersey and the head wrap, Pierce had driven a lot of people to conclude that his time in Boston was done. They felt that way before game seven. Then when the game itself played out, with the Celtics being heckled by their own fans in the second half of a 27-point loss, the talk intensified and became more personal: *Immature. Unprofessional. Not a Celtic. Get what you can for him, Danny, and start over.*

Grousbeck heard the talk as well. In public, he said Pierce was evolving and that he would learn from his mistakes. He was much more direct in private: Pierce wasn't going anywhere. Grousbeck was open about the nuances of the NBA that he didn't understand, but he knew better than to make a reactionary move with the team's best player. Whatever the conversation was, he made it clear that he'd slow it down—or veto it, if necessary—if the solution was to trade Pierce.

They wanted to keep him, and he wanted to stay. But after three straight years of early playoff exits, they were both on the clock. Could the Celtics continue to build this patiently around a star? They'd just used the eighteenth pick in the draft on a six-foot-eight *high school* forward, Gerald Green. Could Pierce continue to patiently wait?

There's a period in an NBA star's career, say, the first three or four seasons, in which the accomplishment of making the league and the lifestyle that comes with it is sufficient. The money, the travel, the attention, the platform. It's intoxicating to play in the best league in the world and be recognized as one of its top players. It's hard to know a real thirst for winning that early in a career because you're often thirsting for other things first: recognition, increased fame, an even bigger contract. It's hard to be at the beginning of a career and think of its ending or even its decline. The only players who actively thought like that were the former ones who were now in front offices.

They thought of three- and five-year organizational plans. They spoke of those multiple years without having to play those years. Ainge and Rivers, for example, didn't have to worry anymore about the minutes they had left in their legs or taking advantage of their peak seasons. It's part of what allowed Ainge to oversee three drafts in a row in which at least one of his first-round picks was eighteen years old. A general manager dreams about that player maturing into a star in three or four years; a veteran teammate is praying that the player can help immediately. Pierce was stuck. He was twenty-seven, a few months away from turning twenty-eight.

Each year, there were fewer and fewer people around him who could understand all the things on his mind. There was his frustration on the court, which was easy for all to see. But there were other things, invisible things that others had moved on from or perhaps had never fully grasped. He had a devotion to the city, never asked to leave it, and wanted to experience a championship celebration down Boylston Street, just as the Patriots and Red Sox had recently done. Though, at times, his devotion to Boston was accompanied by his occasional fear of it.

In the image from Indianapolis that his critics kept returning to, his swinging of that jersey, few focused on the scars on his back. They were the constant reminders of the most frightening moment of his life, just after one a.m. on September 25, 2000.

He'd gone out to Boston's Theater District with one of his teammates, Tony Battie, and Battie's brother, Derrick. There had been a hair show at Symphony Hall earlier in the night, with models displaying the latest hairstyles and fashions. Many of the people there decided to attend the after party at a place called the Buzz Club.

Pierce and the Battie brothers walked in together and were quickly separated: Pierce went to the dance floor, Tony Battie had to go to the bathroom, and Derrick, acting as their muscular six-foot-ten security guard, waited outside the bathroom. He did that to make sure his younger brother, a wealthy professional athlete wearing a diamond necklace and expensive watch, had protection from those who might want to target him.

As Derrick waited, Pierce had moved from the dance floor toward an area with two pool tables. He had a pleasant conversation with two young women. He thought nothing of how this conversation might look to someone who might be jealous of the attention given to a pro athlete. He was just having a good time when a black man, standing about five foot eight, approached him.

"What up, nigga?" the man said.

There was nothing friendly about the question. Pierce was in conversation with a man who was unfamiliar to him but known by the court system. In the previous seven years, the man, twenty-eight years old, had been arrested for numerous charges, including assault with a dangerous weapon, cocaine trafficking, breaking and entering, assault to kill, possession of firearms without permits, and assault and battery on a police officer.

He said it again, and before Pierce knew it, he was falling backward. The man had punched him in the face, and then Pierce felt someone else with arms around his neck, trying to bring him to the floor. There were at least two more men on him now, and he was being attacked in a blur of violence. Someone, he wasn't sure who, hit him in the head with a bottle. The first man who hit him wasn't done. He reached into his back pocket and emerged with a serrated switchblade. He moved forward and began to stab Pierce from the front while someone else, behind him, had another knife and brass knuckles.

On the ground now, at the center of a melee, the Celtics star was being kicked and stabbed. Both Batties returned from the bathroom area and noticed that there appeared to be chaos in the middle of the floor.

"Where the fuck is Paul?" Derrick Battie wondered.

Battie took his role as a protector seriously, and he was adamant about keeping his guys out of fights. He grabbed his younger brother by the arm, pulled him behind the bar, and stood in front of him. *I'm not going nowhere near that shit*, he thought.

With his size, he could see over the crowd, but all he noticed were backs and arms congested in the middle of the room. There were three hundred people in the club, and many of them were running to the corners or out the doors. It was chaos. Seconds earlier, Battie had wondered about Pierce.

He got his answer from the bartender, who shouted, "I think your man is in the middle of that."

The Batties took off through the crowd when they heard that, pushing their way toward the area where the action had been. Pierce was no longer there. With the help of security, he'd been carried away to a back room. Even then, as Pierce was flanked by club personnel, the first attacker was able to land one more punch to his face. Pierce was hurt, feeling the most pain in his stomach.

When the Batties got to Pierce, sitting on a table in a back room, they thought he was hurt from fists alone. Security asked for ice and towels, but this was much more serious than that. Pierce removed his shirt so he could wipe his head, but he also used it to stop the bleeding near his stomach. That was where he felt the most pain. He repeated the same word—*damn*—as he sat in that area away from the crowd, which had begun dispersing; some people were fleeing.

Derrick and Tony Battie's focus was on Pierce and the help he needed, so they told security to stay with him as they retrieved the silver Cadillac Escalade that they had left with a valet just fifteen minutes earlier.

"Get the keys!" Derrick Battie yelled. "We gotta go. Hurry, hurry, hurry. Quick, quick."

He was thinking about Pierce and how they were going to help him, but he couldn't help noticing a group of people near a silver Mercedes. One of the men there moved hurriedly, as if to avoid being caught. Battie told himself that he wasn't going to forget that man's face and clothing. But the in-the-moment priority was help for Pierce.

There was a witness who said she heard more disturbing words from the first attacker. "I'm the only man around here," she heard him say. "Fuck them bitches. Fuck Paul Pierce." Later, she also heard him ask, "Who will be the next victim?" He had blood on his hands and went to the bathroom to get it off. Then he left the club. When Derrick parked his car in front of Buzz and then helped Pierce down the stairs, he placed his hand on Pierce's back. When he pulled his hand away, it was covered with blood.

Derrick Battie began to understand how life-threatening the situation was. He helped Pierce into the Escalade and told Tony to drive to the hospital. The Batties were from Texas, not Boston, so they had to ask where the nearest hospital was. They were told that they were close to a place called Tufts New England Medical Center. But they were on Stuart Street, going in the opposite direction of it, and they were jammed in club traffic.

They didn't have time for this.

Derrick Battie jumped out of the car and sprinted several feet ahead. He stood in traffic to stop it, direct it, and create enough space so Tony could make a U-turn. Then he jumped back into the vehicle and reassured Pierce. He called 911. Pierce was alert in the car, but there was a lot of blood, and Derrick needed specifics on exactly where the hospital was.

At one point, Derrick got out of the truck and walked with Pierce toward what he thought was an entrance. It wasn't. Once they figured out that they were a block away, Tony got them back into the truck and drove against traffic to the entrance. Derrick ran ahead of them into the hospital and bellowed, "We got a delicate situation here! Can we get him in quickly?"

Pierce had been stabbed eight times in his abdomen and back. They were life-threatening injuries. One wound track, for example, extended from Pierce's spleen to past his liver and stomach, hitting his lung. It caused a partial lung collapse and, even more dangerously, stopped just short of his heart. The whole episode was hard to reconcile eight hours later when a stunned Pierce, recovering in intensive care, was awakened by two Boston police officers who wanted to get a victim statement.

Did you know those guys?

Do you remember what the first man who hit you looked like?

How tall was he?

The Celtics star remembered some things, but he was unclear on others. He knew that at least four men had jumped on him but didn't realize that police estimated that at one point it was as many as eight. He was foggy on details. He was pressed for names, faces, and specifics, and he ultimately gave an answer reflective of a West Coast kid—he was twenty-two—at the beginning of a career in an unknown East Coast city.

"I don't even know," he said. "I don't remember. I don't know people in Boston."

He never wanted anyone's pity or sympathy from that incident. That didn't even occur to him. He didn't think anything that they did to him would affect his career, and he was right about that. He played eighty-two games in that 2000–2001 season and averaged 25 points per night. He played wearing a flak jacket, similar to ones worn by NFL quarterbacks. That wasn't an issue.

Why did it happen? There's the side of fandom from the commercials, where the locals are excited to be around their great athletes. Obviously, there was another side to that, a side that he'd never considered. Could he ever go out again without wondering who was coming his way and why?

There were still some realities of the case that were going to be there forever whether he thought about them or not.

That night, after the Batties had gotten Pierce to the hospital, they started to realize how serious things were when they looked in the back seat of the Escalade. It, too, was covered in blood. "We need to go back over there," Derrick said to Tony. "Ya know, get some answers to what's going on. Come on. Let's go." They went back to the club and tried to find out who hurt Pierce. What they got was what amounted to a preview of the trial itself. Did some people know the perpetrators? Yes. Were they going to say all that they knew until justice was served? Not quite.

The club had emptied when the Batties returned. They double-parked their truck in front and remembered that there was a back door that security had used. The brothers went to that door, which was closed, and banged loudly until someone opened it. When they walked in, they saw a group of security guards huddled near the bar. Everyone else was gone.

"I need some answers on who did this," Derrick said to the huddle. "I just need one name. Just one."

Heads turned away.

"Come on, man," he pleaded. "One of our fucking key guys, star guys, just got attacked in this fucking joint. And you all don't know?"

The brothers looked around and made eye contact when they could. They saw information in those eyes. And fear.

"Just give me one name of somebody you saw put their hands on Paul. Just one fucking name . . ."

Finally, one security guard responded. "When I got there, it was already over, man. He was already slammed."

Derrick Battie, an NBA bodyguard now, made his living by reading people. He didn't buy it. "One of my guys is laying all fucked up right now. Ya know you got to give me something."

"I make fifty dollars a day bouncing," one guard responded. "We can't. We have to live here."

Tony Battie asked the guard to talk away from the group. He pulled out a roll of $100 bills and slipped one to the young man. He got a name.

"Thank you," Derrick said. "I really appreciate, you know, you doing the right thing. By stepping up."

During the trial, the prosecution's major witness recanted the testimony that she first gave to detectives a day after the attack and to a grand jury a week later. She told the detectives and grand jury that she had seen a man named William Ragland initiate the attack; in court, she said she saw Ragland there but didn't see him do anything. She said she had seen the knives, the brass knuckles, the punches; in court, she said she couldn't remember those details. And so it went.

There had been some justice in the case, but not full justice.

Pierce didn't think of it most of the time, and playing a professional game he'd mastered, with his friends, brought him joy. He was fine professionally. But he had bouts of paranoia and depression after the attack. He had twenty-four-hour security guarding his house in the suburbs. He became anxious in crowds. Once, while he was out to dinner in Boston, the restaurant manager approached his table with what he said was an urgent phone call from a family member. Instead, when he put the phone to his ear, he heard a stranger promise, "I'm going to kill you." It was only basketball, and the joy that it brought, that provided solace. He believed it would lead to professional fulfillment because he was convinced, in 2002, that the Celtics would keep growing and getting better. Then the job became more challenging.

Antoine Walker was traded in 2003 and reacquired in February 2005. He told Pierce that he was happy to be back with him and wanted to stay in Boston again. He told Ainge the same thing, but Ainge was not motivated by a reunion tour. It wasn't personal from Ainge's perspective, but it was from Walker's.

Back in Boston sixteen months after his first trade, Walker found himself heartbroken again. He loved playing for Rivers and being alongside the youthful Celtics, but he'd have to see them from Miami. Free agent Walker decided to go there, although officially he was part of a sign-and-trade deal. In less than a year, Walker had been included in three Ainge transactions. It really wasn't personal. The organization both welcomed stability and rejected inertia.

Between 2003 and 2005, there wasn't anything close to that Boylston Street parade that Pierce had dreamed of. This was the other kind, the parade of players that he knew and trusted leaving, and some new guys—some talented, some not so much—coming in to see who could stick around for a while.

The slight positive in the basketball side of his story was that he wasn't alone. That was obvious in early 2006, when he was one of at least three great players searching for something beyond individual dominance.

CHAPTER FIVE

THREE LONG NIGHTS

There wasn't always an audience for greatness. Ray Allen lived that on most game nights, but an extreme example happened in Phoenix on January 22.

The Seattle SuperSonics were playing the Phoenix Suns that afternoon, and the best player on the Sonics, Allen, was going off. He was a thirty-year-old guard and a six-time All-Star. He naturally did things that seemed impossible. For instance, no matter how quickly he navigated picks, caught the ball, and shot it—with perfect form, mind you—he never appeared to be rushed. Ever.

When he played in Milwaukee, he tried to coach a new teammate, point guard Terrell Brandon, on the best time to get him the ball. Brandon saw him popping open behind the 3-point line and passed him the ball, and Allen made the shot. Allen then told him, "T, get it to me a little earlier next time, all right?"

No problem, Brandon thought. He got it to him about thirty feet from the basket the next time he had the chance. Allen didn't shoot it from there, but he advanced it and scored. He looked at Brandon again and said, "Earlier."

Brandon thought he was crazy. *Does this dude want it from half-court?* He did exactly that on the next possession, and then he figured out what Allen was trying to humbly say. He could score from anywhere, at any angle, whether it was drifting left or leaning right. Get him the rock and be entertained.

Allen made quick movements while being under control. You could see it while studying his operation at the free-throw line. Total focus. Set. Shoot. Swish. Over and over. He could be counted on to make 90 percent of his free throws mostly because he trusted what he'd perfected in private and didn't overthink it.

Coaches and teammates knew he was a man of routines, so they stayed out of his way and let him reach his inevitable result. He did the same thing before each game whether at home or on the road: He was sure to arrive at the arena at least three hours prior to tip-off so he could begin getting into a shooting rhythm. A rebounder would be positioned under the basket, and Allen, along with anyone else who wanted to prepare with him, would work his way around the court until they felt like they were in sync.

Allen's rule for his workout partners was simple. You're either all in or nothing. He was so into the routine that people with sporadic attendance threw him off. Every ritual he did mattered, even if no one else understood why. When the Sonics were at home, Allen had the same parking spot for practice. Once he arrived to see a teammate's car there before his, and he went inside to joke about it. But he truly wasn't kidding. All these small things helped feed his overall greatness.

On that January afternoon in Phoenix, he looked like the fictional player, Jesus Shuttlesworth, who he portrayed in Spike Lee's 1998 movie, *He Got Game*. Allen scored 42 points that day, hit eight 3-pointers, and played fifty-one minutes in an overtime win over the Suns. Even the people in Seattle who cared about the Sonics likely didn't see it. The team was bad, 16–24, and the real local attraction wasn't happening on a basketball court in Phoenix. It was at a football stadium in downtown Seattle where the Seahawks would play the Panthers for the right to go to the Super Bowl.

For players like Paul Pierce and Allen, discipline was necessary for playing the game and thinking it, too. Four days after Allen scored his 42 in secret, Pierce received what was becoming a biannual alert: The Celtics had made a trade. Ainge and Kevin McHale, the friends who led the Celtics and Wolves, respectively, had pulled off an exchange of disappointing cards.

The Celtics officially moved on from Ainge's first draft pick, Marcus Banks. He'd be joined in Minnesota by Ricky Davis, Mark Blount, and a couple of second-round picks. Once again, the jewel of the deal for the Celtics, a 2009 first-round pick, was on the horizon. The best right-now player in the trade was forward Wally Szczerbiak, who averaged 20 points per night alongside Kevin Garnett in Minnesota. He was a good player, not great, and there was no reason to believe that his presence would do more for the Celtics than it had for the Wolves.

There was no question that the Celtics had become knowledgeable flippers. Essentially, they got two firsts for Walker: one for his trade to Dallas and one for the player they traded him for— Jiri Welsch—when they sent Welsch to Cleveland. They got a free first, basically, for Mike James, who only cost them short money in free agency before they moved him to Detroit. They got another first in this most recent deal with Davis, whom they acquired at below-market prices since the Cavaliers had been so desperate to get rid of him.

All of that was good. Now all they had to do was start flipping some wins.

For the worst teams in the league, improvement had to be measured in silos. It could be the parsing of how a team played under a new coach versus how it played under the fired predecessor. Or the development of a young player from training camp to February. In Seattle, on February 11, the improvement was connected to distraction.

The Seahawks won their conference championship game and appeared in the Super Bowl. They lost it, and the region was still furious over several blown calls that helped the Steelers win. Since it wasn't baseball season yet, and the Mariners were a bad team at that, the balm was the presence of the Sonics and the reassurance of Allen.

Allen got the loudest applause when he was introduced before the game, and fans had so much faith in him that they instinctively rose whenever he shot the ball. From anywhere. The Nuggets were a better team, significantly, but Allen was the best and most relatable player on the floor. Unless you had the most expensive seats in the building, you couldn't get an accurate gauge of just how tall, six foot five, and strong he was. People saw that smooth stroke, that impeccable form, and they had a faultless illustration of how a player was supposed to look when putting up shots.

He did a lot of things right and seemed to be the understated technician. Seemed. Another thing that wasn't obvious from afar was the constant competitiveness. His day had begun so early, with visualization and dribbling exercises and early shooting, that he'd been on for hours before tip-off. There was no revving up necessary; he was just on, always, a show already in progress.

While his outsized talent prevented him from just blending in, he fit in to most situations perfectly. He'd had a lot of practice growing up, when his family moved often due to his father's job with the United States Air Force. Allen had lived in California (twice), Oklahoma, Germany, and England all before turning thirteen. It was then that he moved to Dalzell, South Carolina, about fifty miles from the state capital.

He had a very Allen game on the eleventh, going scoreless in the first quarter and then drilling three audacious 3-pointers in a row to keep the Sonics close in the second. After those 3s, his defenders started to get too close, so they fouled him. Of course, he took four free throws before the half and made them all.

But this was no movie. Despite another game in which he made eight 3-pointers, scored 34 points, and got his team to overtime, Allen walked out of the arena processing another loss. The Sonics were 20–31. Just because he didn't yell about it didn't mean he wasn't bothered, which was a criticism one of his former coaches had for him. George Karl had suggested that Allen was too nice. And with the team playing like this, even if Allen had yelled, was anyone truly paying attention to it?

Two nights later, February 13, Garnett did yell. He did it before every game, at home or on the road. He did it in practice. He said things during competition that were so obscene and offensive that he begged his mother-in-law to consider anything he said on the court inadmissible in real life. This was his job, he explained, and he was doing whatever he could to get an edge. Frothing and cussing was part of the ritual.

Brandon, the point guard, had played in Cleveland with laid-back guys such as Mark Price and Brad Daugherty. He'd played in Milwaukee with the easygoing Allen and Glenn "Big Dog" Robinson. Then he got a chance to play in Minnesota with KG. He'd never seen or heard anything like it. For others, "play like you practice" was a nice thing to say, but it wasn't realistic. The season was too long, and if players like Garnett actually did that, they'd burn out. Except KG did it.

He did on the court what Danny Ainge did in a meeting room. He'd create an argument if there wasn't one, and sometimes he'd talk to himself. Before the game began, there would be a cup of coffee. Snickers. Mountain Dew. Protein shake. Protein bar. He'd be drenched in sweat before tip-off. He was Minnesota basketball and beyond. An array of personalities flocked to him and his games, including the state's most famous musician.

Prince, a student of the game, was often there to speak with Garnett and his teammates. This was during the time when every fan in the state was excited by the momentum of Wolves basketball, and they all believed that the team was headed somewhere great. One night there was a courtside gathering of Minnesota sports and pop culture royalty: KG, Prince, Kirby Puckett, Jimmy Jam, and Terry Lewis.

Prince approached Brandon to exchange KG info and then started breaking down Brandon's tendencies. "I really like the way you approach your midrange game," Prince said. "You never rush on the pick-and-roll. It's smart. Did you learn that in Cleveland from Mark Price?"

Brandon was speechless. He didn't expect to be in Minnesota with Prince talking about hoop. Puckett was nearby listening to the conversation, knowingly nodding toward Brandon and saying, "Oh yeah, dawg. Yeah, dawg. He knows the game. I thought you knew."

Those were the fun days.

Garnett once played with Pierce in a high school tournament when they were both juniors. That had been their loose connection until now. He looked at the old Celtics and new Wolves and understood that he had to display for them in Minnesota what Pierce had shown them in Boston. Even when you know you're going into a game, or a season, with less than what you want, the game—the Game—cannot be cheated.

The season had begun well for the Wolves, and in February 2006 it was well into its descent. Garnett's frustration used to be his team's inability to advance out of the first round of the playoffs.

But just two seasons after his MVP year and trip to the conference finals, this team wasn't going to be close to the playoffs. He took it all personally, the losing, the underachievement of teammates, the waning passion for the Wolves in the community.

The Wolves were 22–28 before their game with the Raptors, and the easily offended still had to stop reading his lips.

There were a handful of players around the league who he tested by talking to them just to see how much they could take. Then there were players who were on-court rivals, players at his position, who he used to sharpen his own game. Toronto's Chris Bosh fit into both categories.

Garnett was the best defender of his generation, and his gift became animated when infused with his original verbal content. He seemed to decide early that he was going to make Bosh a nonfactor in the game, and it happened immediately. The Toronto big man looked uncomfortable with all the pushing—physical and audible— from Garnett.

It was telling to see the individual and team numbers at the end of the night. Garnett had 23 points, 19 rebounds, and 6 assists. Bosh was held to 8 points and 4 rebounds. In fact, Garnett outrebounded the entire Raptors starting lineup. And the Wolves, with ex-Celtics Marcus Banks, Mark Blount, and Justin Reed coming off the bench, lost. Again.

Two nights later in Boston, February 15, Pierce stepped on the court and extended a hand to the kid he had seen back in 2003 at a Summer League game. LeBron James had a body for the league three years ago at the University of Massachusetts Boston. Now that he was playing in the NBA, with elite training and nutrition, he was unlike anyone in the sport.

Whatever the projection was for him, whenever his arrival moment was supposed to be, he was ahead of schedule. It was easy to see the strength and speed advantages he had over his opponents. You had to be on the court against him to realize the mental strain he put on coaching staffs and players because when you tried to take something away from him, if that actually worked, he'd crush you in another area. He wore people down, and he didn't really know all the veteran tricks yet. He was only twenty-one.

Pierce liked the challenge of taking him on. They'd talked with each other on the court, and there'd been a few smiles along the way, but it would be a mistake to call this a friendship. It was respectful but never deferential, neither during the games nor in interviews. There were times it wasn't even respectful. A few years earlier, during a preseason game in Columbus, Pierce and James traded words, and things got heated when Pierce spat toward the Cavs' bench. James had been in the public eye since he was fourteen, and he was now a global sensation. He was averaging 30 points per game, something Pierce had never done, and was already in the conversation for top player in the sport, something that eluded Pierce.

This game, between a good team and a sinking one, had a lot to do with pride. There was some envy involved, too. The Cavs were going to be in the playoffs for the first time in James's career, and the Celtics were going to miss them for the first time in five years. There are some nights, and some opponents, who make you want to remind people not to forget about you. Not only was James averaging 30 points, he'd also exceeded that number a few times in the last month. Before coming to Boston, the Cavs hosted the Spurs, and James scored 44 in a win.

He seemed to be on that pace early against the Celtics, scoring 7 of his team's first 9 points. Pierce, often with James in his face, answered with a jumper over him for his first points of the game.

If there was one thing that the twenty-one-year-old James lacked, it was superior defensive awareness. He'd closed every other hole in his game already, so that was coming soon. But on this night, Pierce took advantage. He ran James into a screen and then made an uncontested jumper. He faked him out on another drive, dribbled past two more defenders, and then finished with an "and one." He had 19 points in the first half to 20 for James.

Both coaches, Doc Rivers and Mike Brown for the Cavs, must have known it then. This was not going to be a night for the men in suits holding erasable boards. This was Paul versus LeBron, with the win going to the star who could be individually resourceful and pull something extra out of his teammates.

James was a problem for Pierce and everyone who came near him. He got the Celtics' new guy, Szczerbiak, twice on the same move: hard head fake to the right—which sent the defender sprawling there—while taking a wide-open jump shot. He made powerful and accurate cross-court passes when players crowded him too much. He used strength and athleticism to snatch rebounds. Late in the game, in what looked like the winning play, he caused a Pierce turnover. Point guard Eric Snow raced the other way on a break and then, smartly, passed to a trailing James. Delonte West was standing there, and James jumped anyway, palmed the ball with his right hand, and slammed it over the falling—and fouling—West.

But no one on the Cavs could figure out Pierce. He got Sasha Pavlovic on a vintage Pierce move: Get you on my hip, turn toward the baseline, fake as if to reset, and then back to the baseline for a clear path and dunk. The shorter Snow decided to guard him on one possession to keep James out of foul trouble, and Pierce just squared him up and shot over him. Pierce had a 17-point fourth quarter, and that didn't look like it was going to be enough after James's late dunk and foul over West. But in the final seven seconds, Pierce got the ball, down by 2, and was fouled by James. He made two free throws to send the game to overtime.

It extended to a second overtime, with Pierce and James continuing to push one another. There was a moment when it seemed to click for James that he could dominate defensively, too. West got in front of the pack, dribbling with a clear lane to the basket. He put the ball near the rim and, in an epic chase down, James rose to block the shot.

After scoring 44 against the Spurs, James finished with a triple-double in Boston: 43 points, 12 rebounds, 11 assists. The only thing Pierce didn't do all night, amazingly, was make a 3-pointer. He finished with 50 points, 8 assists, and 7 rebounds in a Celtics loss.

These nights were long, and although there was some satisfaction in showing that he still had it, that was fleeting. He knew he could play at this pace, although he didn't want to be on a team where he had to play like this for a chance to win. Besides, this was Boston. With all those banners hanging above the parquet, no one was going to give him love for a January showdown against James. For respect here, he'd have to outduel James—or anyone else—in the playoffs, and win.

He was the Truth. A nickname. If anyone asked how the Celtics could go from where they were to where they wanted to be, honestly, he had no idea.

CHAPTER SIX

SEEING RED

In May 2006, once again playoff outsiders, the Celtics had a slide deck that outlined their strategic plan. In the multistep process, the illustration showed how the team could use some of its current players and assets to become a championship contender.

It seemed hard to believe that a thirty-three-win team anchored by Paul Pierce actually owned championship resources, but according to that strategic plan, there was a realistic path to follow:

- They could use Raef LaFrentz's contract, along with some of their young draft picks, to acquire a top-level starter.
- They could use Wally Szczerbiak's contract to acquire a second-tier star to play with Pierce.
- They could simply develop what they had, a talented and young quartet of Al Jefferson, Kendrick Perkins, Tony Allen, and Delonte West, and hope Pierce wanted to stay with that maturing group.
- Or they could go with their least attractive option, which was to trade Pierce and start over.

The organization could feel Pierce's urgency. He was going to be twenty-nine in a few months. He'd averaged nearly 27 points per game the previous season. Reached his career high in field-goal percentage. Listened to Doc Rivers. Encouraged his young teammates. Had that 50-point game against LeBron. Tried to be a good Celtic and all the things people said he wasn't. It earned him a pat on the back and a shutout from the All-NBA teams.

Now what?

Rivers enjoyed talking with Red Auerbach about life and basketball, and he'd often ask thoughtful questions that Auerbach would answer with pithy one-liners. When he asked Auerbach to sum up his team philosophy in a nutshell, he was given an answer that he quickly adopted: "Get the ball. Don't give up the ball."

It was simple and powerful, but Auerbach was astute enough to know that these Celtics struggled to do it.

"Doc, your team is too nice," Auerbach told him one day. "Every good team needs some instigators. If you look at all the great Celtics teams, they had great players. And instigators."

Danny Ainge knew what Auerbach meant, but Ainge could see how it was harder to find great players than instigators. He'd done a good job of discovering talent in less-than-ideal draft slots, and that shrewd drafting brought the Celtics closer to where they wanted to be. A few weeks before the draft, they'd need to keep up their streak of picking solid players who would be useful for them or, most likely, intriguing to other teams in a trade package for an All-Star.

For the 2006 draft, the people in the room with Ainge had different roles.

Just under four years had passed since Morey, then a nimble consultant, helped Wyc Grousbeck understand the NBA salary cap on deadline. It had been two years since he identified Mike

Zarren as someone who could give the organization a new dimension. Now, Morey was leaving. The Houston Rockets, interested in a more analytical front-office approach, hired him as their new general manager.

While Ainge hadn't said much to Zarren in their initial interview, the two talked daily now. One year earlier, Zarren did a clerkship for a federal judge in Columbus, Ohio, by day and sent his detailed statistical reports to the Celtics by night. At the height of trade season, he was probably the only person in the league balancing salary-cap data and details from a death penalty case. Ainge decided that he wanted Zarren as a full-time Celtic, so Zarren was officially and wholly part of the management team now.

Front-office personnel in Boston, Minneapolis, and Seattle were all being scrutinized by their star players. It was going to be tough for Kevin Garnett to be patient and restrained this year. The Wolves traded players with the Celtics last season, and now the two franchises were in the same place. Literally. Both teams were in the draft lottery with identical records of thirty-three wins and forty-nine losses. They held the sixth and seventh picks in the draft. Just a few spots behind them were Ray Allen's 35–47 Seattle SuperSonics, picking tenth.

The three All-Stars from those franchises were all linked and not just as restless lottery alums attached to lottery teams. They were all growing as basketball thinkers and analysts, and if their teams couldn't make smart moves in the next few opportunities to do it—draft night in June, the February 2007 trading deadline, postdeadline free agents in March 2007—they were going to say something about it.

In what had now become a standard part of their scouting process, the Celtics viewed prospects through analytical and traditional lenses. For example, scout Ryan McDonough had returned from Argentina in 2005 praising an unusual player from an under-twenty-one international tournament. He was Team USA's point guard, and his name was Rajon Rondo.

He played collegiately at Kentucky, and he had an atypical profile. He was six foot one, but he played bigger than that. He was wiry, and from a distance, it appeared that he was being swallowed by his headband and jersey. Up close, though, his strength was obvious, and his broad shoulders suggested that a lot more muscle could be added there.

Rondo had the potential to fill both of Red's categories, great player and instigator. That sounded good on a scouting report, but closer investigation revealed that he could be a great player for his team and an instigator *against* his team. He was smart and stubborn, and he could tune out coaches and teammates if he didn't agree with them. His passing was magical at times, while his jump shot was unreliable.

Old-school scouting alone would project Rondo as a late first-round pick. Analytics projected an All-Star. The Celtics found ways to view him at the intersection of both.

They compiled footage of all the guards in the draft, and they kept track of specific categories. Their draft model wanted to know how often a guard's opponent went by him, how often the opponent passed, and how often the guard himself stole the ball or deflected it. This was a draft model that gushed over Rondo. His numbers came out at 12 percent, a mark that tripled the second-place finisher.

But as Ainge said so eloquently in his first meeting with Zarren and Morey, some numbers can be stupid. So the next thing for the Celtics was to see Rondo in person against the other top guards of the draft. Less than a week before draft day, the Celtics hosted Rondo, Villanova's Randy Foye, and Connecticut's Marcus Williams in a joint workout. The other two guards were rated significantly higher than Rondo by most scouts, and the draft was expected to reflect that.

It was a different story in the workout. Matched up against Foye and Williams, Rondo dominated them in every category and drill. It was so lopsided that on that day, at least, it was clear who the future All-Star was. Unfortunately for the Celtics, there was something else for them to consider about Rondo that the draft models couldn't say: He was intensely competitive and peerless in big games and moments, but he could drift if he determined that someone or something—an opponent, suggestion, coach, or teammate—wasn't worth his time.

Ainge clicked with Rondo at the draft workout, and there was something about the player's uniqueness that stayed on his mind. "I really love this little sucker Rondo," he told Grousbeck. "He's aggressive. Tenacious. He's my guy." Grousbeck had heard Ainge mention Rondo so much before the draft that the co-owner decided that he was going to watch on draft day to see where the guard landed.

Boston was unlikely because on the morning of the draft, Ainge made a cap-clearing deal. LaFrentz, who came to the Celtics with a burdensome contract in the first Walker trade, was sent to Portland along with the seventh pick. In return for him, the Celtics acquired the Blazers' backup point guard, twenty-one-year-old Sebastian Telfair.

It made sense that Telfair would be the Celtics' starter since they gave up such a valuable pick to acquire him. But the Celtics also had Rondo rated as the seventh-best overall player. Since he once owned the seventh pick, Ainge could have easily taken him there. But he wanted to move the LaFrentz contract, acquire a player like Telfair, and still find a way to get the athletic Rondo.

As the draft unfolded, it looked like Rondo wasn't going to be picked where Ainge guessed he might be, in the middle of the first round. Grousbeck indeed was watching, and he got an idea outside the top ten as J. J. Redick, Hilton Armstrong, and Thabo Selfolosha came off the board. The co-owner loved watching Ainge work in the draft room because of how strategic he was. He'd seen Ainge create several draft lists weeks before the actual draft and then go back and tear those lists apart. He liked the way that Ainge always had five potential players for each slot and the way he'd make a point to consider all the opinions in the room. Then, sometimes, he'd take off. He'd leave the room briefly and take a hallway stroll before making a pick. He'd reenter the room and make his announcement. Grousbeck called him "Michaelangelo at work."

He motioned for Ainge to step outside the room for a private conversation.

"Go get another pick and get Rondo," Grousbeck said.

"What are you talking about?"

"You love Rondo, he's still there, so you should go back into the draft and get him."

Grousbeck always said that he personally didn't know how to scout players and find unknown talents. But he'd watched Ainge do that every year with the Celtics, so it felt right to give this one to him. This was back to his early venture capitalist days of finding someone to bet on. Ainge was that for him, and Rondo was that for Ainge.

After a few minutes, Ainge had an agreement with his old friends in Phoenix at number twenty-one: The Suns would select Rondo there, and the Celtics would send them one of their extra first-rounders, this one a 2007 first they'd gotten from Cleveland when the Cavs, surprisingly, gave up that capital for Jiri Welsch. The Celtics believed they'd acquired a gem with Rondo. All Rivers had to do was figure out how to distribute minutes and turn the team over to two young point men whose combined age still didn't match Rivers's. They still had a lot to learn.

Kevin McHale also made a trade involving his first-round pick, but it was one that he wanted to undo as soon as he agreed to it. His first move, selecting a guard named Brandon Roy, was a solid one. Roy's talent was obvious, but so were his chronic knee problems. Based on talent alone, he would have gone in the top three. The knee concerns turned him into a bit of a slider. No one would have criticized McHale if he had chosen Roy and stopped.

But that pick was connected to another one he had in place with Houston, picking at number eight. Houston was going to take a player, Foye, there and send him and guard Luther Head to the Wolves. Easy deal. Foye just had to make it to the eighth slot for it to be executed. When Foye was taken by the Blazers with the pick they got from the Celtics at seven, the deal collapsed. That led to one of the strangest agreements of McHale's career. He traded the just-drafted Roy, pick six, for the just-drafted Foye, pick seven.

Roy for Foye.

Six for seven.

Taking a player you don't want at six and then trading for the player you wanted all along—and didn't take—who went at seven.

It wasn't unusual for teams to make pre-draft trades. It was unusual for those trades to comically disintegrate. The only other part of the deal was $1 million going from Portland to Minnesota. There was no other way to put it. The deal stunk for the Wolves. They essentially took $1 million to go back a space. It was not an encouraging draft night for Garnett, who had one more year on his contract.

There was similar tension in Seattle. It was much bigger than draft choices and front-office moves, although those weren't good, either. Rather, it was about the threat of an actual franchise move. The local ownership group was called the Basketball Club of Seattle and was led by Howard Schultz (of Starbucks fame). Schultz wanted to update and expand KeyArena, and he wanted $220 million of the public's money to do it.

The voters and city weren't interested in that plan, so Schultz eventually sold the team to Oklahoma City businessman Clay Bennett. Part of the agreement with Bennett was that he would operate in good faith to find an arena in or around Seattle before doing what many Sonics fans feared.

But that was fall and winter business. In the summer, in the draft, the Sonics selected a twenty-year-old center from Senegal, Mouhamed Sene. Their first-round pick from the previous draft was a twenty-year-old center from France, Johan Petro. The names and countries changed; the ages and positions didn't.

From Boston to Minneapolis to Seattle, there was a similar concern. The veteran players spoke the language of urgency and desperation, and they wanted proof that they were being heard.

Garnett was so frustrated after the draft that he bypassed all diplomacy and got right to the issue in an interview with *Slam* magazine: "One thing that I can't stand is if I'm working hard and the organization upstairs isn't working hard, it's not fair. It's not fair to me. That's not fair to a person who's actually trying to get a championship. I feel like when it works is when both sides are just as active and as hungry. I just wish the Minnesota Timberwolves would work a little harder, or work as hard as I work in the summertime."

The type of executive that Garnett described was not fictional. In fact, Ainge and McHale knew him and had charmed NBA careers because of him. His name was Arnold Auerbach, known in the basketball world and beyond as Red.

Garnett would have loved Red, who was always orchestrating something that wasn't supposed to happen. He'd been doing that since the early days of the league, when the NBA's players were all white and he decided that they shouldn't be: In 1950, he drafted Chuck Cooper, the first black player in the NBA. Six years later, he maneuvered his way to the top of the draft so he could get to his desired destination, acquiring Bill Russell. He selected the center, built the Celtics around him, and set a professional sports record with eight consecutive championships.

Red could read a room.

After that eighth straight title, and his ninth overall, he decided to retire from coaching and work in the front office. He named Russell as his replacement, reasoning that the only coach who could reach Russell was Russell himself. The move was a historic one, as Russell became the first black coach in all of pro sports.

Red could hustle you.

After Russell retired following the 1969 championship season, the Celtics suddenly had a hole at center for the first time since the 1950s. Red scouted Dave Cowens at Florida State and walked out of the gym in mock disgust before the game ended. People thought Red hated him; it was all a ruse so there was a clearer path to drafting him. He did that in 1970 and watched Cowens become an MVP and two-time champion.

Red could work the system.

He had two first-round picks in 1978, at six and eight, and he wanted to draft Larry Bird with that first selection. An Indiana State junior, Bird was eligible to be drafted because his original class began college four years earlier. Bird, though, dropped out of Indiana University and then resumed his career at State. He was a year behind in class but available to NBA teams who were willing to wait a year for him and unafraid to risk losing him to the 1979 draft if they didn't get a deal done in time. The deal got done.

Two years later, Red had an arrangement with Golden State in which he gave up the number one overall draft pick, along with pick thirteen, in exchange for the Warriors' third pick and center Robert Parish. With that third choice, he took the University of Minnesota's Kevin McHale.

There it was, in a savvy two-year whirlwind: the birth of the original Big Three.

It was a different league then. No salary cap. No lucrative TV partnership. No use of analytics. In that league, Bird was the highest-paid rookie in history at $625,000 per year. There was no methodical hoarding of picks with the big reveal coming at the end of year three or four. No, with Red, the reveal came with the announcement of what he'd pulled off. You got a chance immediately to applaud the genius of it all.

Ainge the executive could now appreciate things that Ainge the player could not. What Red did, from traditional acquisitions to creative ones—like his deal to get Ainge in 1981—was brilliant. And difficult. When Ainge told him years later that he would have broken up the Big Three, it was a good line but based on no insight on how to actually get a deal done. The job was much harder than the ever-smirking, cigar-chomping Red made it look. He appeared to be at ease in everything, which the Celtics learned when they tried to collect all sixteen of the organization's championship trophies. Red had casually stored one in a home closet.

One thing Red could not do was outrace time. He was ailing just before the start of the season, and in October, he died of a heart attack. He was eighty-nine. Red Auerbach was the Celtics. Years after he worked his whistle in practices and squeezed his rolled-up programs during games, he gave the Celtics a fighting spirit that many of those teams didn't naturally have. Once, when he was in his late seventies, Red was challenged to a game of racquetball by twenty-eight-year-old Celtic Dee Brown.

"I'll win this one, Red," Brown teased.

"Wanna bet?" the older man replied. "I'll kick your ass."

That was his solution to a lot of things. Outsmart 'em and then kick their ass. But while he was around to see plenty of Celtics lows in his life, he died before he could see his beloved franchise at its lowest. There were so many areas where his presence, his experience, could have helped.

As Rivers entered his third season as head coach, he was struggling personally. He'd kept his home in Orlando while working in Boston. He flew back to Florida as often as he could, taking advantage of breaks in the schedule to see one of his three sons play basketball or to watch his only daughter play volleyball. He missed the mundane, just being nearby for the ordinariness of family life.

Red knew about that, too. In all his years coaching and leading the Celtics, he hadn't moved his family to Boston, either. The Auerbachs were based in Washington, DC, while their father lived for years in Boston's Lenox Hotel. As long as the team was winning, which it was when Red coached, no one cared.

Ainge, showing some of Red's insight, knew exactly how to relieve some of the pressure on Rivers. Unlike Red, Rivers was not going to win often in the 2006–2007 season. Ainge was sure of it.

He wanted to spread the message to the entire ownership group so no one got the wrong idea about what the franchise faced. Ainge, Rivers, Grousbeck, Pags, Bob Epstein, and several limited partners were invited to play at Turner Hill Golf Club in Ipswich, Massachusetts. After golf, the group gathered in a large room for dinner.

"All right, before we get started, I want everyone to write on a piece of paper how many wins we're going to have this year," Ainge announced.

Several people began writing their predictions. Ainge read some of them off—fifty, forty-five, forty—and made another statement after looking over several of the slips: "I have to tell you, this is some of the most unrealistic stuff I've seen in a while. We're not going to be good this year, guys. We're going to struggle. We're going to play hard; we're going to be well coached. But we're young, and it's going to be hard for us."

It was that kind of message and the support around it that was missing from many talk shows, columns, fan sites, and arena seats. During a 24-point home loss to the Knicks in November, Rivers looked behind the bench and saw a couple of homemade signs. "Fire Doc," they read. Just in case he wasn't reading them, the signs grew voices late in the game, and there was a chant. "Fire Doc . . . Fire Doc." The Celtics were 4–8 after beginning the season 1–6. The critics had no idea that what they were watching, by comparison, was as good as the season would get.

Before one game, Grousbeck approached a fan holding a sign critical of Ainge and Rivers. The fan, a young teen sitting a few rows behind the Celtics' bench, didn't know who the owner was.

"What's your sign say?" Grousbeck asked.

"It says, 'Fire Doc and Danny.'"

"Why do you want to do that?"

"Because they're idiots," the kid replied.

"Well, I'd prefer that you didn't have the sign. I really wish you'd put it away."

"Too bad."

"What if I told you that I know the person who assigns seats? And I can get that person to move your seats to the balcony?"

"Never mind, then."

And the sign went away. But the removal of tangible signs, in Boston and elsewhere, didn't change fan anger and resentment.

The figurative signs were there for all to see in Seattle. In a gesture that appeared to be gracious, new Sonics owner Clay Bennett invited Ray Allen to play golf with him. They went to Newcastle, on the city's east side; spent five hours together on the links; and talked all things NBA. They discussed players, coaches, facility upgrades, and the community in which they lived. Or the community in which Allen lived.

Allen came away impressed that Bennett had reached out to him, shared so much, and listened. But what that session amounted to was consulting for Bennett. None of his investors had Seattle ties, and there was nothing in his actions that suggested he was committed to the community. Everything seemed like a warm-up to Oklahoma City.

In Boston, at the beginning of 2007, the results were numbing. Pierce hurt his left foot and was diagnosed with a stress fracture. This was troubling. Pierce had already missed eight games, and the team was 2–6 without him.

Each time a Celtics game was played, a new crack was revealed. The revelation was always paired with a loss. Not sometimes; always. They weren't blowout losses. One by 9, another by 8, this one by 5, yet another by 4. They kept adding up as Pierce watched, surprised and helpless. He thought they needed him, obviously. What he didn't realize was that they weren't able to collectively claw their way to wins without him.

No one had the maturity, yet, to salvage a possession by drawing a foul when the jump shot wasn't there. They didn't know the art of tactfully working the officials ("Good call, Tony . . . watch him on that illegal screen . . ."). No one had the confidence to see it as his team when Pierce wasn't there. Some of them, like the kid Rondo, were just starting to ascend. He was competitive and cocky, with a sprinter's legs and a quarterback's vision. But a rookie couldn't get them out of this. Al Jefferson could score and rebound, and at times he made it look easy. If he kept working, he could make an All-Star team one day. The center from Ainge's first draft class, twenty-two-year-old Kendrick Perkins, was ever capable of delivering that ass-kicking that Red liked to see his big men give. But where do you start the fight when, after a loss in Toronto on January 26, the losing streak is at ten?

Ainge made sure the fight wasn't going to start in the locker room. He knew that his young team might be listening to media speculation about the future of the team or of their head coach. Leon Powe was in the weight room when Ainge walked in to remind players what wasn't going to happen: "I'm not firing Doc. I'm not getting rid of the staff. Don't listen to any of that stuff. Just keep playing hard."

He also encouraged Rivers as the losses began to pile up. At times, Rivers wanted to pull his hat down and not walk around Boston. Ainge tried to accept blame and explain that he had given Rivers "Volkswagens to race against Maseratis." He told his coach what a great job he was doing and how he could see individual players getting better. Rivers believed it and tried to stay positive through it, but any type of optimism was fleeting.

The fans' calls for Rivers's firing began to quiet and not because they suddenly appreciated him. All the losing had changed the focus, and now a benefit to it was in view. College basketball had two dominant players, Greg Oden at Ohio State and Kevin Durant at Texas, and they were seen as the clear prizes at the top of the 2007 draft. If the Celtics continued to lose, they'd be bad enough to significantly increase their lottery chances.

Three more games to close out January, and they were numbers eleven, twelve, and thirteen in a row. Incredible. Rivers was commuting between Florida and Massachusetts for this? He heard those voices from three years ago. *Don't take that job*, smart people told him. *It'll make you look bad.* They appeared to be right.

It was crazy. The Celtics' games, broadcast regionally on Comcast SportsNet, were showing audience growth as the streak continued. The fans cheered for losses. They wanted entertainment, effort, and a close loss. They lost numbers fourteen, fifteen, and sixteen straight with familiar breakdowns. After sixteen, against the advice of Rivers, Pierce returned. His left foot was healed enough, and he'd already missed twenty-four games. It was time to play.

His presence against the Nets, a rival from the competitive days, didn't affect the streak. These days, the Nets weren't very good, at 23–27, but they were more composed than the Celtics and won by 14. What the Celtics needed to stop this madness was a game against themselves.

They got the closest thing to that on February 11 in Minneapolis. It was the current Celtics from Boston against all those ex-Celtics on the Timberwolves. The Wolves were on their second coach of the season, Randy Wittman, and their fourth in two years. The Celtics hadn't won a game in thirty-seven days.

Garnett was upset that national commentators, essentially, told the truth. Doug Collins, Charles Barkley, Reggie Miller, and Kenny Smith all made remarks that amounted to this: *KG has got to get out of Minnesota. He's never going to win there.* It was true, and Garnett knew it. He tried to take the high road in a response to them and redirected commentary back at them.

"They ought to have a drug test before they let some of these people on TV, man. Alcohol tests, see their levels. Everybody has to blow in a Breathalyzer test before you can get on TV."

Pierce and Garnett couldn't change their approach. Even on teams like these, in games like this, they played as if this mattered. Pierce's left foot looked fine as he drove to the basket and hit quick pull-ups. Garnett played like he did in his MVP season, commanding every inch of the court in a forceful display of all-around excellence. Pierce had 29 points in thirty-one minutes. Garnett had 26 points, 11 rebounds, and 10 assists: a triple-double.

The Celtics lost again. Eighteen in a row. It was the longest streak in team history. When they came out of it, finally, in a 20-point win over the Bucks, they were 13–38. There wasn't any aspect of positive thinking, analytics, or big-picture philosophy that could reframe how wretched that victory desert had been.

That is, unless you lived in Seattle.

Every month, there were new clues that the Sonics were leaving town. Fans there knew the team needed a makeover, but at least the flawed team was theirs. It was maddening that every piece of news that came out about the team seemed to be setting up a departure.

Team president Wally Walker was already out, and general manager Rick Sund wasn't expected to stay for long. By March, Allen was out for the year with bone spurs in both ankles.

If there was one thing the relatively connected trio of Garnett, Pierce, and Allen had, it was certainty. They could all look back now to their respective draft nights and smile about the pageantry of it all. Garnett had just turned nineteen, fresh out of high school. Allen and Pierce were twenty, with three years of college behind them. It was their first official NBA introduction, the beginning stage of a lifelong dream.

The idea was never to stay the same as a player or as a person. In the spring of 2007, thirty-year-old Allen could confidently stand up for Seattle in ways that a twenty-year-old Allen couldn't. Garnett, at thirty, could make demands of a franchise while a nineteen-year-old Garnett would have asked permission. Pierce, at thirty, thought like a team-builder; at twenty, he was a passenger who just wanted to prove himself to the team.

After a decade of either waiting to be drafted or seeing whom their team would draft, it was time for a change. The next time the public saw all three of their franchises, it would be back at lottery headquarters for another made-for-TV production. Representatives would be there with awkward smiles and crossed fingers, hoping that yet two more kids, nineteen-year-olds Oden and Durant, could save a team.

The trio had outgrown this. The Lottery Show was programming for kids. One way or another, these men were going to change the course of their careers while they still had the equity to do it. They were going to keep talking and questioning and pushing until they finally found themselves in a better situation. They knew *that* was going to happen. They just never imagined that it was about to happen for all three of them together.

Chapter Seven

BOSTON CONNECTIONS

Danny Ainge looked at the man across from him, Paul Pierce, and could see it and hear it. Again. He had a good relationship with Pierce, and they talked often during the season. While what he heard wasn't new to him, Ainge could sense how obvious it was now: Pierce was losing hope.

That eighteen-game losing streak, inside of a season with fifty-six losses overall, had worn him out. To lose like that all at once was bad enough, but to do it and have some Celtics fans cheer for it was another NBA galaxy altogether.

Ainge and Wyc Grousbeck, sitting with Pierce, wanted to put him at ease.

"We want to build a good team around you," Ainge said. "You've been loyal to this team and this organization, and we want you to be in a good situation here. If we can't do that, we're going to pursue opportunities for you. We're going to move you to a team where you can win."

This was an essential talk, and Doc Rivers knew it. He'd expressed his opinion to Ainge in the last couple of years, with more intensity with each losing season: "We've got another year, *maybe* two, with Paul. And then he's not going to be easy to coach. He's going to be unhappy."

Here, in the spring of 2007, there were parallel NBA seasons running. One, the postseason fight for the championship, was televised every night. The Celtics, playoff observers, clearly weren't part of that world. The other—the season of pleading phone calls, back-channel deals, insider gossip, and reassuring chats with mentally drained franchise players—took place out of public view. It was an easy separation: If your team was good, you were in the first group. Everyone else, including Pierce, Kevin Garnett, and Ray Allen, was in the second.

As thoughtful and forthcoming as Ainge was with Pierce, he didn't tell him everything he knew. He didn't get into the psychology of an NBA team-builder, of how you have to stare eyeball to eyeball with seemingly hopeless situations and see your way out of them. That was part of the job. That was why Ainge and his staff worked the phones so much, looked at numbers, built strategic plans. They were constantly searching for an asset out there that they viewed as better, even if ever so slightly, than an asset that they already had. If they thought it made them even 2 percent better, they'd make a deal.

Honestly, it also helped that Ainge could talk to Kevin McHale any time he needed to. That friendship didn't guarantee that he could make a trade for Kevin Garnett, but it meant the two friends could talk both professionally and casually about what it would take to pull that off.

Rivers witnessed one of those casual talks during a round of golf, and he immediately thought the Celtics were going to find a way to get KG. Ainge, Rivers, and McHale were close to finishing their round, and McHale said something at the seventeenth hole that caused Rivers to raise an eyebrow at Ainge.

"Look, what I really want to do is come out of this with the best young big man in the league."

Rivers and Ainge, who sometimes had silly arguments in which they disagreed on granular points, were aligned now with the same thought: *That's Al Jefferson.* Maybe there was a center in the league better than the twenty-two-year-old Jefferson, but that wasn't the only condition. That player also had to be available, his team needed to have additional players and picks that McHale desired, and KG needed to approve a trade to that city. That was a lot to consider, and even the Celtics didn't have that last part.

With Garnett about to enter the final year of his contract, he essentially had the leverage of a free agent. No sane franchise would meet McHale's price only to watch KG skip town for where he really wanted to go in a year. Boston wasn't on the list. KG respected Pierce and his game, but he didn't think the two of them together would be enough to create a contender. That information alone should have made Ainge stop. Instead, he had two lists that he continually updated in his head: a rundown of what he'd offer McHale in a trade and some talking points that he'd share with KG if he was given permission to speak with him.

Everyone could see the outward gifts of Garnett, who was finishing yet another season in which he led the league in rebounding. He'd already played a dozen seasons, and he was thirty-one. The Celtics needed to do a deep dive and get an answer: How long could he be productive if they did acquire him? When they studied KG's games from last season, they noticed how often he'd been double-teamed on most possessions. He was still able to score after being doubled, and his defense appeared to be as strong as it had been in his MVP season.

The real issue, one week before the draft lottery, wasn't just that Garnett didn't want the Celtics. In fact, he really didn't *want* anyone other than Minnesota. He'd been frustrated at times by McHale and Wolves owner Glen Taylor. He wanted to win again, desperately. But if you plumbed the depths of him, he still hadn't fallen out of love. It was hard to picture him in another state, wearing a different uniform.

On May 22, lottery night, the Celtics prepared themselves for what had become their annual tournament. Once again, the Sonics and Wolves were with them, although the Celtics had the best odds of landing the top two picks.

No matter what happened on this night, Ainge knew he had a corresponding move for it. If the Celtics wound up with a pick lower than number two, Ainge planned to add that pick to Minnesota as part of a package for Garnett. If the Celtics got one of those coveted picks, Ainge didn't feel comfortable making a trade, even for KG. That was because his target was another Kevin, Durant, the super-skinny forward from Texas. All season, Ainge and his staff talked about Durant and his unusual skills, saying they would take him first if given the opportunity. During the college basketball season, Ainge was seen at a University of Texas game, sitting next to Durant's mother. He said it was just a coincidence of arena seating, which it might have been, but he also used the opportunity to tell Mom a few good words about Boston. Just in case.

Durant's selection at the very top of the draft would have surprised the NBA if it had come to that. But as the results were read on TV, a historically bad Celtics season sunk to the ocean floor. They were stunned when their lottery card was in slot number five in a draft with two great players. They were leaped over by two teams that were bad, but not as bad as they were.

One of them, at number one, was the Portland Trail Blazers. The other was Seattle.

Portland would take the center Greg Oden. Seattle, then, would have Durant. He was an intriguing player: a near seven-footer with shooting ambitions and sometimes range, like Allen's. He'd have to work on his shot selection because he'd launch from anywhere, which was part of the intrigue. He didn't lack creativity or confidence.

In Boston, the immediate response to number five caused authentic reactions from Ainge and Doc Rivers. They watched together, and Rivers let a stream of profanities fly when he saw Boston's pick. Then he looked at Ainge.

"I know you can't cuss because of your religion," he said. "But maybe what I just said is how you feel."

Ainge wore a pained smile, and his thoughts fluctuated from in-the-moment disappointment to the phone calls he'd begin to make tomorrow. This was a punch felt throughout the organization. It just so happened that on the business side, the Celtics had a sponsors' summit scheduled for the day after the lottery. Instead of excited companies thinking of creative campaigns for Durant, they found themselves staring at Rich Gotham, the team's president.

"We're not giving up here," he told them. "This is what we're going to do: We're going to get better."

The only thing missing from the conference room was someone saying, "Yeah, right."

Gotham believed what he'd said. He and Ainge began in executive roles with the Celtics the same year. Gotham had seen Ainge's behind-the-scenes mastery enough that the president was convinced, somehow, that Ainge would turn this all into a positive. Gotham's sentiment was popular in-house. Epstein was one of many in the franchise who rested knowing that the smarts of Ainge always gave them a chance, even when it didn't look that way.

Now that the certainty of number five was in place, Ainge began to view the choice as movable property. It was going to Minneapolis, if all went well. The Wolves got the seventh choice in the lottery, so a rebuild with two picks in the top seven would give them options. If not, number five was headed to another NBA city for a veteran player. The Celtics were young enough. A good, not great, prospect wasn't going to bring more wins or peace to Pierce.

For Allen, he knew he could play with Durant and mentor him. He expected to be fully recovered from his ankle surgery and ready for the new season. He planned to meet his new boss for lunch in a couple of weeks to discuss specifics. The incoming general manager was Sam Presti, and at thirty, he was younger than Allen. Actually, he was the youngest GM in basketball, and people who knew him said he was on the path to being among the smartest, too.

He and Allen both had New England ties. Allen attended the University of Connecticut, and Presti grew up outside of Boston in Concord, once home to literary greats like Thoreau, Emerson, and Alcott. He was a fifteen-year-old basketball player—and drummer—at Concord-Carlisle High School on the day that the music stopped. Larry Bird announced his retirement in 1992, ending a legendary career and trio, the Big Three. McHale retired the next year, and so did competitive Celtics teams. For the rest of the 1990s.

But that was old Boston. Presti was aware of new Boston as well. Ainge was no longer the Celtics' number 44, the combo guard who had a knack for getting under an opponent's skin. He was now their free-thinking executive who evaluated players with the same bent that Presti did. If Presti had asked Ainge about Durant, he might have heard Ainge's unashamed love for Durant and envy of Presti: "Two or three months prior to draft night, my whole staff knew I was going to take Kevin Durant."

Based on a bad bounce, Ainge had to move on to other options. There was no question that Presti would receive a call from Ainge before draft night.

Ainge had to talk with McHale first, though.

He needed to be at his negotiating best because this was an attempt to acquire a player, in three movements:

- He needed to satisfy the trade demands of McHale, which he was sure he could do. A package highlighted by Jefferson, the number five pick in the draft, and the return of Minnesota's own 2009 first-rounder was tough for any other team to match. If McHale traded KG elsewhere, he risked being bad without KG and watching the Celtics benefit with what would certainly be a 2009 lottery pick.
- He needed to get permission to speak with Garnett and then convince him that Boston was a great fit for him. He could be at his oratorical best here, but he knew he needed to show Garnett that Boston was better for his career than Phoenix or Los Angeles, not tell him.
- He needed to agree with Garnett on a contract extension.

Ainge and McHale were comfortable with a framework for a KG deal. McHale liked his return, and Ainge obviously liked his. The next step was a one-on-one meeting with KG, at his home in Malibu.

Things couldn't have begun better for the two men. They hit it off immediately, smiling and talking about the game they loved. Ainge met KG's wife and family, and the atmosphere remained pleasant and light. When Ainge brought up the idea of KG playing for the Celtics, they ran into a conversational wall. They were still cordial, with no progress.

"It's not personal," Garnett told Ainge. "There's nothing against the city or team. But I think there are better fits for me than the Celtics."

Ainge left Malibu but didn't close the door. This was the positive he took from the rejection: If the Celtics had more on their roster, Garnett might find them more attractive. There was no trade with Minnesota because there was no agreement with KG. No problem. Soon after, he called Sam Presti.

Allen was the Sonics' star, popular with fans and media, and comfortable in the community. He and his wife, Shannon, had a close circle of friends in the Pacific Northwest, and despite the performance of the Sonics, Allen never considered asking Presti to trade him.

It had been just the opposite in early June. Allen and Presti met for lunch in downtown Seattle, and Allen left that meeting believing that he, Durant, and Rashard Lewis would be a big part of the team's future. Still, there was part of him that remained connected to his family's military background: Learn to pack a bag quickly and be ready to move, because chances are it will happen.

Indeed, the Sonics were willing to trade Allen and some arrangement of late-round picks to Boston, but Presti wanted number five and point guard Rajon Rondo in return. Ainge and Presti, two fierce negotiators, went back and forth on a number of proposals, but they continued to get stuck on Rondo. Ainge refused to be flexible with this request. Rondo's style didn't remind him of anyone he'd seen. A smaller guard who played big and could rebound. Not a great shooter but could take over a game with his defense and decision-making. An iconoclast in a sense, drawn to the offbeat.

This was cross-country juggling mixed with chess. While Ainge negotiated with Presti, he knew he couldn't give away so much that he had nothing left to offer McHale for one more run at KG. Someone, Ainge or Presti, needed to compromise. It was draft day, racing toward draft night.

Finally, the Celtics-Sonics trade was done. Boston agreed to send the fifth pick along with guard Delonte West and forward Wally Szczerbiak to Seattle in exchange for Allen and Glen "Big Baby" Davis, a rookie second-round pick. Part of the Celtics' strategic plan from last year had just come to life. They really had used Szczerbiak's contract to bring in a star.

That star was bothered by the trade, mostly because he heard about it in the media. He wasn't alone. A crowd of about two thousand people, gathered downtown for a Sonics draft party, booed when the trade was announced. They'd planned it as a night of pure celebration for a team that had been connected to two years' worth of negative news. Now they had to say good-bye to a seven-time All-Star, dealt for young potential and contract considerations.

Pierce reached out to Allen as soon as he got the official word, but neither player knew that the deal got Garnett's attention as well. He couldn't have been clearer that Boston wasn't for him when he spoke to Ainge. But now the Celtics had two All-Stars, both going to the Hall of Fame one day, and for the first time, he started to imagine how it might look if he became their teammate.

He was in a different space now, and for the first time in his career, his basketball vision beyond Minnesota was now open.

If he'd thought about it more in Malibu, he would have seen that no other franchise suited him like the Celtics. This was an organization that revered a pioneering and creative defender in Bill Russell. Not scoring, but rebounding and defense. In the history of the Celtics, no player had ever led the league in scoring. It was a stat that spoke to the ethos of the franchise. This was a place where they'd appreciate Garnett's passion, partly because his enthusiasm in and for all things equaled theirs.

As usual, Ainge was on the phone with McHale. Allen was now in Boston, so the Celtics' prior math problem—not enough

All-Stars—was no longer an issue. This was going to be hard for McHale, but now it had to be done.

McHale had watched Garnett grow into a star, and quickly. As popular as Garnett was, with jersey sales and commercials and All-Star appearances, his impact was deeper than that. He was the organization's first superstar, and he managed to do it with a unique sensibility that was raw and still played to middle America. He was a modern star willing to defer and deflect and promote others, all in the name of winning more games. He was well-conditioned, durable, excessive with his energy, a provocative soundtrack.

McHale could and would ask for everything he wanted and still not truly replace KG.

The general manager didn't need one first-round pick; he needed two. Especially that 2009 first-rounder that the Celtics had gotten from the Timberwolves. The "kid" he met in Boston Garden decades ago, Mike Zarren, had written a lot of protection language around the pick, but those protections were going to expire. There was no way the Wolves could be without KG and that unprotected pick. He needed it back.

Ainge agreed to that.

McHale obviously needed his favorite player among all of Ainge's draft picks, Al Jefferson. The six-foot-ten Jefferson averaged 16 points and 11 rebounds last season, and he had room to get better.

Of course Ainge agreed to that. He said yes to Gerald Green and Ryan Gomes, too, but then they ran into a snag. Ainge offered point guard Sebastian Telfair. The Wolves wanted Rajon Rondo.

This was a problem. For the second time this offseason, Ainge faced a Rondo deal-breaker. Ainge wasn't just going to throw him in a deal. Then again, what if it fell apart and he didn't get an all-time great because he refused to give up a second-year guard?

This was now a situation above both of their pay grades. Glen Taylor, the Wolves owner, insisted on Rondo. Ainge was getting weary. This wasn't a trade as much as it was a project. He'd worked this thing for eight weeks now, and as resolute a negotiator as he was, he thought of one word to characterize this process: grueling.

In the meantime, Garnett was in Newport Beach at a ceremony. Gary Payton and his wife decided to renew their wedding vows after ten years, and many NBA players were there to witness it. Payton was a member of the 2006 NBA champion Miami Heat, a particularly close team. He invited all of his teammates, including Antoine Walker, one of their starting forwards. Walker had left Boston twice, angry at Ainge both times. But his love for Boston overwhelmed any bitterness he had toward Ainge, and he told Garnett that.

"Did you like playing there?" KG asked.

"Man, I loved it. It's a great sports town. We won it in Miami, and we still wouldn't get our crowd until the second quarter. Boston ain't like that."

KG asked about Pierce; would he be open to playing with two more stars? He asked about playing for Doc Rivers. Walker had all positive things to say. Then it hit the former Celtic that no deal had been announced, and KG was especially curious about Boston.

He called Pierce.

"Y'all are about to get KG!" he told his old teammate.

They were close to that, for sure. But now this deal was in the hands of ownership.

It was on its way to being a big trade, seven players for one, and that wasn't even the tricky part of it. The league had language in its collective bargaining agreement for an extend-and-trade deal, which is what the Wolves were doing with Garnett, but that language had never been interpreted before. This would be the one to set precedent. There were several clarifying phone calls made to the league office, just to make sure it was being executed properly.

Now it had come to its final stage, one that no one would have predicted at the very beginning of the negotiation. It was Glen Taylor and Wyc Grousbeck, talking about point guards.

"Glen, we almost have a deal," Grousbeck said. "But we need to keep Rondo. He's our starting point guard. He probably sits on the bench for you."

"We really want him in this deal," Taylor insisted.

"But he's my starting point guard. He's all we have. It kind of takes away the purpose of making this deal because we're not going to have a point guard."

Grousbeck quickly realized how this must have sounded to Taylor. The Wolves owner was a smart businessman, so he could clearly see that Sebastian Telfair was on Boston's roster. But Grousbeck had already begun thinking about Telfair as a former member of the team.

Telfair had been arrested in April on a gun possession charge in New York. One year before arriving in Boston, Telfair's loaded gun was found in his pillowcase on the team plane. Grousbeck had the guard's nameplate removed from his locker. Telfair's Celtics career was over, and Grousbeck decided to tell Taylor that.

"Listen, Glen. Telfair is not going to play here anymore. But I'll tell you what: We'll pay his salary. You can have him for free. Think about it. We really have to get moving on this thing. Can you let me know by five?"

Grousbeck was on Martha's Vineyard, and he decided to go for a run on the beach. He kept his phone nearby, and he was hopeful when it began to ring at four thirty p.m. It was Taylor.

"Wyc, let me be the first to congratulate you on winning the 2008 NBA championship."

They had a deal.

Grousbeck called Ainge, and Ainge began calling the co-owner "Papelbon," a reference to the hard-throwing, game-saving closer for the Red Sox.

It was late July, and in no time, training camp would begin. The Timberwolves and Celtics were no longer similar teams, meeting in the spring in that humiliating lottery studio in New Jersey. The Celtics paid their way out of the lottery, and the two veteran Celtics, Pierce and Allen, were ecstatic about welcoming the third.

It was now an all-inclusive summer in Boston. Allen had visited Fenway Park a few weeks earlier, and he watched a Red Sox team that had been in first place all season long. The Patriots, the three-time champion Patriots, had just opened training camp. One of their new acquisitions was the acrobatic receiver Randy Moss.

Now this. The Celtics had flung away their mediocrity. They had a chance to unashamedly sing the championship songs that the Sox and Patriots also sang.

Paul Pierce, Kevin Garnett, Ray Allen. On the same team. Winning, at the highest level, was suddenly all around them. In their excitement, they couldn't stop smiling, interrupting each other with ideas, and promising that this would never be about egos. They couldn't wait to meet and share and train and mentor. They all wanted to win, and it wouldn't be long before they were told and shown exactly how it would be done.

Chapter Eight

UBUNTU

Kevin Garnett's car pulled into the back of Boston Garden, and as soon as he stepped out of it, his new franchise changed. Officially it was the last day of July 2007. It was also the last day of low energy, low volume, and lowered expectations with the Celtics.

It was fitting that a simple thing made KG late for his introductory press conference: looking up. He was ushered through the Garden, and that was the only exercise that slowed his heart rate. He gazed up at the sixteen championship banners and twenty-one retired numbers. He asked questions about the various title teams and absorbed all the details.

He didn't have it entirely, but now he was starting to understand. There was an awakening in him and in the city. He could see evidence of the Celtics' story, hanging there for all to see. And now he, Paul Pierce, and Ray Allen were going to be stitched into this championship quilt.

Rich Gotham and Shawn Sullivan, the team's president and chief marketing officer, met him for the first time. They each shook his hand, and Gotham thought, *This guy is like a nuclear reactor.* His intensity and excitability animated the arena, and everyone there that day caught it and was infused with the same thing.

Gotham, in his fifth season with the organization, had often spoken of a day when the Celtics' raised business floor would in turn raise their business roof. Well, this was that day. Before heading into the press conference, KG had a word with Gotham and Sullivan about marketing, promotion, and people who might come to them saying they represent him.

"One thing for you guys to always keep in mind: In all our dealings, if you don't hear it from me, it ain't happening," he said. "You might see people around me, but no one else is running my shit. I run my own game."

They were going to love working with him. There wasn't anyone in the entire organization like him.

Garnett, Pierce, and Allen hadn't played a game together yet, but Celtics fans were already calling them the Big Three. Those same fans, for the first time in years, joyfully went to websites and mobile phones and virtual ticket windows, making sure they'd have the best seats for the best games of the winter and spring.

Doc Rivers was as excited as everyone else, but he also had to do things that no one else did. He'd be the one managing egos. He'd be the designer of an offense that would, realistically, require sacrifices from each of them. He'd be the *No, we're not doing that* at the end of paths previously filled with smiles and head nods. He'd push them. He'd piss them off.

Those things couldn't wait until camp or even two weeks from now. At the press conference, full of gleaming smiles and summer laughter, Pierce, Garnett, and Allen all said encouraging things. Now he had to make sure those things happened. As they shook hands, told jokes, and made family introductions, Rivers got the trio's attention.

"Hey, guys. Can I get ten minutes?"

The four of them went to his Garden office.

"We're going to win the championship this year," he told them. "I want you to know that. But I'm going to need you guys to buy into me, and I'm going to need you guys to sacrifice stuff. We'll talk about it later, but I need that on record now. I need you to know that you're not going to be able to do things the way you've done them."

They all said they understood, and all said they agreed with the coach. He wanted to plant the seed then because he knew he wouldn't see them again until September. He also realized that saying yes in the summer, surrounded by friends and family, was easy. The challenge would be doing it in the fall.

A few weeks after the press conference, Rivers sat near the window of a restaurant, with a view of Boston's busy Newbury Street. He learned that it was always good to have a notebook nearby because ideas come at odd times and from odd things. As he looked outside, he saw a group of tourists riding in a vehicle that millions of New Englanders knew by its shorthand. It was a duck boat.

He immediately jotted down, *duck boat talk*.

Locally, duck boats weren't associated with tourists. Anyone in the region knew them as the official transportation of championship parades. When the Big Three returned to town just before the official start of training camp, Rivers told them all to meet him one morning at his condo. His place, downtown, was in the same neighborhood where these elaborate two- and three-mile championship parties snaked through the Boston streets.

The first raucous and frigid one, in February 2002, drew more than one million people to City Hall. There was another one in February 2004, and once again more than one million people attended. It got even bigger and flashier six months later when the Red Sox won the World Series for the first time in eighty-six years. Just as that party was cleaned up and quieted, the Patriots inspired another one in February 2005.

Pierce knew what the boat symbolized, but he had no idea what his coach had in mind. And why was he doing it at eight a.m.? KG, forever plugged in and unfiltered, had them all laughing with his skepticism.

"What the fuck is this thing? I'm not getting on that. Where are we going? Are we going in the water? Seriously, Coach. What are we doing?"

Rivers looked at the three stars of his team, already comfortable and enjoying each other's company. He liked that. But they needed to hear what he had to say first, a more in-depth version of the talk he'd begun the day of the press conference.

"This is the parade route," he said. "When you win the title, this is the route we will go on. I want you guys to imagine this. Think about the parade."

The laughter stopped. The players got quiet. The boat began to move. Allen was thirty-three, KG thirty-two, and Pierce a few weeks away from thirty-one. They'd never played in the NBA Finals.

"Listen, I'm going to name you some players in a minute. These are players that I'm saying will never win. You guys are not on the list. But you could be if we don't win. The reason we won't win is the reason these players are on the list—great individual players, but everything about them is what they want to do. And they will not do something different to win.

"They want to win, but they want to win on their terms. You can't win on your terms; you win on the team's terms. If you're willing to understand that, we are going to win it."

Rivers pointed to windows high above Boylston Street and recounted how he'd seen people waving and hanging out of them during parades. He pointed to the Boston Public Library and the spacious area around it. Boston wasn't a city where people lived their lives and loved their sports. No, Boston was more like a city where people loved their sports and then realized they also needed to have a local government and businesses in order to function. If this Celtics team won here, their stories and quirks and jersey numbers—everything—would be forever honored here.

"Let's talk about sacrifice," Rivers said. "What would you give up to win?"

"Whatever is needed," KG answered.

"Okay, what about shots?"

"How many do you need, Coach?"

"I need all your shots, Kevin," Rivers joked.

"You can have all of them," he replied, not joking.

"Really, I don't need them all. But think about it: You've all averaged eighteen, nineteen shots per game. That's not going to happen. It's not possible. Your scoring averages will go down. People might say, 'Ray Allen isn't playing as well because he's not averaging twenty, he's at sixteen.' Can your ego take that? Because if you can't, we can't win."

They could all visualize how it was going to unfold. This was their team map, their blueprint, being detailed on a boat. Rivers had already gotten them to agree to offensive sacrifices, but he wanted to instill a ferocious defensive ethic, too. In fact, no one knew how Rivers had persuaded a top defensive assistant, Tom Thibodeau, to join his staff.

He didn't know Thibodeau, but he knew the tree he'd come from. He'd worked for Jeff Van Gundy, and Van Gundy had worked for Pat Riley. They had the same lineage; it was going to work. But Thibodeau had already agreed to a job with the Wizards. He told Rivers that he'd rather be in Boston with him; he'd signed a contract in Washington, though, and it would take some persuasion of his bosses to get him out of it.

Rivers talked with Washington coach Eddie Jordan and got him out of it. Thibs, as he was called, was known for improving any defense. Now he would have one captained by the force and acumen of KG. Rivers's final point to his stars, though, was that their defensive approach was not going to be only KG's burden.

"I'm not asking anyone, other than Kevin, to be great on defense. I'm asking that you do it right. Be there. Play team defense. We will cover for you if you need help, but I'm not going to cover for you if you won't help yourself."

Allen had never been known for his defense, and he said that he wished he'd paid more attention to it earlier in his career. The conclusion of this ride was revelatory.

"I'm at the point in my life where I need to win," he said. "I'm going to do what I need to do to win."

After hearing the words of Allen, who had to sacrifice the most for this to work, Rivers was convinced: Whenever they next rode in a duck boat, these nearly empty streets would be jammed for them.

Danny Ainge and Rivers had already answered several team questions long before the first practice. One of the frequent issues raised was team depth. They had those three All-Stars, but what else?

Rajon Rondo and Kendrick Perkins would round out the starting five. The bench would have to be a patchwork of homegrown draft picks and well-traveled discount finds. Ainge did some budgeting wizardry and got forward James Posey, thirty-one and on his sixth team, to agree to a one-year deal worth $3.5 million. He was set to join twenty-six-year-old guard Tony Allen, along with Leon Powe and Glen "Big Baby" Davis, a pair of power players in their early twenties.

One day Ainge and Rivers sat in Ainge's office, thinking about the final piece of the roster.

"Man, we gotta add one more shooter," Ainge said. "Do you like Eddie House?"

"I've never liked him," Rivers said. "But he scares the hell out of me. Whenever Eddie House comes into a game, he scares the shit out of you."

"Me too! Every time he comes in, I say, 'Geez, here comes Eddie House.'"

They looked at each other. They knew the book on House. He was exactly the dangerous shooter that they'd said he was, a 3-point craftsman. He'd be their worst defensive player.

"Let's get him," Rivers said. "We can protect him defensively. We've got a great defensive team."

House, twenty-nine, was joining his eighth team in eight years. He was signed for $1.5 million.

This was the team, brought together by equal parts vision, luck, and price tag. Rivers hoped that they would fuse into a real group and not just the Big Three and others. His wish began to happen in training camp due to the schedule. The Celtics were one of four teams selected for global exhibition games. It meant that for two weeks, they'd be practicing and eating and socializing in Rome and London.

Rivers enjoyed getaway training camps. He often spoke of peripheral opponents—hometown buddies, moms and dads, wives and girlfriends, agents, flunkies—who were sometimes more formidable than on-court opposition. The coach let everyone know his first rule: no family and friends on this two-week trip. It was for the team only.

He had other things in mind, too. Five years earlier, while at an event in New York, Rivers met a South African man named Kita Matungulu. They had a great conversation that night, and Matungulu told Rivers about a philosophy that had been referenced by

Nelson Mandela, Desmond Tutu, and many others across the African continent. It could be summarized in a single word. *Ubuntu.* Tutu, the famous South African archbishop, described the concept as the height of interdependence and interconnectedness. It was one person's acceptance that their success, their very personhood, was linked to another's. As Tutu described it, "A person is a person through other persons."

It was a way of being that didn't ask the individuals to lose themselves. Rather, the idea was to see individuality thrive when it was tied to a collective, and, therefore, it helped everyone. That outlook could be applied to education, politics, the economy . . . and basketball. Ubuntu. Rivers had Matungulu speak to the team about it, and its essence became the foundation on which they'd build their season.

Anyone who was around the Celtics in Rome could see how naturally they interacted. They ate meals together and took tours together. They were all unashamedly in awe, together, as they roamed the Vatican and looked up at the detailed artistry of the Sistine Chapel. Perkins immediately thought of his religious grandparents in Texas and said he needed to bring them to Italy to see Michelangelo's work.

They toured the Colosseum and reimagined gladiators fighting before fifty thousand Romans. They all decided to shave their heads in honor of the new bald stars, Garnett and Allen. They all kicked soccer balls and tried to learn about *futbol* from Italian star Alessandro Del Piero.

And like those gladiators, they fought hard. Their first practice was intense, with the veterans of the second team, Posey and House, getting in the faces of KG and Pierce. They were brothers, indeed, but passionate ballers, too. They nearly came to blows in that first practice. Then, afterward, they got on a bus—without cell service—and talked with each other as the vehicle moved slowly through Roman traffic.

By the time they arrived back in Boston, they were a transformed team, immersed in the Ubuntu ethic. They'd begun saying the word as they broke their huddle and approached the court. But as timing would have it, they had to wait in queue before they could present their case to the public.

They returned to a city that was riveted by historic, postseason baseball. Again. Three years earlier, in 2004, the Red Sox were the first team in baseball history to rally from a 0–3 deficit to win a series, against their hated rival, the New York Yankees, no less. It was the signature achievement of their World Series run. While the Celtics were away in London and Rome, the Sox had rallied from a 1–3 ALCS deficit to win a series once more.

Their game seven pennant winner was the climactic moment of the postseason because, afterward, they swept Colorado in the World Series. Which, three days before the Celtics' home opener, triggered yet another million-person party in Rivers's neighborhood.

And that wasn't the only competition. The Patriots were undefeated, 8–0, and crushing opponents by an average score of 41–15.

If the Celtics were a dud, they'd be ignored in this market. Rivers and the players were confident that wouldn't happen, and they'd begin to prove it on the second day of November. The only worry, truly, on Rivers's mind was the health of his father, Grady. The coach had been so surprised by a phone call from his brother in Chicago about his father being taken to the hospital that he'd planned to leave Europe.

His father never complained and never got sick, so Rivers thought this must be serious. He talked to his father, and he said he was fine. There was nothing to worry about, and he wanted his son to focus on work. When he got back to Boston, he thought of taking another trip to Chicago. He could easily get there and spend a couple of days with his dad. Once again, his father talked him out of it. He was assured that things were good. He turned his attention to the season.

Everything about their first game at Boston Garden was different from the recent past, including tip-off time. It was scheduled to begin at eight p.m., a sure sign that it was locally and nationally televised. The ESPN/ABC cameras skipped the Celtics the previous year, so this felt like a league reentry.

Winners, and symbols of winning, were around them and even under them. Before the game, Celtics ownership officially renamed the team's famous parquet floor after Red Auerbach. The franchise architect's signature was neatly inscribed onto the court.

Even the game introduction was different. The marketing team had been busy in August and September, creating new campaigns and hype videos that focused on the now. In the past few years, with all the eighteen-, nineteen-, and twenty-year-old kids, they had no choice but to sell potential and hope. Not now. They'd all been upgraded.

The arena went dark, and the screens above the court showed the recognizable eyes of Allen first, then Garnett, and finally Pierce. There were vignettes from the weight room and the court. There were celebrations and screams. This was going to be fun.

The night really couldn't have gone any better. The opponent, Washington, contributed by giving the fans a fun storyline to follow. The Wizards' leading scorer, Gilbert Arenas, wrote a blog in which he guaranteed that the Celtics would lose their first game. There was already enough emotion in the building, but Arenas's words provided a bonus.

It was over early. And it played out just as Rivers described as they took their tour of the parade route.

In the first few minutes, for example, Allen drove in the lane and immediately drew a double-team. He could have put up a shot but found Perkins alone by the hoop, and the big center converted an easy score. Garnett collected 4 rebounds in the first three minutes and could be heard, nonstop, shouting defensive instructions.

Pierce, meanwhile, played with his usual cool pace and didn't force any shots early. He made a couple of shots in the first quarter of what he used as a feeling-out process. In the second quarter, he and his teammates buried Washington. The ball movement and chemistry were too much for the Wizards, so Pierce had 15 points in the quarter, and the Celtics surged to a 22-point halftime lead.

After that, it was lockdown time and, in the end, playtime. The marketing team showed an old *American Bandstand* video from the 1970s, soundtracked by the Bee Gees' "You Should Be Dancing." Platform shoes, bell bottoms, frayed jackets, colorful miniskirts, and ponchos. The video had it all, and no one in the building enjoyed it more than Garnett. He pulled teammates out of their seats to enjoy the hilarity with him. He lost it when the montage went to a dancing, bearded soloist with "Gino" written on his T-shirt.

The Garden hadn't been this alive on a Friday night in years. The final was 103–83, and even then, each member of the Big Three said the team could be a lot better. As it was, Pierce had 28 points, and he made them all look easy. Garnett showed his diversity with 22 points, 20 rebounds, 5 assists, and 3 blocked shots. Plus, no Celtic since Bill Russell had defended like this. Allen, the one who knew he had to give up the most, showed his willingness to do it. He took just ten shots, nine fewer than Pierce and seven fewer than Garnett, but he still had 17 points and 4 rebounds. He was good defensively, too.

A sign in the stands read, "Too early to predict 82–0?"

The next game was in Toronto on Sunday afternoon. As the team's chartered plane traveled there late Friday night, the players had what was now their normal routine: loud music, entertaining stories, poker games in which the stakes steadily rose. Rivers and his assistants sat in the front, the team's media occupied the back, and everything else belonged to the players. It wasn't just a physical space. Rivers was adamant that he wanted the players to be as authentic as possible, even if their music and language shocked the sensibilities of those outside their group.

In Toronto, it seemed as if Rivers had barely rested his head when his cell phone rang. He looked at the time: four thirty a.m. He looked at the caller: his brother. He began to cry, even before hearing the news.

"Hey, Glenn," his brother began to say.

His father was gone, and that was hard enough to accept. Then there was the thought that he should have left Rome, or Boston, to see him alive one more time. There was practice in a few hours, and he told the team the news. He told the players that he had to go back to Chicago, but before he left, he reminded them about the gift of great parents and how important that was for each of them.

The team would have to take on the Raptors the next day without his guidance.

There was something about this team, and sports in general, that provided a balm. While the Celtics were playing against the Raptors, they didn't realize that their coach was at his parents' house watching them, along with twenty family members. They weren't crying. They were cheering and yelling and hanging on every call.

In his absence, but within his view, the Celtics played well enough to win. This was the luxury, though, of having three stars. With Pierce having an off night on 4 of 17 shooting, Allen was there with a 33-point afternoon, including a game-winning 3 in the final seconds. Afterward, the team dedicated the win to Rivers. Garnett asked reporters and fans to pray for the family. Even in their low moments, this group seemed to get it right.

When Rivers stayed in town for a few days, his mother pulled him aside.

"What are you doing after the funeral, in the morning?" Betty Rivers asked her son.

"I'm sticking around for dinner," he said.

"You guys have a game tomorrow," she scolded.

"Mom, I know. But it's Dad's funeral."

"Your dad's funeral is at eleven a.m. Your game is at seven thirty p.m. No offense, but what are you doing here? Your dad would say, 'Go do your job.' If you want to honor your dad, you honor him by being at the funeral and speaking. And giving us love. You've been here for three days now. It's time for you to go."

It wasn't something that he had said aloud, but he really wanted to win the title, for himself and his father. He listened to his mother and got back to work. The players gave him applause and hugs when they saw him enter the locker room. He didn't realize until halftime that he was still wearing the black suit and tie that he'd worn to the funeral.

And so the Celtics picked up as they were when Rivers last saw them. He was judging them on something specific, and it went back to the duck boat conversation in August. The best teams in the NBA had the best defenses, and his challenge to them was to be the number one defense in the league.

The expectation had been set, and they played as if they were Olympic sprinters trying to outrun the target. They had a dizzying pattern. They'd win in eight- to ten-game clusters, answer a question about their team *before* the question could be fully formed, lose a close game, and then begin the winning cluster again.

They began the season with an eight-game winning streak, lost, and then ran off twelve wins in thirteen games. Before you thought of asking how legitimate their defense was, they held the Knicks to 30 percent shooting and 59 points for an entire game. Before you could wonder if anyone outside of the three could carry the team for a night, there was Perkins tying Garnett for a team-high 21 points—along with 9 rebounds—in a win over the Lakers. How about the bench? Got it: In back-to-back games, Posey went for 17 and 4 and then a nice 10 and 10.

They rolled past the Lakers twice, took out both of last season's Eastern Conference finalists, the Cavaliers and Pistons, and got an 8-point win against the champion Spurs.

Slowly, with no reflection on it or self-awareness of it, Rivers was doing some of the same things as the coaches he admired. Riley and Phil Jackson would have loved the idea and execution of the duck boat talk. Rivers talked about his team so much that it was easy to forget that this was also the best team he'd been a part of. The players had something to prove, and so did he. They heard insatiable critics in their ears, and so did he.

He still didn't want to be part of an analysis on his own coaching. He just woke up and started to move, thinking about some task or another that he had to do. Then he checked it off. His team played basketball in the same way. There was a task, at home or somewhere across North America, and they went to it. Then they checked it off.

Their collective personality was tied into their style of play, fearless and complete. They must have known, didn't they, that teams coming together so suddenly didn't usually win so soon like this. They kept sprinting to that expectation and beyond. At their best, there didn't appear to be a team anywhere that could stop them.

Chapter Nine

GRADUATION

The regular season still had a handful of games remaining, and the Celtics had a surprise. They'd been presented with an assignment sheet of questions, so to speak, and they'd finished their work early.

Way back in July, there were a variety of unknowns about the Big Three. The cautious logic then was that it might take a while for the players to lose their previous identities and create new, unified ones.

Who'd be the one to demand the final shot of a close game? How would they get beyond the way they were raised in the league, three number one franchise players suddenly repositioning themselves into a drama-free one-two-three? Who would set the policies on the team and, realistically, run the room? How would they incorporate the young starters, Rajon Rondo and Kendrick Perkins? And Doc . . . would they trust him to manage and motivate them, the most talented trio he'd ever had on his side?

No one predicted that all questions would be answered so soon—and answered with power and precision.

Maybe it happened because they ignored all the rules. There was no awkward period during which someone saw a problem but didn't know how to verbalize it. No, they'd taken care of that the first week of training camp in Rome. Paul Pierce and some other players had been talking while Doc Rivers was trying to emphasize a point in the huddle.

"Yo, Paul!" Garnett bellowed. "Let's pay attention on this, all right?" Pierce did, and so did everyone else. And so it was: They'd be the stars who would call each other out as needed. The rest of the team took notice.

Or it could have been those film sessions after rare losses. The Celtics had been impossible to classify through fifty games, entering mid-February with a 41–9 record. In all those wins, they were often confusing for opponents: They were both rousing offense and stifling defense, and so it was hard to just press down and control the element that energized them; it was strands of everything. But after those first fifty, they stumbled into their longest losing streak of the season: three games. The coaches would try to highlight a correction on film or at practice, and they'd hear voices louder than theirs.

"Coach, Coach," Garnett would interrupt, "blow the motherfucking whistle. We gotta get this shit right." He'd call himself out, rookies, veterans. It didn't matter. Pierce would chime in with something similar, and then everyone else would get that message, too: *When we stink, we bluntly name our condition and personalize it if necessary.*

Right after their slump, they defended again and won again. They went to Los Angeles and made a bad Clippers team look worse than normal, allowing just 76 points. Then it was back home to Boston against LeBron James and the Cavaliers. Cleveland was the fourth-best team in the conference in the spring of 2008, which meant that a second-round postseason matchup with the Celtics was inevitable. In their last regular-season fight with Cleveland, the Celtics didn't disguise their strategy against the twenty-three-year-old star. What they wanted to do was send waves of defenders at him, forcing him either to shoot jumpers with hands in his face or pass the ball to his less explosive teammates.

He made just 7 of 24 shots during a 5-point Celtics win.

While Garnett arrived in Boston with an impeccable reputation as a defender, he exceeded his rep. His teammates and coaches realized that he was the embodiment of their new defensive spirit and easily the best defensive player in basketball. He was favored to win the league's Defensive Player of the Year award, although the Celtics believed that his ability to transform the style and psyche of the team was MVP-worthy.

What the league saw from the Celtics was the defensive bedrock, because that was obvious. But there were more dimensions than that. The Ubuntu ethic filled the team more than anyone could have imagined. They all got it.

Just two years earlier, the top bench player, James Posey, had been a starting player on Miami's championship team. He wasn't going to start in Boston unless someone got hurt, and that was all right with him. He became the unofficial player-coach of the group, and the players looked forward to his routine: Every game he stood near the pregame huddle and delivered a bear hug and personal word of encouragement for each starter before they took the court. That was the expectation. Every game.

Everyone who entered the green-and-white circle strengthened it. An outsider would have called BS on the whole operation because it either had to be a fantasy or unsustainable. This was still corporate culture, not the welcome innocence and warmth of amateur basketball. A closer look, though, would help explain it. There was nothing warm about the atmosphere. Warm wouldn't have worked.

It was hot.

You could see it during practices, with players challenging each other to be better and more attentive. Garnett's presence elevated

Pierce's practice game and his overall concentration. He'd call out anyone at any time, the medical staff included. Once, during a buffet, KG was offended that a team doctor prepared a plate before any player did. Unacceptable. He chopped the plate out of the doctor's hand, food flying through the air before falling on the floor.

"Players first!" he reminded.

You could see it late at night, when most people were long gone from the practice facility. A light would be on in an office, and Tom Thibodeau would be in there going over his notes and studying film.

"What are you doing here right now?" reserve Leon Powe once asked Thibs, who was there at around two a.m. The coach could have asked the same question. Instead he said, "I gotta get that work in, Leon. Hey, you out there working on your slides? Your rotations? Put that work in. We can always get better."

Ray Allen felt it, too. He liked most of it but not all. He'd incorporated dribbling in front of his locker as part of his pregame routine. He'd done it for several years. But early in the season, KG was annoyed by it. They'd argued over personal rights and locker room ownership in front of the entire team. Back and forth they went, until Allen decided to concede. It was just one more small sacrifice in a season full of them.

As the playoffs began, with the Celtics entering with a league-best sixty-six wins, the players paid more attention to the spotlight that shined at their practice facility. It lit up a space where a banner would be, and the light was a constant reminder: None of this mattered; it was all empty, if they couldn't find a way to deliver a title.

That message was more pronounced than usual in the region. It was April, and New Englanders continued to debate what happened to the Patriots in February. They'd been perfect in the regular season, 16–0, the first team in NFL history to do that. They won their first two playoff games to reach 18–0. Then, as 10-point

Super Bowl favorites, they lost the game and their flawless season. That defeat would sting for years.

With that disappointment still fresh in the local air, it wasn't wise for any Boston sports team to look past any opponent. Though on paper, it seemed to be a comical beginning to the Celtics' title chase. They were the best team in basketball scheduled to face the worst one, the Atlanta Hawks, in round one.

After the first two games of the best-of-seven series, there were no surprises. The Celtics won both games so convincingly that Garnett was rewarded with his late-game Boston Garden video treat: Gino Time, featuring the carefree disco dancers of the 1970s.

It was all smiles and fun in Boston, and as the series shifted to Atlanta, the unspoken goal for the Hawks was to see if they could win a game. To the shock of the entire league, they won two. Somehow, a series between a great team and a bad one was tied 2–2.

Rivers was angry, and he gave the media a clue of how he felt when he said, "This city is tough to beat." He was more specific with his coaching staff: "Atlanta and [notorious gentleman's club] Magic City is kicking our ass right now. These guys are tired. They're exhausted. They should have done away with Atlanta by now. They're fucking around."

Their return to the Garden for game five made everyone forget what happened in Atlanta. They overwhelmed the young Hawks, who didn't have a single player in his thirties, with their defense and intelligence. A trend was beginning to reveal itself in the series, and it was good for the Celtics' tomorrow but not necessarily for their next several weeks. It was simple: When the Celtics were at home, they won, and won big; when they traveled to Atlanta, they played just okay and lost close games.

Since they'd earned the right to play all game sevens at home, they'd be all right if it came to that against the Hawks. But that was missing the point. Why would the thought of a game seven against the Hawks even be required? And with this level of play, a more talented team than the Hawks would be able to walk into the Garden and prevail. After the 25-point win in game five, the Celtics tried to close out the series in Atlanta.

Once again, they failed to take them seriously and win the game.

Following a 3-point loss in game six, Rivers didn't say much to his team. He didn't say much to anyone, including one of the co-owners of the team. When the team got back to Boston, Danny Ainge called Rivers.

"I sent you a text. You didn't respond. Wyc wants to have a meeting."

Wyc Grousbeck was like every other Celtics fan in Boston, puzzled that such a great team could be in such a vulnerable position.

"I'll pass," Rivers said.

"Doc, he really wants to talk," Ainge insisted.

"Danny, I need you to handle this. I don't want to be in a meeting, before game seven, talking to Wyc about who knows what."

Rivers could have said it because he knew what would happen at home, with the Defensive Player of the Year on his team, flanked by two other All-Stars who were sick of their seasons ending in early May. They didn't have to worry about it on a Sunday afternoon, May 4, at the Garden. The game started at one o'clock. Twenty minutes after one, everyone knew who was going to win it.

This was one of those post-film-session games. Those unfiltered reviews during which Garnett or Pierce stood in front of the group, apologized for how awful they had been in abandoning defensive integrity, and vowed to change starting tomorrow. This was the tomorrow of those film-session confessions.

The Hawks shot 30 percent in the first quarter and managed just 10 points in the second. If their paths to the basket weren't blocked, their shots at the basket were. They couldn't find open passing lanes or places to dribble. It was as if everyone in the building was KG, either swarming them on the court or yelling at them, eighteen-thousand-plus, wherever they went in the arena.

It wasn't close. The Celtics won 99–65.

For the first time in his career, Pierce was set to play a high-stakes series against LeBron James.

For James, his eyes had been opened by the previous season's finals. He'd received a two-week crash course in modern basketball history. He learned what dynamic players and coaching staffs can do to teams that have one all-time great and no credible number two or three option. James was the best player in last year's final round, but it didn't matter because San Antonio was able to restrict each of his teammates and therefore win the series easily.

James's 30 points per game led the league, and he led the Cavs in rebounds and assists. If the same cast of players had been led by someone other than James, the team would have struggled to make the postseason. Still, after what they had been through against the Hawks, the Celtics didn't take the Cavs lightly.

The Cavs were not the Hawks, but the series began similarly. At home, the Celtics had lost six games all season and just two since late March.

Game one was an exaggeration of what the Celtics had done to the Cavs in their final regular-season meeting. Thibs, the defensive strategist, had a game plan designed to turn James into a jump shooter. The Celtics' help defense was relentless. And since KG was so versatile on defense, Thibs could use any technique he wanted, knowing that a seven-footer capable of playing three different positions was his defensive captain.

James wasn't ready for it in the first game. He was so out of sorts, so un-LeBron, that he nearly submitted an ugly and impossible quadruple-double. He had 12 points, 9 rebounds, 9 assists, and an unsightly 10 turnovers. The league's leading scorer made two shots from the field, 2 for 18. It was remarkable to watch as the nervous Garden crowd continued to wait for the real James to show up. He never did. The Celtics won, 76–72.

The plan for the second game was the same, and once again, James would have had more success closing his eyes and heaving the ball at the hoop. There was nothing fluid about his shot or his game. He followed his 2 for 18 with a 6 for 24. He went back to Cleveland with dismal shooting on his mind, 8 for 42, and his team facing a two-game deficit.

How strange. Shutting down LeBron was not in the plan; that would be foolish. You don't shut down the top scorer in the league. Until you do.

But game three exposed the obvious flaw in the Thibodeau Technique, and the Cavs took advantage of it during a jolting 32–13 start to the game. How'd they do it? Easy. Players not named James made shots. Cleveland had a fun night in a resounding 108–84 win.

It was Cleveland winning again in game four, the tension and animosity heightening so that Pierce gave James a hard foul near the baseline, a play that carried them both into the first couple of rows of baseline seats. Pierce saw and heard a familiar voice screaming at him. It was Gloria James, mother of LeBron, taking offense at what she perceived as a dirty play on her son. She got close to Pierce and Garnett and had words for both of them.

James didn't want Mom to become a part of this.

"Sit your ass down!" he yelled.

Once again he'd gotten himself and his teammates involved with 21 points, 13 assists, and 6 rebounds.

That didn't happen in Boston, as a trio of Celtics—Garnett, Pierce, and Rondo—all scored at least 20 points. The frustrating takeaway for Cleveland in that game five was that the Cavs had built a 14-point second-quarter lead . . . only to see it reduced to just 3 four minutes later. They lost game five, 96–89. If form were to follow after the Celtics win, a loss in Cleveland awaited. Which it did, an ugly 74–69 Cleveland victory setting up a game seven showdown at the Garden exactly two weeks after the last one.

Pierce wasn't James, but he'd played some good games against him. Rivers likened James in the open court to former Cleveland Browns fullback Jim Brown. When you see someone that big and fast coming at you, the instinct is to duck. But Pierce didn't. In fact, he believed that his array of shots and creative paths to the basket often gave James trouble. He felt good on this day, hours before the game, and it extended to the court.

The series, even at its deciding game, was unpredictable. James, for example, was making an impact even if he'd shot just 33 percent from the field in the first six games. Pierce's offensive numbers were down, but he was a big part of the reason James's shots hadn't been easy. Allen was the only member of the Big Three who looked lost. He'd been crowded on some shots and wide open on others. He missed jumpers and 3-pointers and shot 32 percent overall. The only sign that Allen, the real Allen, still remained in there was free throws. He'd missed one of his twenty attempts at the line through six games.

A sellout Garden crowd, peppered with stars, didn't know which player would step up in game seven. All they knew was that the Celtics were 7–0 at home in the playoffs, and they'd find a way for the streak to continue. They sat in anticipation, along with Patriots quarterback Tom Brady and teammates Randy Moss, Vince Wilfork, and Kevin Faulk. They were all going to get a payoff on this spring afternoon. While the first six games offered no early clues for what would come later, the seventh game did.

In the first quarter, Pierce did all the scoring that helped build Boston's lead to 12. His first basket was a left-side jumper, and his second one came from the right. He hit a 3 and nodded to Moss and Wilfork, under the basket, and the two pros vigorously nodded back. Pierce had been in Boston for a full decade now, and those who knew his game recognized what this was: This was going to be the Pierce who couldn't be slowed because everything he had, the long and short of it, was available to him.

But if Pierce was the one building the lead, James was the determined antagonist slicing it away. Great players, and he was that, figure these things out. James's shot was off early, as he missed four of his first five. He got going by making a layup that ended a five-and-a-half-minute Cavs scoring drought. He followed that with a drive in which he navigated around a screened Pierce, dribbled into the lane, and then powered in a left-handed layup over Garnett and Perkins. Next possession: He went in for an outrageous baseline dunk, only to be stopped by Allen's desperate grab of his muscled right arm. Two made free throws, and the Cavs were right back in it.

This was what the game was going to be. There would be no runaway. There would be no blowout. There would be fine moments of team basketball, but within that team structure, two players were in line to decide who advanced to the conference finals.

For Cleveland, it was James. For the Celtics, it was Pierce. James had 23 in the first half, and all his makes felt like emergencies. The Cavs were down 10 at the half, and without James's production, the deficit would have doubled. Pierce had 26, and if you watched his expression—controlled, calm, expected—his intricate choreography would have been missed. Included in the display was a spin move, leading into a fifteen-foot jumper. There was a split of a double-team, punctuated with a left-hand finish at the rim. And for a shot that foreshadowed the game's final minute, there was a score that bounced high off the rim and then into the basket.

"What do you think?" Thibs asked Rivers at halftime. "I mean, LeBron's on fire."

"I think we keep doing what we're doing. Give him credit: He's made some unbelievable shots."

Pierce versus LeBron. "The Truth" versus "the King." It was the highest level of play, where leads were temporary and, in the moment, every spectacular play seemed perfectly reasonable. The overall third-quarter energy, though, was something Rivers didn't like. He saw the 10-point halftime lead trimmed to 3, and he called his team out during a break.

"Did you think they were going to give it to you?" he asked. "Did you think it was going to be easy? Every loose ball, every fifty-fifty play, they're winning it."

Pierce, of course, responded to the challenge by making a 3 to put the Celtics up 6. James went to the other end of the court and calmly hit a jumper to cut it to 4.

Next, it was Pierce: a jumper, points 30 and 31, to put the Celtics up 6.

Then, it was James: a 3, points 28, 29, and 30, to cut the lead in half.

The back and forth was inescapable, and both players knew it. Going into the fourth quarter, the Celtics were ahead by 5. Pierce had 35 points, and James had 32. They walked toward each other before the final twelve minutes began and bumped fists. Neither could fathom losing a game like this. No, they both thought they'd do enough to get their team to the next round. But it was hard to ignore what the other guy was doing. Respect.

At some point, James understood, the back and forth couldn't be sufficient. As much as he continued to score, the Celtics' lead remained in the 3- to 5-point range. There were six minutes left, and someone—him, Delonte West, Joe Smith—needed to do something dramatic to disrupt the pattern.

Pierce: a pull-up, right over James, to make it 83–77. He now had 39.

James: another 3, just to keep it close at 83–80. He now had 40.

The break that James was looking for happened four minutes later, with two minutes and twenty seconds to play. Following a Zydrunas Ilgauskas basket to make it 89–86, at the 2:24 mark, James remembered that Pierce showed too much of the ball when he was going to pass it off. So he waited for the exposure and then went in for the steal. Before Pierce could react, James was at the other end of the court dunking.

It was 89–88, Celtics.

They hadn't played a game this close at the Garden in months. There was discomfort in the crowd when Garnett missed a layup, and the ball was in James's hands with one hundred seconds to play. Anything could happen now. The dunk had upped his total on the afternoon to 44. If he got to 50, especially in regulation, the Celtics would surely lose. James missed a 3-pointer that would have scared everyone in the building if it had gone down. Instead, the crowd was delighted with a pleasant shock on the next possession.

The newest Celtic was PJ Brown, a six-foot-eleven forward who'd considered himself retired at thirty-eight years old, having not re-signed with the Bulls in 2007. But he was in New Orleans during All-Star weekend walking down the street when he heard a voice from the passenger seat of a car. "PJ! We need you!" It was Pierce, head out the window now, making a recruiting pitch to the then free agent. Shortly after that, he was in Boston, another veteran to provide defense and rebounding.

And unlikely clutch shooting. It didn't make sense to pay a lot of attention to Brown in a game like this. There was no telling what he'd do when the ball swung his way with one minute and twenty-one seconds left and an open twenty-footer waiting for him. *PJ! We need you!* He took the shot, and it was a beauty. There was a Garden eruption as he headed back to the bench with his right hand in the air. His teammates danced and smiled. The last man into Club Ubuntu had made the biggest shot of the season so far, but there were still sixty seconds to play: 91–88.

Cavs coach Mike Brown was sick over that shot. And it wasn't because he didn't expect it. He'd come into the series with two big thoughts about Boston: They were physical, and he never felt comfortable when they went to the bench. *All those guys can hurt you*, he thought. That shot from PJ Brown, of all people, showed just how deep the Celtics were.

Under the Cleveland basket, the six-foot-eight Posey became entangled with seven-foot-three center Ilgauskas. In the fight for the ball, neither of them could possess it, leading to a jump ball. While Posey knew he likely would lose the jump, he saw what was around him. To his right was Pierce, anticipating a tap to James.

That was what happened, and James was late in his response to it. He made a basic mistake. He didn't box out on the jump ball. By the time he recovered from this lapse, the ball rolling toward midcourt, Pierce had inside position and was on the floor scrambling for it. This was going to be something for film study, a championship effort that brought Ainge, the ex-coach, out of his seat and into applause. As soon as Pierce got the ball, he and his teammates called timeout.

There was so much about the team and the organization on that one play. This was Red's *Get the ball; don't give up the ball.* This was

Celtics basketball and knowing every game situation. This was why the original Big Three had success: That team, Ainge's team, was stacked with players who became general managers, head coaches, assistant coaches, analysts. They played the game and thought it through, too.

Pierce clutched the ball and screamed as loud as he could. In the last half-dozen years, there'd been nothing as important or as gratifying as this. When Allen scored just his third and fourth points of the game, at the line, the Celtics were ahead by 5 with eighteen seconds remaining.

Even in those final seconds, James wouldn't let it go. With his team down 6 at the ten-second mark, he found a wide-open teammate in the corner for a 3. Made it. Eight seconds left and, remarkably, the Cavs still had life.

Pierce was fouled intentionally, and he went to the line to secure the game. His first free-throw attempt made him and the Garden crowd groan. It was off-line, a brickish attempt that struck the iron and went high into the air. There was a half second to think that this was a miss and the second one had to be a make to prevent what surely would have been a tying James 3. But in the next half second, the crowd was on its feet and Pierce couldn't contain a wide smile. The ball dropped in. It was a good bounce, good game, and good day.

Pierce had unashamedly asked for games like this in the national spotlight. LeBron had forty-five, he had forty-one, and the best basketball was still to come. Just four teams—the Lakers, Spurs, Pistons, and Celtics—still had something to play for.

Yes, the Celtics.

They were finally moving on.

Chapter Ten

ANYTHING IS POSSIBLE

His boxing videos were popular with the players, so Doc Rivers continued to show them to the Celtics between playoff games. A fan of the fight game, particularly of Muhammad Ali, the coach made sure that any montage he shared stuck to a similar theme.

He never showed the ones where Ali's opponents seemed to be lulled by the promotional hype and rhymes. "The Greatest" would go into his familiar *Float like a butterfly, sting like a bee, his hand can't hit what his eyes can't see* act, and some awestruck brawler would be psyched out before entering the ring.

Those weren't the ones that spoke to Rivers. He was more of a Thrilla in Manila type. Ali versus Joe Frazier. A scheduled fifteen-round fight that went fourteen, a fight where the winner—Ali—said that it was the closest to death he'd come. He'd said that he wanted to quit, but Frazier's corner conceded first.

Those fights were amazing. Rivers could use them to tease out lessons for each player, from the Big Three to the last man in. He could also use them as reminders for himself and Paul Pierce.

They'd seen a lot in their four Boston years together, and at times it was hard to imagine that they'd stand in the spotlight when it was over, with a referee holding up their fatigued arms in victory.

They'd both had long conversations with Danny Ainge about leaving Boston. They'd both been picked apart, and often slammed, for their supposed lack of an essential thing.

Their relationship had swayed between similarities and extremes. Rivers pointed to their joint October birthday as an explanation for their occasional conflicts. Their birthday was also their annual signal for a remodeled Celtics roster. Starting when Rivers took the job in April 2004 to where he was in May 2008, just two players remained: Kendrick Perkins and Pierce.

Here they were now in a proud city whose residents understood the life of absorbing hits, literal and figurative. This was Detroit on a Friday evening, minutes before the start of game six of the conference finals. The Celtics, ahead 3–2 on the Pistons in the series, were just a win away from going to the NBA Finals.

So many new questions had been answered in the last two weeks. Even though the Celtics captured a game seven against LeBron in the previous round, they did it without winning a road game. Between Atlanta and Cleveland, they were 0–6. Could they win on the road? Yes. When they needed to.

They learned that about themselves when they were finally put in that position. They won the first game of the Detroit series only to lose the next one in Boston. The consequences immediately became stark: If they couldn't win on the road, they couldn't go to the NBA Finals. They went to Detroit, won game three, and regained control of the series.

This entire Boston-Detroit matchup was played before a backdrop of freakish connections to the past. Some of those connections went back four years. For others, it was twenty.

Kevin Garnett had a bond with Flip Saunders, the Pistons coach. Like KG, Saunders left Minnesota for a better situation in the Eastern Conference. He landed with veteran players who didn't need to be taught to win because they'd already done that. His role was to steward them back to the finals. It was a good job but also a time-sensitive one. He had more wins during his three years in Detroit than he did during any three-year period in Minnesota, and no one in Detroit gave a damn about that. They wanted to taste more of the finals, where they'd been and Flip still hadn't. This might be his last chance. Flip loved KG and vice versa, but this was the first time they'd be on the same playoff court knowing that if one of them advanced, the other would be left behind.

There was a generational element to the series as well. Boston and Detroit used to fight in the playoffs, seemingly every year, in the late 1980s. Two of the original Big Three—Larry Bird and Robert Parish—actually traded punches with Pistons center Bill Laimbeer. The Celtics won the conference in '87, and the Pistons won the rematch in '88. The Detroit win was significant because it was an official transfer of power. Boston had been to four consecutive NBA Finals, blocking Detroit and everyone else in the East. The win meant it was time for the Pistons to do what the Celtics did, winning two titles in four straight finals appearances.

In 2008, the inverse was forty-eight minutes away from being official. Boston had to get through Detroit, grind and wrestle and—there was no way around it—fight their way through Detroit until they could be considered the best of the East.

Rivers was always looking for an edge, and he thought he found one as he walked into the arena several hours before tip-off. He and Jeff Twiss, the Celtics' longtime vice president of media services, saw it at the same time. Chauncey Billups, Rip Hamilton, and Tayshaun Prince walked out of general manager Joe Dumars's office.

"This series is over," Rivers said. "Three players coming out of the GM's office and the head coach isn't in there? That's not good."

Twiss smiled and said, "I hope you're right, Boss."

These proud Pistons may have been splintering a bit, but they were still going to make the Celtics scratch for it. Billups, perhaps the strongest point guard in the league, wore out young Rajon Rondo in the first half, scoring half of Detroit's points. In the third quarter, Billups and Hamilton continued to push their teammates, and it appeared that yet another game seven showdown in Boston was inevitable.

Nothing went right.

Pierce made a 3 with a defender leaning and falling all over him, and the Boston bench celebrated, thinking that a possible 4-point play was seconds away. But official Bennett Salvatore saw something that no one in the building did—an offensive foul—and the Celtics walked away from the possession with nothing. Of course, the Pistons answered with a basket. It had become that type of game.

With ten minutes to play, Detroit led 70–60.

Rivers watched with his arms folded and began to instinctively nod. This was it. Right now. If they had it, now was the time to show it. They turned the next ninety seconds into their own biopic. It included the Big Three, but not exclusively, because that was the most accurate description of who they were.

Rondo made a floater. James Posey blocked a shot. Pierce got into the lane and found Perkins, who dunked and was fouled. KG went to post up and forced Rasheed Wallace to commit his fifth personal foul, a sequence that sent Wallace to the bench. As one camera followed Wallace, he threw a towel over it and yelled, "Get that fucking camera out of my face."

Garnett made two free throws. The Pistons traveled. A Celtic exclaimed from the bench: "We gotta take this shit—it's ours!" KG hit a turnaround. Perkins got a steal. Detroit went silent.

That 10-point lead was gone. The game was slipping away from Detroit, obviously, but the wise watchers of these things knew what this was. This was that power transfer. Teams are never ready to hand it over, even when their time is up, so they furiously grip it until someone hungrier and more talented rips it away.

It was happening. And quickly. A beautiful step-back jumper by Pierce, and due to the desperate situation, Wallace was back in the game . . . missing a layup. KG, at least eight inches taller than his buddy and old teammate Billups, shot over him and scored. A pull-up jumper by Rondo . . .

The Celtics were ecstatic, rising, and free. They could admit that now. The Big Three, and their thirty-two collective years of NBA experience, could exhale. They'd beaten themselves up at times, trying to understand why they'd never made the finals. Now that they were on their way there, they could appreciate that the self-doubt may have been one of their strengths. It made them all work harder.

"Yeah, baby," Rivers said as he hugged Pierce. He gave him a glance that only the two of them could grasp. There were tears in that glance, but they'd be released later. Defiance had to come first.

"Hell yeah," Pierce said, hugging back. They held each other for a few seconds, smiling about where they were going and where they had been. Pierce needed his coach to hear what he was saying, and how he was saying it.

"*We* did this, Coach," Pierce said into his ear, hugging him again. "*We* did it. No one thought we'd be in this position."

He wanted Rivers to know that he'd heard him during these four years together. He heard him that day Rivers told him to move the ball, and he heard the message of unselfishness on the duck boat.

They were their own team, eager to escape the shadows of Celtics history so they could solidify their own memories. Still, they had one more throwback to the 1980s before they walked out of the arena in suburban Detroit.

The Lakers had finished off the Spurs in the Western Conference Finals the night before, and so Pierce instigated a "Beat LA" chant in the locker room. It was ironic because Pierce, the LA kid, grew up loving the Lakers and hating the Celtics. He was also chanting for something that needed to be remastered and remixed from its 1982 origins.

Back then, "Beat LA" was a gracious Boston Garden crowd's response to losing game seven of the conference finals. They hated the 76ers, for sure, but they hated the Western opponent—the Lakers—even more. They'd root for anyone to beat the Lakers.

The power of the 2008 Celtics was that "Beat LA" was a word of encouragement *for* them and *from* them. They knew they could say it and do it themselves. In 1982, the Sixers actually didn't beat LA. They lost in six games and had to wait until the following season to beat the Lakers.

That wasn't an option for these Celtics. They all felt as if they'd spent enough time dreaming and hoping and waiting. It was time to take on the Lakers and follow the instructions of the chant.

It may have been a function of playing in the East, but the Celtics' NBA-best sixty-six wins didn't position them as favorites against the Lakers. Nationally, Los Angeles was given extra credit for everything in its profile: the top seed in a tougher conference; league MVP Kobe Bryant; and head coach Phil Jackson, who already owned nine championship rings.

Danny Ainge thought it might have been the Atlanta series, too. The backstory didn't matter to people who hadn't watched the Celtics closely all year. They saw them pushed to a seventh game by the worst team in the playoffs.

Before the series started, Ainge asked Lakers assistant coach Tex Winter what scared him about the Celtics.

"I'm not sure Kobe can handle Ray Allen," Winter answered.

No one, outside of the Lakers' coaching staff, was thinking about some of the difficult matchups the Lakers faced against the Celtics. All discussion of Bryant was about his offense, not whom he would have to guard.

Every chance he got to speak with his players, Rivers found a way to download a few of his favorites. He praised Bryant and his 28 points per game just as he had praised LeBron and his 30. But he was quick to note that the Celtics' strength was in their depth and trust. He never passed on a chance to say what he felt was obvious: *We're better than they are.*

Whether with his players or staff, Rivers never wavered in his belief. "There's no way the Lakers are tougher than us," he said. "One game, maybe, because they have the ace of spades: Kobe. But in a seven-game series? There is no way physically that they can take the heat that we're going to bring. Offensively, they're pretty good. Defensively, they're not a great defensive team, even though the numbers say they are. We should be able to get whatever we want on offense."

In the opening half of Boston's first finals game in twenty-one years, there was a nervousness and timidity to everyone in the building, even with players and coaches who had been on this stage before.

It might have been nerves that sent Pierce first to the floor midway through the third quarter and then, stunningly, into the arms of his teammates seconds later. It was a close game, with the Lakers ahead by 4. Pierce, in a cluster of players, went up for a rebound and had his right knee or ankle bumped by Kendrick Perkins.

Pierce screamed and then grabbed his knee. He thought a ligament had snapped, and although team doctors didn't make any quick diagnoses, they told him to stay down. Seconds later he was in the arms of reserves Brian Scalabrine and Tony Allen, followed closely by a group of team employees and . . . a wheelchair. For Celtics' fans, the circumstantial evidence was overwhelming. Pierce was grimacing in that wheelchair, pointing to his knee, as the group hurried him to the locker room. It was there on the ESPN cameras for all to see. Depressing.

Team trainer Eddie Lacerte quickly told Rivers that Pierce was out. This was not the situation for follow-up questions, so Lacerte and Rivers had a miscommunication. Rivers thought he meant Pierce was out for the season with a torn ACL. Lacerte meant that he was out for the game.

Neither was true.

The Garden crowd continued to watch the game and, now, their phones. *Any updates on Pierce?* Was this it? The Celtics had torn through the regular season, survived the Eastern playoffs, and been brought to the doorstep against the Lakers, only to lose Pierce?

It didn't take long for the dire thoughts to be replaced by cynical ones. Just a few minutes of game time later, Pierce could be seen bouncing out of the tunnel, shouting and clapping his hands. This was the Pierce Revival Meeting. He had been scared, truly thinking he had torn something. His shouting and clapping was for that more than anything else.

The confusion was cleared up now: Rivers looked at Lacerte, Lacerte gave the coach a thumbs-up, and Brian McKeon, the team doctor, told Rivers that Pierce was structurally sound. There was a standing ovation from the crowd, back-to-back 3-pointers, a game one win, and some disbelief from the Lakers. One minute in the third quarter the guy is crumpled near the baseline. By the end of the third, he'd posted a 15-point quarter.

Rivers was asked about it after the game, and he answered all questions without awareness of one key detail: the wheelchair. He hadn't seen it. When he was asked a question about Pierce's theatrics, he thought it was a bizarre suggestion of Pierce faking an injury. Why would he do that? Once he got home and watched the game highlights, he finally saw it for the first time. So did Thibs, who called him.

"Can you believe it?" Thibs said, laughing. "I didn't know that he was in a goddamn wheelchair!"

"I didn't either," Rivers said. "I didn't even know we had a wheelchair. Where'd the wheelchair come from?"

They had to call Dr. McKeon and get him in on the laughs, too.

"Doc McKeon, where in the hell did the wheelchair come from?" Rivers prodded.

"We always have one back there. I'm telling you, I thought he tore his knee."

It had gone from a humbling moment to a hilarious one. Once Rivers got the scope of everything that happened and how it looked to the Lakers on TV, he had to admit, "Yeah, that would have pissed me off, too."

The story got a lot of attention in the two days off before game two. For the Celtics, relief. For the Lakers, more eye rolls.

Late in game two, the series took another turn that seemed strange at the time. The Celtics were crushing the Lakers with just seven minutes left in the game. The feeling-out phase was over, and now the teams were just playing ball. It wasn't going well for the Lakers, down by 24.

The Celtics were going where they wanted, and doing what they wanted, all over the court. Rondo had been criticized several times during the postseason, but he was a hitmaker in game two. Each pass he threw found a hot hand, and he was stacking assists at video-game rates. Leon Powe sprung from the bench and attempted more free throws, thirteen, than all of the Lakers combined. He had 21 points in fifteen minutes of work. Pierce's knee looked just fine; he was perfect on four 3-pointers and also had 8 assists.

What was there not to like with a 95–71 lead? It was a party. There was still nothing to worry about one minute later with the lead at 21. Or a minute later when it was 16.

Right?

Even after Bryant made a long 3 with three minutes left, the Celtics were still up by 11. And Rondo had been fouled, giving him an opportunity to extend the lead with at least one made free throw. But when Rondo missed them both, Rivers started to feel that sickness. He did believe that the Celtics were better; what he didn't mean to imply was that they were so much better than the Lakers that they could relax against them.

"Don't let them get comfortable," he warned during a timeout. "And I'm not just talking about this game. I don't want them to get comfortable for the next game. Especially their role-players."

It was too late for all of that. This game, an easy win a few minutes earlier, was going to be a struggle until the end. With the Celtics up by 9 with less than two minutes to play, Pierce had the ball stolen from him, and Sasha Vujacic hit a 3 to cut the lead to 6. Pierce threw a sloppy pass on the next possession, and that turned into a Vladimir Radmanovic dunk. Four-point game. After Rondo missed a jumper, Bryant made two free throws with thirty-eight seconds left. Two-point game.

Finally, Pierce and James Posey were able to make their free throws, as well as a block by Pierce, to secure a 6-point win. While the Celtics were officially halfway to the championship, they'd also shown some vulnerabilities in game two. Indeed, they had given those role-players confidence.

Everyone knew the Lakers were going to adjust in LA. It would begin with Jackson using the off days to point out free-throw discrepancies. He'd bring attention to the inherent craziness of a world in which Powe—whose name he intentionally mispronounced to make it rhyme with "wow"—could get nearly twice as many attempts as Bryant. If his lobbying worked, and it usually did, it would set the tone for Bryant and his teammates in game three.

Perfect plan: The Lakers won game three by 6, Pierce shot a miserable 2 for 14 from the field, and Bryant attempted eighteen free throws, more than the Celtics' entire starting five—and sixteen more than Leon Powe.

The Lakers had played nine playoff games in their downtown LA home and won all of them. It was all so routine there, with the best seats occupied by those who were either on the Hollywood Walk of Fame or destined to be there soon. Musicians and actors and comedians and influencers, all there to see their favorite NBA creative, Bryant.

He elevated in that environment, seeming to inhale all the energy and improvisational skill surrounding him. Bryant was tough for the Celtics to contain anywhere and nearly impossible in LA. He was the biggest reason there hadn't been a hint of disappointment in the postseason at Staples Center. If the Celtics couldn't deliver the Lakers their first home loss, they'd return to Boston needing to win two consecutive games for the title.

After the first half of game four, there was nothing that suggested a trend change. One quarter in, and the Lakers already held the record for the largest lead—21 points—after one quarter in NBA Finals history.

Halfway through the second, the lead bulging to 24, and still not a hoop from Bryant. This was, this was . . . this was something. Yes, that's what Kris Rivers was trying to say as she texted her husband while she watched his team. She knew he wasn't reading them and probably wouldn't until postgame. But she'd watched him play and listened to him analyze and coach for twenty-five years now. Sometimes they sounded alike. As she sat next to their four children at Staples, she began firing off texts every time she saw something from the Celtics she didn't like:

"This team is soft."

"You guys need to move out of the Four Seasons and into a Motel Six."

"My God! Move the ball! Tell your team to move the ball!"

"Play some defense."

They were down 18 at the half, 58–40. Bryant had run into foul trouble and had just 3 of those 58 points. Applying basic logic and history, that wasn't going to continue in the second half.

"We've got to relax and just play," an assuring Rivers told the team.

Nope. No relaxing. No good basketball. They got a combination to the face in the third: Bryant finally scored from the field, and the lead was growing. It was 20, 68–48, five minutes into the quarter.

Rivers scanned his bench. He was looking for answers and taking suggestions. Rondo, who had been so active and confident in game two, seemed to be in a haze. He'd been replaced by Eddie House. Pierce asked to guard Bryant in the second half, knowing that he wouldn't need any defensive help to slow Bryant down. If Bryant started to go off, Pierce was determined that it would happen against great defense.

Gradually, elements of game two in Boston seeped into game four in LA. Then, the Celtics nearly blew a 24-point lead in the fourth quarter. Here, it was happening earlier. A 3-point play by Pierce cut the LA lead to 9. There was a stirring in the crowd. House made a 3, and now the advantage was only 6.

During a break, Rivers looked at Garnett and said, "Never stop believing, baby."

The almost retiree, PJ Brown, the big shotmaker against Cleveland, dunked, and they were down 2. With just over ten minutes left, a play was called in the huddle for Powe. He was surprised by it, and so were the veterans.

"You better make this shot," Garnett told him.

It was a post-up against Lamar Odom, and Powe put in a bank shot to tie it with ten minutes to play.

Jack Nicholson, the devout Lakers fan and Rivers's golfing buddy, was seated near the Celtics' bench. He could hear the actor freaking out. "Oh boy, oh boy . . ."

The Celtics had been given too much time. When they went down by 4 halfway through the fourth, they were confident because they had enough space to make it up. That's what happened two minutes later when a House hoop gave them their first lead of the game. It went from Lakers blowout, to Celtics playing competitively, to LA shock and desperation, all on the same night.

What happened? How was it that a Garnett hoop had the Celtics up by 5? In this building? With these stakes? It's one thing to *almost* give back a 24-point lead. It's akin to *almost* winning a game. But the Lakers had actually done it. They'd given up that lead, lost the game, and effectively the series.

"Doc, we're dead men walking, aren't we?" Nicholson said.

The coach didn't want to be cocky, and he didn't want his team to be that, either. But there was no way the Lakers were going to win three straight against them.

"Yes," he answered his friend. "You are."

No one in NBA Finals history had trailed by 24 and won that game. No finals team had ever been down 3–1 in a series and come back to win it. Pierce walked toward the locker room in his hometown, shouting. "That's how you fight," he said. "That's how you do it, Cs."

Down the hall, Bryant was succinct.

"We wet the bed," he said. "It was one of those bad ones that can't be covered up."

Rivers checked his texts and saw a series of furious ones from his wife, with one at the end of the thread that read:

"I'm sorry. I hope you didn't read any of those texts. Congratulations."

It wasn't surprising that the Lakers managed to win game five, temporarily taking the sting away from their game four collapse. Their next challenge was to go to Boston and beat the Celtics in consecutive games there. Forget about the long-forgotten games in the league's distant history; in 2008, the Celtics didn't lose two games in a row at home.

If they could only make it home. That was the challenge for the Celtics as two planes, a team plane and family plane, waited to depart from Los Angeles on Monday morning. The old Lakers used to be convinced that Red played mind games with them for a competitive advantage, and this had echoes of LA revenge.

The Lakers and Celtics shared the same hangar for their four planes, two for each team. The Celtics watched the two LA planes take off on time in front of them, at eleven a.m. One, two, three hours later, and the Celtics' planes were still in LA. They waited so long that they were all able to watch Tiger Woods, with a left-knee injury, play his entire round during the U.S. Open at Torrey Pines. All the Tiger fans on the team were excited that he'd played his way to a Monday playoff. They were in LA so long that they wondered if they'd see *that* on the plane, too.

They finally landed in Boston just after one a.m. on the day of game six, when they were scheduled to be there around six p.m. the previous day.

Just as Nicholson and Justin Timberlake attended Lakers games as representatives of LA industry, the celebrity attendees at Celtics games spoke to what was at the heart of Boston: sports.

The nonplaying stars of the night were Patriots coach Bill Belichick and a quartet of NBA Finals MVPs who lowered themselves from the rafters and into courtside seats: Bill Russell, John Havlicek, Jo Jo White, and Cedric Maxwell.

The crowd was there long before the game began, creating a persistent buzz. This was KG's kind of crowd, and it had been all year. The Garden was loud, shaking with anticipation. KG was at his locker in a lead-up to the game that was too charged even for him. The team's equipment man, "Johnny Joe" Connors, interrupted him.

"KG, Coach wants to see you in his office."

Minutes later, he was in there, breathing hard and talking fast.

"Wassup, Coach? What you need?"

Rivers had his head down. He could hear the locomotive that was Garnett. He sounded like a boxer midworkout, giving his best to the heavy bag.

"Coach," KG repeated. "You need something?"

Rivers looked up briefly.

"I'll be with you in just a minute, Kevin."

He put his head back down again, writing a few notes. He waited two or three minutes for KG's shifting and superpowered breathing to slow down a bit. Then he looked up.

"I'm good," Rivers said. "You good?"

KG got it.

"Thank you. I needed that."

This was the night for a championship.

Rivers decided to go with a different pregame speech. He knew that the malfunctioning planes and early-morning arrival threw off schedules. He didn't want the distraction of that, so he went with a blunt, predictive approach. "Guys, tonight we're not going to just win. We're going to win by a lot. We're going to win big. Don't think about just playing; think about dominating and destroying."

Three minutes into the game, Bryant made his own prediction: This was going to game seven. He laughed with a courtside fan and declared, "Not tonight."

He, of all people, should have known better. His opponents were not the Celtic legends, or the Celtic crowd, or even the Celtics he had faced in the previous five games. No, he and the Lakers were the only obstacles separating the Big Three from unqualified success and recognition. No more, *If they only had a championship* . . . No more, *Yeah, but* . . . No more, *good-but-not-great marginalizing* . . .

Russell, the most decorated winner in the sport's history, had befriended Garnett and was so struck by him that he'd made a promise. He told KG that if he didn't win as a Celtic, he'd give Garnett one of his rings. The gesture from the seventy-four-year-old Russell made Garnett want to win it even more.

For Pierce, he'd been in Boston for a decade. He could answer almost every significant question in team history. One thing he didn't know was what it was like to play a game in Boston in mid-June. He didn't know the protocol for a home game, his home game, where the Larry O'Brien Trophy was there, possibly within the grasp of his team.

Ray Allen, the man of ritual and organization, looked at what was before him and tried to put it into its proper slot. It had been a difficult week for his family. His two-year-old son, Walker, had some health issues. When Allen wasn't on a court, he was in a hospital. He'd played game five, gone to the hospital, and taken a red-eye flight back to Boston for game six. This would be a good time to take care of this small compartment, the game, so he could fully devote his time to his family.

These players and their coaches and their fans could feel it. It was one of those nights where the score was just there to confirm the feeling. Back-to-back 3s by the bench guys, House and Posey, put the Celtics up 9. The lead was 11, and the chant was "Ed-dee, Ed-dee . . ." when House ran into the stands for a loose ball. A 14-point cushion and a new chant—"MVP, MVP . . ." for Pierce at the free-throw line.

How high would it go?

It was at 21 when KG swerved into the lane, cupped the ball with one hand, and banked it in. Twenty-three, yes, 23, when Perkins scored on a layup from KG.

They maintained that lead, 23 points, at halftime.

"What do you think?" Wyc Grousbeck asked the man standing next to him at the bar in the Garden lounge. "Are you going to calm me down here?"

The man was Belichick, the Patriots coach who had trained the entire region to be methodical and assume nothing. Even when you're ahead by 23.

"What are you drinking?" Belichick said.

"Tequila."

"All right," the coach said. "Tequila for the whole bar!"

This was Belichick? Grousbeck looked confused. Belichick explained.

"Let's celebrate now. You're winning the championship tonight."

Maybe Bryant's comment about the night was for the Lakers and not the Celtics. They were going to win a championship tonight, for sure. They just had to answer the last two questions of their season: How many points would they win by? And who would they play as they won? KG was Russell. Pierce was Havlicek. Allen was Sam Jones. Rivers and Ainge were both sides of Red Auerbach, coach and executive.

It was wild. They were up by 29 after three, and it was starting to sink in now. Another member of the Patriots, team president Jonathan Kraft, was there with Steve Pagliuca. Kraft had an African safari planned with his family, so he had to leave early. It was obvious by now that the city would celebrate its sixth championship parade in eight years.

Pags walked Kraft out, and he didn't even mind that at just that moment a photographer had snapped a panoramic shot of the entire arena, championship in progress. For all time, his family would see the picture with themselves, but with Pags's seat empty. It was all right. This made the story even better.

The Celtics hadn't been together for a calendar year, and they'd already forged a brotherhood that they'd sworn was unbreakable. They'd assembled a new team and watched it immediately coalesce. They'd pulled off the biggest single-season turnaround, a forty-two-win improvement, in the history of the sport.

They weren't easily summarized, even now, after 108 games, and it's what made them great. They had passion, and that's what made them relatable. They were showmen, pouring it on against the hated Lakers, and that's what made them irresistible in Boston. When Allen hit his fifth 3 of the game, it was 101–70. He took another and made it: 104–70. He made his seventh of the night, and the Celtics were at 113.

Finally, Rivers had seen enough. He brought his three stars out of the game together, and together they stood there with him in a group hug. Rivers had tears in his eyes because the person on his mind was his father. He imagined what Grady might say as he watched all of this: *Well done, and it's about time.*

As he had that thought, he simultaneously heard a splash and felt something cool around his shoulders and neck. Pierce had dumped a container of Gatorade on him, staining his crisp white shirt. Rivers smiled and said through his tears, "I don't mind it."

He was going to hold on to that shirt, just as Pierce was going to hold on to the NBA Finals MVP trophy he'd earned. With a couple of minutes left, Mike Zarren hugged Pierce. KG and Allen hugged Danny Ainge. With just seconds to go, Rivers looked around and became emotional at the scenes. So did Ainge. The theme of all the things around them was unmistakable. Family matters.

The last time Ainge won a championship was twenty-two years earlier, with the Big Three. He played great that night, and like these Celtics, his teammates won game six convincingly. But as Ainge, executive, let the atmosphere sink in, it occurred to him that this championship with the new Big Three was more rewarding than that one.

As an executive, you know more stories. As an executive, you're thinking more about what it took for so many people to get to this moment. So he thought of all the players, coaches, members of his staff, and ownership group. He could feel his emotions heighten and then wash over him as he looked around the arena and identified everyone whose story he knew, and even those he didn't. This wasn't a bond with teammates; it was a bond with an entire franchise and region. More people than he'd ever realized were feeling this joy.

All the players had either siblings or wives or parents or children there. Little Walker Allen was there, being held by his father. Rivers's fifteen-year-old son, Austin, who had dreams of playing in the NBA one day himself, draped an arm around him.

The Celtics were champions, and Rivers sang along as the music of Queen blared through the jubilant Garden. The final score, 131–92, captured each emphatic thing that happened in the game and season.

It was all over now, and Garnett stood for an interview.

"Anything is possible!" he said, tilting his head back. He said it again, this time louder and more melodious: "Anything is possi-buuuulll!"

He found Russell, and the two men embraced.

"Thank you for everything," Garnett said to the great center. "I've got my own ring now. Now you've got to tell me where to go tonight. I was going to go home."

One day last July, Pierce, Allen, and Garnett sat together at a joint press conference and made promises to themselves and New England. Then their coach took them on a run-through of a parade route. It would have been gimmicky if it hadn't worked. But it did, and they'd become such total Celtics that their stats, in season or postseason, never mattered.

Indeed, Tex Winter, the eighty-six-year-old Laker assistant, had been on to something. Kobe Bryant's defense on Allen didn't get a lot of attention because the Lakers used him more on Rondo, daring him to take jumpers. But Allen's series had been similar to his game: worthy of a shout, but so smooth that it was taken for granted. He was the only player in the series who made over 50 percent of his field-goal and 3-point attempts.

It was after midnight, and the real fun was still an hour or two away. Eventually, Zarren went to the Garden floor and played pickup basketball with some Celtics staffers and members of the media. In the locker room, players chugged champagne and beer and sat around trying to describe what they'd just done.

As it got later, and every Celtic employee had taken a picture with the trophy, Grousbeck picked it up and went home with it. He wasn't going to leave it there when the party was still going strong. He left at three a.m., and the collective fatigue hadn't hit yet. Friends of players, family members, team employees, media members—people were everywhere.

In the back of the locker room, KG, Leon Powe, Eddie House, and someone's inquisitive friend talked about their first few hours of a championship existence. The friend went around the table.

"E-House, how do you feel about being a champion?"

House answered with a couple of quick superlatives.

"Leon Powe. How about you?"

Powe told him that it felt good to see everyone's hard work pay off like this.

"KG. Tell us how you feel."

Garnett wasn't so caught up in the atmosphere that his sensors were off.

"Hold up," he said. "House, is this dude with you?"

House shook his head.

"Powe, is he with you?"

Powe shook his head.

"So tell me—who in the hell are you?"

The friend, who was actually a random, passionate Celtics fan, had slipped unnoticed into the locker room.

"It was so awesome just to talk to you guys. Bye."

Boston revolved around sports on normal days. For championship moments and championship teams, the lore lived forever. Garnett still didn't get all of it, so when he told Russell that he was going to go home, he didn't understand how his and all of their lives had changed. Winning in Boston meant that your house might be home, but so is every other crevice of the city.

Chapter Eleven

GROUNDED

Wyc Grousbeck's phone conversation couldn't have been more perfect, both for what it was and what it symbolized.

He'd gotten to sleep close to four a.m., with the championship trophy next to his bed. Then the house phone rang a few hours later, at seven.

"This is the White House calling. Please hold for President Bush."

Before that congratulatory call from the president, who mentioned the Big Three and Ubuntu, Grousbeck had asked himself about the dream season that they'd just experienced. It hadn't been a dream due to any flukiness. The Celtics had the talent to match any team in the league and a unified purpose that far exceeded that talent and everyone else's.

That was both the beauty and difficulty of winning. How often does everything intertwine so perfectly that one morning you awaken to your reflection in a championship trophy as you talk hoops with the president?

The entire season, from the press conference in July to the final blowout in June, had been one in which everything went in their favor. There were no upsets, no frayed relationships, no regrets over building a team around three veteran players in their thirties. That was something to both celebrate and put into perspective.

Of course, to complete the circle that Doc Rivers began to draw on a duck boat ride, the celebration came first.

It was the Celtics' turn now to parade through the old city and finally see how it was transformed into a sprawling festival. Grousbeck was so excited about it that he asked Daryl Morey, one of the first people he hired six years ago, to join the parade with him. Morey was grateful but pointed out that it would look bad for the Houston Rockets' general manager to be parading with the Celtics. They'd have a bunch of questions when it was over, for sure. They'd be the same questions that the Patriots asked in their first three citywide parties and ones the Red Sox asked in their two. For the sixth time, with blaring horns, confetti, and duck boats shaking from jumping players and thumping bass, the questions remained relevant. And often unanswerable.

Where did all these people come from? Did they shoehorn themselves into already narrow streets? How did they seem to travel in sets, endless dozens, waving from Boston Common all the way to Copley Square? Were they employees in these places? Is that how they got to the perfect buildings at precise heights for winning views of the route?

This was the sports city that was always there, but one you couldn't fully access until you'd found a way to be the best in your sport. That was Paul Pierce and his girlfriend, Julie—today, the king and queen of the NBA.

For the league, Pierce clutched his NBA Finals MVP trophy in one hand. For Boston, teeming with sports scholars and historians, he held a cigar. On this day, local cigar shops reported that their sales were up. It was what Red Auerbach would have smoked if he had been there, so everyone in Boston understood

Pierce's message when he lit up and enjoyed the ride. (Unlike the incessantly smoking Red, Pierce didn't know cigar technique. He had a brief sick moment in the duck boat and then resumed the party.)

It was not the time for business, but business needed to be done soon after the celebration. It was not the time for tough questions, but they needed to be asked. Eventually. As all the Celtics were escorted through Boston, there was nothing more important than those two-plus miles of accomplishment and league supremacy. All Celtics weren't equally responsible for it, but they all had a part of it, and that fact alone made everyone believe that the joy of it would last a lifetime.

Shortly after that flamboyant win over the Lakers, Pierce accepted the trophy and mouthed to the crowd, "I told you." It was true of many things in his Boston career.

He told everyone from his family to his team that he wasn't looking to leave Boston, even after one of the most frightening nights of his life. His attackers' behavior was neither produced by Boston nor exclusive to it.

He told management that all he wanted was to be placed in a championship environment. He told Doc Rivers in their early meetings that he was a great shooter, despite a then-low field goal percentage, and then he proved it by coming out favorably in series with LeBron James and Kobe Bryant, two of the top five players in the sport.

He told the fans what they wanted to hear, following a period where many were down on him because he said what they didn't want to hear. *I'm a great player on a bad team, and it sucks.* He played like a captain all season.

Everything worked out all year. Realistically, could that be done again?

After the Celtics won, with players celebrating loudly nearby, Rivers went to his office, sat down at his desk, and wrote the following: *Winning a championship is hard!* He thought of the madness of the Atlanta series, game seven against Cleveland and the best player in the sport, and beating the Pistons in Detroit. Against the Lakers, what if they hadn't come back and won after being down 24?

The other thing that affected him was the look on Tommy Heinsohn's face after they'd won it. He saw tears in Heinsohn's eyes, and seeing that made him tear up, too. He'd spent a lot of time with Heinsohn and many Celtics from the early championship years. He was particularly struck by how all of them talked about Bill Russell. It gave him another thought: *Usually guys have some jealousy. But being a Celtic is not about being in competition with each other. It's a family.*

Shortly after winning, Ray Allen had a conversation with Michael Jordan, who had six championship rings. Jordan told him that winning one championship was lucky and that winning two wasn't. He warned that the role-players wouldn't want to play their roles anymore after their championship success.

Could jealousy or hostility infect the Celtics? Was Ubuntu deep inside of them, or was it a talking point to guide their season?

In the summer of 2008, the Celtics' necessary good-byes were business related, not personal. The team's two oldest players, PJ Brown and Sam Cassell, both thirty-eight, stepped back from their roles. Brown retired; Cassell hung around but was more coach than player. James Posey, who was a bargain signing in 2007, got a raise in '08. New Orleans gave the thirty-one-year-old forward the security and dollars he wanted, so he signed a four-year deal there that nearly doubled his salary.

Danny Ainge hadn't fundamentally altered who he was just because they'd won. He'd still have to look at a player's age, skill, and demands and then figure out if the investment made sense. He didn't think the cost and four-year commitment to a reserve player made sense. Besides, he'd drafted Tony Allen four years ago. It was time for the twenty-six-year-old wing, five years younger and $4 million cheaper than Posey, to step into the vacated role.

Business. It was present as much as Ubuntu was, and they could never lose sight of it.

The afterglow of the championship remained, even if everything else—the season, the perspective, the relationships—was beginning to change.

It all looked the same at the end of October on opening night. Officially, the seventeenth banner in team history was raised. Pierce bawled as he watched it hanging there, alongside ones earned by Celtics greats. A few of those players were in the Garden, smiling at him, hugging him, encouraging him to keep going. Larry Bird once said that he got the feeling that if he didn't win multiple titles in Boston, it was as if he didn't have game. Pierce had his single title and a new ring to go with it, but the flapping banners silently confirmed Bird's feeling: *Keep them coming.*

The night was perfect. Members of the staff got rings, too, and the players presented the rings to them in the locker room before the banner ceremony. Mike Zarren, the man KG nicknamed "Numbers," got his and brought it with him to his familiar three-hundred-level seats. He took his father's hand and placed the ring with the "Zarren" inscription there. Harvey Zarren and his son burst into tears. Harvey held the ring the entire night.

The night's opponent was familiar, as LeBron was back for another parquet session with Pierce. It wasn't nearly as compelling as the game seven semifinal, but seeing the two players match up was telling. Pierce was patient and confident, knowing that James had watched him receive something that James didn't have.

It would have been a very good night for most players, 22 points, 7 rebounds, and 6 assists, but it was only all right for James. He was almost twenty-four going into his sixth season, and, incredibly, his game still had considerable room to grow. The league was now much more global and lucrative than it had been in the 1990s, when James watched as a kid. One thing that carried over was the instinctive twitch for a title that all great players had.

James watched perceptively as the dramatic ceremony took place, with Cedric Maxwell and John Havlicek personally welcoming Pierce to the club. You had to play for a while to get it, to really understand what a gravitational pull that was for a great player. That thing, whatever it was that Maxwell and Havlicek and Pierce shared, was more powerful than regular-season MVPs and All-Star appearances. It just was. It wasn't aggressively pulling James yet, but it would soon.

At thirty-one, Pierce was still making NBA discoveries entering his eleventh season. He was content to let his play speak for him and not to force anything in the presence of a national TV audience. If they were basketball fans, they knew about him and they'd seen him elevate last year. He played under control and finished with 27 points in a 90–85 win.

If the previous year started out perfectly, this year was better. Allen, at thirty-three the oldest of the Big Three, set the conditioning tone for the group. He looked five years younger than he was and was hyperconscious of his diet. He'd visualized the offense in 2007 before playing in it, but his actual on-court time helped him grasp what kind of adjustments he'd have to make. He got it now, so he was more comfortable and was getting even better in-rhythm shots. Some of that was a credit to him, and some of it was from the emergence of Rajon Rondo.

rry Bird, Kevin McHale, and Robert Parish—known as the Big Three—powered the Celtics for a zen years. Their 1986 team, the organization's sixteenth title winner, is considered one of the best history, for both its physical talent and basketball savvy. (Steve Lipofsky / Contributor / Getty ages)

Auerbach was many things: visionary dealmaker, championship team-builder, and willing itor. He's here with a twenty-eight-year-old Danny Ainge, whom Auerbach admired for his skills because "he's lucky." (*Boston Globe* / Contributor / Getty Images)

Doc Rivers and Ainge played the same position and made their first All-Star team in the same y[...]
When they finally worked together on the same team, often sharing similar thoughts, it see[...]
inevitable. (Dick Raphael / Contributor / Getty Images)

Most people thought the Celtics' future was promising with two young stars in Paul Pierce and Antoine Walker. From afar, Ainge saw one fewer star than everyone else; in his first year as a Celtics decision-maker, he decided to make a bold move. (David Yellen / Contributor / Getty Images)

Just two years into his career, Pierce experienced the dangers of celebrity life. Here, as a witness, he describes the events of September 25, 2000. (*Boston Globe* / Contributor / Getty Images)

Wyc Grousbeck (right) called Steve Paglicua (center) and Bob Epstein shortly after he'd asked the Celtics' previous owner, "If I pay you $360 million, you'll give me the Celtics?" (Courtesy of the Boston Celtics / Brian Babineau)

The first time Pierce saw LeBron James, in the summer of 2003, the Celtics' star was actually there to see someone else. He continued to run into James, often contentiously, for the next decade. (Brian Babineau / Contributor / Getty Images)

Ray Allen could shoot from any angle, over any opponent, from anywhere on the floor. He once gave simple ball-delivery instructions to a new point guard: "Get it to me earlier." (Barry Gossage / Contributor / Getty Images)

Kevin Garnett brought passion, national attention, and an MVP to the Minnesota Timberwolves. But as he got older, the team around him got leaner, leaving him in an uncomfortable role: soloist. (David Sherman / Contributor / Getty Images)

Ainge had one word—"grueling"—for his quest to acquire Garnett. No one thought of that on July 31, 2007, when the Celtics' new Big Three happily agreed to change the way they played. (Brian Babineau / Contributor / Getty Images)

e Celtics' trip to Rome brought them closer together and gave them an identity that made them
tial to ancient warriors. (Jesse D. Garrabrant / Contributor / Getty Images)

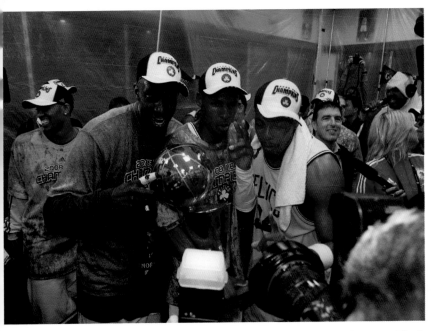

There's no time on this championship night photo, but it had to be before three a.m. That's
when Grousbeck took the trophy home, leaving the Big Three and dozens of others to celebrate
in the Garden until sunrise. (Nathaniel S. Butler / Contributor / Getty Images)

Rivers, in a Gatorade-drenched shirt, with a championship tribute to the one who once gave [
a memorable basketball summary: "Get the ball. Don't give up the ball." (Jesse D. Garrabra
Contributor / Getty Images)

Pierce, Garnett, and Allen had a duck boat preview, with Rivers, before the season started. W
they did it for real in June 2008, they were able to see a new side to an old city. (Brian Babine
Contributor / Getty Images)

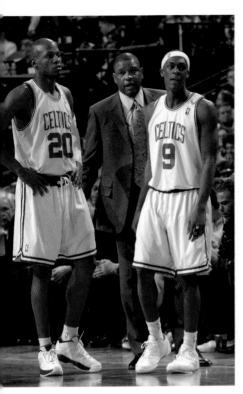

Rajon Rondo was the temperamental artist; Allen was the accommodating statesman. Their clashes escalated to a point where even Rivers couldn't help them. (Andrew D. Bernstein / Contributor / Getty Images)

e Celtics, up three games to two on the Lakers in the 2010 Finals, seemed to have numbers and nt on their side. But after game seven in Los Angeles, one of the team's owners said, "I've never n so many tough guys so despondent." (Andrew D. Bernstein / Contributor / Getty Images)

One controversial decision by James led to a new team-building approach in the NBA; a new conce
from midmarket owners; and a new and intense rivalry that featured James, Dwyane Wade, a
Chris Bosh versus the Celtics. (*Miami Herald* / Contributor / Getty Images)

Ainge wanted Rivers to coach the Celtics for life. After he left, Ainge asked three members of his s
to submit their top choices for the next head coach. When all three had the same name at num
one, Ainge said, "I guess I'd better call Brad Stevens." (Jared Wickerham / Staff / Getty Images)

Ainge couldn't have drafted anyone more suited to star assistance than Rondo. Rivers was awed by Rondo's recall and how he seemed to have the multiple actions of the offense at his fingertips. The coach methodically ceded more offensive control to him; Rondo rewarded the gesture by consistently regulating the offense at its ideal pace. There were times when Rivers would be on the verge of calling out a play only to hear Rondo announce it a split-second before Rivers did.

He was a pass-first player, exactly the valet the team needed. Now in his third season, he demanded to have the ball because no one was better at unchaining the talents of his star trio. Thinking and playing the way he did, he was a whisper away from stardom himself.

Thirty games into the season, no team could touch the skill and power and aesthetics of the Celtics. They lost a rare game at home, to the Nuggets, on November 14. Their record was 8–2. They won their next game. Then another. And another . . . Different tools, same results.

Sometimes a game might need the Allens, Ray and Tony, for a win against the 76ers. Ray had 23 in his usual starting spot, Tony redefining the Posey role with 10 points, 5 rebounds, 4 assists, and sublime defense off the bench. Rondo got a producing credit with 6 points, 12 assists, 6 rebounds, and 3 steals.

For an easy win over the Magic, the formula was 24 for Pierce, 21 for Ray, and 13 rebounds for Kendrick Perkins.

Two nights later at the Garden, December 3, the sellout crowd was surprised to learn that it hadn't seen every little thing in the Big Three era. This group had been together well over one hundred games, and no one had gone for a triple-double. There was a delightful one in their win, their tenth in a row, over the Pacers.

It was arranged, produced, written, and performed by Rondo: 16 points, 17 assists, and 13 rebounds.

In a rematch on December 7, the Pacers might have been thinking about controlling Rondo. It was a good idea, but it left out others. Including Rondo's backup, Eddie House. He had 15 off the bench. But this was a throwback game for KG and Ray—a throwback without the heartbreak of losing.

Honestly, some nights KG really did have the ferocity and spirit of Bill Russell in him. He finished with 17 points, 20 rebounds, 5 steals, and a fusillade of expletives for anyone who attempted to score on him. Ray puzzled the Pacers defenders, making them commit to him when he was twenty feet from the basket and even twenty-five and twenty-six. One hand in his face or two, it didn't make a difference. Their closeouts were either late or sloppy, so they watched him make seven 3-pointers and score 35 points.

When the Celtics played the Jazz at the Garden a week later, on a night when Perkins submitted 15 points and 14 rebounds, they turned everyone into researchers afterward. How many times had this happened? When was the last time a Celtics team went a month—thirty-one days exactly—without a loss?

In those thirty-one days, they'd played fifteen games and won them all. A win, roughly, every other day. And some days were tougher than others. In a reprise of last season's first-round playoff tug with Atlanta, they were back in that city trying to pry a win from the Hawks. With three seconds left, they led by a point, 86–85, when Ray Allen was fouled by Al Horford. As usual, Allen made his free throws, but it still wasn't over. House's brother-in-law, Hawks guard Mike Bibby, missed a 3 at the buzzer that would have tied it.

They made it look easier than it was the next three games, as if they could summon these masterpieces on demand. They beat the Bulls by 18 and silenced the Knicks and 76ers by 19 apiece.

Somehow it was two days before Christmas, and they'd last lost a game two weeks before Thanksgiving. That was nineteen wins in a row. Their record was 27–2. They had the entire league's attention due to the way they won and how they erased a storyline. There wouldn't be a championship hangover. They were more sudden, more energetic than last year. LeBron James, who was having an MVP season, was amazed by what he saw. His team had begun 25–4 and still trailed the Celtics by two games.

The Lakers were waiting for them on Christmas Day in LA, eager to stop the roll before it reached twenty. The game six loss in Boston haunted Kobe Bryant's summer. His workouts, his messages to his teammates, and his statements in the media all tagged back to that loss. Getting a win on Christmas wouldn't avenge it, but it also wouldn't hurt. He scored 27 points, and a national audience saw the run end at nineteen with the 92–83 loss.

Going into a new year, there wasn't much debate about the best team in basketball. The best player? That was an endless subjective argument between Bryant and James. The best team was the Celtics.

Rivers often teased Ainge about the original Big Three and about how many of those teams Ainge played on had arrogance. "You guys thought you were better than everyone else," Rivers told Ainge. "The funny thing is, we're the same way."

From the outside looking in, they didn't have many weaknesses. Inside out was another story.

Part of Ainge's job was to make and take calls about his own players. If some of them would have shadowed him for a day, they'd have been fascinated and offended. It wasn't personal; it was a relentless business. That approach allowed them to get the Big Three in the first place. You made phone calls when your team lost ten in a row or won ten straight. You took a rival GM's call about a player even if you just finished having a pleasant conversation with him about his wife and family.

Ray Allen knew about the corporate nature of the sport more than anyone in the starting five. He was the oldest, and he'd been traded the most. He considered Rondo his little brother and enjoyed mentoring him when he'd come to his house asking about the business of basketball.

It was February, and the deadline was near. Allen never relaxed during these times, even if the Celtics had followed their nineteen-game winning streak with a relatively modest twelve-gamer. That's what happens when you've been traded twice and blindsided both times.

They were in Dallas, playing their final game before the All-Star break. It was their fifty-fifth game, and they were 44–11. Rondo gave everyone something to think about before their few days off. It was another triple-double, with this one checking in at 19 points, 15 rebounds, and 14 assists.

He wasn't an All-Star yet, but that was going to change soon. The only thing that could get in the way was his stubbornness. He and Rivers had a good relationship—most of the time. But when they argued, it was intense, and there were times when players slid between them during practice just to be sure nothing crazy happened.

Sometimes Rondo would get so frustrated that he would leave the practice court, go to the locker room to vent alone, and then return—only after he heard the unmistakable come-back commands of his coach. Rivers coached the players hard, and with honesty, and Rondo often didn't want to hear it. Especially if he was the player being criticized.

There was nothing to complain about after that win over the Mavericks, but it was still good for the coaches and players to take some time off.

When they met in Salt Lake City after their break, it was as if they were back in training camp. The mood was light as they hugged one another, played poker for cash, and talked trash. Unspoken and clearly understood was how they perceived themselves. They'd played 137 regular-season games together since the launch of the Big Three and were 110–27 in those games. They hadn't seen a team—not the Lakers, not the Cavaliers, nobody—who they worried about. There wasn't any good reason to pick against them.

In the second quarter against the Jazz, a fear from training camp made a sobering revisit. Garnett was alone under the basket, about to catch a lob that was going to lead to a dunk. He'd done it dozens of times this season. Except this time when he caught the ball, he felt something strange in his right knee.

Back in camp, he'd had some knee soreness, but the Celtics managed it, and he began the season as the same KG. This was a different pain, and he knew immediately that it wasn't normal. Forget about the dunk. Before he got to the top of his jump, he began to descend and quickly thought to protect the knee. He landed on his left leg and hopped, careful not to put any pressure on his right side. He couldn't diagnose it, and he didn't care to. It hurt like hell, and it scared him.

So many times he played the role of warrior, and that meant there was often a citadel covering his fears. He'd said that years ago in an interview, that he didn't like showing vulnerability because he didn't like being exposed. He couldn't let those players out there, teammates and true brothers, know how frightened he was and how hurt he was. He couldn't.

He walked to the locker room on his own and stretched outside of it. The knee was stinging. At halftime, during warmups, he was out there with his teammates taking shots. The knee still didn't feel better. The Celtics held him out in the second half and officially called his injury a knee strain. Well, it wasn't just a knee strain. They didn't know exactly what it was then, but it wasn't as casual as that. Their defensive tower was down. And although they could still be a very good team without him, he was the difference between good and great.

The KG mystery, and that's how it unfolded, became the story of the rest of the season. There were just twenty-six games before the start of the playoffs, and Celtics reporters and fans thirsted for Garnett updates. The Celtics shared nothing substantive. Their updates were essentially clichés: *We're going to be cautious because it doesn't make sense to rush anything . . . He just needs to rest . . . He's doing some conditioning, but the games now are not as important as the ones later . . .*

But the real story was that every time he increased his activity, his knee would throb and he'd have to stop. He'd feel better a couple of days later, repeat the process, and have to stop again. He'd been a durable player his entire career and hated missing games. But after Utah, he missed thirteen in a row. The Celtics went 7–6 without him. Not great. Not ten, eleven, or even twelve of thirteen, which everyone knew they were capable of when healthy.

With thirteen games left in the season now, Rivers had a plan. With the blessing of Garnett, he'd bring him back on limited minutes to see how he looked. There would be no thirty-five- or forty-minute nights. He'd be a starter getting the minutes of a reserve, fifteen to seventeen minutes max.

That plan lasted three and a quarter games. The Celtics won the first three because that's what they did when Garnett was on the floor. In the fourth game, against an Orlando team that was no match for them with a healthy KG, Garnett went up for a rebound. No one was around him. He felt that familiar pain from the right knee, the knee that didn't seem to care that the Celtics were trying to win back-to-back championships.

It was clear now. His season was over. This called for more than a self-diagnosis. Eventually, he'd need surgery.

Two days before the Celtics prepared for their first-round opponent, the Chicago Bulls, Rivers had a media announcement. No KG for the playoffs.

"I don't see it," the coach said. "I hope I'm wrong, but I don't think so. I knew it was the right decision when I told him and he didn't fight me on it."

It was just last year that Garnett screamed a statement—"Anything is possible!"—that stuck with Boston sports fans. They said it long after the championship, and they applied it to the Celtics, other Boston teams, or anything else. Anything is possible. But Garnett's knee needed surgery, and his statement needed a realistic revision when applied to the Celtics: Anything is possible . . . with the Big Three.

The whole organization knew what they were with KG and what they were without him. They weren't champions without Garnett. They played a thrilling seven-game series against the Bulls, taking game seven at home. The best player in the series was Rondo, who nearly averaged a triple-double in those seven games. They went seven more against the Magic before being run off the Garden floor in a humbling 19-point defeat. They'd led the series, 3–2, and then crumbled.

No, there would not be another banner raised in the Garden in 2009. But by May, that was only surprising to the naïve. The championship was headed to LA, where Bryant and the Lakers had to settle for beating the Magic, not the Celtics, after last year's disappointment.

But there were bigger issues in Boston, issues that would speak to who the Celtics were next year and beyond. There was the medical mystery of Garnett and what would become of his right knee. Every Celtics fan knew about the sensitivity of that.

What they didn't know about was a different type of sensitivity—a fragility, truly—that chafed the Ubuntu dynamic.

As the NBA draft approached, Ray Allen heard some information that he wanted to share with his mentee, Rondo. He heard that they both might be traded to Phoenix for six-foot-ten Suns center Amar'e Stoudemire, guard Leandro Barbosa, and the fourteenth pick in the draft.

There were several problems with the Allen-Rondo information exchange. Some could have been prevented, and some were the result of different personalities and evolving relationships.

First, the information that Allen had was a rumor. Teams talked with each other constantly, with a deal-completion rate lower than 5 percent. Allen shared the information from the perspective of a mentor who had been traded and was just looking out. But Rondo didn't receive it that way. He was growing into his game and gaining even more confidence. He wasn't the little brother of 2008. Besides, he didn't take criticism well; he took it personally.

When Allen told him what he heard, Rondo heard something else. It seemed as if Allen was trying to blame him for being mentioned in a trade discussion.

The whole thing was not something that split the team. It was just awkward. Strained. Weird.

At the very least, the relationship between Allen and Rondo began to change. Socially, Rondo was more a part of the Big Three than Allen was. Plus, his game was surging toward All-Star status.

If Garnett returned healthy, the Celtics had more than enough talent to win again. They'd just have to do it with slightly different execution and identity. They could certainly be championship Celtics. The Ubuntu Celtics were a thing of the past.

CHAPTER TWELVE

THE HARD WAY TO LA

Their trip to Rome was just two years ago. That's it: two years. It wasn't so long ago that the Celtics couldn't remember all the details of it or that they looked any different back then. No, that wasn't it.

But there had been changes since the bonding trip there, changes that couldn't be detected from their Roman pictures. Their most memorable one, the one Doc Rivers loved and had framed, was taken outside of the renowned Colosseum.

They were all in the best shape of their lives then. Hungry. Humble. Strong. Gracious to those in their group, cautious of all others. Connected to one another in ways that they didn't expect and struggled to explain.

"Warriors," Rivers said when he thought of the photo. "The symbolism of that picture couldn't have been more perfect. Listen, God was on our side; I don't know. To go to Rome with seventeen guys—only a few of them had played together before—to go somewhere and get sequestered with that team was so perfect.

"The bus rides to and from practice took forever. It was the greatest team-building trip because no cell phones were working, and the guys had to talk to each other. That team—that was a *rough* team. I wouldn't want to play against that team. Forget about the Big Three. Start thinking of some of the other guys that you had to deal with: Perk. Rondo. Tony Allen. Posey and Eddie were the spiritual leaders of our second unit, and they weren't having nonsense from anyone.

"Danny will get credit for the Big Three, but he really should get credit for the other players he brought in, too."

They hadn't won a title yet, so back then maybe they thought this type of closeness was the championship norm. They knew better now. What they did then was a stand-alone rarity. No NBA team, certainly not a twenty-four-win one, had imported so many new players—starters and role-players alike—and galloped to the top of the sport. The league had been celebrating champions for more than sixty years, and none of them had a profile like that. Never happened. Until they did it.

It wasn't possible to do that again, for the Celtics or anyone else. Where they were now, with bodies being repaired and relationships in need of repair, was the place everyone else lived. That was the story of the rest of the NBA. That was the story of the global workplace, regardless of industry.

Whatever it was, the Celtics were all in on it. They'd determined that Kevin Garnett's right knee wouldn't stop him from being an excellent player. He'd have to discover a different path to excellence because that knee and his age—thirty-three—clipped some of his quickness and buoyancy. Perhaps the biggest challenge for him, his bosses, and his peers would be a mental one. They all needed the driven Garnett, but a driven player with refocused expectations.

For example, the three-thousand-minute/eighty-game seasons were gone. The seasons in which he casually stacked rows of double-doubles because that's just who he was were probably gone. He wouldn't be able to consistently rely on some of his perfected techniques: He'd always been able to use speed to slip past other big men, who he was faster than, and then lean on his gifted combination of athleticism, strength, and passion to leap over them.

While he said, and everyone knew, that he didn't like to show vulnerability, could he accept that he was now exactly that? Vulnerable, unquestionably. He'd had the injury, the reinjury, a spring 2009 surgery, and now a Celtics' maintenance plan for him in the fall. His career wasn't over; his career as MVP KG was.

He remained the conscience of the Big Three, and he could still play.

For the Celtics to win the finals this season, they'd have to be true to their talent and their personalities. If they tried to bring their Rome insights to this year's team, it would fail. They were different players and people now. Everyone could see it and sense it. The Big Three's collective ability was crisper two years ago, but the team's overall talent was better now. Rajon Rondo hadn't taken a star turn two years ago. Big Baby Davis wasn't getting starters' minutes and winning playoff games two years ago. Tony Allen hadn't fulfilled his calling as an all-league defender.

There was also more tension and less trust since Rome.

Ray Allen and Rondo were friendly for business purposes, but they weren't friends. It's not that friendship was required on any pro team, but this had the potential to be personal and nasty.

Maybe it was how different they appeared to be: Rondo, the finicky contrarian, and Allen, the compatible pro. Or it could have been Allen's sensitivity to being the third wheel of the Big Three. That was difficult on its own and trickier now because there were signs that he was close to losing that unofficial number three slot to Rondo.

There were money matters for Allen as well. He was entering the final year of his contract, and he knew what that meant. He was due to make almost $20 million, so his expiring contract made it—the contract, not necessarily him—an attractive trade commodity. He'd have to brace himself for lots of trade rumors and legitimate trade discussions.

Rondo and Doc Rivers had plenty of arguments, the frequency and tone of them seeming to increase the better Rondo played. Sometimes they argued because Rondo wanted to push the offense and team to places where Rivers didn't think it was ready to go. There were arguments over Rondo's listening. That is, he didn't always do it. And made no apologies for it. He picked up everything quickly and became bored and annoyed when others didn't. There were times he crossed the line and had to be called out on it.

In what may have been a first in NBA contract announcements, Rondo's agents volunteered that what slowed negotiations with the Celtics on an extension for the point guard was Rondo's attitude. The agents said that the Celtics were concerned about their client's leadership and wanted him to show more of it if he were going to be a long-term player with them.

Imagine. That was included in the prologue of a new, five-year, $55 million agreement between Rondo and the Celtics. It would have been completely fair if Celtics fans had made the corresponding leap: If the people who work *for* Rondo are willing to admit this about him, the real stories must be even worse than this.

Fifty games into the season, and Rivers was exhausted by . . . his life.

That was the simplest way to put it. He put so much of himself into the job that there wasn't a lot of time to reflect on what he was doing. In the times he did, he wondered if he should continue to coach.

He had four kids, all heavily involved in sports, and he wanted to support them all. The oldest, son Jeremiah, was playing college basketball at Indiana. His only daughter, Callie, was a University of Florida volleyball player. His two younger sons, Austin and Spencer, were high school basketball players near Orlando. Austin was one of the best players in the country and would be in position to pick any college program he wanted. On visits to Boston, seventeen-year-old Austin would find himself in pickup or one-on-one games with the Celtics. When he was a freshman, Austin was at the Celtics facility with his siblings. Ainge said to Rivers, "That's the pro right there. He's got 'pro' written all over him."

Rivers wanted to be there to witness it, so he spent thousands on personal travel between practices, games, and off days. That was part of the physical exhaustion. But there were issues on the job as well. What was wrong with his team? Why weren't they a pleasure to coach as they had been his first two years with them?

The team's biggest acquisition was thirty-five-year-old forward-center Rasheed Wallace. A whole Celtics group, including the Big Three and Rivers, had gone to Detroit in the spring to recruit him. They thought the former Piston would be the perfect fit on the team, with his ability to rebound and shoot with range and defend.

The reality, though, was that he hadn't played to expectations, so there was a lot of waiting for the real Wallace to show up. His range was suddenly gone, so his 3-point percentage tanked. He had lost quickness, desire, or both on defense because that wasn't a plus for him anymore. He was also out of shape.

Wallace had been part of the Pistons' contending core, a group that had been involved in dozens of playoff games. In his opinion, all his deficiencies would disappear in the postseason, and that's what he was pacing himself for. But this wasn't pacing. There was no buildup, no gradual process of Wallace getting into better condition. It never happened, and anything positive he did was accomplished on sheer talent.

It wasn't all on Wallace. It was a combination of everything: lack of concentration, injuries, trade rumors, arguments, petty jealousies. The team was wrapped up in a constellation of issues, and that explained why Rivers found himself probing the team's psyche, thinking of something that would get everyone's attention and draw them closer together.

After the fast start to the season that had become typical of the Big Three era—the team began 23–5—the Celtics slumped. In their next twenty-two games before their All-Star vacation, they went 9–13.

Garnett was voted to the All-Star team, but in those first fifty games, he'd already missed eleven because of knee pain. His absence could be felt in the numbers; the team was 5–6 without him. Pierce made the All-Star team as well, the eighth appearance of his career. He seemed to savor his selection to the game in Dallas because, at thirty-three, who knew how many more were coming? He'd missed seven Celtics games already with knee and ankle injuries. The third Celtic All-Star didn't have any injury concerns. He'd emerged as the team's best and most unpredictable player.

It was the first All-Star appearance for Rondo, who clearly had worked on his body during the offseason. He was noticeably stronger, and he played like it. His biggest change was on defense, where he used muscle, quick hands, and memorization of opponents' tendencies to neutralize opponents. His Rondo Games, usually high-profile or nationally televised games in which he piled up head-spinning statistics, were happening more often. It was obvious that he was getting better on the court. Off it, he continued to be a work in progress.

The only mention of Ray Allen in Dallas was the type of conversation that he'd gotten used to. Trade talk. There was chatter among players and media that Allen was going to be moved to the Washington Wizards. Another deal had him going to Chicago. Yet another to Sacramento. The trade deadline was still a week away, and with the way the Celtics were playing, a trade wouldn't be surprising to anyone.

On his way to Los Angeles for a game against the Lakers, Rivers spoke with Ainge and listened as the general manager briefed him on potential trades. The deadline was hours away, and doing nothing would be foolish. The men agreed that this team wasn't going to magically correct itself. Ainge told Rivers that he had a chance to bring in a younger backup point guard—the Knicks' twenty-five-year-old Nate Robinson—for Eddie House, who was thirty-one. The deal would include a couple of young players, J. R. Giddens and Bill Walker, who weren't getting time in Boston anyway.

Rivers hesitated. Objectively, the trade made sense, and the Celtics would win it overwhelmingly. The problem with the view from that lens was that it removed emotion. Players and teams could never be looked at objectively.

House had become one of those guys. He was a confident shooter who didn't back down from anyone. He was one of the players who understood what the team needed from him, and he was always ready to provide it. He'd helped deliver that historic finals comeback in game four two years ago with his accurate second-half shooting.

While the team headed to LA in February 2010, House left in the opposite direction. He was a member of the New York Knicks, his ninth team in a ten-year career.

The Lakers weren't having any of those problems when the Celtics visited. They were the defending champions, and now, at 42–13, they were the popular choice to return to the finals for the third straight year.

Rivers agreed with that assessment. He also wanted the Celtics to believe that they'd be playing them, and he had an idea to illustrate it. He asked everyone in the team's traveling party to give him $100. Garnett, who'd made more money than all of them in his career, was initially resistant. He asked Rivers what he was getting at. When the coach told him the purpose, Garnett was not only willing to chip in his own $100; he offered to pay for several others.

The intention was to collect some cash and hide it inside the visiting locker room at Staples Center in LA. Rivers selected assistant coach Kevin Eastman for the job of climbing up to the level of the ceiling panels, removing one, and placing a $2,600 envelope where no one would look for it. The Celtics weren't scheduled to play the Lakers again in the regular season. Which is what Rivers's point was: We'll see the money when we return here for the finals.

It was an idea, bold and steeped in intrigue, that stuck with the players. If Rivers believed it, they thought, maybe he was crazy enough to be right.

They learned something about themselves in the game against the Lakers, even with Kobe Bryant taking the night off. With just over seven minutes to play, they trailed 84–80. Over the next seven minutes, they held the Lakers to 2 points. One for 11 shooting and 2 points? Over seven minutes?

If they could defend like that the rest of the way, they'd get those bills back; if they defended like that, those bills would be tip money for an all-night championship celebration in LA.

If we can play like this . . . Several players said it over the course of the regular season, but the truth was they couldn't on most nights.

Rivers was constantly on planes, whether it was with his team or by himself on a quick visit to Florida. On one of those trips, with a handful of games left, he made the decision to reset. Why were they all, himself included, stressing themselves about long-forgotten parts of the season? They no longer mattered. He liked who they were headed into the playoffs.

Fortunately for the Celtics, they were familiar with the roster construction of their first-round opponent. The Miami Heat won the NBA title in 2006, but just one starter remained from that championship team, twenty-five-year-old guard Dwyane Wade. He was a great player, surrounded by well-coached role-players. Essentially, that was the profile of the Cavaliers, except the Cavaliers had a greater player in league MVP LeBron James and better complementary players, too. The Celtics easily brushed aside the Heat in five games, with the lone Miami win fueled by an entertaining 46-point eruption from Wade.

Due to their fourth-place finish in the conference, the Celtics had known for weeks who and what was coming next. The "who" was James. He didn't seem to be aging quickly enough: He was in his seventh season now and still only twenty-five. He seemed to add a new wing to his empire each time the Celtics saw him.

When he and Pierce had a regular-season duel in 2006, James was still weak defensively. He'd closed that hole by 2008, when he and Pierce had a shootout in game seven. Even then, in a season in which he led the league in scoring, there were some shots he wouldn't and couldn't take. And his defense was good, not stellar.

That had all changed by 2010. All of it. He was a first-team all-league defender; he was a more efficient scorer; his passing had improved; he spent more time deconstructing coaching staffs and the strategies used to stop him; and, his own coach believed, James's voice and personality powered the Cavaliers more than anyone realized.

Mike Brown had coached him for nearly five years and saw the various ways he pushed teammates to be better than they thought they could be. During one game, the Cavaliers were being torched with their pick-and-roll defense. Brown called timeout.

"Guys, we're a 'show' team, and we're getting slaughtered out there," he said. "What do you guys want to do? Do you want to switch? Drop? Iso? What do you want?"

James interrupted.

"Nah. Fuck that. We're a 'show' team, so we're gonna 'show,' and we're gonna do it right. And this is how we're gonna get it done."

James began calling out different teammates and telling them how to improve their coverage. It sounded like something KG would do. James had a lot of that fire in him, too, but it didn't manifest the same way. And besides, people were distracted by something else in his career.

There had been a season-long traveling road show focused on James's future. As James neared the end of his contract, the mystery revolved around his next stop. Everything he said and did was news, locally and nationally. There was a nervous, manic energy in Cleveland, a city that hadn't won any championship in James's lifetime. There was urgency for him to win and anxiety for him to stay.

For the Celtics, this was a significant advantage. They already knew how to play against James and his deferring teammates, and that wasn't going to change. But Rivers had spent so much time talking about the mental side of the game that the players recognized—in themselves and opponents—when someone was in a good head space or not.

No matter what James said about not focusing on anything but the game, they knew that couldn't be true. He did a good job of bringing his teammates together, hosting dinners at his house and organizing team activities such as bowling and Halloween parties. James wanted these to be truly inclusive gatherings, so he was sure to invite players, coaches, and staff members. The inside was not his issue. Outside of the team, his future was an inescapable topic.

Each postseason win would be framed as one more reason for James to stay. Every loss would get Cleveland fans closer to a panicked LeBron Watch. Local officials, including the governor of Ohio and the mayor of Cleveland, produced a music video begging James to stay. The song was set to the tune of the mid-1980s international hit "We Are the World," which was created for worldwide humanitarian aid.

If that didn't make it obvious that James, seen as a one-man economic engine, was facing pressure beyond basketball, it was clear when the games started. Whether the Celtics won or lost, it was about basketball. When the Cavs won or lost—especially when they lost—it was about the future of James.

The Celtics looked like their regular-season selves—old and average—in a game three loss to the Cavs that had them trailing the series, 2–1. They lost by 29, the worst postseason home defeat in team history. Pierce was miserable from the field (4 for 15), from 3-point range (1 for 5), and even from the free-throw line (2 for 5). It was bad, and no one suggested that there was anything beyond that.

It was just the opposite when the Celtics did something similar to the Cavs in game five. They went to Cleveland and won by 32, giving the Cavs their worst postseason home loss in team history. James was . . . Pierce-like. He was 3 for 14 from the field and missed his four 3-point attempts, but he did manage to go 9 for 12 from the line.

The postgame commentary was a mix of shock, fear, rage, and psychoanalysis. James's summary statement was not viewed as sufficient or believable.

"I just missed a lot of open shots that I'm capable of making," he explained.

He was asked about his sore elbow, his lack of aggression, and being booed by his home fans—which had a double meaning for him since he was the only player on his team actually from the Cleveland area. "We played awful. They have every right to boo us if they want to." There was the inevitable question, the Question, about his future. He said he wasn't thinking about it. But after the next game, in Boston, the Celtics forced him to.

For the first time all season, the pillars of the team were united. There was the Big Three, the foundational trio of this championship era. And there was Rondo, representing the Celtics' present and their future. All four of them had their fingerprints on game six, and there were smiles—sincere, joyous smiles—on the floor and throughout the satisfied Garden.

This was fun: Rondo had 12 assists; KG had 12 rebounds; Rasheed Wallace made big shots off the bench and had 13 points. The crowd enjoyed teasing James along the way. He stepped to the free-throw line in the last three and a half minutes, and the Garden fans bellowed a mocking, rhythmic "*New York Knicks*" in a collective guess at his next team.

The fans' joke was telling. This was Boston, and the disdain for New York—all things New York—was real. LeBron James could actually *save* the Knicks, who hadn't won a title in nearly forty years. In theory, Celtics fans should have been rooting for him to turn away from New York, Cleveland, Chicago, and just keep heading West until he was safely clear of the Eastern Conference.

But the fans didn't think that way, and neither did the Celtics. They had two series wins over him, and they didn't believe he alone could do anything to change that against them. They knew how to play him, and despite his genius, they'd advanced past him. They were half right: There was nothing James could do, in Cleveland, to get through Boston. But he and a few others were the only ones who knew the plan he had in mind, a plan that would alter the next generation of NBA team-building and the previously unimaginable future of the Big Three concept. Everyone would learn about it, in a stunning way, during the summer.

For now, the public knew where he wasn't going—to the conference finals. His last game of the season featured one of the strangest stat lines in team history: 27 points, 19 rebounds, 10 assists, 9 turnovers. A triple-double/almost-quadruple-double good-bye. As he walked off the court and into the visiting locker room, he walked by Celtics president Rich Gotham. James removed his jersey before the Cavs' door opened.

Wow, Gotham thought, *this really is happening. We've seen him on this team for the last time.*

When the Celtics won the game and the series, taking down the top team in the East, there was so much focus on James that a postgame confession from Garnett was underplayed.

"You have to understand that chemistry is a hard thing to come by," Garnett said. "All year, we've been dealing with chemistry problems. Rondo is getting better, and we're fitting him in. At some point he's going to take this team over, and that's a big adjustment for us. I think the chemistry is starting to be sound now."

Chemistry problems. Garnett spoke those words on May 13. Nine days later, no one in Boston—or in the country—knew what he was talking about. There were no chemistry problems and never had been. There had been no feud between Allen and Rondo. Wallace was exactly what the team needed. The Celtics didn't need to be motivated to play to their potential.

That's what three quick wins in the conference finals can do to you. The Celtics, the old Celtics from April, might have blown a 3–0 series lead. But not the new Celtics from May.

The old Celtics from way back in January might have blown a 14-point fourth-quarter lead on their way to a 2-point loss in Orlando. Not these new guys. They confidently jumped on the Magic at the beginning of game three, holding them to a 12-point first quarter. The truth was they didn't respect this team. Not enough to have even a slight trace of doubt or fear. They pushed a 15-point lead to 20, and then 25, and all the way up to 32. They won that game in Boston by 23. The biggest indication that the Celtics had changed was that no one who played in the game, or watched it, wanted to talk about stats.

Instead, what stood out was a moment.

Four minutes into the second quarter, there was a loose ball, and Orlando's Jason Williams had a sizable head start on everyone and should have had it first. But Rondo didn't think so. He sprinted to the ball where Williams jogged, and he belly slid on the floor for it while Williams barely bent his knees. This was effort. This was athleticism. Rondo took the ball, did a crossover dribble on a surprised Williams, and then banked in a one-handed shot.

Danny Ainge, watching from his baseline seats, was brought out of them. He knew how he felt about the team's season— "lethargic and up and down"—but this Rondo play was breathtaking: "It's one of the greatest individual plays ever. Incredible."

When they watched Rondo, Celtics fans didn't care about the numbers. They knew that he was mesmerizing to watch, and he wasn't a momentum player as much as he was one who captured surges. There was a moment in the game—like in game three—where you just understood that the surge was there. His shooting (4 for 14 that night) was irrelevant. He was their unsmiling hustler and conductor.

They took down the Magic in six games as well, setting themselves up for a trip to LA to meet the Lakers. And to pick up their money.

On paper, the Celtics were most committed to Rondo, whose five-year contract would begin next season. Allen would be a free agent. Pierce could opt out of his contract. Kendrick Perkins would be in a contract year next season. Rivers had a contract, but he still wasn't sure if he wanted to come back and fulfill it.

This road to LA had been harder than anyone in the organization, from ownership to the players, had thought possible. Winning the series might hold the core of the team together, personality clashes be damned. A series loss would make Danny Ainge retreat to his office and revisit the question that stuck with him at all times: *How long do I hold on to the Big Three?*

Beyond the Big Three, there was the talent of Rondo in one column and the maintenance of him in the other. Could another coach deal with Rondo as well as Rivers had? It was not an exaggeration to say that the next seven games determined who the Celtics were going to be for the next several years.

Both teams were better than they were two years before, even if their records told a different story. Pau Gasol was more physical now than he was then, and the addition of forward Ron Artest gave them a strong, tough player who could match up with Pierce. For the Celtics, Rondo's development not only changed the way the team played; it made the Lakers think of him differently, too.

Two years ago, in game four, a healthy Rondo didn't play in the second half. That would never happen now. Tony Allen, Big

Baby Davis, Nate Robinson. They'd all be expected to contribute to something they either mostly watched or weren't here for in 2008.

After four games, with the series tied at two, there were several events that previewed where this was headed. Kobe Bryant and Gasol did whatever they wanted in game one. Bryant scored 30 points, which was expected, but Boston hadn't seen this Gasol. He was persistent in every aspect of the game and finished with 23 points, 14 rebounds, 5 assists, and 3 blocks. In game two, Rondo had a triple-double, and many of his assists were to Allen, who set a finals record by sinking eight 3-pointers. He had 32 points, and the Celtics won, but the Gasol-Garnett matchup was worth noting. KG was in foul trouble and finished with 6 points. Gasol had 25 points and 8 rebounds.

Game three was a reminder of how maddening pro basketball can be. The same man who sets a finals shooting record in LA can return to Boston and miss everything. Allen made eight 3s in game two and missed eight—0 for 8—in game three. He was 0 for 13 on the night. Garnett did have 25 points and looked more like himself, but the Celtics were down 2–1.

In game four, Rivers and Phil Jackson leaned in different directions. Jackson rode his starters hard; Rivers went to his bench and stayed with the unit well into the fourth quarter. In a coincidental tribute to the player he was traded for, Nate Robinson helped his team win it. Eddie House had done the same thing in this game in 2008. Davis, who once called himself the Ticket Stub compared to KG's Big Ticket, delivered 18 points and 5 rebounds. Robinson had 12 points and 2 assists. After one emphatic stretch of play, the five-foot-nine Robinson jumped on the six-foot-nine Davis's back. Afterward, they joked that they were Shrek and Donkey from the animated movie.

That left three games potentially, with two of them in LA. The winner of game five, statistically, was likely to win the series.

Dwyane Wade, eliminated by the Celtics in the first round, was in Boston attentively watching game five. So was the new owner of the soon-to-be Brooklyn Nets, Mikhail Prokhorov, who piqued the NBA's interest when he announced that he expected his team to win a title in five years and presumably be kings of New York. Prokhorov didn't realize that all the smart general managers in the league would be calling his GM in a few years, aware that ownership pressure often leads to bad deals.

The Celtics controlled most of game five and probably knew they were going to win it in the third quarter. Bryant put on a show there, scoring 19 points in ten minutes, several on well-contested shots. They could have been buried by an outburst like that, but they still led by 6 heading into the fourth quarter. They led by a dozen with four minutes to play, and when the lead began to shrink in the final ninety seconds, Jackson called a timeout. He knew ABC's mics were on him, but he didn't care. He used the opportunity to motivate his team and to take a cheap shot that was also true.

"This team has lost more games in the fourth quarter than anybody in the NBA," he told the Lakers. "They know how to lose in the fourth quarter, all right? And they're showing us that right now."

He knew the Celtics weren't going to do that in game five. But he wanted the sentiment out there as the Celtics made their final trip to LA of the season, up 3–2.

Wyc Grousbeck hadn't been listening to Phil Jackson, but he was still uncomfortable. He thought his team would win it. He just felt it needed to happen in game six. There was something about going the distance with the Lakers that made him uneasy.

In LA, seven minutes into game six, the Celtics learned that part of their identity was broken. Perkins, their only true center, tried to grab a rebound between Bryant and Andrew Bynum. He fell to the floor screaming, and he grabbed his right knee. It was as bad as it sounded and looked: a torn ACL.

We win it if we have him, Steve Pagliuca thought as he watched Perk being helped to the locker room.

He was finished for the rest of game six and for game seven. Of course there would be a game seven. The Celtics were down 20 at the half and 25 after three quarters. There would be no special comeback tonight. Jackson said the Celtics blew leads. He should have added, *When they can get them . . .*

They were never in it. Boston's "Beat LA" chant wasn't heard anywhere. With a minute to play, the Staples crowd broke out in "Boston sucks."

One more game in downtown LA and a cap would be put on the season and, appropriately, the NBA's first decade of the century. The season would have its champion, and one type of NBA—with its legacy franchises and iconic players sticking with them—would become an anomaly.

The league was changing. Bryant's fourteen-year stay in LA and Pierce's twelve-year run with Boston was going to be the exception. Everything was more lucrative now—team values, TV contracts, global media rights, player salaries—and therefore everything was more fluid. Bryant and Pierce were not Magic and Larry, but they were more connected to that era's sensibility than this one's. It was all about to change. The last game of the season, and last of its era, had to be memorable.

Just a few minutes into it, the tone was set. It was going to be a physical game. Players and coaches always appreciated knowing that early so they could figure out how to play. The message from the veteran officials—Dan Crawford, Scott Foster, and Joe Crawford—was clear: *Play as hard as you can; we'll whistle the obvious and play through everything else.* Both teams were fine with that because both of them liked the contact.

The problem for the Celtics popped up in the first two minutes, and it wasn't going anywhere. They were too small. The Lakers were slinging bad shots at the basket, and missing badly, but it didn't matter because they kept retrieving offensive rebounds. It was a real math problem for the Celtics. Simply, they took better shots than the Lakers, but the Lakers had three times as many opportunities for all shots, whether they were good or not.

After thirteen minutes, the Lakers had 11 offensive rebounds. They couldn't shoot, but they could defend and rebound, and it kept them close. They trailed 40–34 at halftime, and they were making 26 percent of their shots. Bryant was 3 for 14. Doc Rivers and Tom Thibodeau decided to throw a different look at Bryant: They doubled him. With numbers like his, the Lakers could have been down by a dozen.

They were down by that—actually 13—with twenty minutes left in their season. Five minutes later, they still trailed by 9, 56–47, after a Wallace jumper. Fifteen minutes remained in the game, and Wallace, starting for Perkins, grimaced.

This was going to be an issue in the final minutes, and it was connected to what had been discussed all year. Wallace was too out of shape to keep up. He didn't have the conditioning to push the Lakers' big men, and he struggled up the court. His first five minutes of the game were inspired, and now he glitched.

Entering the fourth quarter, the Celtics held a 4-point lead. This is where Jackson hoped his nationally broadcast cheap shot could seep into Boston minds. They had another fourth-quarter lead; would they lose this one, too?

Really, with nine minutes to play and the Celtics still ahead by 4, the winner of this game would need basketball skills and Jedi wisdom. Nobody could hide their weaknesses anymore, so the struggle was to work around them.

Bryant wasn't going to suddenly get hot. He was 5 for 20 after three. Allen wasn't going to start making 3s. All the energy in his legs was devoted to slowing Bryant, and he had nothing else to give. Rondo wasn't going to start making free throws; in the series, he was 5 for 19 from the line. The Celtics weren't going to outrebound or outmuscle the Lakers. They couldn't box out Gasol. Couldn't. He was too much.

This was digging time for both teams. Find something, anything, that will squeeze a few more opportunities for your teammates. Both the Celtics and Lakers thought they had something with six minutes left. Allen made a couple of free throws—he'd missed just one all series—to put them up 3. Then Lakers guard Derek Fisher made a 3 to tie it.

Even when the Lakers appeared to cut off all Celtic options, when they controlled all rebounding, didn't allow shots in the paint, and dared someone to score, the game was close. The Lakers were up 6 with ninety seconds left, but Wallace came out of a timeout to hit a 3 from the left side to cut the lead in half, 76–73.

It was the final series, Celtics-Lakers, so everything that happened from here until the end of the game would be exaggerated. And permanent. No two franchises had finals moments that were so seared into the memories of pro basketball fans. In their head-to-head matchups, both teams had delivered solid basketball lessons over the years; it was not always the primary stars who were capable of making closing plays. There were winning plays by Larry and Magic and also by Gerald Henderson and Michael Cooper.

Ron Artest had essentially played two different styles for the Lakers within one series. In the first five games, he was a 30 percent shooter who was a liability with the ball. But he was much better in game six and made three 3-pointers. In the last minute, Pierce played Artest like he was that 30 percent shooter, and the Celtics paid for it.

Pierce played off Artest, who hung around the right 3-point arc. Artest had an open 3 and took it, long before a surprised and late-arriving Pierce could close.

It was either devastating or a game winner, depending on your allegiance. But seconds later, some hope was found when Allen finally found his legs and countered with a corner 3 over Odom.

It wasn't a pretty game, but it was close. Just over thirty seconds remained, and the game revealed its basic pattern on a simple sequence. Bryant took a 3, missed it, and Gasol grabbed the offensive rebound. His retrieval gave the Lakers another opportunity, and Bryant was fouled. His free throws gave them a lead that they wouldn't lose.

Gasol walked away with 18 rebounds, exactly half of them offensive. That was more than the combined total of Garnett, Wallace, and Baby Davis. These forty-eight minutes had been a game of keep-away, and the season had become that as well.

The Celtics stood in a circle in their locker room, arm in arm, and cried. What they'd lost was a game, but the tears had more depth than that. They cried as if they were grieving something. Grousbeck and Pags saw it and got out quickly so they wouldn't cry themselves. Bob Epstein stayed and was reminded of why he'd become a co-owner. He hadn't done it solely for the money, and the distraught players—all well paid—hadn't either. "I've never seen so many tough guys so despondent," he said. "It was devastating to each of them. You stand in the middle of it, and you realize how much winning means to them." The Lakers had the title that the Celtics thought they'd win, and now each of their memories would be filled with different game images that would haunt them for weeks, if not years.

Summer had begun abruptly, and it was decision time. For Ainge, Rivers, and many of the major players in a soon-to-be-reconfigured NBA.

Chapter Thirteen

DECISIONS

What was it about catching a ride out of this city?

Two years ago, with the Celtics in Los Angeles for the finals, they tried to take their two planes back to Boston for game six. They were convinced that someone was messing with them, as the two Lakers' planes departed smoothly, and the Celtics fiddled in their two on the runway for hours. That story eventually turned into a fun one, because it became part of 2008's championship tales.

In 2010, getting out of LA and far away from Staples Center was now difficult because a vehicle was on fire. It was meant to be a celebratory burn. The Lakers won the championship, 83–79, and moved one title behind the Celtics in the all-time chase, seventeen to sixteen. The Celtics' bus was slowed down by the fire, and that allowed for extra time to think about missed opportunities.

It was going to be hard for all of them tonight, next week, next year. Everyone was going to have one-on-one time with his own demon.

For Paul Pierce, it was those 20 points from Ron Artest, including that savage 3 in the final minute. For KG, it was rebounds. The Celtics were pummeled there, and KG had just three boards all night. For Ray Allen, one of the greatest shooters in history, it was simply that: his shot. He was 3 for 14. In his mental replay, he'd probably view his missed jumpers as if they were missed layups. For Rivers, it was at least two demons, one from the game and one from the entire season.

In the game, if he could have found a way to sneak in more rest for KG—somewhere—he could have had him fresher down the stretch. Garnett hurt the Lakers with his post-ups, and maybe with more rest, he could have hurt them even more. As for the season, Rivers could have been more insistent with Rasheed Wallace about his conditioning. Wallace gave what he had in game seven, but what he had wasn't all that he could have been.

Danny Ainge, probably the best golfer in the organization, drew some parallels from one of his favorite sports:

"To put it in a golf analogy, you felt like you shot seventy-five and lost. As opposed to, you shoot sixty-eight and someone else shoots sixty-five to beat you. We shot three over par, and we weren't at our best when we needed to be at our best. Which is the back nine on the last day, and the fourth quarter was not our best fourth quarter. It was a frustrating way to lose a championship.

"That was one of the toughest losses I've been associated with. I thought we were better. I thought we had the game in hand. We did a good job of defending Kobe, and we just got beat on the glass. And Ron Artest. He had been outplayed most of the whole series, but he had a big game seven. That was just really a tough one to lose."

It was especially tough for Pierce.

Four days after the loss, he could visualize how game seven was being relived in LA because he used to do that himself. Growing up there, he loved Magic and Kareem and couldn't stand that instigator from the Celtics, Danny Ainge.

It was wise to avoid TV now. Kobe, Magic, and Kareem were all there, smiling and celebrating for the two miles of the parade route. Everyone and everything was draped in purple and gold. All the streets and landmarks on the route, part of Pierce's old home: Figueroa, the Convention Center, Pico, Jefferson, USC.

The good news was that the loss likely ensured a Rivers return. That game, against that team, was not one of those walk-off-gracefully moments. That was the kind of game that could spoil your first couple of years of retirement, so it was better to coach instead.

The draft was exactly one week after the loss, and Rivers still hadn't said anything publicly about a comeback. He did know that if he were to coach next season, he'd endorse Ainge's first-round draft pick. They both liked Avery Bradley, the combo guard from the University of Texas. Players like him—athletic and dogged on defense—could fit into this culture, and Rivers's rotation, quickly.

He was in San Antonio watching his son Austin play in a tournament when a *Boston Globe* reporter tracked him down. Austin was on the path to a top school—for a year—and then to the NBA. His father would be in the NBA with him.

"I'm coming back," Rivers told the reporter. "I want another crack at it with this group."

It was good that Rivers made his decision in June because the first week of July was the space for player decision-making, and it promised to be one of the most significant weeks in recent league history.

The league had never had such a decorated free agent class. Pierce had exercised his player option, so he was technically part of it, although everyone knew he'd return to Boston. Allen was in it, too, and despite hearing his name annually in trade talks, he also wanted to return to the Celtics.

But it wasn't so simple for other players, including the winner of the last two MVP awards. LeBron James was a free agent, and there was no precedent for anything that was happening with him. When Cleveland offered him a five-year extension in 2007 and he elected to take three instead, many teams decided then to start clearing salary-cap space.

You know, just in case.

The best player in basketball, twenty-five years old, might be on the open market for any team to sign. A player, in his prime, *might* leave the area in which he grew up and take all that he was—player, pitchman, entertainer, franchise savior—and move it elsewhere? The teams that had the space and James's attention were all for it. The rules were set up so that James, and any other player re-signing with his own team, could make more money in that city. It was an incentive to stay put and keep franchise players with the teams that drafted and developed them.

If offering more money couldn't stop their players from leaving . . .

Some owners and GMs often didn't finish the thought because the answer was uncomfortable. They were all approaching a new NBA that the iconic stars of the previous generation—Michael, Magic, and Larry—had never experienced.

Take the cap itself, for example. The last time Magic and Larry met in the finals, 1987, the salary cap for an entire team was about $5 million. The very idea of one player turning down *$30 million* to play somewhere else, in the same league, was incomprehensible. And frightening. Because if the players turned down the money, then the cliché—that it was all about the money—was no longer valid.

What was it, then?

It wasn't just one static thing, and that scared teams, too.

Teams watched Cleveland and saw their own insecurities illustrated. A league follows the patterns of its best players, and James was doing something revolutionary. The euphemistic way to say it was that a new partnership between players, coaches, GMs, and owners was taking place. The truth: Players were becoming more strategic and exercising more power. The veil between the front office and the court was dissolving; some of the top players thought and made moves as though they were GMs themselves.

By July, the Cavs were one of six teams who James invited to make presentations to him. He'd weigh all the offers and then make his choice.

As the league waited on LeBron, the Celtics took care of their own business. Pierce signed a four-year contract, which would take him through the 2014 season. Allen's deal was for two years, which meant it would expire in 2012, the same year as Garnett's. The Big Three wanted to stay together, and it was especially important for Allen and Garnett.

They'd been aware of one another since high school. During his game introductions, Garnett was always announced as being from Farragut Academy in Chicago. He loved Chicago, but he and Allen were both from South Carolina, or "South Cack," as Garnett called it in his emotional championship speech in 2008. They entered the NBA one year apart. Before the Celtics, they'd been at the same All-Star Games and on the same All-Star teams. Their wives were friends. They were brothers.

No matter what the separation was, at times, with Rondo, Allen wanted to be in Boston. He and his wife, Shannon, sat on the board of a local hospital that was known for its treatment of juvenile diabetes. Their four-year-old son, Walker, had a trusted team of doctors and nurses throughout New England. They often vacationed on Martha's Vineyard. They were Bostonians, New Englanders, Celtics.

Allen was at peace. Even the team's decision to spend first-round capital on Bradley, theoretically his replacement, didn't bother him. The way he saw it, Bradley would be another talented young player who would help the team and extend his career.

The price of winning is sometimes saying good-bye to good players, and that's what happened with the other Allen, Tony. He'd taken over when James Posey left after the championship, and he played the role well for two years. He was a tenacious defender, and he thought he should have been paid better and earlier for his skills. The Memphis Grizzlies offered slightly more money than the Celtics, but he went to Memphis because the delay in negotiations with Boston angered him, and the business became personal.

When Tony Allen signed his deal, there was a familiar face at the negotiating table. Chris Wallace, the Celtics' general manager who preceded Ainge, was entering his fourth season as the Grizzlies' GM. When Ainge was hired in 2003, Wallace didn't know what to expect. As he put it, "I didn't have the highest approval ratings at the time" due to his doomed trade for Vin Baker. But he stayed in Boston for four additional years, leading to an irony that made him forever grateful: He was the least athletic and NBA-connected person from the old Celtics regime—which included Rick Pitino, Jim O'Brien, and Antoine Walker—yet he stayed in Boston longer than all of them.

Every year, the Celtics' crew from 2008 became smaller. They were down to six: the Big Three, Rondo, Perkins, Big Baby. This year they lost Brian Scalabrine, the backup forward who had a knack for breaking up any tension with a smile or joke. He went to Chicago to play for the Bulls' new head coach, Tom Thibodeau.

Perkins's injury concerned Ainge enough that he acquired two O'Neals, Shaquille and Jermaine, to play center. They had needs there due to the injury and Rasheed Wallace's decision, after one Boston season, to retire. The center plan for the season was to ride the O'Neals, thirty-eight-year-old Shaq and fifteen-year veteran Jermaine, until Perkins got healthy. The weakness of the roster, top to bottom, was that it had star power. Old star power. Of all those big names, no one was in his prime.

Now that they knew who they were going to be, it was time for the Celtics to see about their competition. James had a half-dozen teams pacing, waiting for the King's kiss. There was a big hint of where he was going when Miami retained Dwyane Wade, a close friend of James's, and enticed Chris Bosh to leave Toronto for South Florida. All three of them were part of the same draft class, 2003, and they'd structured their contracts to expire simultaneously.

In another first, James didn't plan to simply say where he was going. ESPN released a statement to announce *The Decision*, an exclusive, onetime television special in which James would reveal where he was headed and why. It was a basketball decision in reality TV packaging. All corners of the league openly wondered about the absurdity of it while also being drawn to its center. Everybody in the NBA ecosystem waited for the decision on *The Decision*.

The logic, nationally and especially locally, was that it had to be Cleveland. There was no way James would go on TV and say anything else but Cleveland. But then, the event was being held at a Boys & Girls Club in Greenwich, Connecticut. That was Knicks country. Maybe he was going to New York? A New York newspaper had reported the day before that James was going to Miami. TV personality Stephen A. Smith reported the same thing a week earlier.

Sure enough, a fidgety James sat across from *Decision* host Jim Gray and, in front of an audience peaking at thirteen million people, said the words that lit a firestorm, literally, in Cleveland: "This fall, I'm going to take my talents to South Beach and join the Miami Heat."

There were gasps around the country and gas in Cleveland. Did he just say that? Did he just *do* that? James's number 23 jersey was in flames, and police lined the streets to make sure there was no vandalism due to the bad news. It wasn't actual fire, but the open letter posted to the Cavs' website by Gilbert, the Cavs' owner, was toxic enough to end reputations and relationships. He called James a "former hero" and called his choice a "cowardly betrayal." He called him selfish, narcissistic, disloyal, shameful, and someone who kids should not want to be. The screed included a shouting promise, in all caps: "I personally guarantee that the Cleveland Cavaliers will win an NBA championship before the self-titled former 'King' wins one. You can take it to the bank."

As that letter continued to quake the next day, James was in Miami for a "Welcome Party" at the Heat arena, along with Wade and Bosh. There, in the street-fair atmosphere of it all, Wade claimed that they were "the best trio to ever play the game of basketball." When James was prompted that he wasn't there to win "just one" championship, he took the moment and went wild with it. "Not two, not three, not four, not five, not six, not seven . . ."

James was on notice, and so were the Heat. *The Decision* was popular in Florida and despised elsewhere. The public didn't like the method, the meetup, the arrogance, none of it. The concept of a super team was not new. The league's history was dotted with them; Red Auerbach and Jerry West and Jerry Krause and Danny Ainge created them. But players didn't do that. Or they hadn't.

While other owners didn't share Gilbert's specific fury, they were as concerned as he was. The NBA was in the final year of its collective bargaining agreement, and this was the kind of act, the kind of rebel spirit, that could lead to a lockout.

The Celtics were unmoved by the shift in Eastern power. They had their group back, and they weren't afraid of anyone. Pierce respected James, but he also reveled in matchups against him. He'd taken on the challenge of guarding him. He'd never lost to him in the playoffs. Why would this be different?

Of course, the first game for the new-look Heat was at the Garden against the Celtics. The fans and the Celtics got what they wanted.

James's last game with the Cavs and first with the Heat were both in Boston, and he did similar things in both. He'd turned the ball over nine times in his final Cavs game, and in his Heat debut it was eight. He scored 31 points, but the other parts of the trio looked uncomfortable. Wade had 6 turnovers and 13 points. Bosh appeared lost, got the fewest shots of the group, and finished with 8 points and four fouls.

Oh, if they only knew the secret that Allen did. In a trio, someone would have to be prepared to reduce his game dramatically for it to work, and no one would understand or fully appreciate it. In Boston, that had been Allen. In the original Big Three, it had been Robert Parish. In Miami, it would have to be Bosh. He either didn't know it yet or didn't know how to do it. The Celtics won, 88–80.

Two and a half weeks later, it was Celtics-Heat again, this time in Miami. Not only was it a vintage Big Three night, it was one where Rondo was featured prominently with them. Rivers loved these games. He didn't think there was a better team in the NBA when his players were operating like this.

No one could keep up with the thirty-five-year-old Allen. Wade was a great defender, but not on this night. His chasing of Allen got him out of rhythm (2 for 12 shooting) as Allen found his. He made seven 3-pointers and had 35 points. Garnett had a 16-point, 13-rebound double-double; Rondo had 16 assists; Pierce scored 25 points.

The amazing Heat had yet to reveal themselves to the league. They didn't look like the greatest of, future of, or any of the comments they made during their grand Welcome Party. What they resembled was one of James's Cleveland teams that lacked dynamism outside of him. He had 35 points, 10 rebounds, and 9 assists. Terrific. Every other starter was unremarkable, and Miami lost by 5. The Heat were 5–4. And the Celtics, as usual, were about to go on one of their early-season runs.

One month after they'd left Miami, the Celtics had a fourteen-game stretch in which they won twelve. Their offense was the best it had been in the Big Three era, and that could be seen both in style and stats. Each member of the Big Three was shooting the best field goal percentage of his career.

This was Rondo's offense now, and he handled it impeccably. It was standard for TV mics to pick up his urgent and high-pitched call for the ball ("KG! KG!") once someone else got the rebound. He wanted it because chances were he saw or felt something that they didn't, and most often the right thing happened with the rock in his hands. His assists were at such levels that his name continued to be mentioned next to Bob Cousy's. The legendary "Cooz" was the franchise benchmark for exquisite passing, and Rondo was on pace to break his single-season assists record.

All of this, and Perkins still hadn't returned to the court. There were encouraging reports there, too. He was progressing so well from his reconstructive knee surgery and rehab that he'd be back in January instead of February. The Celtics didn't need him now, given their 19–4 record, but they would soon.

Shaq, meanwhile, had fit into the city and team nicely. He'd hung out at Harvard Square and gone to the bar from the Boston-themed TV show *Cheers*. The crowd there was amused and entertained when he did a sing-along with them, belting out the familiar lyrics to "Where Everybody Knows Your Name."

He was Shaq, who already had his four championships and string of endorsements. He'd done things his way for a while. One practice, he didn't like the way the team approached its pick-and-roll coverage. Even after subbing out and sitting down, he still had some things to say about it. Garnett, as he was wont to do, stopped practice from his position on the court.

"Hey, Shaq," he yelled. "You are on the Boston Motherfucking Celtics. This is how we play defense. All right?"

Shaq said he got it, and everything was cool.

Garnett still was as intense as ever, commanding the Celtics' attention wherever he was. Although his 2009 knee surgery had cost him some game stamina, everyone in the organization valued any time he could give. His will to win—and to be a Celtic—made up for any athleticism loss that the injury had taken from him.

Overall, there wasn't much for the Celtics to worry about. At least nothing for them to worry about in Boston. But in Miami, the Heat finally started to live up to the promise of their hype.

To the delight of the country, the Heat began slowly with a 9–8 record. But the Heat went 25–6 after that sluggish start and were 34–14 on February 1 after a win over a truly beaten franchise. The Cavs had come to town and been blown out by 27. James's old team was 8–40.

This was what the critics didn't want to see: The Heat were still improving and discovering.

The Celtics were in stride, too, and for Ray Allen, the stride was historic. Before a nationally televised home game against the Lakers, Allen was within reach of the NBA record for successful 3-point shots (2,561). When he made the record-breaking 3, he was able to share the moment with his mother, his wife, his children, and even the previous record holder, Reggie Miller, who was working the game as an analyst for TNT. The assist on the historic shot had come from Rajon Rondo, and the night was so special that even those two shared a warm embrace.

The Celtics were three games ahead of Miami, 37–11, at the beginning of February. Perkins had returned from his injury and looked leaner and better than before. He was the team's most reliable center, and his teammates trusted his ability and mentality. He was the enforcer, the bouncer, always ready to, well, enforce and bounce. He arrived quickly and angrily whenever someone crossed him or his teammates.

With more than half of the season gone, three teams looked strongest in the East: Thibodeau's Bulls, the Celtics, and the Heat. But even Thibs knew that if his young team played Boston or Miami, those teams would have the advantage. The intensity, the sizing up of one another, the nastiness was between the Celtics and Heat.

That played out in a nationally televised game just before the All-Star break. The teams had virtually the same record then, 38–14 for Boston and 39–14 for Miami. It was still too early to talk about being the first-place team in the conference, but the winner would be that.

Things got personal in the fourth quarter. Dwyane Wade was called for a flagrant foul after elbowing Kevin Garnett. As the Heat huddled on the court, waiting for a detailed foul explanation from the officials, Rondo stood near the huddle as if he were going to join it. He was pushed away by James, while Allen stood between James and Rondo to calm the situation.

The afternoon took a gleeful turn for Boston when James had a chance to tie the score in the final twelve seconds. All he had to do was make his free throws. He missed one. Big Baby Davis went to the line six seconds later, made two, and the Celtics won, 85–82.

They were 3–0 against the super friends from Miami. Pierce was gracious in his postgame Heat assessment.

"They're going to be a different team in March and April, the more important months, when we'll probably have to see them again."

It was a prophetic statement, but not the prophecy that the Celtics wanted to hear. Indeed, there was going to be a different team in March and April, but it was going to be the Celtics.

The players thought Perkins's value was obvious to anyone who knew the game and their team. In that win over Miami, he'd contributed 15 points and 6 rebounds. Trips inside against him were not enjoyable ones. His defense, rebounding, attitude, and time with the team—seven and a half years—all factored into his value.

But "value" was the word Danny Ainge had to think about and the players didn't. Perkins was in the final year of his contract, and since he and Ainge knew each other so well, they'd had informal talks about what Perkins might be willing to take in a deal. The team's identity still was the Big Three and Rondo, and all of them had contracts. As Ainge saw it, the only way to keep Perkins and to keep his team out of a financially untenable situation was to pay him about $6 million per season.

Perkins was not going to accept a contract like that. He loved Boston and Ainge, so he wasn't offended by the offer. He planned to leave in the offseason for his best business move. In the meantime, he looked forward to staying with his brothers and trying to get back to the finals.

Ainge wasn't thinking that way. He saw how the team played in those games without Perkins. The offense had run beautifully, and although the O'Neals weren't the same kind of players as Perkins, the team could win a title with them—if healthy. Ainge understood the risk of that last part, health, and it's why he built that into his trade talks.

Yes, trade talks. He'd spoken with Sam Presti when the young GM was beginning to install his vision for what used to be the Seattle SuperSonics. They were the Oklahoma City Thunder now, and Presti had turned them into winners. They'd drafted as well as any team in the league by selecting Kevin Durant, Russell Westbrook, James Harden, and Serge Ibaka.

Oklahoma City wanted Perkins and backup point guard Nate Robinson. In turn, the Thunder would give up six-foot-eight forward Jeff Green—who was part of the Ray Allen deal in 2007—along with seven-foot center Nenad Krstic and a 2012 first-round pick.

Perkins awoke in his Denver hotel room on February 24 to the sounds of ESPN's *SportsCenter*. He slept with his TV on because he didn't like a completely dark room. It was early when he heard the announcement of a big NBA trade, and he sat up when he heard "Boston Celtics." Then he heard his name mentioned, something about going to Oklahoma City. He called his agent.

It was sinking in now with all the details. He started to feel sick when he was told that he'd hear from Ainge, and then Presti, that the Thunder were happy to have him . . .

He sat there and thought of his years in Boston. He was just a high school kid, eighteen and raw, when he came to the league. Then his whole career, his whole life, changed when Doc Rivers was hired and the Big Three became a thing. Garnett was his mentor and big brother. He and Rondo were brothers, too—more like twins. This whole group was family.

He sat there and cried, uncontrollably. He was supposed to leave *after* the season. The timing was terrible. What about his wife and kids in Boston? What about housing arrangements? What about the finals?

Rondo was somber when he heard about it, and KG and Pierce were angry. Why? And why now? They all understood the business end of it by now, but this seemed like the kind of move that helped future Celtics teams, not this one.

The whole team met in Perk's room and just talked through everything, laughing and crying. They were down to five now from '08, and the reality of those dwindling numbers made them even more emotional. They'd never thought to look back at '08 because they were still in their championship window; looking ahead made more sense. But when a scan around the room finds more and more new faces, it's only human to reminisce.

There was nothing against the new players, personality-wise. In fact, the team's veterans noticed how friendly and agreeable Green was. He never complained, not once, about going from a starter in Oklahoma City to a contributor off the bench in Boston. He wasn't as seasoned as James Posey and wasn't the defender that Tony Allen was, but Ainge and Rivers wanted him to reside somewhere between those guideposts. He'd averaged 15 points per game with the Thunder, and at twenty-four, his game had room to grow. Still. It wasn't the same.

Rivers was in the three-stage position of understanding why the trade was made, guiding the players and keeping them focused during a period of disappointment, and being disciplined enough to not blurt out how we really felt about the deal. "It was an awful trade for us. It killed our spirit. Perk wasn't a superstar, but he fit our team. We could see teams almost saying, 'You lost your identity. You're not the big bad Celtics anymore.'"

This was about chemistry. Trust. Togetherness. Shared experience.

It wasn't there. The team was not the same.

Within a week of being with the Thunder, Perkins had a four-year contract worth $9 million per season. Meanwhile, it seemed all the Celtics were doing was waiting on injury news from all their centers. Jermaine O'Neal didn't play for an entire month after the Perkins trade. Shaquille O'Neal missed twenty-one straight games with an injured Achilles'. It sounded serious, a major threat to the career of a man Shaq's age and size. But he returned for a game against the Pistons, and he allowed the Garden crowd to dream for five minutes.

Then they all got quiet when they saw him suddenly hobbled with no one around him. It was the Achilles', and everyone knew it. He hopped toward the bench, toward the tunnel, and then out of sight. His regular season was over.

Finally, there was the newest center, Krstic. He flashed talent when he first arrived in Boston. But with nine games left in the season, he grabbed his right knee under the basket and squirmed in pain. It was called a bone bruise, not a tear, but it was something that was going to affect him the rest of the year.

The season had become disastrous. The veterans still seethed over it. They didn't have much time left to win a championship, and fair or not, the Perk trade became their go-to touchstone when they needed to recall why they were so pissed off.

Going into the playoffs, behind Chicago and now Miami, this was where they stood in the middle: no Shaq, a questionable Jermaine, and a brittle Krstic.

There was true disdain for the Heat, so the proudest Celtics—KG, Pierce, Rondo—would never say it aloud. They'd die before admitting that the Heat was the better team. But with that interior softness and uncertainty, it was true.

That was still tough to reconcile when they saw Miami again in the conference semifinals. Both teams had glided through easy first-round matchups, and the winner of their series was likely to represent the East in the finals. Because of a pivotal Heat blowout win over the Celtics at the end of the season, Miami slipped by Boston in the standings. The first two playoff games were in Miami, not Boston.

By the time the Celtics got back to Boston after those games, the whole organization was on edge. It had little to do with the games, both Miami wins. It was the response to them. In game two, the Heat's trio went off. Back in Boston, at the team's practice facility, Rivers wanted to analyze it all on film.

A fifty-inch monitor was in the middle of the room for all to see, and the teacher went to work. Rivers never used sweet words to cover major issues. He said what he saw and trusted that the criticism would be taken in the spirit given and that corrections would be made. This system went both ways, because he expected his players to call him out when he was wrong. In this case, his criticism was specific and straightforward.

He told Rondo that he needed to get back on defense and have better body language. There were coaching points for others, but Rondo didn't respond the way they did. Body language? His body language in this session wasn't much to see, either. He wasn't interested.

This wasn't going well. Rondo was agitated. He'd been boiling since the All-Star break with the Perk trade. He was angry about the two games in Miami, losing like that to players he didn't even like.

Now Rivers was going in on him.

And by then, there it was in the air, hurtling toward that TV monitor.

Rondo had fired his water bottle, full force, at the TV. He was a strong young man with a good arm, so when the water bottle hit the TV, the TV broke. Shattered. Now there were two angry men in the room, Rondo and Rivers.

"Fuck that," Rivers said. "I want Rondo the fuck out of here."

Rondo kicked the door on his way out, and KG followed him, physically carrying him out of the room. Rivers and Rondo argued often, but this was different. The players and coaches in the room couldn't believe it.

The Celtics series was important, but this situation was bigger. They'd talked about Rondo's outbursts and his leadership in those contract negotiations, and he said he got it. All the teammates from 2008 saw how KG modeled accountability then, how he'd sit down to watch film and berate his own effort before a coach could get to it.

Then again, this wasn't '08. Most of the guys who watched Rondo flip out weren't Celtics then. They wondered how Rivers and Ainge would handle it. Pierce wondered, too, and his first thought was that Rondo should be suspended for the next game.

But Rondo played in that game, a win. He not only played but also dislocated his left elbow after being taken down by Dwyane Wade and remained in the game.

If anyone wanted to understand this team at a crossroads, all it took was a forty-eight-hour snapshot: The talent of Rondo gave the Celtics hope; the immaturity of Rondo gave them headaches; the toughness of Rondo gave them inspiration; and an opponent's perceived dirty play—in this case against Rondo, but it could be anyone—was unchecked because a main enforcer, Perk, was gone.

That dirty play happened on the same side of the court where Red's name was written elegantly in cursive. One could imagine him in basketball paradise, looking on and imploring some Celtic, "Kick his ass! Or do I have to do it?"

That tense Celtics win was followed by two losses and a playoff exit. Disappointing, but not something that would shake the franchise. Dealing with Rondo was the priority. And that's what it was going to come down to: Either they were going to deal with him or deal him.

CHAPTER FOURTEEN

BROKEN BROTHERHOOD

They often met in the gym to talk, one-on-one. There didn't have to be anything wrong for Danny Ainge and Rajon Rondo to have their conversations. No one talked with Rondo, advocated for him, or interpreted his actions like Ainge.

He took the time to see things from Rondo's perspective when others might stop at his cockiness or brooding. He'd gotten beyond that veneer long ago and learned how passionate Rondo was about winning and how—despite his reputation—he'd be self-critical after losses, sometimes too much.

And that was the problem. Not many people saw or knew that Rondo. A whole team had seen something else in a meeting room, where the mildest criticism of his play led him to throw a tantrum—and a water bottle. Ainge was one of the rare people who could acknowledge Rondo's immaturity and aloofness and love him anyway.

But Ainge didn't love this conversation that they had to have. He was disappointed, and he wanted Rondo to know it.

"You need to apologize to your team and apologize to Doc," Ainge said.

"I'll apologize to the team, but I won't apologize to Doc."

He thought Rivers was singling him out for the performances in Miami. Where Rivers had seen constructive criticism, Rondo saw an unfair ambush, an attack.

"Well, you're going to have a tarnished reputation for the rest of your career, because I'm going to have to suspend you. If you don't apologize to the team and Doc, you'll have a stain on your career that goes against the player I know you to be, and I know you don't want that."

Ainge clearly saw that Rondo didn't agree with him. At least not in the moment. But one thing he knew he could get from Ainge was full and fair criticism of any basketball-related incident. The general manager had seen everything in his career. Ainge didn't like what Rondo had done during the film session, but he also didn't think it cracked the top ten of all the authority-challenging things he'd witnessed on good teams. He believed these things needed to be handled, but he was also against overreactions. He continued.

"It's a simple thing to do, and you should actually *want* to apologize. You should feel remorse for how you acted, because whether you were right or wrong, it's the wrong way to behave under any circumstances.

"You could have addressed Doc one-on-one. You could have come to my office. You could have dealt with it in a lot of different ways. But that was the wrong way to deal with it. And you have to feel sorry for that. That was a terrible mistake."

This was no sudden transformative moment. It was going to take some time for Rondo to come around. Ainge had made his points, though, and he was hopeful that they would sink in before the Heat series was over. He wasn't going to put him back out there without an apology, because then Ainge would have a problem on his hands with Rivers, as it would send a horrible message to the entire team.

There was combustion in the New England air, for sure, but tensions and contradictions enveloped the entire NBA, as well.

Rondo's story was a fraction of a larger league issue. In both cases, discomfort and grievances had been building for years, and eruption—before resolution—was inevitable.

For Rondo, the basketball profile didn't match his behavior. He was a generous and creative on-court helper, someone who would go through people, and seemingly the laws of physics, to get the ball to a teammate. He'd recently rewritten the team's record books with the two best assist seasons in Celtics history. His game play suggested community; his off-court approach accelerated conflict.

The Celtics were going to have more time to think about that than they wanted. Rondo apologized to the team and Rivers, paid for a new TV, and played against Miami. The Heat ended their season in five games and then did the same thing to Tom Thibodeau's Chicago Bulls. That meant millions of people, either in the NBA or devoted fans of it, could be united as they rooted against Miami in the NBA Finals.

It was hard to keep up with the instant allies that had been produced, all aligned because they hated *The Decision* and the Heat. From the wealthiest owner to the fan with the cheapest seats; from old-school Lakers to millennial Celtics; from small-market general managers to GMs with escalating payrolls (some of whom missed out on signing LeBron James), the goal was simple: Root like hell for the Dallas Mavericks to win the championship.

For all of them, a Mavericks win would restore some measure of NBA justice. It would highlight an MVP talent, Dirk Nowitzki, who spent thirteen years playing for one team. And it would show that a team could win it all without All-Stars lining up their contracts so they could present themselves as a package deal.

But the leaguewide togetherness against Miami was just a disposable script. Because after the Mavericks won the team's first title and James disappeared in some fourth quarters, many of the allies abandoned one another to pick new and more predictable sides in a bigger fight.

Just two and a half weeks after the finals and one week after the draft, the NBA was headed toward a lockout.

League commissioner David Stern and his owners wanted control, and money, back from their players. Stern revealed that of the league's thirty teams, twenty-two of them lost money in the previous year. To make up the losses, the league proposed a fifty-fifty split between players and ownership. In other words, they wanted the players to take a significant pay cut. Under the previous agreement, NBA players received 57 percent of basketball-related income, and owners suggested that the fifty-fifty proposal would make the league more profitable.

Business blended with bitterness with some of the midmarket owners. One of the angriest of all was Dan Gilbert, owner of the Cavaliers. He and other owners didn't want to draft players, watch them become stars, and then have them run off to the most desired teams and cities in the league. James was from Ohio, and even he didn't say, *Hey, let's all play in Cleveland.*

If he didn't do it, how many players would? One of the proposals was for a "supermax" contract, which would provide players even more financial incentive to stay with their original teams.

The players pushed back on a lot of it. The supermax was fine, but the players didn't want to lose some of the salary-cap exceptions that allowed players of all talent levels to be paid. Some owners still didn't get it, really, with great players switching teams. James had opened a portal that wouldn't close any time soon, if ever. Players now used executive language and made executive decisions.

It was business, not personal.

Naturally, it was perceived publicly as a fight among the 1 percent: the infinitely rich versus the rich with limits. Instead of July free agency, there were negotiations. Instead of training camp in September, there were accusations lobbed from both sides. Instead of games in October and November, there were threats of a canceled season and lawsuits. Ten days into November, Stern said talks were finished and that it was about to be a "nuclear winter."

Finally, two weeks later, the lockout was over. It lasted 149 days. The season was scheduled to start on Christmas at Madison Square Garden, with the Celtics taking on the Knicks. It didn't leave Ainge much time to figure out which free agents to sign . . . or whom his starting point guard would be.

There was a fight over that as well, and once again Gilbert had something to say about it. Technically, the NBA owned the New Orleans Hornets until the team got a new owner. Their star player was Chris Paul, who was in the final year of his contract and didn't plan to re-sign with the team at the end of the season. Paul's availability made the market frantic. Both Los Angeles teams were interested, and so were the Celtics.

Ainge was a Rondo fan, but his affection for Paul went back further. Paul was a first-team All-NBA talent, and the Celtics were eager to get him. Ainge and Rivers told Rondo that their pursuit was not personal. They'd talked and thought out their issues from last season and were confident that nothing like that would ever happen again. But the chase was on.

Boston tried to involve other teams to fill in the gaps where the Hornets wanted assets and the Celtics didn't have specific matches. After some furious maneuvering, twisting, and pleading, there was no deal with the Celtics.

At one point, Paul was traded to the Lakers in a move that had many screeching that the Hornets had been robbed and that Paul was gifted to the team. Stern rejected that trade, and soon Paul was on his way to LA again, this time to the Clippers.

In an e-mail to Stern, Gilbert wrote that the almost-deal to the Lakers was a "travesty."

Ainge had a lot to consider with his own team. He was optimistic, a man of strong faith, but he was also a realist based on the totality of his NBA experience: Teams constructed like his usually didn't win titles. Yes, maybe he had been a little too flip when he laughed and joked about the original Big Three. But no one said he had been wrong to fear holding on to Hall of Fame players too long.

Now in the chill of December, it was easy to see that this team was in a winter of its own. Allen was thirty-six; Garnett, thirty-five; Pierce, thirty-four. If they were to win a championship in 2012, it couldn't be like 2008's. The trio couldn't carry the team now as it had then.

Rondo would have to continue to be a rising star, with more leadership and maturity. It wouldn't be long before last year's first-round pick, twenty-one-year-old Avery Bradley, would be counted on to contribute more as well. They couldn't afford to pay Big Baby Davis the money he wanted, so they traded him to Orlando in exchange for Brandon Bass, a twenty-six-year-old forward.

What they were trying to do was tricky, close to impossible. They wanted the experience, wisdom, and pedigree of the Big Three to remain foundational, while the younger portion of the roster would provide the energy and flight.

The challenges were everywhere.

Green, acquired from the Thunder in the Kendrick Perkins trade, was a big part of the team's plans. He was another youthful forward who could help with difficult matchups against small and power forwards. But during a routine physical, doctors noticed an enlargement of his aortic valve. He was grateful that doctors caught it when they did, and suddenly basketball was no longer a priority. He needed heart surgery and would miss the season.

The player acquired with Green, Nenad Krstic, decided that he couldn't wait for the lockout to end and joined a team in Russia instead. With Davis gone now, four players remained from their championship team.

In their final game before the All-Star break, the Celtics traveled to Oklahoma City and saw young, elite talent in person. If anyone deserved to be bitter, it wasn't Gilbert; it was Seattle fans. GM Sam Presti took the remnants and resources of the old Sonics and showed what can be done when you don't settle for drafting high school centers year after year.

The strength of the Thunder was in their three A-plus draft picks from 2008–2010: Kevin Durant, Russell Westbrook, and James Harden. The oldest of the trio, Durant, was twenty-four. Perkins was the perfect complement to them because all those players needed the ball and he didn't. He was on a team headed to the finals, and he knew it.

His best friend, Rondo, was in trouble again. This time it was a two-game suspension for hitting an official with a basketball. Rondo didn't like a call, and out of frustration, he flipped the ball at the official and hit him. Rivers tried to deflect some of the Rondo criticism by pointing out the ironic timing: On the day that he was serving a suspension, Rondo was named to his third straight All-Star team.

"Now we know the league doesn't hold grudges," Rivers cracked.

He didn't play against the Thunder, and the Celtics lost their fifth game in a row. They went into their break with a 15–17 record.

The trading deadline was three weeks away, and Ainge had to make some decisions about the roster. The season was already strange with the lockout, even more injuries—this time to centers Jermaine O'Neal and Chris Wilcox—and more discord between Rondo and Ray Allen. It had gotten so dysfunctional between the two that Allen believed that Rondo was freezing him out of the offense. He'd run the play, look for the ball, and the ball didn't come to him.

It was difficult to imagine Allen and Rondo finishing the season together peacefully. And for a few moments, it looked like they were going to be former teammates: Allen was being traded.

The deal was done, all set and ready to go. Allen even got a phone call from Ainge informing him of it. He was in the last year of his contract, and so was the player he was traded for, O. J. Mayo. Allen was the better player, but he was also a dozen years older than Mayo. The Celtics were acquiring a draft pick in the trade as well.

After all the rumors, they'd finally done it. They'd traded him. It was easier to count the seasons in which he didn't hear any trade rumors. There was just one, 2007–2008. That was *the* year for a lot of his current and former teammates. He knew it was special then, but that word wasn't enough to capture all that it was. Forget about the statistics; it was the most fun he'd ever had playing basketball.

He could walk away from Boston knowing that he'd given the team hard work, sacrifices to his game, and professionalism. He was better than advertised in the '08 finals: He made half of all his shots and more than half of his 3-pointers (52 percent). He tried not to take the trade personally.

Yes, he was nearly gone. Nearly. Because just as it started to sink in for Allen, he got another call with the latest update. The deal was off.

It wasn't until a month after the collapsed trade that the first media reports on it appeared. By that time, the Celtics had won twelve of sixteen, their best run of the season. When Rivers was asked about the failed Allen trade, he put on a performance for the ages.

"I don't see what the big deal is," he said. "It was a month ago. It was a scary moment for all of us. If you lose Ray, that's a scary moment. He's pretty good. I wouldn't want to see Ray, Paul, or Kevin ever moved. That's just how you are. Even if you got the best deal in the world, you're still losing a guy you have an attachment to, and it's pretty scary."

His finishing kick was even better: "The guys are great. We just moved forward. That's what I love about this team."

But the main thing moving forward was time. The guys, particularly Rondo and Allen, were not great. And the big deal, for Allen, was the collapsed deal. Plus, there was his awful relationship with Rondo. It reached its breaking point, surprisingly, after a win in Indianapolis the first week of April.

The surprise was not that it happened after a win. Rather, it was that Rondo and Allen weren't initially involved. There was an argument between Brandon Bass and Paul Pierce in the locker room, and it rose to the point where teammates thought the two men were going to come to blows. It never came to that; Bass and Pierce squashed it, and everything was temporarily calm.

Out of nowhere, Rondo began verbally attacking Allen. It was nasty. It was personal. They'd both been holding in thoughts about one another, and they all came tumbling out.

Rondo said Allen was jealous of him; Allen said Rondo was "bullshitting everyone on the team" by not playing his hardest consistently and by playing for assist numbers rather than what was best for the team. Rondo said he was going to get Allen out of Boston; Allen said he'd leave before ever letting Rondo do it for him. They went back and forth, and some players and staff winced at what was said because they knew, no matter what apologies happened, those words couldn't be taken back. And that was another reality: Everyone knew there wasn't going to be an apology. Of the two, Allen was wired to be politic. There was just no way Rondo was going there. This relationship was dead.

It was awkward for teammates. Pierce and Rondo had become quite close, and so had Rondo and KG. The four of them couldn't all hang out together, though. The nastiness between Rondo and Allen was too deep. They weren't living in Ubuntu, and they were far from Rome. They weren't even in the state of mind of those close-knit Celtics who had come before them.

After the season, one of them had to go.

Allen's right ankle was in pain from bone spurs, and he knew it would require surgery as soon as the season ended. But he was going to give this group what he had. He'd get cortisone shots, whatever he needed to do. He'd do it for Pierce and Garnett, and he'd get through it with Rondo.

Realistically, this was the last shot for them all. Ainge had already agreed to deal one of the Big Three, albeit temporarily. Garnett and Allen would be free agents in July. Next year's team might not include any of them.

There was hope entering the playoffs because as part of their late-season run, the Celtics faced the Heat three times over three weeks and finished 3–0. The third game was a rest game for both teams, but the other two wins were instructive. They matched up well with Miami, and their mission was to reach them—in the conference finals—in one piece.

The Celtics knew they'd have to do that in the early rounds without Allen, who was hopeful he could play in the second round.

They were disappointed when, for one game, they had to do it without Rondo. He chest-bumped official Marc Davis in the playoff opener against the Hawks, a loss, earning a league suspension and a seat for the game two win. Pierce picked everyone up with 36 points and 14 rebounds.

Boston was able to win three of the next four games and the series. Miami eliminated the Knicks the night before, so the Heat was moving on as well.

Heat-Celtics had become a series with player rivalries, but there was some hostility in the front offices as well. Heat president Pat Riley coached the Lakers during the height of the Celtics-Lakers trilogy (1984, 1985, 1987). Larry Bird and Magic Johnson emerged from those games as close friends, but they were the exception. Fighting for the title every June took a lot out of you and put something in you, too.

Twenty-five years later, some of the current Celtics could relate to the old hostility. Pierce, KG, and Rondo could never imagine being friendly with the Heat. Allen, who grew up in environments in which he was always trying to fit in, could. He believed in diplomacy, and those three couldn't care less about it.

After the Celtics and Heat each won their second-round series, a broken Boston arrived in South Beach for the conference finals. The Celtics beat the 76ers and lost Avery Bradley in the process. The guard, who'd become the starter over Allen, dislocated his shoulder and was out for the postseason. Allen, bum ankle and all, was back in his usual slot.

In 2011, the Heat won the first two games of the series, and the Celtics never got back in it. The first two games of the 2012 rematch, even with a higher entertainment value, seemed to be going in the same direction.

The first game was tied at halftime, and then Miami ran away in the second half and won by 14. Game two was a Rondo jewel. Even standing on the same court as James, the best player in the world, he didn't look out of place. Smart teams played off Rondo so they could give him jumpers and clog passing lanes. He wasn't nearly as dangerous when relegated to outside shooting, but he was in game two.

There was also no slippage in his handling of the offense. The Celtics went up by 15 in the second quarter, and it should have been a sign of what was coming when the 15-point cushion was cut to 7 in the next four minutes.

Again, perhaps as an indication of how much they'd drained their depth, the Celtics wavered in the third quarter and lost their lead altogether. But with four minutes left in the game, they seemed to be trending toward a win. In a great sequence, Pierce hit a jumper to put the Celtics up by 5 and then went to the other end of the court to block a Mario Chalmers shot. Eventually Rondo got the ball, and he fed Allen for a 3-point attempt that would have been devastating had it gone in.

No good.

One minute later the game was tied on a Shane Battier 3. Allen did save the Celtics from a loss in regulation. His team down by 3 with thirty-five seconds left, Allen made a 3 to send the game to overtime. But the Celtics lost it there, and a 44-point, 10-assist, 8-rebound Rondo game became a pleasant footnote.

So much for the rivalry. In the last seven playoff games, the Heat had won six.

While the Heat may have quietly conceded that the Celtics were too proud and talented to be swept, there's no way they saw any path to what happened next: two wins in Boston, including one of the oddest overtime periods in playoff history. That was in game four, when the Celtics got off to a roaring 18–4 start and led by as many as 18 in the second quarter.

But it said something about the Celtics, as well as the nature of binary basketball analysis, that some of their flaws were being ignored. It was as if the bottom line, a win or loss, was the tell-all in each game even if long series don't work that way.

Eventually, a deficiency that you have will be attacked until you can either fix it or hide it. There was no hiding those poor Celtics third quarters, and they didn't have enough players to fix it. The Heat went at them in the third and reduced that previous big lead to 5.

The game evened out in the fourth quarter, and then it was as if both teams lost data. It was a surprising and almost comical power outage in which both of them combined for just 6 overtime points. It was worse for the Celtics, who won a playoff game by totaling only 32 points in the final twenty-nine minutes.

More shocking, though, was game five. Back in Miami, the Celtics had the Heat contemplating playoff elimination. Leading by just a point, 87–86, with a minute left in the game, the Celtics had the ball and got it to Pierce. He was being guarded by James, who Pierce believed allowed him too much space to operate. It hadn't been a good shooting night for Pierce, and it had for James. It didn't matter. Pierce briefly stepped back and launched a 3. As soon as it went in, Miami head coach Erik Spoelstra wanted a timeout. Pierce jogged to the Celtics bench and announced, "I'm cold-blooded."

The Celtics led the series, 3–2, and that was a call to action for the temporary allies. That is, once again, millions of people with various agendas coming together to root against the Miami Heat. In the minutes after the loss, Spoelstra all but acknowledged that he knew what was coming before game six in Boston.

"It's a loss, and that's all it is. And that's what our focus is right now, to fight any kind of noise from the outside . . ."

The noise from the outside was at nonstop concert levels. There was general Heat mockery; questions about the legacy of LeBron; debates about whether the Miami trio would be traded if it lost game six; wondering about the job status of Spoelstra; praise for the toughness of the Celtics; and, again, a reminder from those in the Dan Gilbert camp that James was forty-eight minutes away from no title.

The Boston Garden crowd was anticipatory. Last year notwithstanding, the fans were used to being in this position against James teams and having celebratory drinks afterward. Before his players took the court, Rivers looked at them all and said, "They still haven't seen our best yet. They're going to see our best tonight. I can feel it . . ."

James was feeling something else, and he had been since Pierce hit that shot in his face. He respected Pierce and liked his game; he didn't like the guy all that much, though. James was annoyed at Pierce's trash talk and the snapshot summary of that game itself. The Heat hadn't won, and that was all that mattered. But if the suggestion was that James should have been better, maybe the critics should have been expecting something historic and favorable for Miami.

James had finished with 30 points and 13 rebounds in the game, and Pierce was 6 for 19. So if James indeed had more to give, it was likely to be delivered forcefully in game six.

Which is what happened, and it was over fast. James was stoic most of the night, not at all resembling the player who enjoyed getting others involved in the game before he took it over. He was impatient and aggressive, and everyone could see that this was going to be ugly for Boston.

Sometimes those power-to-power transfers happen as a team clinches a series. It was that way when the original Big Three Celtics passed the power to the Bad Boy Pistons and the Pistons passed it, reluctantly, to the Michael Jordan Bulls. In 2008, the Big Three took it from the Pistons in Detroit to wrap up the series. And now, even though this thing was going to a winner-take-all game seven, a separation had taken place.

If LeBron could do what he was doing to the Celtics, they couldn't beat his team anymore. Not with who he was becoming and what they were becoming. Right here, this night, was the intersection of his championship ascent and their championship fall. It was over. The transfer was unofficial, and to retrieve it, all James and the Heat had to do was keep playing.

In the first half, James hit them with his shots and moves reminiscent of others. He dribbled toward Pierce, waited for the double-team, and then sped by when he noticed it was late. One second later he was in the air, with Garnett watching, and then he punched in a dunk. That was his. He went baseline and then hit a jumper off one leg. That was Dirk Nowitzki's. He did a spin move on another jumper: Earl Monroe. A teammate missed a free throw, and here he is, out of nowhere, cupping it and slamming it. Scottie Pippen used to do that often.

He had 30 in the first half. He finished the game with 45 points, 15 rebounds, and 5 assists. The fans in the Garden appreciated what they'd seen from both teams. No one had had a playoff line like James's since Wilt Chamberlain, so that was historic. For the Celtics, aged and competitive, the crowd chanted "Let's go, Celtics" throughout the fourth quarter, even when they were down by as many as 23. They had more to say than that, of course, but the chant covered it all: *Go win game seven because this series isn't over— but if it is, thanks for all you've done the last five years.*

Celtics fans knew their team intimately, so they understood what was at stake in game seven. It was impossible to lose game sevens with a core like this and expect to just run it back one more time.

There was no shame in how their final game together as contenders unfolded. It followed the pattern of a team that was very good and not great: excellent first twenty to twenty-two minutes with a double-digit lead; a slide in the middle where the lead shrinks; and the fade to black in the final three to four minutes.

For the first and maybe last time, it was Miami and Boston for the right to go to the finals. The younger star trio beat the older one. The Heat were now thinking about their immediate future—against the Oklahoma City Thunder in the finals—while what was ahead for the Big Three and Rondo was more uncertain.

Rivers was emotional postgame. The season had turned him into a conductor, of game plans, lineups, and squabbles. He was highly respected for his basketball mind, so before leaving he had to confess what was a painful truth for all of them: "I thought we had nothing left."

Even if they had gotten to the finals, Allen would have had to tap out of them, leaving the Celtics further depleted. His bone spurs had become so bothersome that he told himself that he had one more game—game seven—before he would ask the team doctors to shut him down. Maybe Allen would have been rejuvenated playing in the finals against a team he had a historical connection to—before Boston. Seattle was probably the only non-Miami market passionately rooting for James to win the title since that would mean the Thunder—also known as the stolen Sonics—didn't.

James and the Heat won their title quite easily, in five games, and James completed a year in which he won the MVP, got by the Celtics, and won the NBA Finals MVP as well. The Celtics either didn't watch it at all or watched it with a sneer. Garnett and Pierce particularly wanted another shot at them. They respected James but had no fear or hesitation about playing against him.

They also had the privilege of thinking that way because they both had Celtics contracts now that Garnett had re-upped with Boston. Allen sent Garnett a congratulatory text on his deal and then added, "I don't think they're going to pay me."

Garnett told Allen not to worry about it. Of course the Celtics would bring him back. He'd come off the bench, most likely, because Bradley was their future at shooting guard. Allen would still be an important part of the team, though.

Allen thought about his free agency in 2010, how everyone in the organization seemed to call him and say how much they wanted him to return. It was different this time. It was more transactional; more, *Here's the offer; what do you want to do?*

What he wanted, honestly, wasn't realistic. It was realistic for employees, just not employees in his business. He wanted to be able to call Boston home and know that it wasn't going to change. He wanted to know that his family was here, their doctors and nurses were here for his son Walker, and that the community of Boston would be as important to him as his employers.

It was never going to happen. Not in Boston, not anywhere. They'd traded him during the season and even taken calls about Pierce and Garnett. If he came back, he wouldn't be coming back to security. And that made him wonder what exactly he was coming back for.

He and Rondo were too different to ever be close. Besides, the organization continued to promote him despite all the things that he'd done, behind the scenes and for the public to see. Allen compared what he was hearing in Boston, a response that he considered halfhearted, to the recruitment he got from Miami. He'd come off the bench there, too, but they sounded excited for him to be there.

At dinner, he and Spoelstra excitedly talked basketball while Pat Riley raved about a book he was reading, *The Four Agreements*, about pursuing freedom and happiness based on ancient Toltec wisdom. This seemed like the right fit for Allen, even if he understood what the Boston fans would think of it.

He got the irony: He would have had the fans on his side if he had been traded to a bad situation, like Memphis, with no choice in his future; the fans would be against him for going to a good situation, Miami, with a say in what was best for him.

He'd been around long enough to anticipate the fan response. It was vile in some cases. They were understandably emotional, and he knew they didn't consider the business and workplace issues of their favorite sport. What he didn't expect was the response of his brothers, Pierce and Garnett. He'd thought what they had was bigger than basketball. He'd thought it was a friendship.

But when he signed with Miami, they cut him off. Five years together, and it was all gone. He thought he was just signing with the Heat, but to everyone else, he was making the decision to send their relationship up in flames.

CHAPTER FIFTEEN

THE FINAL PUSH

Doc Rivers stood near the baseline of the Celtics' practice court in suburban Boston. He had notes in his hand, but he barely glanced at them as he spoke to the men in front of him. It was October 27, three days before the start of a new NBA season.

These mostly new Celtics wouldn't have to wait long to see how good they were; coming up on opening night: the Miami Heat, in Miami. That would have been a good game purely based on the Heat's win over the Celtics in game seven of the conference finals last season. But when they won the NBA title and signed Ray Allen, too, it became the matchup that everyone had to see. It was the promise of great basketball mixed with messy family business. Allen left Boston in July, and no one here pretended like the move was insignificant. Rivers gave one of the rare unprofane quotes about him, but it also wasn't complimentary.

"You know what it was like here with Ray," Rivers said to the group. "It was all about him. But I'm telling you why I'm here—why we're here—and it's to win a fucking championship. That's what it's about. We've got a lot of depth here, and sometimes you're gonna be pissed at me because you won't play as much as you want. Just remember that it's all about winning."

Allen versus the Celtics had been happening since July, in obvious and subtle ways. Rivers didn't miss it when Allen commented in his first Miami press conference that the offense in Boston was "more traditional" and that he couldn't wait to play in Erik Spoelstra's more flexible "position-less" scheme. Paul Pierce was angry that Allen never called to talk about what he planned to do. Kevin Garnett said that he wasn't going to call Allen because "I lost his number." And everyone knew the history of Rajon Rondo and Allen.

The point was clear to all here: Allen was not a friend anymore even though he continued to say that his business decision didn't cancel his personal relationships. He was beginning to learn that his old teammates, for better or worse, didn't know how to compartmentalize. It was all personal to them, and if they didn't approve of the way you left the club, you were an outsider forever.

Besides, honestly, Allen went to the Heat. They hated that team, and he went to them for more guaranteed years but less guaranteed money. What did he expect? Part of Rivers's summer was spent studying the Heat. He and his assistants rewatched the series several times.

Standing there facing the team, Rivers brought up some of last season's issues with Miami.

"LeBron is LeBron, and Wade is Wade. There are no surprises there," he said. "But Chalmers and Battier . . . those motherfuckers killed us last year. We don't just have to control them this year. We gotta shut those fuckers down."

He was convincing as he spoke, and all the eyes on him were indicative of how much weight he had in the room. His players believed in what he said, although most experts didn't. No one was picking the aged Celtics, now without Allen, to get by the Heat and to the finals. They had chances to do it the last two seasons and failed. If they were able to pull it off, it would be recorded as an upset. More important, if they were to do it, this season would be their final shot at it.

One of their weakest positions, for a variety of reasons, was the one Allen vacated. They projected Courtney Lee to be the starter and Jason "Jet" Terry, thirty-five, to back him up. That could all change when Avery Bradley recovered from his shoulder surgery, but he wouldn't be ready to play for a couple of months.

In front of the group, Rivers anointed Garnett, Pierce, and Rondo as his leaders. He also gave the trio a warning: "Sometimes being a good leader is knowing when to follow, too. Understand what I'm saying? Y'all have got to know the difference."

They all nodded, even Rondo. He was entering his seventh season, and Garnett and Pierce no longer viewed him as a kid. In fact, they saw the twenty-six-year-old point guard as the key to their season. When he and Allen coexisted uncomfortably as teammates, it was the Big Three and Rondo. Not only was he one of three now, some nights he was expected to be *number one* of three.

Danny Ainge watched his team as practice began, and he had no illusions about Rondo. The general manager had been fascinated by the guard since he first saw him play in high school. He liked everything about him, from his vision on the court to the way he viewed the world.

"He loves to be different," Ainge said in appreciation, pointing in his direction. Every other Celtic was wearing either a green or white practice jersey. The muscular Rondo, looking like an NFL slot receiver, was shirtless. Ainge was close with the players, and it wasn't unusual for him to joke with them, shoot against them, or counsel them. They also knew that his office was nearby, overlooking the court on which they practiced. He was going to get and make a lot of phone calls about them this year, so they all had to be ready.

The season hadn't even begun, and a blockbuster had been finalized that morning. Ainge and his assistant GM, Mike Zarren, were amazed that the Thunder traded James Harden to the Rockets. Ainge and Zarren knew both GMs well. They'd done business with the Thunder's Sam Presti in 2011 to complete the Kendrick Perkins deal, and the Rockets' Daryl Morey worked with Ainge and hired Zarren. Morey had observed well, because his blizzard of transactions to store assets and free up salary was Ainge-like. Morey never tried to hide his influences, saying of Ainge, "Danny is the killer GM. He's open-minded and super smart, a former player who knows the game and understands analytics. It's hard to think of one better than Danny." His old boss thought about the trade and seemed jealous of what Morey had accomplished.

"James Harden is a foundational player that you're trying to sign, not trade," Ainge said. "He's a young Paul Pierce; that's the guy I'm trying to sign."

Ultimately, the Thunder fell short of offering the twenty-three-year-old Harden a max contract after big commitments to Kevin Durant, Russell Westbrook, and Serge Ibaka. Morey, in turn, did what Ainge would have done. He collected every valuable thing he had and offered it to Presti. He sent veteran guard Kevin Martin, rookie guard Jeremy Lamb, two first-round picks, and a second-round pick to the Thunder. Plus he said he'd give Harden a max deal. After all that . . . analytics said the Rockets won the deal.

Ainge and Zarren agreed on the analytics but sparred good-naturedly elsewhere. They had opinions on everything, from the league to the media to the pros and cons of the Affordable Care Act. They argued often and with passion. Zarren's politics leaned toward left-center, and Ainge was usually on the opposite side, on the right. A trip to his office usually meant Fox News playing on the TV. At times, he and Zarren would debate so energetically and loudly that people would stop by and ask, "Are you guys all right?"

As if a well-rehearsed comedy duo, they'd pause on cue, quizzically look at the questioner, and say, "Why would you ask us that? We're fine."

They never lost sight of timing, though. When the practice was tense and focused, they paid attention to it.

As the team went over sets for Miami, Garnett never smiled once. He pushed his teammates to talk on defense. He followed up an assistant's coaching point with a point of his own, adding, "I think it's important to include that." When a spirited scrimmage lost its flow because it was taking too long for subbing players to change from green jerseys to white (and vice versa), Garnett snapped at the support staff, "There's a bunch of motherfuckers standing around the court, and not one person can throw a jersey out here?"

There was then a scramble by a couple of kids to grab a fistful of green and white jerseys, simply to avoid the glare of Garnett. The practice lightened as it neared its conclusion, and Rivers was happy to wave over a tall, white-haired man in his seventies. He stopped practice, called over two rookies, and promised, "I'll give you both fifty dollars if you can tell me who this man is." They both had vacant stares. Neither of them could do it.

"This is John Havlicek," the coach said. "A true Celtic. You know how we always talk about Reggie Miller running around and always moving without the ball? This guy did it first. Let's bring it in here, guys, with Hondo. On three, let's repeat it, 'Havlicek steals the ball . . .'"

They'd spent the entire offseason talking and projecting. Rivers had done that more than anyone. There hadn't been much time to unplug from the NBA. He'd been a proud father on draft night when his son Austin was selected tenth overall by the New Orleans Hornets. It was pure joy as a father and sobering as a coach: Austin was his then-fifteen-year-old boy, arm slung over his shoulder, in the closing minutes of game six against the Lakers in 2008. It all seemed so far off then: his high school graduation, college at Duke, and now being chosen in the lottery. Austin would be playing against Garnett, Pierce, and Rondo, guys he grew up admiring.

Rivers hadn't had much time to reflect on it because he'd also been thinking about getting the Celtics ready for at least one more year of contention. He was overjoyed when Garnett returned, albeit with a no-trade clause, which gave him control of where he'd go next. He was disappointed when Allen left, and when news began to trickle out that Allen had a problem with Rondo, Rivers stood in front of that train. He redirected the conversation and told the media that since he was the coach and he gave Rondo authority, Allen's problem was with him.

Rivers was a summer broadcaster as well. The Olympics were in London, and he was a TV analyst for the games. Watching the league's best players was instructive, and it was also a smart place to be for those interested in projecting future super teams. The owners didn't like it, particularly the small-market ones, but this was where player friendships and alliances were strengthened. This was where great players, who played and practiced and socialized and won gold together, got confirmation that they could be teammates in the league as well. Chances were high that some pairs—or trios—from the Olympics would be NBA teammates one day, too.

Finally, it was time for Rivers to worry about his own team. The truth was that he really didn't know them at all. Not as a collective, he didn't. He knew how much he could push three guys and how deep they could reach down to find something—anything—to help the team win. He'd seen them all hide injuries from the media and opponents, play hurt, and win games. The three had institutional knowledge that the others didn't, so even with this first game at the Heat, three of them could get to and recall Miami-related intensity levels that the rest of the team couldn't understand.

Four years ago in Boston, LeBron James stood in a darkened Garden as David Stern handed out championship rings to the Celtics. They'd gotten those rings, in part, at his expense. It was his turn to return the favor on October 30. The rings were distributed, and for the first time, James had jewelry to tie all his accomplishments together. This season, the Celtics were attempting to stop him and the pattern of league history: Once all-time great players win one championship, several more usually follow in bunches.

Really, that was the simplest way of describing what the season was for Miami and Boston. The Heat were trying to restate their greatness, and the Celtics were trying to repress it. In the first game of the season, the Heat were closer to meeting their goal. It was the first minute of the season, so Rivers didn't overreact to it, but the first 3 points of the game arrived when Mario Chalmers found Shane Battier for a 3-pointer. *We don't just have to control them this year. We gotta shut those fuckers down.*

The game settled down, and with just under three minutes left in the first quarter, it happened. Allen checked into the game, wearing the number—34—that he always had before becoming a Celtic. It was startling to see him there with the familiar Heat villains. He got polite handshakes and hugs from most of his former coaches and teammates. But when he approached Garnett, KG looked straight ahead with no acknowledgment, and Allen tapped him on the shoulder.

One minute later, Allen drifted to the left corner where guard Norris Cole found him. His first attempt for the Miami Heat was a 3, and he nailed it. He'd had surgery on his right ankle in the spring, and in the fall, he looked like a refreshed player. When he went to the free-throw line, the Heat crowd broke into a chant of "We love Ray."

They were having fun, and so were the Heat players. They led by 17 points after three quarters and cruised to an 11-point win. James, Wade, and Chris Bosh played like stars in the win. While Chalmers had 11 assists, he didn't kill them. Number 34, coming off the bench and putting in 19 points, did.

It was too early to make any definitive statements about what each team was and what to expect in the postseason. Each side still had a long way to go before developing its personality. But one month later, the Celtics gave one of their first clues about who they were going to be.

Playing at the Garden against the Brooklyn Nets, a week after Thanksgiving, the Celtics didn't seem ready for the game. They fell behind by 21 points midway through the second quarter, and it appeared they were on their way to a long night against a better team. Late in the first half, Garnett attempted a shot near the baseline, and the Nets' Kris Humphries fouled him hard, hitting his left shoulder instead of the ball. As soon as Humphries turned around, there was a player with both hands around his throat: Rajon Rondo.

There was more pushing and shoving, and the commotion led to some players being pushed into fans' seats under the basket. It took players and coaches from both teams to get things back to normal. Rondo was ejected, the Celtics lost the game, and the NBA announced a two-game suspension for the Celtics' leader. The team hadn't developed any offensive consistency, but what it would and could do was fight.

Most nights, there was no artistry to the way the Celtics played. They ended 2012 with three losses, all by 20-plus points. They added another loss, this one by 10, in their first game of 2013. They were 15–17 when they left town for a quick two-game trip to Atlanta and New York. They were able to get themselves straightened out, but not without another suspension and unplanned Madison Square Garden fight.

The Hawks were first, and when Rivers arrived at the arena, he was given a presidential greeting. Many of the workers at Philips Arena lived in Atlanta when Rivers played there in the 1980s, and they gave him familiar smiles as he entered.

"I've never seen anything like it," former Celtic Cedric Maxwell joked after Rivers had gotten through the crowd. "Everybody talks to Doc like they go back years with him. Doc makes everybody feel good, makes them laugh, asks how everybody is doing. And then you ask him later, 'Doc, who was that you were talking to earlier?' He'll smile and say, 'I have no idea.' I've never seen anybody do it better."

There were thousands of Celtics fans, wearing green, spread throughout the Philips crowd. Another former Celtic, M. L. Carr, was at the game as well. He sat in the stands, entertaining clients for one of his businesses. When Carr played for the Celtics in the 1980s, he had two primary roles: While on the bench, wave a towel to get the home crowd involved (or to taunt rival fans on the road); while in the game, do what's required—often a shove or hard foul— to slow the other team down.

Carr watched the game and was asked if he missed being in the NBA. At that moment, the game became physical, and Carr perked up. "I do now," he said with a smile.

The Celtics won the game and didn't think anything of an incident where Rondo asked official Rodney Mott about a call and, while questioning the referee, made contact. The NBA reviewed the footage and didn't like what it saw. The league called Rondo and wanted to speak with him about it but was stonewalled. The verdict, then, was that Rondo was uncooperative and that he was suspended for the Knicks game.

It was his third suspension in eleven months. He was developing a reputation, the wrong kind. With all the speculation about Pierce and Garnett and their future, there wasn't enough conversation about Rondo. Ainge's decision on him wouldn't be age related like the others. The questions had been lurking since Rondo threw the water bottle at the TV: If this was the real Rondo, and always would be, how long could they put up with it? And was their approach with him—usually an immediate public defense—a model of loyalty or enabling?

In New York, most of the Celtics' energy against the Knicks came from the oldest player on the team. The thirty-six-year-old Garnett still played with an edge, and that was apparent as he and Carmelo Anthony wrestled for position in the paint.

The wrestling, and talking, went on for a while, and double technicals from the officials didn't stop it. Even timeouts didn't stop the talking. Anthony cussed at Garnett as both men went to their respective benches, and Garnett naturally cussed back. When Garnett was questioned about it after the Celtics' win, he brushed it off as just basketball intensity. But Anthony disagreed.

As Rivers walked the outer concourse of Madison Square Garden, heading to the area where the Celtics' bus was parked, he saw an agitated Anthony trying to get on to the Boston bus to confront Garnett.

"Come on, 'Melo," Rivers said to him. "Don't do this, man. This isn't you."

"Nah, Doc. Fuck that. There are some things you just don't say to a man. That was some disrespectful shit."

Rivers tried again to calm Anthony, and this time he listened. In the meantime, Garden security had formed a wall between Anthony and the vehicle. Rivers took his seat at the front of the bus and exhaled as players, toward the back, buzzed about what would have happened if Anthony had boarded and put his threats into action. It was comedy and chaos wrapped into one.

On the short flight back to Boston, as most players played cards or slept, glowing lights from the coaches' laptops illuminated the front of the plane. They'd won three games in a row, and they'd done it with their defense, which was still a team strength.

As the plane landed, one of the assistant coaches was excited to share a defensive insight he'd picked up from his in-flight study. After all, the team had forced Anthony into a putrid 6 for 26 shooting night. On the ground now, approaching one thirty a.m., the impromptu coaching point from the assistant continued. Players gathered belongings and prepared to go home.

"Are you kidding?" reserve guard Leandro Barbosa, from Brazil, said to the coach. "*Vamos*! It's late."

That could have been Rivers's silent urging of these Celtics as well: *Let's go*. They'd appear to do just that and then retreat. After the Knicks win, they won three more in a row to push their overall streak to six. Then they followed that with a six-game losing streak. It was the first time they'd had a skid like that in six years.

It was going to be a season of "firsts" for Rivers, and soon he was going to have to honestly answer what that meant for his future with this team.

In late January, Rondo hurt his knee in Atlanta, and he and the team thought it was just a sprain. After further tests, doctors confirmed that the point guard had torn his ACL. He had been named to his fourth straight All-Star Game, this time as a starter, but he wasn't going to play in that game or any other this season. His year was over after thirty-seven games.

Rivers was defiant, publicly, when he explained the news. That was just his way. He'd been that way since he was a kid; his parents never allowed him or anyone around him to cover themselves in excuses. It sounded good, but he knew it wasn't realistic. No one in the locker room was going to give them what Rondo did. It was almost February, and they were in trouble.

As Ainge began to make calls around the league, seeking the best short-term fix for his hole at point guard, other names on his roster came up as well. Teams wanted to know how he felt about dealing Pierce and Garnett. It was what GMs did most of the time. Everyone in the Celtics office knew the annual joke: "Every year we call Miami and ask what it will take to get LeBron. Either we laugh, or they laugh at us. But one day they might not laugh."

Ainge listened. The thought of trading his fading stars didn't scare him. No one ever accused him of being sentimental. He just didn't want to rush into anything. Any trade of KG and Pierce, even at this stage of their careers, would require a huge return.

Garnett heard the chatter and found a way to gain even more Celtics fans when he spoke about it.

"I bleed green; I die green," he said. "That's what it is. But it is a business. If it crosses the path, I'll deal with it. Trades are a part of this league. Every year you're going to hear things."

He had the savvy to say it that way without pointing out that a trade wasn't going to happen unless he wanted it to. It's precisely why he had the no-trade clause inserted into his latest contract. It's also a detail that made his dispute with Allen all the more fascinating. The no-trade clause is something that Allen didn't have in his five Boston seasons, and the absence of it, along with the insecurity it brought, was one of the reasons he didn't trust the Celtics at the end.

Allen's teams, his new one and former one, couldn't have been more different. As the Celtics struggled, the Heat soared.

It may have been a coincidence, but the Heat's play approached historic levels after a team-bonding Super Bowl party. Two weeks after it, they still hadn't lost a game. They'd gone to Oklahoma City, watched Kevin Durant drop 40, and still won their seventh straight. A full month after the party, still no losses.

Forty-six days after their party, they were in Boston. Their winning streak was at twenty-two. They were on the second night of back-to-back games and on the road for the fourth consecutive game.

It looked like a good spot to predict a loss.

The Celtics, 16–12 since losing Rondo, hadn't collapsed without their star guard. But there had been no flash from the locker room, no revelation of a great player who just needed an opportunity. It looked like that player could be rising against the Heat. Jeff Green missed the previous year due to heart surgery, but he was back and playing well—and exceptionally well against the Heat as the Celtics built a 17-point lead in the first half.

Green, often matched up against James, seemed to have access to LeBron's tool kit. He made 3s from the corner. He drove to the hoop with his right hand and finished with a soft floater from his left. When Shane Battier drove toward him, he blocked his shot and started a break. He had 26 points at halftime, and the Heat didn't slow him down in the third.

He poured in 12 more third-quarter points, and you could see thought bubbles over the heads of eighteen thousand fans in the Garden: *Ah, so this is why Danny traded Perkins.* Green—what a name for this team—was exactly what the team needed going forward. No one was talking about the old Big Three or anything else. Garnett was sick and didn't play. Pierce was content running the offense and had 8 assists. Allen had just 6 points and missed all his 3s for the visitors. This was all Green.

He had 38 after three, but the team's lead had been reduced to 13. It was still 10 with just over seven minutes to play. That was also when the fun stopped. Green had 43 points then, and he didn't score again. The Heat won in the final ten seconds on a jumper by James.

Twenty-three wins in a row. For a single season, it was the second-longest streak in league history. They added four more wins after Boston before the run stopped at twenty-seven. The Celtics, as they had all season, went the other way. They were 36–30 after their loss to the Heat and then finished the regular season 5–10.

It was back to New York for the playoffs, and it was the first time since the advent of the Big Three that Boston had begun the postseason in the lower tier of the bracket. Garnett and Pierce were spent, and they were doing that thing that Rivers had seen for the last few years. They were telling half truths about their injuries, trying to play through and cover up the things that hurt the most.

They were down 0–3 to the Knicks and clinging. Realistically, getting one win was the goal to avoid the shame of it. They got two.

Rivers knew it from all of his boxing videos: It's hard for fighters. Most of the time everyone else knows it's over, big picture, before they do. The instinct to scratch, defend, block, clutch, throw jabs is all there even when their time is up. He knew it about them because he was one of them, too.

This had been the final push for the Celtics, and they hadn't made it out of the first round. It was the end of the season already, and it was the first week of May. It wasn't fair to compare the end of their previous season to this one without considering context. Still, last year they were one win away from keeping Miami out of the finals, and this year Miami wasn't thinking about Boston.

Ainge delayed a rebuild the last couple of seasons, trying to get all that he could from the Big Three. Now it was time. He'd begun to plan for a fresh start, which would obviously mean new players. One thing he hadn't planned for was a new coach.

Chapter Sixteen

RENEWAL

Danny Ainge knew he'd spend a lot of phone time with Doc Rivers in the spring of 2013. They talked and texted all the time anyway, but this was the offseason of renovations.

The Big Three era was unofficially over after six seasons when the Celtics lost in the first round to New York. Wyc Grousbeck couldn't resist a one-liner about it: "There's no bigger wake-up call on the planet than losing a playoff series to the Knicks."

Ainge planned to keep his head coach updated on Kevin Garnett and Paul Pierce trade possibilities, solid free agents to acquire, and draft prospects. In their nine seasons working together, Ainge and Rivers had dozens of passionate debates about potential Celtics, and this seemed like an especially important time for that.

Except Rivers wasn't sure if he wanted to remain a Celtic himself. And he wasn't sure that he didn't want to. He'd talk himself into circles like this with his agent, Lonnie Cooper. Just in case Rivers wanted to get back into TV, Cooper had already begun talking with TNT about a role there for the 2013–2014 season.

"I always hear you say what you don't want to do," Cooper told him. "You don't want to do this to Danny. You don't want to hurt the Celtics. You don't want to let down the fans. Tell me—what do you *want* to do?"

He wanted to think about it.

What Ainge wanted was for Rivers to stay on the job as long as he liked. They got along great, even when they had deep disagreements. They counted just one time that they'd had a real, out-of-control screaming argument. Most of the time, on their long back-and-forth discussions, they'd agree to end it by declaring someone a winner—and to never say, "I told you so."

"I don't know how we agreed to that," Rivers once joked, "because 'I told you so' is definitely in both of our personalities."

Rivers's conscience might have said that to him when he signed a contract extension with the Celtics, an extension that took him past the All-Star years of his Hall of Fame players. That contract had three years remaining, and now he could see how this could play out. KG and Pierce would be in some other city, playing for a contender. He'd be back here with Ainge, restarting the painstaking game of roster rebuilding: draft hoarding and flipping, a flurry of roster moves, drafting some eighteen- and nineteen-year-old kids, and then taking a Sharpie to measure their yearly progress.

That worked once, and he was grateful that he worked for the rare NBA team-builder who believed in coaches when they were at their best and not. They'd won a championship with that approach. He could do it again and enjoy the pain of that journey. Or he could ask Ainge to help him pursue the opportunity with the Los Angeles Clippers. They had a young roster led by Chris Paul and Blake Griffin, and they wanted him.

Although Rivers was his friend, Ainge still had to consider his coach as an asset. He was an asset for them or someone else, so that's what needed clarification. What Ainge knew for sure was that there was just no way—not a chance—that he was going to let him walk away from the Celtics and into the arms of the LA Clippers. If he left for there or elsewhere, there would need to be compensation.

What do you want to do?

Rivers was conflicted.

He still was a Celtic, with all the familiar faces around him, when the team held its pre-draft workouts at its practice facility. He watched and listened as one of his assistant coaches, Jay Larranaga, explained defensive concepts and the Celtics' way of doing business to a group of prospects.

"Listen," Larranaga said, pointing to a spot on the floor, "in the NBA, no matter who catches the ball here, they're likely to score. So our goal is to not let them catch it."

Rivers watched as a half-dozen point guards tried to prove that they had the brains and skills to do what Larranaga said. Time really was going quickly. Phil Pressey was one of the prospects, and Rivers had played in the NBA against his father, Paul, who was also one of his assistants for two years. Shane Larkin was out there, too, and Rivers had watched his father, Barry—a Hall of Fame short-stop—play in the majors. Austin Rivers and Shane Larkin used to play on the same AAU team.

There was another drill, this one for the big men, and it was more about will than basketball. The idea was to grab basketball after basketball and dunk until you just couldn't do it anymore. One center from the University of Pittsburgh, a seven-footer named Steven Adams, seemed to go through the entire drill smiling. He was tireless as he grabbed and jammed endlessly. On the flip side, there was a seven-footer from Kansas, Jeff Withey, who was wilting. This wasn't the drill for him. In the latter part of it, the ball appeared to be a fifty-pound weight in his hand. He could barely get it to the rim.

All of them, guards and centers alike, were raw. The Celtics held the sixteenth pick in the draft, and while there was always a chance to select a game-changer anywhere from any draft position, as Ainge had proven over the years, the chances at sixteen were still as low now as they were when Daryl Morey showed everyone his draft-research chart in 2003.

Rivers watched and left the building. Did he have the patience to put up with the kids he'd just seen? Was he really a Celtic outside of that gym?

Because that was what the team was going to be, and it was what he had to confront.

Ainge, meanwhile, had a lot more to manage now. He'd have to work out a trade for Rivers if the coach really wanted to go to the Clippers. And if that happened, he'd need to find a new head coach. Plus, the Brooklyn Nets had begun calling, primarily about Pierce.

Everyone in the league knew Brooklyn wanted to make a splash in all that it was doing because the team's owner, billionaire Mikhail Prokhorov, desperately wanted the Nets to have a relevant footprint in New York. When he bought the team in 2010, Prokhorov said he wanted to win a championship within five years. The Nets' previous season was good, but they weren't championship contenders. They had a couple of years left before the time on the owner's promise expired.

The Nets had actually asked about Pierce the previous summer and offered a first-round pick for the Celtics' captain. That offer wasn't taken seriously, and the Nets were told that it would take at least two first-round picks to acquire Pierce. When Brooklyn called back in May 2013, there still hadn't been much movement on their proposed compensation: a single first-round pick.

It wasn't unusual for conversations to begin this way in the off-season before they evolved into serious negotiations. What Ainge and

Nets general manager Billy King were doing couldn't even be considered exploratory. It truly was talk going nowhere because the Celtics had set a price, and the Nets gave no indication that they'd meet it.

Grousbeck knew firsthand that Ainge was an adept negotiator, so he didn't say anything about Ainge's approach in May. Grousbeck was more interested in Prokhorov's stated desire to win and his willingness to spend to do it. The approach, honestly, reminded Grousbeck of himself when he and his group aggressively embraced the Celtics. "He bought into the league because he wants to be a champion," Grousbeck said. "He has the right motivations. He doesn't care about the money; he just wants to win. If you don't care about money, what's the difference? If you happen to see two aces on the table, you want them both." That passion was necessary and contagious, but it could also be taken advantage of if it was too unrestrained. Grousbeck, an experienced dealmaker, kept that in mind.

The Clippers made their call about Rivers. Their best player, All-NBA point guard Paul, was headed to free agency. They needed a coach with credibility, one with the cachet to inspire Paul to stay. Like many NBA players from opposing teams, Paul respected Rivers. Players liked his energy, his insightful game recaps, and his extensive experience.

It had begun to get serious with the Clippers, and the two teams began to discuss draft compensation for Rivers. But they were the Clippers. They had a bad reputation: second-rate and unintentionally funny. They were at it again. They'd made their inquiries on Rivers, and they'd also asked about KG. Those were two separate deals, and the Celtics knew they had to be viewed in that light. You couldn't just make it a package because the collective bargaining agreement wouldn't allow it.

Even after being told that it couldn't happen, the Clippers leaked a story that suggested the teams were in talks about Rivers and KG in exchange for players and draft picks. That led to a rebuke from David Stern, who went on a radio show to say that he'd reject any attempt at a deal like that. It was the equivalent of getting yelled at for something you'd explicitly told your kid brother not to do.

Whew. If Rivers really wanted to go there, he'd have to put up with things in LA that he'd never had to worry about in Boston.

Rivers was excited about turning around a franchise that was known for consistently going in the wrong direction and often doing it on the cheap. The one year Rivers played there, the Clippers won forty-five games. In the next twenty years, they'd topped that slightly above-average standard just once.

As May turned to June, the Clippers needed to get moving on a deal for him. If not, his plan was to return to the Celtics and coach them. A return to Boston would mean he'd certainly do it without Pierce and, now, KG.

King, the Brooklyn GM, said the Nets wanted them both.

The deal was growing now, which meant the GMs would have to agree to it, and the owners would have to close it. There were many swirling factors that raised its level of complexity: KG's no-trade clause; Pierce's contract, which became guaranteed on July 1; the number of contracts coming back to Boston to make the deal salary-cap compliant; and the compensation from Brooklyn.

Even with KG added to the deal, the Nets' offer was two first-round picks.

Grousbeck was well into his Prokhorov scouting report now, so he operated as if he were dealing with his 2002 self.

"They have deal fever," Grousbeck said. "They're nowhere close to their max. We're going to keep going until they say no. There's no risk for us: We're on Mount Everest, and they're trying to get there."

Unfortunately for the Celtics, the current fight for the top of Everest was happening in Miami. There had been audible groans in the Celtics' offices after what happened during game six of the finals.

The Heat trailed the Spurs 3–2 in the series. With 28.2 seconds left in game six, they had no timeouts and were down 5 points. They were still down 3 in the final seconds when LeBron James missed a 3 and saw Chris Bosh get the rebound and pass it to the corner for Ray Allen.

Even a coach who didn't want to see it happen knew what to expect next. Allen looked like himself taking the 3 and sounded like KG after he saw it go in.

"Get those fucking ropes off the court!" he yelled to security. They'd prepared to rope off the court, anticipating a Spurs win. Instead, the game went to overtime, where the Heat won it to force a game seven.

Putting the season-saving flurry into perspective, James looked at Allen and said, "Thank you, Jesus," a reference to Allen's movie character.

Both sides had officially moved on. Allen had become a champion again, and the Celtics were officially disassembling any championship hopes they'd had left.

Going into mid-June, the Nets were two picks short of meeting the price. They offered two first-rounders, and Grousbeck wanted Ainge and Mike Zarren to insist on four. Grousbeck suggested that one of those four could be a pick swap, which would allow both teams to have first-round picks but permit the Celtics to choose the higher pick of the round.

"Insist on that swap," Grousbeck instructed.

Everyone in basketball operations had the same idea: They wanted as many picks as possible from the Nets, because they were hopeful that one of them could land in the midteens. The Nets were better than they were last season, and they expected that to continue for a while. The way they saw it, two picks would be in the twenties and the additional two—if they could get them—would be in that midteen range.

As for the Clippers, Rivers was convinced that the deal with them was dead. And it was probably best. He'd wanted to coach LA, the team's best player wanted him to coach there, the Celtics were willing to trade him there, and the Clippers still couldn't close it. He shouldn't have been surprised. They hadn't changed from the old days as much as he'd hoped.

On June 23, a Sunday afternoon, Rivers watched his daughter play a volleyball game. It was a family affair, and Rivers kept his policy of keeping his phone off when his kids competed. He wanted to watch them play without distractions.

After the game, he had fifteen missed calls and texts from Cooper, his agent.

"Where are you?"

When he called Cooper, he got the latest: After all the negotiating and soul-searching came to an end, he was not just the new head coach of the Clippers; he had vice president after his name, too. The deal was done. The Celtics got a 2015 first-round pick in return.

He told the news to his children, who grew up around the Celtics. They'd never lived in Boston, but they saw it as home. Some of their best memories were being at the practice facility and the Garden and seeing all the other families there as well. When Rivers took the job in 2004, his son Austin was in grade school, and one of Ainge's sons, also named Austin, was playing college basketball. Now both of them, Austin Rivers and Austin Ainge, were in the pros (Ainge as the Celtics' director of player personnel).

Rivers's three sons gave him appropriate but understated congratulations when he told them about the Clippers. His daughter, Callie, was more direct. "Do you think this is a good idea?"

Good question. He felt that he needed a change, even if the Boston job was the best one he'd ever had.

"I'd found a special place," he said. "One of my teammates from Russia, Sasha Volkov, used to have this great phrase. It was, 'Once you've found a good life, you should stop looking for another one.'"

He'd found it, for sure. But he needed a new adventure. And because he needed that, so did the Celtics.

Shortly after he'd agreed with the Clippers on the Rivers trade, Ainge asked three members of his staff—Zarren, Austin Ainge, and Dave Lewin—to come into the office the next morning, June 24, with the names of their top three coaching candidates. On that Monday morning, Ainge surveyed the room for the number ones, and everyone there, including him, had the same top choice: Brad Stevens at Butler University. There was no need to read the other names on the list.

"I guess I'd better call Brad Stevens," Ainge said.

Stevens and Ainge had spoken a few times before, usually about potential draft picks. Ainge and Pags had attended the national championship game between Butler and Duke in 2010. Pags adored Duke, so he thought he understood what Ainge meant when he pointed to the court and said, "There's the best coach in college basketball."

Pags was beaming. "Yep, Coach K."

"No," Ainge said with a smile. "The other guy."

The other guy was thirty-three years old then, and he'd led the small school in Indianapolis to heights that no one had imagined. The university had given him the head coaching job when he was thirty, and he'd won more games in his first six seasons than any coach in college basketball history. He was so appreciative of Butler, its program, and its culture that he'd decided that taking another college job didn't make sense. *Why win there when we can win here?* he thought.

He was aligned with Butler, from its president to its athletic director to its students to its understated facilities. His hard sell to prospects, if it could be considered that, was an appeal to their decency and sense of purpose: "This building doesn't have all the bells and whistles, but if you like tradition and history, you'll probably be drawn to it. If you like that, it means you understand that there's something bigger than you, and you can be a part of a team. If somebody isn't all in, you can really feel it." He had a lifetime contract there. Two other NBA teams had called in the past couple of years, and he'd turned them down, too. Still, Ainge wanted to talk.

"I really want you to think about being the head coach of the Celtics," Ainge said. "Just really think about it. I'll call you after the draft. I've got some things to do in the next few days."

Stevens felt like an NBA insider when Ainge didn't wait to contact him postdraft. He actually called him back the day before, the twenty-sixth, and told him about plans to move KG and Pierce. Stevens shared the explosive news with the only person he could trust: his agent. She also happened to be his wife, Tracy, a labor lawyer who prepared all his contracts.

Brad and Tracy talked about how flattering it was to be contacted by the hallowed Celtics and how it would take a unique place to pry them from Butler. They thought about the history and the opportunity.

And then Stevens said no.

He loved the school, his team, his midwestern life. He was staying in Indianapolis.

Ainge wasn't through with his pursuit of Stevens, but he wanted to close part of this deal with Brooklyn first. In fact, Tracy Stevens would have enjoyed the gristle of this agreement; there were lots of nuggets for a lawyer to look over.

A lot of players were coming to Boston from Brooklyn, strictly for accounting purposes. The Celtics wanted their contracts more than them. A perfect example was Gerald Wallace's contract, one of the worst in the league. He was four years past his All-Star days and still being paid like a star. He was due more than $10 million per year for the next three seasons. Brooklyn hated that deal, and shoveling it to Boston was a relief.

Brooklyn wanted Pierce and Garnett, and they also got guard Jason Terry. What the Celtics really wanted from Brooklyn was the organization's future.

Going to Boston, along with the players, were first-round picks in 2014, 2016, and 2018 and Boston's option to swap draft positions in 2017. There were no protections on those picks. That meant if the Nets became a bad team in the next few years and wound up with top-three or top-five draft picks, they'd send those to the Celtics. With no restrictions.

No one in the Celtics' war room celebrated the possibility of lottery picks in this deal. They weren't expecting *that* much. They were just happy that they'd set a price and stuck to it. Danny Ainge had done that to Grousbeck and Pags way back in 2003. Now he was doing it with them a decade later.

It was a shocking deal. The first-round picks had to be spread out every other season because of something called the Ted Stepien Rule. Teams are not allowed to trade future first-round picks in consecutive seasons. Stepien, a former Cavaliers owner, did that in the early 1980s, and one of those choices became the number one pick in the draft.

At worst, the trade ensured that Boston would have a storehouse of draft picks for the next five years. At best, these picks—seedlings of potential—put the Celtics in position to renew themselves and draft a new Big Three or select the Next One.

When Garnett agreed to waive his no-trade clause, the bulk of it was done—the deal and the era. The Celtics' most successful block of the last twenty-five years was over, and the payout was three Hall of Fame players; two finals appearances; one championship; a culture of toughness, intelligence, and creativity; and a first-round pick for every day of the workweek. As the Celtics approached the end of June, their draft pantry was refilled:

2014: Brooklyn's first
2015: Clippers' first
2016: Brooklyn
2017: Option to swap with Brooklyn
2018: Brooklyn

They weren't completely done with all the Nets' small print. The trade wouldn't be official until July 12, in two weeks, when the Celtics would be at the Orlando Summer League. Viewed another way, Celtics rookies and free agents would be playing basketball in two weeks without a head coach.

Ainge was still thinking about Stevens, and Stevens was open to the Celtics still thinking about him. He and Tracy had put an offer on a house in Indianapolis, trying to get a good deal, and their offer wasn't accepted. So they packed up their things and went to Stevens's mother's house, about twenty miles outside of the city, in Zionsville. When Ainge said he and the Celtics' brass wanted to fly out and visit Stevens in Indianapolis, he told them where to go: Mom's house.

Grousbeck, Pags, Ainge, and Zarren chartered a jet and flew into Zionsville, Indiana. Their giant SUV pulled up to the house on a quiet cul-de-sac, and out tumbled four men in suits. One of them was six foot four and had won championships with Indiana hero Larry Bird. And they were trying to keep the trip confidential.

They sat down at the kitchen table, with a playful dog nipping at their feet. They all talked about things that were important to them, and it wasn't their pitch that began to change Stevens's mind about coaching the Celtics. It was two things. The first was Tracy's comment to him: "You'll never be as good as you can be unless you're uncomfortable."

Yes, they were comfortable at Butler, and that place was in their hearts for life. But what was the worst that could happen coaching the Celtics?

"I'll go and get a PhD in basketball, and if I get my brains beat in and being myself isn't good enough, I'll go and be an assistant somewhere else. We'll figure it out later."

The other thing that impressed him was them. It wasn't just what they said in the moment; it was what they had done for nine years.

"The way that Danny talked about Doc. The way that he loved him. And the way he said, 'It's good for him to do this now. This makes a lot of sense.' There wasn't one moment of ill will, and there easily could have been. They supported him in the championship years, but in the years leading up to that, too. That really spoke to us."

It helped that those represented at the table had all been with the franchise, in some capacity, for ten years. This was a group that believed in stability. At one point, Stevens asked how the group felt about having family at the practice facility, because that was important to them.

Zarren burst out laughing.

Grousbeck shot him a look. *What's gotten into you?*

Zarren explained that what Stevens just described was Ainge's favorite thing in the world, to be surrounded by joyful, laughing kids.

Speaking of that, the agent got a call and had to leave the high-level kitchen table meeting. The kids at the basketball camp they were running needed her to come and unclog the toilets.

They were getting close. They could feel it. Now all they needed was the contract. Except they didn't have it with them. If this had been another candidate, he might have flipped out about it. *You don't have the contract?* Instead, Stevens pointed Zarren toward his and Tracy's unpacked belongings, where a printer was. Zarren reinstalled the drive, connected it to the home computer, and printed the contract. "I didn't know I was the IT guy on this trip," he joked.

The dog. The clogged toilets down the street. The laughter at the kitchen table. The unhooked printer. This was home. They believed they had their guy.

One thing Stevens was sensitive about was leaks. He needed the Celtics to keep this quiet on their end, and he'd keep it quiet on his. The last thing he wanted was his players to hear about a meeting like this through the media.

On the plane, Grousbeck told Ainge, "We should stay here overnight. Let's not leave here without a signed contract."

"No, I'm not staying," Ainge said. "I'm not going to stay and beg him to coach us. I want him to come only if he wants to. He's got all the information, he's met us, and if he really wants to come coach in the NBA, then I think he will."

As soon as they landed, Tracy Stevens called Zarren. This was a good lawyer-to-lawyer conversation. She never talked about money, just as her husband never had at Butler. His approach there was, "Yeah, sure. I can't believe I get paid this much to do this." It was all about contractual language.

The final request from Stevens was the ability to make the announcement to the Butler community before the Celtics broke the news. So he went to talk with his athletic director at five p.m. and then attempted to talk with his players at five thirty. He never made it through that speech. The Celtics released the news at 5:31 p.m.

Brad Stevens didn't know how he'd adjust to the pro game or how he'd make the switch from practicing one hundred times in forty games in college to, potentially, fifty practices for one hundred games in the pros.

He knew that the infrastructure of the franchise was in excellent shape. Grousbeck, Pags, and Bob Epstein were still excited about their purchase, and they'd pulled off a franchise remake while preserving its soul. They didn't buy for the money, but the money—and a title—had come. The Celtics became a top five revenue team in the league, with more room to grow due to media rights fees and a still-growing international market. For Ainge and Stevens, the new task was to build on and learn from the footprints and mementos left by the Big Three and Rivers.

There was a banner. An African word that centered them. A dispute that splintered them. A phrase, *Anything is possible*, that rallied them and their city. A Gatorade-stained dress shirt. A 3-point form so perfect it was worthy of records and movies.

There was something different about being a Celtic. Stevens wasn't sure exactly what it was yet, but he was drawn to it after initially turning it down. It was why Rivers was so tormented while stepping away from it. It was why Ainge, contributor to the Big Three class of 1986, returned to be Ainge, creator of the Big Three class of 2008.

It was why, on July 12, a Celtics fan teared up as he simply did his job at the Orlando Summer League. The Orlando Magic set

Zarren up in a security office so he could officially execute the trade with Brooklyn. Part of what makes a trade official is a recitation of all a player's injuries with the franchise. Pierce had been with the Celtics for fifteen seasons. There had been sprains and strains and bruises. Then there were the horrifying injuries reported from that awful September night in 2000.

Pierce had given a lot to the city, and the city had taken some of his blood. Now the man who made so much Celtics history was leaving the organization. Zarren cried as he read that list about Pierce. It was sad to see Pierce go. But being a true Celtic meant you could say good-bye to one chapter and return, someday, in another one.

Epilogue

Two weeks into his new job, Brad Stevens didn't know what to expect from the league that he'd just signed up for. He'd returned from summer league ball in Orlando, and now he was in suburban Waltham, Massachusetts, trying to figure out how to be a pro coach. And whom to coach.

He and one of his assistants, Ron Adams, stood in the Celtics' training facility and looked at each other. What now?

Doc Rivers, Paul Pierce, and Kevin Garnett had been traded. Everyone else on the roster expected to be traded. And the Celtics' most treasured valuables were historical banners above the court and future draft picks inside of a mythical vault.

Stevens understood it was going to be a long year and that the season would rough him up efficiently; he was almost guaranteed to lose more games in his first six months here than the forty-nine he had lost in his entire six-year head-coaching run at Butler. His understanding of that, and his trust in Danny Ainge's methodology, gave him an advantage over Jim O'Brien, the first coach Ainge inherited in 2003. But O'Brien's advantage was that he'd been in the league for a while. Stevens, the first-year coach, had to learn everything.

"I'll never forget spending the first month realizing that I couldn't teach the defense that was so good for us at Butler," Stevens says. "It didn't fit our team. And it didn't work in the NBA. It gets you spread out, and you can't guard the three-point line. Our big men at the time never would have been able to play that way; they were bigger guys, so they had to be more back and protecting the paint.

"So I had to teach myself a defense I'd never taught, and I'm teaching myself this with Ron Adams every day. Then there's coaching in the NBA for the first time, when you know the big question is going to be, 'Can this college guy make it in the pros or not?' And you know, I'm thinking about things like where our body position is when we close out. I'm losing sleep for two weeks in freakin' August about that. Luckily, I learned that it's not that big of a deal. You figure it out as time goes on."

Stevens had already learned the most important thing he needed to know about the Celtics at his mother's kitchen table in Zionsville, Indiana. There, in July 2013, Ainge reaffirmed his belief in coaching stability. He was willing to be patient if Stevens was.

When Stevens agreed, he soon discovered why no one was ever bored or static in the ever-shifting transactional world of the Celtics.

The first clue of that actually happened in Orlando at the summer league, but few people paid attention to the detail. At the last minute, the Celtics tweaked the margins of their giant trade with Brooklyn. They included a player named D. J. White, who played twenty-eight minutes the previous season, in the deal. His inclusion increased Boston's trade exception from $7 million to $10 million.

Somehow, that deal helper would be useful for them later.

As Stevens learned on the job and piled up losses, fifty-seven of them, the legendary players he'd heard so much about were settling in to Brooklyn. The sight of KG and Pierce in the black and white of the Nets was jarring enough. Beyond that, it was clear that the championship aspirations of Brooklyn were a bit of a reach.

The Nets were a good team, not great, and they finished with forty-four wins. They were affected by injuries to two of their top three players, Deron Williams and Brook Lopez. They also didn't get what they expected from Pierce, thirty-six, and Garnett, thirty-seven.

KG was never about the numbers, but it was the first time in his career he didn't average double digits in scoring. Pierce was good, but he found himself looking for some of the younger players to elevate the Nets—and they in turn looked at him as if he were that guy. The team did win its first-round series before being eliminated by a familiar and hated—to two of them, at least—opponent: the Miami Heat. LeBron James was especially devastating against his mouthy rival, Pierce. He averaged 30 points and seemingly couldn't miss from the field.

But that wasn't the big story of the playoffs. That was happening in Los Angeles with Doc Rivers's new team, the Clippers.

The team's owner, Donald Sterling, made several racist remarks that were recorded by his girlfriend. When the recordings became public during the Clippers' playoff series against the Warriors, the entire league responded with anger, shock, and protest. Some players discussed a boycott; some Clippers employees, of all racial backgrounds, were embarrassed to work for the team.

Rivers knew that going to work for the Clippers would be challenging, but he didn't realize Sterling's problems were as deep-seated as those tapes revealed. Since Rivers was seen as personable and stable, people looked to him to resolve a variety of issues during the crisis. After he spent part of one day trying to uplift the spirits of employees who didn't work in basketball operations, he got into his car and made a call.

Adam Silver, the new NBA commissioner, once told Rivers to call if he ever needed anything. Well, he needed him at that moment. The organization was crumbling. He explained to Silver how bad the situation was and how, with the Clippers, he'd become the unintended spokesman.

Silver assured him that he was doing a great job and that things would change soon.

They would not change before Rivers's players heard him, before a playoff game in Oakland, screaming at someone on the phone before the game. He was admonishing the team's president, Andy Roeser, not to bring Sterling to the game. Even after the release of the controversial tapes, Sterling was at the San Francisco airport en route to see the Clippers.

"Are you crazy?" Rivers's players could hear him say. "Do not—and I want to make myself clear on this—do not have Donald come to this game!"

They went back and forth so long, and so animatedly, that Rivers didn't take his seat on the bench until a minute before tip-off. In the end, Sterling didn't come to the game. Nor did he keep his team much longer. At the end of April, Silver made a stunning announcement.

"I am banning Mr. Sterling for life from any association with the Clippers organization or the NBA," Silver said. He fined him $2.5 million and said he was going to force him to sell the team. The commissioner said he was also "particularly grateful" for the leadership shown by Rivers.

In June 2014, the Celtics had their first opportunity to use a Brooklyn first-round pick. It followed their own selection, at six, of six-foot-four guard Marcus Smart. At seventeen, Boston drafted another guard, Kentucky's James Young. It was also trade and free agent season in the NBA. Pierce left Brooklyn to sign a two-year contract with Washington; LeBron James returned to Cleveland four years after *The Decision*; and the Celtics, on the strength of the salary-cap exception they received in the Brooklyn trade, were able to acquire guard Marcus Thornton, center Tyler Zeller, and a future first-round pick from the Cavaliers.

Ainge and Mike Zarren were just getting loose. They made deals aggressively, always looking for the slightest positive in an acquisition that would be good for something one day. In their latest trade, they were able to absorb the full salary of Thornton because they tucked it, so to speak, into the salary-cap exception space. The draft-pick vault was filling up to eye level, but the players still came in and out, transfer-station style.

That couldn't have been clearer to anyone watching two months into Stevens's second year. His career record on December 17, 2014, was 34–71. It would have been easy for anyone to look at that record, without context, and say that whatever Stevens was doing was not working. Ainge saw beauty in it.

"So Danny is this nasty competitor, right?" Stevens says with a laugh. "You go back and watch his games. He's chucking balls at people. On the golf course, he's relentless; he'll take anybody's money that will go out there with him. But nobody is more of a glass half full, optimistic person than Danny Ainge. I'd be down in the dumps, we'd get beaten by twenty, and he'd call and say, 'Man, I saw some good things out there.'"

Ainge usually saw good things and trade opportunities. On December 18, 2014, he traded one of his favorite players—and people—ever in Rajon Rondo. He sent him to Dallas in exchange for a bundle of players, including forward Jae Crowder and yet another first-round pick. Rondo's new coach would be Rick Carlisle, a reserve guard on the championship Big Three Celtics of 1986.

With Rondo gone, Ainge couldn't stop in January 2015. He moved his leading scorer, Jeff Green, to Memphis as part of a three-team trade. One of the pieces he got back, of course, was a future first-round pick. There was also a kid in the trade, one he'd watched grow up. It was Austin Rivers. But he wasn't going to stay long, either. Ainge traded Rivers to the Clippers, to play for his father.

In February 2015, at the deadline, there were even more trades. The Nets sent KG back to Minnesota to end his career there. Just nineteen months after the Brooklyn-Boston deal, the Celtics had yet to get into the meat of their picks, and the Nets already were left with nothing to show from doing business with Boston. The Celtics were spending from all parts of that trade. That's how they acquired Thornton and Zeller from Cleveland. So just before the deadline, they traded Thornton and that Cleveland first-rounder they'd received and brought in a five-foot-nine guard, Isaiah Thomas.

They were excited by their new guard.

Carlisle, Rondo's coach, was already sick of his.

Rondo got himself benched by Carlisle after he wouldn't listen to the coach's play call. They'd yelled at one another in front of the bench, on display for all to see. Rondo was in his contract year, and there was a good chance he wouldn't re-sign with the Mavericks.

On March 1, 2015, Stevens's team was 23–34. But the Celtics finished 17–8 and made the playoffs. The new player, nicknamed IT, was sensational. He found his game playing for Stevens, and he became the team's top scorer.

Stevens, unquestionably, was a pro coach. He'd been able to make a team out of a group that Ainge had never intended to be a team. He was making trades for assets, so that brought an eclectic bunch of players to Boston. The fact that Stevens was able to take those odd fits and spare parts and forge a traceable identity was miraculous.

"It's not much different from when you have a young rookie who you know is going to be a fantastic player, but he's not going to be a fantastic player in his rookie year," Ainge says. "It's going to take some learning. And I knew that about Brad. Coaching is hard, and coaching in the NBA is even harder. I knew that we didn't have a great team and I was very open and honest with him about all of those things.

"I think Brad is one of the top coaches in the NBA right now. And I think that he's getting better every year. He's going to be even better five years from now. It's funny: From his standpoint, he thinks there were some definite growing pains when he first started. But not from mine. I knew he wasn't perfect as a coach, but I knew he was good, and he has been good from day one. But now I think he's one of the better coaches in the league."

In 2016, a few notable things took shape. After twenty-two seasons, KG retired. Pierce wasn't far behind. He'd played for Rivers and the Clippers in '16 and planned to extend his career one more year. The Celtics had become good again, winners of forty-eight games. Their leading scorer, and All-Star, was Thomas. As warm as that story was for the franchise, the development in Brooklyn was staggering.

The Nets were awful. Really bad. They won twenty-one games and were headed to the lottery. The trade had put them on a treadmill that would take them a couple of years to escape; they'd be bad enough to enter the lottery, but because of the trade, they couldn't improve from those lottery picks. Those were for the Celtics to use.

In the 2016 draft, with the third choice via Brooklyn, the Celtics took California forward Jaylen Brown. Red Auerbach had been right about Ainge. How lucky was this? The rebuild lasted one year, and now they were a good team being gifted high draft picks. There was no pressure on Brown to lead the team because of what Ainge had done in the offseason.

He'd managed the salary cap well enough that there was enough room to pursue two prime free agents. One was Atlanta center Al Horford. The other was Oklahoma City forward Kevin Durant. The Celtics were one of the few teams who earned a one-on-one meeting with Durant in the Hamptons. They even brought his favorite football player, the Patriots' Tom Brady, on the recruiting trip to sway him. Durant picked the Warriors instead. The Celtics continued their ascent and won fifty-three games. Thomas, who averaged 29 points, became the shortest All-NBA player in history.

Brooklyn? The Nets won twenty games. This was the 2017 draft, so it was the pick swap year insisted on by Wyc Grousbeck. No matter where the Nets landed in the lottery, there was no doubt that the Celtics, picking twenty-seventh, were going to swap with them. After the lottery balls bounced, the Nets finished with the number one overall selection.

Incredible. Ainge, who'd hoped the Brooklyn deal would lead to some decent late- to mid-first-round picks, acquired number three and number one in successive drafts. He knew the player he wanted with that pick, and it wasn't Markelle Fultz, the consensus top choice. He had his eye on Duke forward Jayson Tatum. He realized he could still get Tatum and acquire a future first if he traded down from one to the three slot, held by the 76ers. The Sixers wanted Fultz, and the Lakers, choosing second, wanted guard Lonzo Ball. The Celtics added Tatum and said goodbye, officially, to the Truth.

Pierce signed a one-day contract and retired as a Celtic.

With one more Brooklyn pick in their care, the Celtics decided to cash in. They'd added forward Gordon Hayward in free agency, drafted Tatum, and now wanted another championship move. Cleveland guard Kyrie Irving requested a trade, and the luck of Ainge struck again. He had another Brooklyn pick to offer, and that was a valuable chip. It was going to be in the lottery, and it could be as high as the top three. He also had the benefit of insight. The Cavs' former general manager was David Griffin, who used to work for Ainge in Phoenix. If anyone could tell him everything he needed to know about Irving, it was Griffin.

The deal was in motion, and the results from one of the most stunning transactions in league history were complete. The Celtics traded their veteran stars to Brooklyn and received the youth of James Young, Jaylen Brown, Jayson Tatum, and Kyrie Irving.

It all looked good in print, but Ainge, a lifelong Celtic, recognized the sacrifice necessary to be successful in green and white. He saw numerous examples of it in his playing and executive career. Rivers saw it, too, and summed it up by describing the 2008 version of KG.

"If you had never seen us play or practice that year, if all you knew about us was what you saw from the team plane, team meetings, interactions in our locker room, you would have thought that Kevin was a role-player.

"He was that player who basically said, 'You can have my body, my brain, my talent. Use me as you see fit.' He was special. He didn't care about stats, ever. It was all about winning."

It was why he looked so long at those rafters, delaying his first press conference by twenty-five minutes. All those players up there, with their numbers retired, weren't there because of individual stats alone. They'd been honored because they played and thought a certain way.

In 2018, Pierce returned to the Garden and had his number retired while KG and Rondo watched. (Allen wasn't there and instead tweeted a photo of himself and others at a previously scheduled golf event.) Later that year, Allen was inducted into the Hall of Fame. (Pierce and KG weren't there.) In 2020, KG was inducted into the Hall and officially learned from the Celtics that his number, like Pierce's, would also hang above Red Auerbach's signed floor.

Allen still plays golf with Ainge and continues to have strong ties to New England. There are no plans for his number to hang above the court, even if what he, Pierce, and KG established on it is undeniable.

AFTERWORD

On April 6, 2021, minutes after the Celtics lost to the Philadelphia 76ers at Boston Garden, a single tweet caused a stir on the Celtics' roster.

Its author, former Celtic Kendrick Perkins, wasn't trying to be provocative. As part of the team's local television coverage, Perkins had watched the game. He'd noticed, like many Celtics fans, that there was a certain lethargy to the team's performance and its best player—Jayson Tatum—was being sucked into that abyss. The team, six months removed from the Eastern Conference Finals, held a disappointing 25–26 record. Neither hard coaching nor subtle coaxing freed it from its rut. That's why the tweet and the reaction to it was so revealing.

"Jayson Tatum, you got paid the big bucks! You have the body language and energy level of an underpaid player and it's hurtin the team," Perkins wrote. "Time to step up and live up to your role."

While Danny Ainge and Brad Stevens hadn't spoken exactly like that in the season's first fifty games, the sentiment was there for the collective roster. Everyone could see it. The Celtics lacked want-to and focus. That their best player got it, in part, from a former player's tweet was both insightful and foreboding.

Soon after reading the tweet, Tatum initiated a phone call to Perkins, with the current player and former one respectfully exchanging their perspectives. A couple days later, Tatum scored a career-high 53 points against Minnesota. He followed that game with a 28-point, 10-rebound night. And a week later, he had 44 points and 10 rebounds against the Warriors. The Celtics, meanwhile, won six games in a row, their longest winning streak of the season.

There was nothing coincidental about the obvious cause and effect. Stevens, in his eighth season as head coach, struggled to capture the team's attention. It was a rare position for the coach, who was known for his magical whisperings to underdogs. These Celtics, shaped by Ainge, had marginal talent as well as emerging superstars like Tatum and Jaylen Brown. Yet, at times, Stevens couldn't connect with either faction of his odd team. Stevens never played in the NBA, and that had never been a talking point, inside the locker room or out. The 2020–2021 Celtics, though, seemed to want and/or need the one thing that their head coach couldn't give them. There was speculation that Stevens would either return to the college game or be fired at the end of the season.

Neither happened.

Instead, the Celtics' postseason and its aftermath featured irony, revenge, history, and a couple of jaw-dropping surprises.

The team's first-round opponent was the Nets, whom the Celtics once filleted and left for dead by taking their high draft picks and flipping them into All-Stars Tatum, Brown, and Kyrie Irving. But Irving, after publicly declaring his desire to stay in Boston in the fall of 2018, changed course in the spring and joined the Nets in 2019 instead. By the spring of 2021, Irving, Kevin Durant, and

James Harden suddenly formed the core of a team that was superior to Boston's.

The Nets easily won the first two games of the best-of-seven series. Immediately after the second game, the big question was if the Celtics could manage to secure a single victory. Then the question shifted after Irving spoke at his postgame press conference. In a demeanor that was strangely just short of whimsical, given the subject matter, Irving said he hoped to avoid belligerence and racism in Boston for games three and four. When asked if he experienced those things as a Celtic or at any other time, Irving shrugged and smiled his way off the dais. What followed was an extended media and fan discussion on race in Boston and whether the city is hostile to its black athletes.

Irving started the discussion and then coolly slid away from it. His performance, as a spokesman and as a star, was a reminder of how enigmatic he was as a Celtic. In the weeks leading up to Irving's free agency, the franchise essentially held its breath around him. Some team officials ignored it when Irving ignored them during road trips or at home in the locker room. They nervously told the media relations staff not to ask him anything that might upset him. They continued to hope, despite his quirks, that he'd make the decision to remain a Celtic. He clearly had other plans.

As a member of the Nets, Irving's last act against the Celtics, following a game four win, was to wipe his feet on the team's iconic logo. Shortly after he did that, a fan foolishly threw a water bottle at him as he walked toward the Nets' locker room. This breakup between star and fan base, nearly two years old, remained mean-spirited and spiteful.

But that was the old breakup, and in retrospect it was predictable. The newer one was shocking. After the Celtics were eliminated from the playoffs in five games, the team made an announcement:

Ainge, who'd guided basketball operations for eighteen years, was resigning his position.

He wasn't fired.

He wasn't retiring.

He was making the decision to walk away from the job.

Consequently, he'd be replaced by his head coach, Stevens.

This was quite the seismic shift in Boston: a new lead basketball executive for the first time in a generation, and a new head coach for the first time in nearly a decade. It was hard to reconcile that Ainge, who had a hand in everything the Celtics had become since 2003, was exiting. Under his leadership, the team hired two of its most successful coaches in Stevens and Doc Rivers. It acquired Kevin Garnett, Ray Allen, Tatum, Brown, and Irving. It won the 2008 championship and established a championship standard for a dozen years after. It brought groundbreaking diversity to the front office and bench, hiring black women in player development (Allison Feaster) and coaching (Kara Lawson). It became known as a team that knew whom to draft when it was situated high in the lottery but was also adept at navigating the myriad loops of the salary cap to collect sizable trade exceptions to make smart deals (such as the one for Isaiah Thomas).

Ainge's departure officially began a new era for the team's ownership group. When the owners hired Ainge, their mission was to find someone who could build a championship organization. He left the franchise in better shape than when he found it, so the new mandate was difficult but simple: maintain a championship organization.

Stevens didn't wait long to make boss moves. He traded the player who'd replaced Irving, Kemba Walker, and received former Celtic Al Horford in the return package. Stevens had always gotten the most out of his point guards, but the combination of Walker's knee injuries and occasionally ill-timed ball dominance made him a bad fit by the end of the '21 season. He then consulted with his former players and considered their opinions on the next head coach. All involved agreed that Ime Udoka, a longtime assistant and former NBA journeyman, was the man for the job. Udoka knew Tatum and Brown from their work together with USA Basketball. The new coach's confidence with them and the overall situation was on display in his first press conference. He promised to challenge his superstars and shared that they asked him to do it. He teased Stevens about how poorly the team passed the ball in the previous season. He said he wanted a hungry team that had some "dog" in it.

He and Stevens clearly were aligned with their vision of reshaping the team, with rough edges intentionally included. A few transactions made it obvious. Marcus Smart, the grittiest player on the team, was given a four-year contract extension. Udoka also told him that he was entrusting him as ball handler/decision maker. Two other players, Josh Richardson and Dennis Schroeder, were acquired in part for their brazen reputations.

As the Celtics prepared for the 2021–2022 season, Stevens found himself in the middle of a familiar Celtics narrative. His predecessor, Ainge, had inherited Paul Pierce and had to creatively find stars to put around him. Stevens inherited Tatum and Brown, whom he coached, and is now tasked with unearthing a star to make the duo into a trio.

Said another way, he's now looking for a new Big Three.

Notes

This project began in 2012 and then was tabled for a while. At the beginning of it, the focus was on Doc Rivers and the Celtics as they attempted to make one more championship run. There was access to several meetings and events that the author was present for (such as Carmelo Anthony's attempt to climb aboard the Celtics' bus in Madison Square Garden in 2013).

Most of the information in this book is based on the author's interviewing and reporting. The following are examples of either news reporting from other sources or court reporting:

Prologue: Information used from Jack McCallum, "Thank Heaven for Danny," *Sports Illustrated*, April 20, 1981.

Chapter 4, "Attacked": Information used from Boston Police incident report, victim statement transcription, and witness statement, all from September 25, 2000. Suffolk County Superior Court Records: Commonwealth of Massachusetts v. William Ragland, November 14, 2000; Commonwealth v. William Ragland, Trevor Watson, and Tony Hurston, January 9, 2001; Commonwealth v. William Ragland, March 14, 2002; Commonwealth v. William Ragland, April 17,

2003; Commonwealth v. William Ragland, June 14, 2003; Commonwealth v. William Ragland, Appeals, October 14, 2008. S. L. Price, "The Truth Revealed," *Sports Illustrated*, December 8, 2008. Jackie MacMullan, "The Courageous Fight to Fix the NBA's Mental Health Problem," ESPN, August 20, 2018, https://www.espn.com/nba/story/_/id /24382693/jackie-macmullan-kevin-love-paul-pierce-state -mental-health-nba.

Chapter 6, "Seeing Red": Frank Hughes, "Day on Links Gives Allen Insight into New Owner," *Tacoma News Tribune*, November 24, 2006. Steve Aschburner, "Speculation by Pundits Riles Garnett," *Minneapolis Star Tribune*, January 27, 2007.

Chapter 7, "Boston Connections": Eric D. Williams, "Cheers Turn to Jeers in Seattle When Team Unloads Allen," *Tacoma News Tribune*, June 29, 2007.

Chapter 8, "Ubuntu": Information used from Shira Springer, "Celtics Build a Bond in Ancient Rome," *Boston Globe*, October 7, 2007. "2013 Templeton Prize Laureate Desmond Tutu on Ubuntu," November 19, 2013, video, 12:00, December 13, 2013, https://www.youtube.com/watch? v=yQnm_P0TBzE.

Chapter 9, "Graduation"; Chapter 10, "Anything Is Possible"; and Chapter 12, "The Hard Way to LA": In-game comments or coaches' miked-up segments gleaned from ABC/ESPN coverage.

Chapter 13, "Decisions": Kendrick Perkins's trade anecdote from his appearance on ESPN's *The Jump*, February 7, 2020.

Chapter 14, "Broken Brotherhood": Information used from Baxter Holmes, "Rajon Rondo: Good at Math, Bad at People," *ESPN the Magazine*, April 8, 2015, https://www.espn.com/espn/feature/story/_/id/12587848/old-questions-surface-new-dallas-mavericks-point-guard-rajon-rondo. Ray Allen with Michael Arkush, *From the Outside: My Journey through Life and the Game I Love* (New York: Dey Street Books, 2018).

Acknowledgments

I've never been through a book process like this one. And that's really a nice way of saying that I pushed a lot of people to their limits with my self-doubt, last-minute changes, and publication delays.

I love reading acknowledgments from other authors just so I can learn from their journeys. I usually walk away feeling guilty. *They're so organized; what's my problem?*

That thought first occurred to me as I scanned notes and emails from the beginning of what was going to be the first book. There was a congratulatory email about the birth of our daughter, Ava. She is now eight years old.

So, truly, thank you to all the publishers, editors, publicists, marketers, copyeditors, bookstores, and readers who were more patient with me than I would have been. I'm grateful for everyone who didn't cuss me out—in person—after receiving those, "Well, here's the thing . . ." phone calls.

My editor, Brant Rumble, was understanding and resourceful whenever I told him what I was going through. I'm sure he took some hits that I should have taken. In fact, I once begged him to tell his bosses that he was dealing with an unreasonable author, and he refused to do it. Thank you, Brant, for your calming reassurances.

Hachette has a great team with Susan Weinberg, Michelle Aielli, Mollie Weisenfeld, Quinn Fariel, Michael Giarratano, Megan Schindele, and many others.

There are four people who had all access to every stage of the book: my wife, Oni, and our children, Robinson, Beckham, and Ava. This is the seventh book project I've been blessed to be a part of, and Oni has been with me for six of them. She is able to offer loving encouragement when she sees me down, and she knows just the loving—and forceful—way to say that it's time to get to work. She runs our house well all the time, but she does it with particular precision during my long stretches of inaccessibility, moodiness, and time spent walking around talking to myself about some transition in the narrative.

Oni is one of those supremely organized people, and she often has the kids' schedules—what they're doing and when—posted on a board in the house. For example, one will read, "Robinson—Piano, 3:00 p.m." Or "Beckham—Soccer (of course), 5:30 p.m." For me, the sign says, "Daddy—Write."

No time. Just write. Always. How direct is that? I fall into another layer of love with her daily. I'm grateful for our kids, too. They gave me a push at the end of the book when they told me that the three of them got together and prayed for me to finish. When I told them that I was done, they wrapped me in the greatest hug of my life.

It's not easy to open your organization to an outsider, especially when you're unsure of what exactly will be written. Thanks to the Celtics for their openness during all phases of the project, including the first one in which I traveled on the team plane, rode on team buses, watched team practices, and even got a salary-cap tutorial that I still need to study (how Daryl Morey was able to master it in a weekend is beyond me). There are numerous people, in several roles, who were helpful: Wyc Grousbeck, Steve Pagliuca, Bob Epstein, Jim Cash, Rich Gotham, Shawn Sullivan, Danny Ainge, Mike Zarren, Christian Megliola, Doc Rivers, Brad Stevens, Tommy Heinsohn, Chris Wallace, Antoine Walker, Leon Powe, Jeff Twiss, Annemarie Loflin, Heather Walker, Brian Olive, Cedric Maxwell, M. L. Carr, Sean Grande, and Mike Gorman.

There are many others who put in extra effort just to make my life easier: Raymond Ritter—it's no wonder the Warriors are at the top of the league in public relations year after year (what a pro); Mike Brown; Al Michaels; Dan Masonson; Tracey Hughes; Sean McCloskey; Daryl Morey; and Terrell Brandon, who not only got a chance to play with KG and Ray Allen but also got a personal scouting report on his game from Prince himself. Amazing.

I began teaching at Boston University in 2018, and it's been a thoroughly enriching experience. My colleagues and students there have challenged and inspired me to be better. Three BU researchers, who are all working journalists now, were rigorous in their information gathering for this project: Alex MacDougall, Greg Levinsky, and Trevor Ballantyne. It got to the point where I couldn't get Ballantyne away from the Boston courts because he was so determined to get detailed information on Paul Pierce from September 2000. I hesitate to name specific professors, because you know how that goes; someone is inevitably left out. Still, the university has been in great hands with the last two deans in the College of Communication, Tom Fiedler and Mariette DiChristina; my neighbor, Chris Daly, who shared all of his classroom tips; Bill McKeen; Michelle Johnson; Sarah Kess; Damon Carlson; Jenn Underhill; Tina Martin; Marisa Moseley; my family at the Howard Thurman Center, including Kenn Elmore; Katherine Kennedy; Nick Bates; and Mitch Zuckoff, a superb professor and author who gave a narrative presentation that unlocked a lot of things for me.

Several current and former colleagues at NBC Sports Boston have been supportive: Kevin Miller, who helped me find full TV copies of old games to dissect, such as Pierce versus LeBron in 2006; Princell Hair; Chris Wayland; Kayce Smith; Tom Giles; A. Sherrod Blakely; Chris Forsberg; Abby Chin; Kyle Draper; Danielle Trotta; Tom E. Curran; DJ Bean; Courtney Gustafson; Paul Lucey; Jim Burgoyne; and Jim Aberdale and his team on the Emmy-winning *Anything Is Possible* documentary (Jason Brown, Josh Canu).

There's no way I'd be able to function during these intense times without prayer and the sound teaching across the country of men and women of God. I've never physically attended some of these churches, but I've been blessed as a virtual congregant. Boston: Myrtle Baptist; Bethel AME; Morningstar; Marsh Chapel; St. Mary of the Assumption. Alexandria, Virginia: Alfred Street Baptist. Richmond: St. Paul's Baptist. Goldsboro, North Carolina: Greenleaf Christian. Chicago: Trinity United Church of Christ. Minneapolis: Christ Presbyterian Church. Akron, Ohio: Mt. Calvary Baptist (founded by my great-grandfather); Arlington Street Church of God. Houston: Wheeler Avenue. Louisville: Bates Memorial; Pleasantville, New Jersey: Mt. Zion. Biblical scholars: Judy Fentress-Williams, Renita Weems, Abraham Smith, Valerie Bridgeman, Frank A. Thomas.

My family, whether biological or my *Brother From Another*, Michael Smith, has always given me strength. The Holleys, Sales, Soberanises, Prestons, Robinsons, Igartuas, Shakurs, and Greens . . . I love you. When I told Smith about this book's dedication and the meaning of it, he gave me a directive: "Just write it. Don't worry about anything else; it's bigger than basketball."

The book is dedicated to my grandparents, Kathryn Sales Darnell and Goldman Booker. My grandfather was fearless and wise. I think of some of the things he told me when I was a kid, and I'm just now understanding some of his powerful lessons.

My grandmother was one of the best storytellers I've ever met. I used to tease her and say I knew I was getting better at it because she'd finally let me get to the end of my stories (tough crowd—if the thing was boring, she'd shut it down). She was hilarious and well versed in laughter, the Lord's Prayer, and the (non-NBA) lottery.

I'm grateful for the gift of being placed in their care. My grandmother, Nana, used to read every basketball article I wrote as a young reporter for the *Akron Beacon Journal*. She never missed a single one, and she enjoyed quizzing me about what I'd seen around the country as I covered the NBA. This is my first book on basketball, and when I close my eyes, I can imagine her reading it—and making it to the end.

INDEX